Sheriff
&
Priest

Nicky Moxey

Dodnash Books

Published in paperback 2017 by Dodnash Books

ISBN:
978-1-9997832-0-4

British Library cataloguing in Publication Data

A CIP catalogue record for this book is available from the
British Library.

ACKNOWLEDGMENTS

This book would not have been possible without the generosity of Carol Gurney, who provided access to his library and his first-hand knowledge of the job of Sheriff, and who maintained a calm certainty over many years that the book would be published.

I am also indebted to Rupert and Sara Eley, who were the first people I told the story to, and who listened interestedly enough to make it seem possible to write it all down.

Some vital clues in the detective trail were to be found in the library at Helmingham Hall, and I would like to thank Lord Tollemache for access, and his archivist for his help - Vic was just as excited as I was by some of our discoveries!

I have been blessed with a lovely band of beta readers and cheerleaders; all faults in the book are my responsibility, and no-one else's.

Finally, to my family, who lost me for long stretches of time whilst my head was stuck in the 12th C – love and apologies!

WIMER, AGE 9

DODNASH, MAY 1143

Wimer thumped the tree trunk hard, just missing a moss-stained pair of feet, scrawny calves disappearing into a homespun tunic. He sighed, and looked down at his own finery. Climbing up himself just wasn't worth the risk, however boring it was down here. Well, not boring. He had plenty of cheerful scenes in his head to keep himself amused. Usually he felt completely safe in church, the one place where his brother couldn't reach him; but today, there were so many things that could go wrong. Every time he thought about what would happen when the Bishop arrived, he had to swallow a fresh flood of spit. *I will not be sick...* What if he threw up in the middle of the service? Fainted from fright? Or dropped the Host? He swallowed, and looked up again.

"Anything?" he called.

"Oh, shut up, Wimer, you asked that about two heartbeats..."   "There! Look! There's the knight's pennants!" The lowest boy's reply was drowned by someone with a better view calling out the news they'd all been waiting for.

The whole flock of boys fell out of the trees, and started pelting down the road towards the church. Wimer started to walk after them, then his legs took over, and he put his head down and ran as hard as he possibly could. To his surprise, he was in the middle of the pack when they arrived, and feeling much more cheerful. *Maybe today won't be too awful after all...*

Where was Hervey? It was always safest to spot him first. Not part of the big group of parishioners, just getting up from their gossip-session sitting on the church wall, their Sunday best clothes making a bright splash of colour in the shade. His mother caught his eye, and made little flicking motions down the front of her dress. *What?...* Oh! He got the idea, and brushed the dust off his long white tabard. She nodded and smiled, and he waved back.

Father Philip was alone in the doorway of the church, looking very smart in his best albe and robes, fussing with his sleeves. *Huh – the Father's looking nervous too!* Somehow that made Wimer feel more confident. He wasn't being stupid, if Father Philip felt scared too! *So where...*

There he was. Talking to Will the tanner, who must be visiting his family, he'd moved to Ipswich just a few months ago. Standing surprisingly close, most people stood as far away from Will as possible. Maybe they were doing some business? Hervey looked up, pointed at Wimer, and said something. Will sneered, and said something that made Hervey go red and ball his fist. He visibly relaxed, and punched Will on the shoulder. Wimer suddenly knew what they were talking about. SURELY Hervey wouldn't apprentice him to the tanner? To spend his life up to his waist in stinky pee, hauling hides for that horrid man? Please God, no.

He jumped as someone grabbed his arm.

"Wimer! There you are. Come on! We have to go to meet the Bishop NOW!"

Father Philip pulled him into position in the parade, next to the other altar boy. Wimer stood waiting, switching between worrying about the service, and being apprenticed, until everything was just one unhappy blur. *I suppose I could run away…* Finally they all started off.

He had to squeeze between people to put his tabard away. The sacristy was full to bursting, with a nice buzz as everyone relaxed after the service.

"Well done, lad!" Father Philip said, and clapped him on the shoulder.

He sucked breath, hard. Father Philip frowned and looked at his hand. It shone slightly, then dried to its normal colour. Wimer blushed. *My back must be leaking, how yucky!*

"Has he beaten you again?"

Wimer nodded. Father Philip frowned once more, then waved him on. Wimer ducked round a couple of the Bishop's servants, then tried to melt into the wall as the Bishop himself went past.

He could hear Father Philip;

"Your Excellency, I have a troubling Parish case I would like your advice on, if you'd be so kind?"

The Bishop mumbled something.

"It's about the lad who assisted Father John at the altar

today when he stumbled?" Wimer could feel his cheeks getting hot. *Why is Father Philip talking about me?* Had he messed something up? The priest had tripped and nearly spilt the wine, was it a sin to have steadied his elbow? Wimer wriggled a bit closer, to hear better.

"Yes, he did well. What about him?"

Whew - not in trouble, then!

"I am concerned by the treatment he receives at the hands of his brother. He has a foul temper, and takes it out on the boy – and the lad is frequently prevented from coming to Sunday school, although he's devout, bright, and willing. He's Saxon, of course, and will come to nothing here. I'd like you to talk to his brother…"

"Boy! Where does this go?"

By the time he'd sorted out one of the Bishop's servants, Father Philip and the Bishop had gone. He leant against a pillar, careful of his sore back, and looked through to the church. *I'm going to get such a beating when the Bishop talks to Hervey, he's bound to think I complained. Hey, maybe I could just live in here… claim sanctuary? That would be wonderful. So peaceful! I don't think you can stay forever, though. And only bread and wine to eat!* His tummy rumbled. *Wow, I'm starving! Hey, I'm missing the feast!*

Hervey and Wimer stood in the hall waiting. They'd been summoned by one of the Bishop's soldiers at dawn, asking for "the altar boy and the priest's witness, so that the Bishop can thank them for their service", and had quickly stuffed themselves into yesterday's finery again. Hervey's robe of fine blue wool still had folds from the chest, and his bleached linen shirt looked a little worse for wear. Mother had got out Wimer's best dark-yellow tunic and woollen hose, and tutted at a hole in his right boot. She'd been making him a new pair without telling him! They were a great colour, warm dark brown, and she'd felted the wool so there was a band of darker brown around the top. Wimer looked down at them. *They look very smart! Good old Mother...* The boots were a little big – Mother had made them that way on purpose, so he would grow in to them. He'd had to do the lacings up really tight, to keep them on, and that had squeezed a fold of felt into a knot over his right ankle. Every so often, when he thought Hervey wasn't looking, Wimer lifted his foot up and tried to rub the knot out on his other calf.

Hervey was alternating between hissing threats at Wimer through the side of his mouth, and nodding politely to anyone passing who was above a certain rank. He was beginning to look a bit frayed, as though he was worried he might get it wrong. Wimer had to swallow a sudden giggle, as he imagined Hervey saying *Stop that, you little turd* to someone like Sir Charles.

Watching everything that was going on was interesting; he didn't mind the wait. The hall was crowded with knights and priests from the Bishop's entourage, Sir Charles' people trying to go about their daily routine, and plenty of people like themselves waiting for an audience with the Bishop. The Bishop's Chaplain had taken Hervey's name, then ignored them; they were clearly far down the list.

First to go up the stairs to the solar had been a priest with an armful of parchment scrolls tied with linen strips;

from time to time he reappeared at the door and beckoned up one of the waiting men. Wimer was amusing himself trying to work out what they were all doing here. Paying his rent, he decided, watching a harried-looking man clutching a small purse close to his chest. There was a little run of people with purses, none of them particularly well dressed. After them, the local lords were in luck. Wimer was getting quite good at guessing who would be next – it seemed to have something to do with how much embroidery there was on their cloaks. *Master Tollemache's lovely dark blue velvet cloak, hey, how do you embroider those interlocking silver squares, that's clever - or Richard of Boynton's fine red wool and huge shiny brooch?* He bounced smugly when they were called in together - and then nearly fell over when Hervey forced him into a bow as they went past. Eventually, when there was almost no-one still waiting apart from them, the Chaplain called Hervey's name, along with Father Philip's, to Wimer's surprise.

After they had all kissed the Bishop's ring, Eborard began briskly:

"Thank you for your witness service yesterday, Hervey of Dodnash. The Church depends on good men like you to ensure rectitude in the Parish." Hervey bowed slightly and looked pleased with himself. "Father Philip tells me that young Wimer here is an excellent altar boy." Wimer stopped admiring the Bishop's red pointy shoe, and looked up in surprise. Hervey sounded surprised too.

"The boy spends his days dreaming, Your Excellency. He's of little use on the farm."

"Good. I propose to take him to Norwich, to test his potential. I may put him into the school; or I may retain him as a servant. From what you say, I assume you have no objection?"

Wimer stared at the Bishop in shock, then swivelled round to see Hervey's reaction. *Norwich! What an amazing idea!* Hervey, taken aback, half shook his head automatically, then stopped.

"I cannot afford to pay you for taking him in, Your Excellency – and my mother would be distraught. And who will..." Hervey trailed off.

Wimer caught the use of 'will' instead of 'would be', and his heart started to beat faster.

"I will waive the entrance fee, should he test high enough to enter the school. Your mother has other sons at home, does she not? She'll get over it. He's of an age to be apprenticed, anyway. The Church will make use of him. Any further objection?"

Hervey stood looking as though he had found half a maggot in an apple, but stayed silent. Wimer turned to look at Father Philip, who was smiling at him. *He must have planned this! Was that what they were talking about yesterday, that the Bishop was going to talk to Hervey about?* He grinned back, as wide as he could, then turned back to face the Bishop.

The Chaplain made a note on some parchment whilst Eborard blessed them; then hustled them back out into the hall. Wimer was walking on air. He was going to Norwich!

"Lad! For heaven's sake, keep yer leg still!" the carter poked him.

Wimer pushed down on his leg until it stopped jumping up and down. "Sorry, Sir."

"and don't call me Sir! I've told thee my name." The man crossed his arms, and scowled.

"Sorry, Aedgar!" Wimer half stood and folded his leg underneath him on the driving-bench, so it couldn't start jiggling again. *Maybe the other leg will jiggle, though… he's getting very cross. Better not upset him, he's in charge of me for weeks, until we get to Norwich!* Wimer tucked the other leg up so he was kneeling, just to be safe. WHEN were they going to move? They'd been ready forever. *This is a great view, all the way up here!* There were a lot of people in the courtyard - lots of the Bishop's servants were rushing around, carrying boxes out of the house and dodging the knights, who were all on horseback, looking just about as fed up as the carters. Every window had a few faces looking out, and there were people pushed back against all the walls, trying to stay out of the way and still see everything.

A squeal from an angry horse made him jump. One of the knights had let his horse drift close enough to bite another. The scuffle was raising a cloud of dust. He sneezed. When it settled, he saw his brother on the other side of the space. Hervey, as usual, had his arms crossed, glaring at him. *I'm glad I'm up here! He'd be cuffing my ear if I was down there, he looks in an awful mood. I suppose he'll have to fetch his own firewood now, and get the hens in, and look after the oxen. At least he doesn't have to pay an apprentice fee for me now.* Wimer looked solemnly back. *He looks smaller somehow. I wonder why?*

In case his brother could still change his mind and order him off the wagon, he consciously looked away. No point in upsetting him. All the family had come! Thomas was teasing a neighbour's daughter, taking no notice of

Wimer. *No change there. Bye, brother. You won't even notice I'm gone.* His mother was a little behind them, wiping a tear on her apron, smiling up at him at the same time. He stood up, waved to her and blew her a kiss. *I'm going to miss you...* He looked away, and plonked down onto the bench again. *I'm going to miss you a lot...* he gulped. *I am NOT going to cry now!* He gave the bundle of best clothes she'd packed for him a big hug. His eyes were a little wet. He rubbed his face in the bundle, and looked sideways up at the big carter. *I don't think he noticed anything.*

WHEN will the Bishop be ready, so we can all get going? His leg was jiggling again.

WIMER, AGE 9

NORWICH, JUNE 1143

Wimer had been standing up on the high wagon bench at the top of every hill for miles, to get the first possible view of Norwich. At last, the road crested a hill, and there straight ahead was a gleaming golden rod, pointing straight to heaven. Looking down its length, to the graceful Cathedral below, shining like a beacon against the dark greens of the hill behind the town, made him dizzy.

His eyes were drawn to the left, and to the square mass of the Castle; built of the same coloured stone, but a statement of power rather than of grace. He thumped down into his seat, almost afraid of the castle, and looked back to the beautiful spire. He slowly became aware of the town, its buildings insignificant in comparison, clustered around the Castle, with the Cathedral slightly to the side.

All the way down the slope, his eyes were taken one way to the Cathedral, then to the Castle, flipping between the two great powers. Gradually, as they went lower, the Cathedral spire dominated, and he had to tilt his head more and more to admire it. Aedgar gave the reins a shake, slapping the horses' rumps, and they went rattle-splash over a ford. The Cathedral was hidden by some trees, and Wimer's attention jerked back to the wagon. They were driving alongside a completely straight river!

"Aedgar, what's happened to the river here?"

"It's not a river, lad, it's a canal. Our first Bishop built it so he could get stone for the Cathedral up from the river proper there. The limestone came all the way from France, you know!"

Then the Cathedral cleared the trees, and he was lost again. Soon they drew level with a house, and Aedgar brought the cart to a halt.

"Well, here you are, lad, there's the Prior's house – in you go and wait for him; and good luck!"

Wimer scrambled off the cart, starting to feel all the worry that had been pushed aside by the beautiful buildings start to well up again. *Got to do well in this test. Would they send me home again if I mess it up? - No, the Bishop said I would be a servant. I'd rather be a servant than go back to Hervey, anyway - or be apprenticed as a tanner...* He looked up at the grand house in front of him, then looked back as Aedgar called to him.

"Here, lad – thanks for your help!" and the cart moved on.

Wimer caught the small object arcing through the air to him. It was half of a silver penny, cut neatly down the middle. Riches! He'd never owned any money at all before. *Where can I put it to keep it safe?* He thought for a bit, and then tucked it down the side of his felt boot. He looked up again. Aedgar and his wagon had moved on, out of sight.

Nothing for it, then. Unless he wanted to start walking

back to Dodnash, he'd have to do this test. If he stood here much longer, too, he'd throw up. He licked his palms, brushed his hair as flat as it would go, and tugged his tunic down. *Please God, make me pass this test and let the Prior take me into the school!* Before he lost his courage, he ran to knock on the door.

Wimer stood in front of the desk, hands clasped behind his back to hide their shakiness. The man behind the desk - Prior William de Turbeville - was taking his time studying him. He thought it would be rude to stare back, so he was looking behind the Prior at the lovely tapestry hanging on the wall. He was beginning to get drawn into the picture, feeling less terrified; it came as a little shock when the Prior spoke, in English.

"You are Saxon, are you not? Parles-tu français?"

"Oui, mon Seigneur, un peu."

"Tell me then, in French, about your journey here."

Wimer took a steadying breath, then started to try and describe the daily routine. It was easier if he talked to the lady on the tapestry, the Prior was just too scary. He didn't know some of the words, and it didn't take very long before he dried up. He bit his lip and stole a glimpse at the Master, but he didn't look too cross.

The probing changed direction:

"Can you read?" - he was handed a list of school expenses from off William's desk.

"Item: 15 balls of wax, each one pound weight..."

"Can you guess what that's for, lad?"

"Candles, Sir?"

"No." - with a smile. "Can you write?"

"Only my name, Sir."

"Then you might be spending a lot of time on my wax tables! It's spread on a frame, so you can practice your letters, smooth it out if you make a mistake, and try again. Look, I have a small wax tablet here, I'm making notes on your performance." *Oh my. He's not going to forget any of my mistakes…*

"Now, have you been confirmed? Good. Recite the Lord's Prayer, in Latin."

Then he had to do some arithmetic. The Prior had asked in French, but he'd got confused, and the Prior had asked again in Latin. That he could do. He'd spent enough time asking Father Philip to show him how the ancients had used the numbers in the Bible.

At last, de Turbeville put his stylus down, and Wimer knew the test had finished. He had answered to the best of his ability, and thought he had done reasonably well – except for the French, and the singing test. His ears burned again, thinking of the mess he'd made of the simple song he'd been asked to sing… He knew what the Master was going to say before he said it. He held his breath anyway. *Pleasepleaseplease God, let him take me as a scholar – Please…*

"So, lad, I'm afraid your French isn't good enough to join the school – all the lessons are either in French or Latin, you know. I'm not entirely sure why the Bishop wanted you tested; we're not really set up to educate Saxons. Pity, your arithmetic is acceptable. If you could sing… we're short of trebles at the moment. No mind, we'll see what else we can make of you. Let's get you settled in now. Boy!" he called through the open doorway.

Wimer studied his shoes. *A servant then.* He shivered a little, suddenly cold. *What did he mean, "not set up to educate Saxons"? What did that have to do with it? Would I have passed if I'd been Norman? Although I suppose I'd speak better French if I were...*

"Ah! Jean! Excellent." Wimer looked up and saw a boy of about the same age. "This is Wimer; he's joined our community. Both of you are free until Vespers, on my sanction; please show him around. He'll need to report to the Chamberlain after the service. Oh - and get him something to eat and drink." and with a grin at the way both boys had brightened at the last instruction, he blessed them and let them go.

"Food first?" Jean asked. Wimer hadn't realised how hungry he was until the Prior had mentioned food, but now his gut rumbled loud enough for the other boy to hear. Jean laughed. "See the corner of that building? Race you!"

Rosie looked up from kneading her dough to see that scamp Jean strutting in. He often hung around the door of the lay kitchen, and Rosie sometimes fed him scraps. She had a soft spot for him, he had tight dark curls and an easy grin like her own William used to have, God rest his soul. He had another lad with him, a stranger, and a bit shy-looking.

"Cook, this is Wimer. It's his first day today, and the Prior says that he – um, that is, we" - with a cheeky grin - "need food and drink."

Rosie raised her eyebrows at the 'we', and automatically complained, "Where's your 'an it please you', scamp?" Then she took in how skinny and sad Wimer looked, and relented immediately.

"Oh dear, you poor chick, you look washed out! I've some game pie left over, would that do? Oh, and a jug of ale – and here's a couple of apples, they're wrinkled but still good – cheese? Bread?" and she piled the two boys' arms high with a feast.

"Now shoo – be off with you!"

"Thanks, Rosie!" yelled Jean, from the door.

"Thank you very much." Wimer smiled sweetly, and followed Jean rapidly.

"And don't forget to bring the jug back!" she called after them. The new boy looked as though he could do with feeding up. She made a mental note to add another pastry or two to the tray she often left cooling on the windowsill as the boys came out of school...

Jean led the way to a large oak tree in the infirmary gardens. They leant against the trunk and munched contentedly.

Eventually, Jean burped and patted his stomach.

"Ah! That was good." – in French. "Where are you from? What's your full name?"

Wimer opened his mouth to reply, but Jean was talking again.

"I'm from Rouen, are you Saxon? My father sent me here because it's a really good school, but I'm not very clever, I think. I'd like to be a jongleur, except I can't sing..."

In a gap, Wimer said "Yes, I'm Saxon. I can't sing either. I failed the Prior's test, so I'm to be a servant, I suppose." Jean didn't seem to have heard.

"The Prior can be a bit strict." said Jean, around a mouthful of apple, "But he only gets angry if he thinks you're not trying. He does sometimes teach – he used to be the Domini before he was Prior – but we usually have Father Ricard, the Prior's too busy. You'll get his lecture though about how everything that happens here is so that we can serve God better – and that includes our school work. Are you going to be a chorister?"

Wimer blushed and shook his head, his mouth too full to repeat himself.

"Me neither – good thing too, they have to do all kinds of extra services and practice. They think they're better than us, though – you need to watch out for Guillaume, he's the head chorister, he's a mean one. "

"Jean, didn't you hear me? I'm to be a servant. My French isn't good enough."

"So? You're still going to be living here, aren't you? And you're not having any bother understanding me, what's the problem?" Jean grabbed one last pastry, whilst Wimer gaped at him. *Is he mad? Surely he can't make friends with a servant?*

Jean wiped his mouth on his sleeve, and stood up. "Have you had enough to eat? - come on, then, I'll show you where everything is. Grab the jug, we'll drop it off on the way..."

He gave Wimer a tour that would have bemused the Bishop. He covered the pantry and the buttery, the place

in the stable where the brindled hound had her pups,
which horses could be petted and which would bite, half a
dozen places where a boy could keep out the way of
people looking for idle hands, the privies – and as an
afterthought, the Almoner's school building by Ethelbert's
gate, the monks' refectory, and the Chamberlain's offices.

Wimer was aware all the time of the Cathedral, rising
gloriously above all the chaos of the wooden buildings
clustering around it, and the busy to-ing and fro-ing of the
ant-like people at his level. *It's holding up the clouds! What a
place to worship God...*

When the Vespers bell rang, they were at the far end of
the close.

"Oops! Come on, we'd better hurry up, or we won't get
a good spot." Jean set off at a jog.

Wimer stayed where he was, and Jean ran back.

"Come ON! What's the matter with you?"

"Am..." Wimer bit his lip. "Am I allowed in to the
Cathedral, as a servant?"

"Yes! Of course you are, silly! Everyone is allowed in!
And we boys HAVE to go to Vespers! Come on, we have
to hurry!" They sprinted off, overtaking a few stragglers.

That first view down the Cathedral nave stayed with
him for the rest of his days.

They went in the great door at the West, and the
columned pillars, galleried arches and soaring rib vaults
tore his eyes upwards. He stood rooted in the middle of
the doorway, lost in the wonder, until Jean pulled his arm
to make him move. Then his gaze dropped from the
heights to the end of the church, where a Bishop's chair on
a pedestal at the end was made a tiny toy by the distance,

then back past the long double row of wooden choir stalls, and up to the high altar. The far end of the church – the monastery end – was bright with the last of the evening sunshine lighting the painted walls; but the stone nearest to him was plain, a soft pale gold.

"Why aren't there any paintings here?" he whispered to Jean, who was still trying to hustle him down the steps and into the crowd of people standing in the nave.

"Cos it's only just been built, now shhh!" he whispered back, just as the first notes of the psalm began. The music was glorious, the deep tones of the men soothing his soul, then the high notes from the boys sending it soaring. He moved forward, wanting more than anything to be close to that music, until the crowd stopped him. *I want to stay here forever…*

When they knelt for prayer, he gave thanks for the Cathedral and its music first.

The boys were sat behind the kitchen, making use of Wimer's free time whilst Rosie was serving the midday meal. Jean quite often came round; usually they'd sit and chat - or, rather, Jean would talk and Wimer would listen - but today Wimer was having another go at teaching Jean how to do arithmetic.

"No, look, here where you've added vii to v – you've made it viii; but v and v make x, so it's xii, see?"

Wimer rubbed out Jean's scrawl with the end of his stick, and neatly wrote the numbers out again. Having everything in columns, so you could see what you were doing, made it so much easier – why couldn't Jean see that?

"Oh I hate this – how come you find it so damnably simple? Talk me through it again, will you – I have to be able to do this in class later, or the Prior promised me a beating – he says it's so easy even a babe in arms could do it – some babe – what do I have to do first?"

"It is easy. Look at the columns. You just need to add them up…" It was difficult to explain. When he looked at it, the answer was just there in his head. Even if the answer could get into Jean's head, it would be drowned out by all the hundreds of other things buzzing around in there. He sighed, and tried again.

"Look, how I've written a column of Vs and a column of Is. Add up the Is and you get?"

"Two. I'm not that stupid."

"And the Vs?"

Jean rolled his eyes and started to speak –

"Wimer! Come and get these pots, and take them down to the river to scour clean, please."

"Yes, Rosie – coming!" He switched back to French. " – Good luck with the Prior. Just remember to put everything into columns before you start!" and he sprinted off.

There was a bit of food– that was stuck fast – he scooped up a fresh handful of damp sand, scrubbed hard, and grunted in satisfaction as the crust broke off cleanly. He shook the sand out of the pot, and sat back on his heels to admire the view. He'd come to love it, these last few weeks of being the kitchen pot-boy. It was always so noisy down by the river, and so full of life... there was a kestrel, body absolutely still above the marsh, wingtips frantically fluttering. *Good hunting, Brother!* A family of swans flew overhead, wheezing with each downbeat of their wings at the effort of keeping their great bodies aloft. As he turned to watch them, a flock of rooks swirled up from the trees lining the lane, squawking in protest at a disturbance. *Hello! Someone's in a hurry! Hey - it's Jean!*

""Wimer! - Wimer! - Oh there you are! Come quickly - I'm really really sorry - come on, quick, leave that, the Prior wants you, please hurry!"

He grabbed up the pot and jumped to his feet.

"Why? What's happened?"

"I don't know! I finished doing that stupid sum for him and he just told me straight away to go and get you! I have no idea why! But please hurry!"

The air puffed out of him as though Jean had punched him in the stomach.

He's going to throw me out.

It felt exactly like his first day. Wimer was back studying the tapestry in the Prior's office whilst the Prior studied him. The only difference was that Jean was beside him this time. He wasn't sure whether that made it better or worse. And he was still holding the pot.

I wish he'd get on with it... Wimer sneaked a look at his face. He didn't look angry - more surprised than anything; his eyebrows were as high as they'd go.

At last, the Prior shook his head. *Here it comes...* but all he did was to write something on a tablet, turn it round, and push it towards Jean.

"Try your newfound mastery on this, lad."

Wimer sneaked a look at it. It was arithmetic! Jean had to add iii to iii. He did it the long way round, writing down all the ones, then making a five and a one out of them; but Wimer was proud of him.

The Prior took the tablet back, wrote again, and turned it back round. *vi plus viii - almost what we practiced, he should manage this?* Sure enough, Jean wrote the answer down quickly.

de Turbeville shook his head slightly, and retrieved the tablet. ix plus vii - *oh-oh, he's going to mess that up...* Jean picked up the stylus and licked his lips. He looked up at Wimer, then at the Prior. Neither said anything. Slowly he wrote the numbers out in columns;

```
i     x
v     ii
-----------
vi    xii
```

He looked up again. The Prior smiled at him. Wimer frowned as hard as he could, to try and get him to start again. He half-got the idea, and wrote quickly in a corner;

```
v     i
x     ii
-----------
xviii
```

He stood straight, "Eighteen! It's eighteen, right?"

The Prior spoke to Wimer. "What advice would you give him? - no, don't do it for him, just tell him one thing to help him out."

"Jean, you need to split the 9 into a five and a four, then put it in to columns."

Jean looked at what he'd written, and his mouth silently made an O of surprise. He picked up the stylus, rubbed everything out, and started again.

```
v        iiii
v        ii
-------------
x        iiiiii vi
```

"Sixteen!" Jean said, triumphantly.

Neither Wimer nor de Turbeville looked at him; for the first time, Wimer was looking straight at the Prior, who was matching his gaze. *Am I in trouble for teaching Jean arithmetic? Surely not? But maybe there's some rule about who can teach here? What's he going to do – I wish he'd do something!*

As if on cue, de Turbeville stood up, and began pacing the length of the study, hands behind his back. He made four or five turns, his head-shaking getting stronger each time. Finally he stopped in front of Wimer, legs apart and arms crossed, and glared.

"Tell me what you've been doing for the last two or three weeks."

"Well, Sir – I've been helping Rosie in the kitchen. Mostly washing pots, but sometimes I've turned the spit. Helping her clean, wash vegetables, that kind of thing. And I've been going to services in the Cathedral, of course; and seeing Jean occasionally…" *Oh! Is that it! Maybe I'm not allowed to make friends with the scholars!*

De Turbeville started pacing again.

"I have never done this, in all my years as Prior. But you leave me no option…"

Wimer stood still, too numb and sad for thought.

"Do you realise how long I've been trying to teach Jean to add one and one? And this entire conversation has been in French. You clearly haven't been wasting your time, either." – another turn up and down. "Go and get your bedroll from the kitchen. You can move up to the scholars' dormitory tonight."

Wimer realised that his mouth was open only when Jean's hug made him bite his tongue. "But – I - " he gawked at the Prior, dazed. de Turbeville nodded approval at him, gravely.

"Be off with the pair of you!" the Prior growled. "Don't make me regret this decision, or you'll be back in the kitchen before you can blink!"

The spell was broken – and Wimer tore outside, whirling with joy.

The only sour note in the day was as the boys were settling down for the night. Wimer had of course been the centre of attention, answering all the questions thrown at him as best he could, but that had died down now. He had taken his boots off and was just rolling up in his blanket in a spare space when the choristers came bustling in from practice, led by a big boy with blond hair.

"Hello! What's this then – who are you? You're in my

space, move!" - and the boy nudged Wimer with his foot.

"Leave him alone, Guillaume." said Jean. "He's new."

"No he's not – isn't he Rosie's little Saxon slave?"

"He was a servant, yes – but the Prior's made him a scholar!"

"God in heaven, what is the world coming to – look at this, you fellows, we're educating Saxons now! Why are you still in my space, Slavey?"

Wimer had been unwinding himself from the blanket. He didn't mind moving if he actually had taken someone's place – but he had a strong suspicion that Guillaume would have found some reason to pick on him whatever he'd done. He had gone very calm and quiet inside – not thinking at all; just ready. Part of him watched with interest to see what would happen. Guillaume lifted his foot to kick him again. Wimer watched him bring it back – and noticed that he was wearing clogs; it would hurt if that kick connected. Suddenly Guillaume's actions seemed very slow. Wimer had plenty of time to dart in, bend under the kick, and straighten his legs and back really fast, shooting Guillaume's leg high in the air. For a second or two they stayed like that, Guillaume teetering on one foot, Wimer with both feet planted strongly, balancing Guillaume's leg on his shoulders. Guillaume's clog fell off, still in slow motion. Then the world speeded up again. The clog bounced and clunked, horrifyingly loudly, against the door.

"What's going on in there?" came the voice of the novice who was supposed to keep order in the boys' dormitory. Wimer could hear him coming down the passage.

"Don't ever kick me again." he said to Guillaume, very

quietly, slow, and steady; then released his leg by bowing low. By the time the novice appeared, Wimer was back in his blanket roll looking innocent; Guillaume was still standing, completely bemused.

The novice got everyone bedded down and then pointedly took their candle and sat in the passageway, leaning against the wall. It was clear to everyone, even Guillaume, that no further discussion was possible that night, and soon the dorm was full of snores.

Wimer tossed and turned for a bit, worrying about what Guillaume would do the next time they met, but soon he slept too.

The next morning, Wimer woke early. He thought he heard a bell, very faint; and he could see the outline of the window shutters. It must be nearly dawn. He had to take a piss, so he quietly got out of his blanket and went outside. As he finished, he noticed a glimmer of candle light from the cloisters – it was a line of monks, making their way to the Cathedral. Wimer ghosted across the open space, and ducked into the cloisters, a little way behind the last monk. He needn't have bothered being quiet, because as the monk turned to close the Cathedral door, he noticed Wimer and smiled an invitation; Wimer smiled back and went in.

The monks were in a small, welcoming cave inside the cathedral formed by the soft glow from their candles. He settled down next to a spiralling pillar as the monks began to chant; music of a piece with the golden light and the perfumed incense, slow, rich, and very beautiful. Their voices rose and fell, and Wimer became lost in the prayer. The feeling stayed with him as the monks drew the service to an end and filed out; only the candle on the altar was left, and as he stared at it, he seemed to be lifted out of himself...

It seemed as though it were just a few minutes later when Jean was beside him, nudging him in the ribs. The sunlight streamed through the east windows.

"Hey, where have you been? Come on, you're almost in the monks' part of the church, you'll get in trouble – we need to be this side of the altar. You were MAGNIFICENT last night, but oh!, you're going to pay for it – Guillaume and his little gang are going to be out to get you – where did you go anyway?"

Mercifully, the stream of talk was stopped with the first notes of the processional hymn. Wimer glanced around him; the Cathedral had filled up. He recognised the boys from the dorm and the kitchen staff; but there were plenty more people he hadn't met. Suddenly the treble voices joined the hymn, their steely beauty rising above the initial tenor, and his attention snapped back to the procession. Wimer spotted Guillaume at the same time that Guillaume saw him; from the look he got, Wimer was in no doubt that he was in for it. Still, Guillaume was a bit busy just now. Wimer relaxed into the service, and more wonderful music.

"I really liked that service," said Wimer enthusiastically, as they were waiting in the breakfast queue. "It just seemed to go straight up to heaven..."

"Well, that's what it means! It's Lauds, short for

Laudate, praises. Way too early for me though, you do know we only have to go to Prime and Vespers, don't you? Although I suppose the monks would be happy if you turned up for any of the other services. Oh-oh, there's Guillaume. You made him look a real idiot last night, it was worth watching, how did you do it?"

"I just ducked under his kick and lifted." Wimer folded his arms and planted his legs. "I won't let him kick me, or bully me. My brother used to do that, and I had to put up with it because our father is dead. He made me promise to obey Hervey before he died. But I won't let Guillaume do it. I don't care if he's bigger than me. I'll fight him back, if he starts anything!" and Wimer looked mulish and scowled towards the back of the queue.

"Hey, that's more words than I've heard you put together since you've been here! Well, good for you." and Jean turned to hold his bowl out for the acolyte who was serving the oatmeal.

The trouble started as they were making their way past the queue to a space on the benches at the long table that ran down the middle of the room. Wimer had been expecting Guillaume to do something and had been watching him carefully, but just as they drew level, an acolyte climbed backward from the bench without looking where he was going, and Wimer had to step back to avoid him. Guillaume cried out, as though Wimer had stepped on him, and pushed him away hard. Wimer's bowl of hot oatmeal landed full on Guillaume's chest. Pale ooze dripped from his tunic to the floor.

Guillaume looked down, not understanding what had happened – and then the heat from the oatmeal hit him.

Wimer watched, fascinated, as he wriggled a bit, then pulled the skirt of his tunic down and away from his body... then quickly jerked it up and over his head as the full heat burned through. Guillaume blushed beetroot all over, clutched the dry bits of his clothes to his front, and sprinted toward the door– his buttocks still bright red as he disappeared from sight.

Wimer looked at Jean. He was staring back, eyes wide as Wimer felt his own to be, solemn as an owl.

"I didn't mean..." "He looked so funny!"

They spoke together, then all at once, laughter burst out of them like hiccoughs, and they laughed until they cried. All through the clean-up punishment duty, all they had to do was whisper "red bum!", and the giggles came back.

Wimer was doing his afternoon job, happily mucking out the stables. He was using each stroke of the shovel to practice his Latin, as Father Anselm had rather pointedly suggested during lessons that morning...

"Iacio stercore! I throw shit!" A heap of straw went onto the pile.

"Iacis, iacit! He, she or it throws!" He used each word to scrape muck out of the corners.

"Iacimus!" Another load onto the pile.

Um... what's next? It goes like servus - ah, yes!

"Iactis!" He stopped mid scoop, and leant on his shovel. It was hard to believe that a year ago, he had been a servant - and now it felt like he'd been here forever! *How strange...* He shut his eyes, and tried to remember what it had been like, home in Dodnash. One particular spring day came to mind.

The fat black tadpole was doing a most peculiar wriggle-flip thing, making it change direction in very unexpected ways. Wimer inched forwards on his tummy a bit more, careful not to get his shadow over it. *Is it just about to grow legs, and it's trying to itch the spot?* It swam behind a school of lesser tadpoles, and he leant in just a bit more to find it again. There it went, jinking around a frond of weed. *How on earth did it do that? How wonderful God's creatures are!*

He pulled his knees and feet together to make a tail and... "Aaaah!" *Ooops...* He hauled himself out of the stream. Water poured from his tunic. He wrung it out as best he could, and lay on his back in the sun to get dry. He pointed his toes and pulled his feet together, and wriggled his "tail". *I must've looked a right idiot falling in –* he grinned at a bumble bee buzzing over his head. Good thing no-one had seen him! He'd never live it down. The bee buzzed up into the white froth of the blackthorn. It looked so pretty against the pale blue sky... He closed his eyes to soak up the sun, just for a minute...

Hervey had caught him sleeping, and had beaten him. There had been lots of beatings! *Thank the Lord that the only bully in my life now is Guillaume, and he's easily avoided...* He tried to remember something else. How quiet and sleepy Dodnash seemed! No school work, no chores, no services - how had he spent his days? *Now I'm busy from Prime to Vespers. And thinking of busy...*

"Amo... amas... amat..." The shovel was getting

heavy, and he stopped again for a rest. *This has to be easier than being an apprentice, though.* He'd walked past the tannery on his way over to the stables. Most of the boys had been scraping away at hides, with the master screaming at them to hurry up before the flesh dried. One boy, though, had been hauling hides out of a vat of something that smelled absolutely disgusting - he'd thrown up as Wimer watched, the master cursing him not to get any on the hides. Wimer had caught a whiff of the vat, and had moved on quickly. *I escaped that by a whisker! Deo gratias!*

He went back to his shovelling. The stables had to be clean before he could go, and he didn't want to be late for Vespers. *That's another weird thing about home - only going to church once or twice a week! I'd really miss it if I couldn't hear the services now. How did I clear my mind, before?*

He checked that each bay had fresh water and a bundle of hay, and started to get the horses in.

"That's another thing, isn't it, Poppy," he said, to the little chestnut mare who was his favourite, "No horses at home, only smelly oxen!"

He rubbed the soft nose, thoughtfully, and twisted up a wisp of sweet grass for her.

"You know what? Maybe this is home now."

WIMER, AGE 17

NORWICH AND DODNASH, SUMMER 1152

The whitewashed cob was warm and comfortable against Wimer's back. He re-read the last sentence again; the finer points of canon law just weren't sinking in today. He was finding the silence from Jean deafening. All these years, he'd had Jean's stream of consciousness as a constant background; now there was no chatter, the silence hurt like a missing tooth. Finally he gave up, carefully re-wrapped the book in its kid leather cover, and put it on the top of the low wall. Jean was picking bits of straw apart with a determination bordering on manic.

"Come on, tell me what's wrong. You're so quiet it's hurting my ears."

Jean threw down his handful of chaff and sighed. "It's my brother. I got a letter from him this morning. He says that it's time I stopped spending his money getting an education, he's got a business trip to Ipswich planned in September, and we're to go home to Rouen together. Oh,

Wimer! He wants me to keep his accounts! What am I to do?"

Jean's face looked as though he'd bitten on a sloe. Wimer manfully didn't laugh.

"Well, you'd better write back and tell him that you can't add two numbers together the same way twice! He'll see for himself how dire your Latin is. Maybe he'll beg Bishop William to make you a monk and throw away the key to your hermitage."

Jean brightened. "Hey! Maybe I could become a monk! Then -"

He stopped, affronted, as Wimer fell over sideways laughing. "What's wrong with you? I could easily be a monk?"

"Jean – have you ever read the Rule of St Benedict? Especially the bit where he says that leave to talk should be given as infrequently as possible? You'd burst, the first day!"

Jean jumped on him, and Wimer wrestled back; the game only ended when both young men were out of breath.

"I suppose I have to go home." Jean sighed. "I do actually miss the old place – and it would be good to see my mother - and I'll be able to ride whenever I wanted again. Hey! I could buy one of those seriously beautiful saddles in the market place. Louis will need to buy me a new horse, ergo I need a new saddle!" he bounced in place, grinning. "What are you going to do when they throw you out? Can't be too long now, you're the same age as me? Look for a cleric's role somewhere, I suppose?"

Wimer smiled across at his friend. "Ah, I'm never going

to leave here. I really am going to be a monk; I've already asked the Novice Master about being a postulant."

Jean stared. "Wimer! You never did! Without telling me? But you can't be serious. What are you going to do about the vow of obedience? Are you really going to solemnly vow to give up your free will to smelly old Prior Elias? You know you're about a hundred times brighter than he is! For heaven's sake, be a priest instead – at least that's only a vow of obedience in law to Bishop William, and he's all right."

Jean sat upright like he'd been pricked with a pin, and spoke again: "Ah, ah, ah! I've just had a really good idea! Become a priest, move to France with me, and be my confessor! After all, you're used to listening to me... I'm sure my brother can cope – and you could do his horrid accounts! This is better and better the more I think about it! Say you'll come. Please?"

Oh my – I can just imagine how pleased his brother would be!

"Why do you rate a personal confessor, second son? Very keen to spend your brother's money, aren't you. He'd love that!" and things deteriorated into wrestling again.

They settled back down, and Wimer picked up his book again. The words blurred, as the pros and cons of being a monk continued to echo round his skull. It felt like there were at least two people arguing in there...

He's partly right. The vow of obedience is just plain scary.

But isn't that the point of such a vow, to do my small bit towards redeeming the fall from grace, by living each day a little more Christ-like, knowing that all men are imperfect beings trying to reach towards perfection? The greater the trial, the greater the victory, who said that?- the sternness of the discipline is attractive in itself. And the whole reason for the postulancy and the novitiate is to make sure that the applicant is ready, and able, to take the unbreakable vows of a monk.

Yes, but – they are unbreakable. What if I can't stand it? The choice would be to die a little every day, or to run away and be damned in hell…

He stroked the cover thoughtfully.

The other thing is the Lectio Divina – I'm so lucky to be able to just wander into the library here, and pick any book I want. How would I cope with being issued just one book a year, and be expected to spend the whole twelve months meditating with it alone? I suppose the opposite is true, that as a clerk, I might end up with no access to books at all! And I draw just about as well as I sing, if I was put in the scriptorium, they'd have me grinding ink, not copying books…

But still, there's something very noble about a life spent in prayer, seeing the seasons change in the colours of the vestments, and the hours in the cycles of the Psalms.

I'm just not sure… I'll try being a postulant, and see if I can cope. If I can't, maybe I could try Jean's brother! He sent up another wordless plea for courage, then turned his attention back to the intricacies of the law. The quiet didn't last long.

"Hey, did you hear about Guillaume? His father's died, he has to go and be a farmer somewhere, he's gone home already. Lucky sod. He'll be knighted soon. I bet he owns half a dozen villages with pretty girls in each one… Oh! If you become a monk, there's no nookie – ever!" Jean's eyes were round as an owl's, matching his mouth. Wimer roared with laughter.

"Oh, Jean, you are an idiot. Do you think I haven't thought about that? But I'm Saxon; I've no land, no family money, I've never even learnt a trade – I'm stuck with the Church, now. There'll be no pretty wife for me, nor squalling babies. Makes no difference, monk or clerk, either way I'm doomed to chastity." He shrugged, then wrapped the book again, this time carefully tightening its laces, and stood up. "Come on, let's go and see if there's any spare pastries, I'm starving."

The 3rd Bishop of Norwich looked up at the knock on his door. Two men entered at his call, the Prior and the Master Almoner.

"Ah, thank you for coming, my friends. Please take a seat; I just need to close this letter and I'll be with you."

Very shortly, William came out from around his desk and joined the pair, seated on the benches around a wide window enclosure. They made small talk whilst one of the boys from the school served wine, then William asked the lad to leave the flask and close the door. He came right to the point.

"I have had an interesting letter from the Earl of Norfolk. He writes that Father John's health is deteriorating, and he wishes to replace him as the Earl's personal priest with, and I quote, 'someone who is capable of withstanding the rigours of extensive travel'. So, what do you think the old fox is up to? And how do you advise me to deal with his request?"

Elias snorted. "'Replace', like a worn-out shoe! I see the Earl's still exercising all his talent for personal relations. Poor old John – actually he's not that old, you know, he's only a couple of years older than I am. It wouldn't surprise me if having the charge of Hugh Bigod's soul has contributed to his ill health. Do you know what's wrong with him, Your Grace?"

"No, not really. If you remember, he fainted when he came to the Easter Synod; but he seemed to be fine after a bit of a rest. That's the other question, of course. Should I recall John, get him out of there, or would he be happier in an environment he knows, particularly if the Earl is away? There's the heir to consider, too – he must be, what, four or five by now? Certainly ready for religious instruction. I think I'll ask John to visit, and see how he looks after the journey here. So that's him taken care of; what about a priest capable of travelling for Hugh?" and William looked expectantly at the Almoner then the Prior.

"Don't look at me, Your Grace! None of my boys are currently training for the priesthood. And besides, would you throw one of them at the Earl, to be gobbled up by him?"

"Elias? One of your monks?"

"I can't think who. I don't know why, but very few of my younger monks are priests at the moment; I can only think of Brother Luke off the top of my head, and he's just broken a leg falling out of a pear tree. No hope he'll be up to travelling any time soon. The next youngest is Brother Gregory, but he's no spring chicken – and he has a stutter; he and the Earl would drive each other mad, you know Hugh has no patience."

"Yes, there's none of the parish priests I'd consider bright enough or strong enough personalities to cope with our Earl. That brings us back to your boys, Andrew."

"Who, though? Jean, Wimer and Ricard are all coming up to the age when they need to make decisions on their future; but Jean will return to France in a couple of months, and neither of the other two have shown any inclination towards the priesthood."

"Actually, Wimer has asked about becoming a postulant." said Elias.

"Has he, indeed! Will you accept him?" asked William.

"Yes, I'd be delighted to. He is truly devout."

"Andrew, what's your opinion of him?"

"He's very, very bright. Excellent at arithmetic, and developing a broad knowledge of the law. If he were Norman, I'd like to see him carry on his education; he would benefit from going to Padua or Paris."

William raised his hand, fingers closed. "I have also noted that he is an excellent listener;" – he lifted his thumb, then a finger; "people like him; and he refuses to be bullied. So, in summary, we have a devout man, who would be an asset to a monastery, perhaps in time a Cellarer or a Bursar." He raised another finger. "He is also possible priest material, with the intellectual ability to meet any clerical challenge the world may throw at him, and he wins the trust of people around him." Two more fingers raised. "Saxon is a count against him, however – he cannot have the contacts a Norman has." The little finger went down. "Can we overlook that? I think so, if we can place him in the Bigod household, their power base is broad enough to give him good exposure to the world." He waved his hand, fully open, and used it to scoop up his goblet. "We are not in particular need of more postulant monks; but we do have need of a bright, strong-minded priest." He lifted the goblet in toast, and sipped.

"Now, to the last matter; what is taking the Earl of Norfolk, in his mid-sixties by my reckoning, away from his estates and his family on an extended journey? My guess is that he goes to France, to offer support to Henri FitzEmpress. Is that your reading also?"

Two nods in reply.

"Then I really think we must do what we can to support that endeavour, given the current relationship between King Stephen and the Church. His behaviour is close to risking an anathema on all the land... a situation I would risk much to avoid. I will talk to young Wimer, and see whether he can be persuaded that he has a vocation to the priesthood. If he can be ordained Deacon swiftly, he would have a short time for Father John to advise him; Hugh will not join any campaign this late in the year. Thank you for clarifying my mind, my friends."

The pair bent to kiss his ring, and left.

There had been no time to himself on the journey down to Ipswich, as he helped with the horses during the day and was included in the carters' circle around the fire at night. Now, though, he purposefully chose the quieter route home, taking the ancient footpath south through Belstead instead of the carters' roads. *I need some proper time to think. Got to make my mind up...*

The Bishop had given him a lot to think about. The

two visions of his future kept elbowing each other aside; the serenity and austerity of the monk, versus the picture the Bishop had painted of what life would be like as the Earl's chaplain, out in the wide world. *What do I know about either Earls or soldiers? They'd both eat me for breakfast! But I'd be in charge of their souls - what if I messed up? Being a monk would be so much easier! Maybe too easy, maybe that's the coward's way out...* Other people on the track gave him a wide berth, as he stomped along, ignoring everyone, and occasionally muttering to himself.

He started to come out of his absorption as the woods he was walking through became more and more familiar. His mood lightened, and he gave up worrying; he was nearly home, he was going to see his mother again, and maybe things would be clearer in the morning. All he had to do was not irritate Hervey... *I guess my dear brother will be less than overjoyed to see me. Still, at least this time he can't beat me black and blue, like he did at any excuse, or none, when I was a boy. Although I suppose he did me a favour, really, otherwise the old Bishop would never have rescued me. I expect I'd be a journeyman tanner, or something, by now – what a strange thought!*

He pulled a handful of cherries from his pack, and walked on, munching pensively. Journeymen could marry, with their master's permission – if he had been apprenticed, would he now be bringing a future wife home to meet his mother? Or maybe to show off a son or daughter? He tried to imagine a girl who could put up with the smell of a tanner, and wrinkled his nose in disgust. *She'd look like the side of a barn, and it wouldn't matter if she could cook or not, we'd never taste anything, it would all smell the same...* He crunched the last cherry with relish, and spat the seed into the wood.

He was here! He turned down a side path, and patted the huge old oak that stood at the edge of the clearing. *Hello, old guardian – I can remember when I couldn't reach this branch! I'm glad you're still doing well.* He stood and looked across the clearing at the family house. *That thatch is looking a bit tired...* there was someone sat on the bench outside.

He called "Hello!", and walked towards him.

A boy of 7 or 8 put down the tack he was cleaning, jumped to his feet, and asked "Can I help you, Sir?"

"I'm looking for Hervey or Thomas."

"Me, sir?! Oh, no, sorry, you must mean my father. He's out in the fields at the moment. I could run and get him?"

Wimer looked down at the lad with a mix of amazement and amusement.

"Which one are you, Hervey or Thomas? And which one's your father?"

"Hervey son of Hervey, I am. My Uncle's called Thomas."

"Then well met, Hervey son of Hervey! I am your other uncle, Wimer – although I must admit to not knowing I had a nephew until this moment!"

"Oh! My Grandmother used to talk about you! You went away when you were little, didn't you?" *She used to talk about me? Is she visiting somewhere? What bad luck to miss her!*

"I went to school when I was your age, actually. She used to talk about me?"

"She died last winter. Oh, I'm sorry! She was your mother, wasn't she! Didn't you know?"

There was a black pool of sorrow and loss rising inside

him, threatening to overwhelm him.

"No. I've had no letters or messages at all, whilst I've been at school. Perhaps you'd better run and get your father now. Wait - is your mother around?"

"She's in the house with the babies. I'll go and get Father, we won't be long." and Hervey junior sprinted off.

Wimer slumped onto the bench his nephew had vacated, and put his head in his hands. *Last winter! I'll never see her again… Dear Lord, please cherish the soul of your dearly beloved daughter, Eadgifu of Dodnash!* He rubbed his face with his hands, to rub away a tear. If he sat like this any longer, he would bawl like a baby – he stood up, and glared at the thatch. How like Hervey not even to send word she was ill! *I so wanted to tell her how well I've done at the school, and ask her what she thought I should do… But maybe she died suddenly, and Hervey couldn't send for me in time? I shouldn't pre-judge.* Feeling a little more positive, he went and knocked on the open door.

"Hello, the house!"

A half-familiar woman came to answer, a baby in her arms and a toddler at her skirts. "God give you a good day, Sir! How can I help you?"

"Good day to you too! I'm Wimer, Hervey's brother. I have been at the Cathedral school in Norwich, and I've come home to say goodbye; I may become a monk, and so couldn't come again…"

His voice trailed off as Hervey himself barrelled into view. He was now almost bald, and seemed much stockier and squarer somehow. He was also brick red, and stopped at the edge of the clearing to catch his breath. The pause allowed Wimer to bring his eyebrows down to something like their normal level.

The woman called across,

"Husband! Look, your brother Wimer – he is to become a monk. Isn't this a lovely surprise?"

Hervey strode over to them, breathing hard. "Still a skinny runt, aren't you. I'm not surprised you're to be a monk, still sponging off people who do real work, eh? Well, come in, have a mug of ale, and tell us all about it before you go."

I hate you, you narrow-minded, ignorant oaf. Good Lord. Where did that come from? *Um. Leviticus? "You shall not hate your brother in your heart"- going to have to work on that one.*

Wimer silently followed him inside, and took the offered seat on the bench. The house seemed smaller, and darker. He took his ale over to the window.

"I remember Mother sitting here sewing. Your son tells me she died last winter."

Hervey had the grace to look a little embarrassed. "Yes, God rest her soul. She just seemed to fade away over the winter, then the last frost in February took her. Such a shame. I'm sorry I didn't send a message, but things just piled up, then there didn't seem much point. Well, let me introduce you to my little family here. You remember Sal, from Bergholt? And you've met Hervey; this is William, and Maurice. An heir and two spares, eh? Good job you're off to be a monk, I can't afford any more mouths to feed!"

Wimer moved to put his mug back on the table with careful force, and nodded to his sister-in-law.

"Aye, Brother. Well, I'll say farewell, then. Good to meet you, Sister; and you, nephews. Please pass my good wishes to Thomas, when you see him next. God give you all a good day."

He involuntarily looked up as he went out of the door; there was still a rod there, ready for use. He shivered. *Thank the Lord I'm no longer under Hervey's thumb...*

He had planned on spending the night – maybe even a few days – at Hervey's house; but he couldn't stand being in his brother's presence even a minute longer. *Fratricide would not get either of my prospective careers off to a good start.* He set off to walk the seven miles back to Ipswich, to beg a meal and a place to sleep from one of the religious houses there. He felt sure of more of a welcome, and a place where he could pray for his mother's soul in peace.

The walk back, through the long summer twilight full of birdsong, calmed him. At first, he stormed along unseeing, rehearsing all that he might have said. Then, as he became aware of the scents on the air and the textures underfoot, his gait became slower. He stopped for a drink at a stream, and knelt beside an ancient beech tree to pray. Afterwards, he lay with his head pillowed on its roots, gazing up through the branches. Slowly, his eyes closed.

There was a small figure, far below, dressed in a black woollen habit, belted, a black scapular worn loose over it. The toy figure's head was bare, as was proper in the presence of God, and his dark hair made his tonsure clear. The figure moved around the cathedral in a fixed pattern, sometimes lighting candles at the altar, sometimes kneeling in prayer, sometimes seated in the choir stalls. Sometimes it was dark, sometimes light; sometimes the figure was dressed in sandals, sometimes heavy boots. His steps left a trail of light; a small groove in the stone floor was beginning to glow. The tonsured head grew less dark, then grey; the little figure became slower and slower, the trail of light dimmer and dimmer. Soon it stopped, and an angel came and lifted the monk to heaven. All that remained was a rut in the stone.

Time shifted, and the dark-haired figure was back, this time dressed for riding in hose and tunic. He knelt in a part of the cathedral the monk hadn't visited, and when he had finished praying, he left. The view widened and Wimer saw him again, riding towards a castle. A thread of light attached him to the cathedral. Inside the castle he sat at a desk and wrote a letter, and sent it off, carrying its own thread of light. The figure spoke to a man in rich clothing, and then rode off again to another place, then another, his paths criss-crossing the land. The thread was beginning to weave itself, lighting dark places where once beggars had hidden to rob wayfarers. The figure stopped to celebrate Mass in a church, and people left from it with their own threads lighting the way for more to come to God. Again, in time, the figure grew slower, and greyer, and its light faded to nothingness, and was gone. A fabric of light remained in the hearts and minds of the people, and that light continued to grow.

The morning sun woke him. The light was split into rays by the leaves, and for a moment he knew it to be the thread of light in his dream, connecting him directly to God. Suddenly, the world of a monk felt claustrophobic. The thought of never again being able to go for a walk in the woods without asking someone's permission was unbearable.

Chaplain it is, then! Thank you, Lord, for making my path so clear.

The Bishop sent for him at the end of October. He was more than ready to leave school; after Jean had gone (still laughing at him, always careful to call him "Father Wimer" so he would become used to it), the place felt flat and dull. Not boring! He had spent the time frantically studying, cramming the usual months or years of preparation for ordination into a few short weeks.

De Turbeville had actually performed the ordination service as soon as he had returned from Dodnash, in case the Earl came in haste; then set him to grow into the role. Now the rehearsal time was over.

He stopped outside the door and ran his hands through his hair, then pulled his clothing straight. He took a deep breath and knocked, fast, before his courage failed him. As he rose from kissing the Bishop's Ring, the elderly man seated to his left rose with him.

"Good grief, Bishop – this is a babe in arms you've given me! And a Saxon name – is he house-trained?"

Arrogant old Norman fool...

The man walked round him, looking him up and down. Wimer clasped his hands behind his back, braced his legs, and jutted his chin, feeling as though he were a sheep at auction. When the Earl reached the front again, Wimer enquired politely;

"Shall I open my mouth so that you can see the condition of my teeth, Sir?"

The man scowled, his face reddening with anger.

"Don't be impertinent, boy!"

de Turbeville intervened, smiling slightly.

"Lord, let me introduce your new Priest, Wimer de Dodnash. Father, this is Hugh Bigod, Earl of Norfolk. Uh – you are Earl currently, are you not, Lord? I gather that between them, King Stephen and Empress Maud have each granted and revoked that honour, I'm not sure of your current position?"

Wimer looked suspiciously at de Turbeville, but kept his mouth shut. *Why's he smiling? What's so funny?*

The Earl turned his ire from Wimer onto the question. *Hah! The old fox. I shall have to remember that trick. Even I know that it doesn't matter what his title is, the crusty old fool controls most of East Anglia.*

Whilst he talked, Wimer studied his new employer. If he hadn't been told his age, he wouldn't have guessed it. The Earl's hair, falling straight in front, and shaved so as not to catch in a mail hood at back, was a uniform dark grey. His body was lean and upright, muscles moving smoothly under his striped hose, less visible through the thick brocade on his tunic. His face gave more of a clue, with hints of loose skin pouching along his jaw. The lines on his face accentuated the impression, all drawing downwards. *This is not a man who smiles easily, or often.* At the moment, he was scowling fiercely, a formidable set of frown lines between his brows.

"So when Henri FitzEmpress makes his move, my banner will be beside his. Which brings us back to the matter at hand. I have need of a chaplain to serve my army in the field, and of a cleric who can take care of my personal correspondence. Is this - boy - really the best you can do for me, your Grace?"

"Lord, he has one of the sharpest minds the Cathedral school has produced for many years, is skilled in letters, numerate, and with a wide knowledge of Roman and canon law. He has also an easy manner with people, and is a true man of God. Youth is something that time mends; I am confident that you will find him up to the task."

Wimer could feel a blush rising. *My goodness! I wouldn't recognise me, if I met myself in the street!*

"Well, I have no time to quibble, events are moving apace. When can you be at Framlingham, boy?"

Wimer spread his arms. "I am at your disposal now, my Lord." *And the Lord help me! Well, I shall just have to show M'Lord Oh-so-Norman Bigod that this Saxon is competent. I hope.*

"Then we ride in an hour."

He re-read the letter again, just to be sure.

"*Willelmus, Episcopus, ad Wimer Capellanus.* William, Bishop, to Wimer the Chaplain.

My son, I meant to give you this package before you left Norwich, but it slipped my mind. It contains a small portable altar, which I am sure will be useful in your service to the Earl, and I also send something to aid your meditations – a copy of Folcard's *Vita Sanctus Botulfi;* it came into my hands on the very day I dedicated the altar with a small quantity of the bones of St Botulph, so I feel sure that it is meant for you. A Saxon saint for a Saxon priest, and one who lived in East Anglia; it feels most fitting!

If you press the altar's images of St Luke and St John at

the same time, you will unlock the relic compartment. I pray the saint will watch over you in your travels, and will impart to you some of his virtues; to be humble, meek, and affable. You must work on all three, you know, my son; especially towards the Earl.

Go in God."

Wimer scowled. *I thought I'd escaped his nagging… No, that's not fair, he's right - and right to remind me.* He knelt and said an Our Father, and added on a prayer for the health of the Earl, the source of his daily bread. *And, dear Lord, help me to be - what was it - humble, meek and affable!*

He rose to his feet, and touched the package. *I suppose I will have to get used to being so close to holy relics! What an amazing gift!* Reverently, he slit the ribbon close to the seal, and unfolded the linen. Inside was another wrapping, of pale blue silk, and lying on top, a slim book. He lifted the book, kissed it, and laid it aside for later.

He slowly opened the silk, admiring its suppleness as it slipped from the precious object within. At last the altar was revealed. The polished depths of the sheet of porphyry gleamed, its mottled purples contrasting intensely with the creamy bone surround. At each corner were small startlingly blue enamelled plaques, each with a symbol of the four Apostles.

He sucked in breath, *This is a truly beautiful thing…* he stroked each of the plaques. *Dare I? Oh come on, stop being silly…* He put his forefingers on the Ox and the Eagle, and pressed gently. There was some give, but nothing happened. *Have I broken it?! – no, it must be protected against an accidental knock.* He pressed more firmly, and felt the plaques move downwards. With a soft click, a drawer opened to the front. Inside was a small scrap of linen, tied with a label.

He lifted his hands, and rubbed them down the sides of his tunic, to wipe them clean. Before he could change his mind, he lifted the package reverently, and read the label aloud. "Ex femur os sancti Botulphi…"

He sank to his knees. *Sancti Botulphi, ora pro me…* No, wait, this is a Saxon saint, I can pray to him in English! *Dear Saint Botolph, please help me. I really want to be a good priest, and to look after my flock; and I hope my work will satisfy the Earl. Please, please help me not to make an idiot of myself!*

He rose, made the sign of the cross, and reverently put the package back into its place. The mechanism slid smoothly back, finishing with a satisfying click. He wrapped the altar back up in its silk, and turned to the book. *How kind, to send me a book of my own!* He settled himself comfortably in the window seat, and began to read.

HENRI, AGE 9

SOUTHERN ENGLAND; WINTER 1142/43

The crossing had gone on forever, and Henri was so cold that he wasn't sure where his hands and feet ended, and so tired that he didn't care any more. Another icy wave broke over the sides. A horse shifted uneasily. He bent to bailing efforts again. After a while, he became dimly aware of a change in the rocking of the boat and the rhythm of the other people working with him – then someone took the bucket from him, and boosted him onto a dock. He stood swaying, grey with tiredness, then the realisation of where he was snapped the world into monotone clarity. Behind him, in Wareham itself, there was a clash of steel and a cry cut off in mid-yell.

He spun to see. There was movement above him; he glimpsed a woman, her white wimple clearly visible in the gloom of an upstairs room, as she slammed the shutters across the window. He spent a heartbeat admiring the pattern of wood and plaster on her house; the deep orange plaster panels appearing thinner and thinner as the building stretched away from him towards the back of the square. Under the jetty at the far end of it was the source of the cry, a man crumpling to the floor as a mercenary, in mail from the knees up, withdrew his sword. More mercenaries were running across the cobbles, towards warehouses painted red and yellow, and the wide gap between them. *That must be the road...*

"Get the horses and weapons off!" came a fierce whisper from below, and he ran to take a place in the line of people unloading the boat at speed. When his uncle's charger surged up the steep ramp, he took its reins, moved to a mounting block, and tacked it up; Leon was still muzzy from the valerian mixture the horses had been given to calm them for the crossing, and stood still for him, for a change. As he finished cinching the girth, his uncle the Earl clattered over in his hauberk and helm, mounted with a nod of thanks, and galloped off towards the growing noise of fighting.

Henri looked around. All of the mercenaries were over on the far side of the square, engaged in hand-to-hand battles with figures that looked identically dressed from this distance. He could see one or two mounted knights using their spears to pick off targets. *Where are all the other knights? – They must have ridden into the town. Ah, yes, Uncle said that no word of our landing must reach the King, or he'll attack. They'll have gone to secure the gates.*

At a shouted command, some of the mercenaries broke off from the fight, and came trotting back towards the boats.

"Form up to move out!" Henri and the other non-combatants with the party – clerics – were hustled into the centre of a wedge of armed men. Behind him, the boats started to cast off from the wharf. Henri wished for a sword, and drew his eating dagger as they neared the fighting. *How are we going to get through? There's no gap!*

The mercenary beside him stepped to one side of a duelling pair, and plunged his spear down across the shoulder of the enemy, almost severing his arm. The man wheeled away, clutching at the hole where his arm should attach and screaming in curious, high-pitched waves. Henri stood still and watched him go, trying to understand what had happened. *He should have had stuffing coming out of that hole, he was like that doll I broke the arm off...* "Move on, damn you!" and the wedge swept him onwards again through the new opening.

They reached the street leading out of the square, and the escort reformed into a line on either side of the houses. With no opposition in front of them, they picked the pace up. Henri began to feel safe. The blisters on his hands started to throb, and his legs felt almost as heavy as his eyelids.

A soldier charged out from a swirl of smoke in an alleyway, screaming, his sword stabbing towards Henri. He raised his dagger in reflex, the blade of the sword growing huge. On either side of him, his uncle's men turned in unison *like a dance!* and thrust their weapons into the soldier's body. The man's eyes widened in surprise, his mouth a soundless O. Henri caught the acrid stench as his bowels voided. He retched, and one of the mercenaries wordlessly pushed him into moving again. He held his dagger at the ready.

They swept on, the daylight beginning to fail. As the houses ended, they came to a whitewashed wooden church, tucked away under the protective shadow of the town wall towering above, built on a natural bank. Road, and church, would be completely hidden from the other side.

"We stop here and wait for the Earl." ordered the leader. "Clean out the church."

A mercenary kicked the door open, and then stood back as two more wove past him, swords at the ready, eyes darting to the corners of the nave then down to the end of the chancel. Henri saw them relax and lower the swords. One jerked his thumb towards the door, and a single old man sidled out, looked in horror at the bloodstained fighters, and took off at a stumbling run along the lane.

In you go, you non-combatants!" the captain waved at the church, and turned away, pointing out guard posts to the mercenaries. Henri sheathed his dagger, and followed the clerics in. Several knelt to pray.

Henri also went to his knees, and tried to ask God for the continued success of their mission. As he shut his eyes, he saw again the blood gouting from the man in the square, and heard his keening. He realised, as though he had been struck a blow, that the man must be dead by now. *I nearly got spitted too…* Suddenly feeling sick again, he made a brief mumble of thanks for a safe landing, and went out into the fresher air.

"Oh, no, you don't, young master - inside." ordered the captain.

"Why? It's safe enough here."

The captain looked at him as though he had just been

spawned by a toad. He pointed to two of the soldiers.

"You, you – get this little fool inside and keep him there. Don't be too gentle about it."

Henry felt a black tide of rage starting to swamp his control. If those louts touched him, he would...

"Thank you, Pierre, I'll take him." A voice from the top of the wall made them all start. Leon leapt off the wall and slid down the slope. The Earl extended a hand to Henri, hoisted him onto the front of the saddle, and nudged Leon into a canter, all in a few seconds.

"So, nephew – had I been one of Stephen's men, and seen a well-dressed boy at the centre of a band of strange mercenaries, you would be, at best, a hostage now, and at worst, wriggling on the end of my spear. It was unworthy of you to put the men at risk; think on it."

Henri did think about it, or tried to; as he warmed up under his uncle's cloak, it got harder and harder to stay awake. He spent the ride in a sort of half-nightmare, spouting blood and severed limbs being kept at bay only by the speed of a good horse, with swords dancing in candlelit churches.

Someone kicked him, not ungently. "Come on, lad, shake a leg, you're wanted in the chamber."

He jumped up and stretched, looking around at a large hall, bodies wrapped in cloaks on benches or on the floor, a few men warming themselves at the fire. For an instant he felt lost, then remembered where he must be – Corfe Castle. Yesterday's events came back to him, and he realised he was still wearing his uncle's cloak. He shook it free from straw, folded it over his arm, and followed the servant across the hall and up the stairs. Several of the men by the fire turned to watch. *Why are they all staring at me?* He tried to walk tall.

The Earl stood frowning thoughtfully at a sand-table, eating-knife in his hand, jabbing it at his companion to emphasise a point. The other man looked more tired than irritated, as though they had gone over this same ground many times before. Henri bobbed a bow to both, put the cloak on a stool by the door, and came closer to listen.

"Ah, boy, come here. My lord Constable, let me present Henri FitzEmpress; Matilda's heir."

Henri made his best courtier's bow, and then stood straight for inspection. To his surprise, the man bowed back.

"Ah, our potential solution. Yes, he resembles the King his grandfather. He's what, nine, ten? I weary at the thought of the years we must remain at war, before he can come into that inheritance." The man stared sombrely down at him. *Well, I'm sorry, but it's not my fault I'm nearly 10!*

"Aye, well, we have a more pressing problem, I remind you – we need to rescue the lioness before elevating the cub. Should Stephen have Matilda killed, and mends his relationship with Canterbury enough for his son Eustace to be crowned, Henri's chances grow dim. Come; show me again the approaches to Oxford castle. - Boy, have you eaten yet? There's bread and ale over there, then come and join us at the sand-table."

Henri bit his lip, and went to get some food to cover his frustration. *For all we know, Mother could be dead by now! If I were the King, I'd kill her – why leave another claimant to the throne alive? He could kill her now, and worry about all the nobles who swore to protect her, later.* He munched mechanically, hunger blunted.

To distract himself, he thought again of the Constable's words – "our potential solution". *What have they got planned for me?* He turned his attention back to the table, and watched, fascinated, as the two men wiped the sand flat and used their knives to draw the important features of the landscape.

"Oxford here; Wallingford there. I still say that you should make for Wallingford, regroup, and attack from a fortified position."

"No, Stephen is too volatile. I want my sister out of Oxford at the earliest opportunity. What castles does Stephen hold if we came up this way?"

The lines in the sand grew deeper as the conversation grew more animated. Finally the Earl drove his dagger through the dip representing Oxford, and left it vibrating gently in the table.

"Agreed. We move at dusk. Time for a show, I think?" Both men turned to look appraisingly at Henri.

What?!

Henri's pony shifted uneasily, and the Earl's great charger bared his teeth at it. Henry grimly brought the pony back under control. *These men don't care whose side they're on – and they'd slit my throat and package me up for King Stephen, quick as winking, if we stop paying them...* he shivered, and steadied his pony again.

His uncle was telling the bailey-full of armed men

about the great wrong done to Henri's mother by the barons when old King Henry died. They had forsworn their oath to put her, as Henry's rightful heir, on the throne. Many of the men were mercenaries, who simply listened politely, not caring one way or the other; but here and there were local men nodding and scowling. Henri tried to note who was scowling.

The Earl was telling them how much better off they would be with Matilda on the throne instead of Stephen, and how she would bring an end to the endless civil wars. Henri's gaze was caught by an old man and a youth standing together. The young man had been one of the nodders as the Earl talked about the oath-breaking; but at the thought of peace, the old man ran his hand over his face and sighed. *Poor old fellow. He's seen too much fighting in his lifetime. These people need a ruler who can bring them a peaceful future...*

As if in echo of his thoughts, the Earl wound up with:

"And I give you the future – Matilda's heir, Henri!"

Henri had been told just to stand in his stirrups and wave, but suddenly he couldn't bear not to talk to these men. He turned his lively grey pony and made it climb the first, broad step of the motte stair, so that they could see him better. He supposed he was an arresting sight – the two nobles had put some effort in to his appearance earlier in the day. He had been bathed, much to his disgust, and dressed in a richly brocaded yellow tunic and red hose. He carried a pole with his grandfather's colours tied to it, the flag snapping gratifyingly in the breeze.

He took a deep breath, and remembered to try and talk slowly, so his nervousness wouldn't show through. He spoke loudly, trying to pitch his voice to the men standing at the back, hoping the wind would carry it:

"Fighting to right a wrong is a great and noble thing to do. On behalf of my mother, and in my own name, I thank you. When we come to power, we will right the wrongs that King Stephen has done to you, and bring peace to all the land. I, Henri, swear this." And now he stood in his stirrups, and raised the flag high:

"Who will fight with me?"

First one, then a few, then most of the men raised their fists and shouted "Aye!" "Henry!"

The chant settled to "Hen-ry! Hen-ry!" in a wall of hungry sound that made Henri shiver. The Earl, surprised but quick to take advantage of the situation, gestured him to ride out the gates. Men parting to let him through reached out to touch him or the horse for luck. A small army followed him out of the gate, and Henri turned the pony onto a low mound and smiled and waved as they went past. He managed not to throw up until the Constable's men had everyone busy with some marching practice, and it was safe to dismount.

Henri's pony jinked a little, and he absent-mindedly stilled it with a gentle shift in weight. He had listened to his uncle's speech so many times that he could have repeated it by heart. They were coming up to the bit where he would normally take over, but this time, thank goodness, he was just there to support his mother. He watched with pride as she nudged her horse to the front, and began to speak to the men.

He had been so relieved and happy when she'd turned up at Wallingford after escaping from Oxford Castle - all by herself, simply walking through King Stephen's guard lines in the snow. Then she'd spoilt it by patting him on the cheek. He'd been telling her about the performance he and the Earl had done, so often that he had lost count of the castles and manor courtyards they'd visited. All she had said was how pretty he must look, with his red curls! He had nearly gotten angry with her again, but his uncle had thumped him on the back, and said that the men followed him, he had something about him. Henri was still pleased about that.

His mother was embroidering the speech a little. Henry looked out at the men, trying to count how many would follow them this time. Most were standing solidly, arms crossed.

"...and so, my brave warriors – who will follow me, to fight for my throne?"

His mother stood up in her stirrups and waved an arm in the air. Henry stood too, and raised the flag. There was a polite smattering of applause, then most of the men turned away. His mother sat back down in the saddle with a thump. Henri looked around. *What was happening? Why aren't they rallying to the flag?*

"Well, that was a huge non-event." His mother snatched the goblet of wine Henri offered her, and drained it in one gulp. She held the goblet out for a refill without even looking at him.

"Yes, I don't understand it." the Earl was watching

him. Henri hurried to fetch him some wine; he took it with a smile. "The lad here has certainly had better luck."

His mother whirled round, and stalked to the window. "Well, I don't have the leisure to stay here and recruit these English peasants for you; my husband the Count requires my presence at home as a matter of urgency."

Henri frowned. *I can't imagine Father requiring her to do anything – he'd have to notice her, first!* He glanced over at his uncle, and saw the same frown.

"Well, m'dear – whatever you think best. May I keep the boy for a while longer?"

His mother waved an arm, languidly. "Yes, yes, if you think he'll be of any use – fetch me some more wine, would you please, mon petit chou?"

Henri fetched the wine ewer absent-mindedly, not even rising to the hated pet name. *She's giving up!* Actually, she had failed, and she wasn't admitting it. He could not afford to do the same. He was going to have to go back to the endless round of rallying – *and baths*, he thought, mournfully – one of them must stay, and build an army, or else their cause was lost.

HENRI, AGE 14

CAEN - DECEMBER 1147

The young red-head flipped his leg over his horse's neck and leapt lithely down from the saddle. He tossed the reins to a waiting boy with a smile.

"Walk him for a bit, would you, Jacques? He and I have had a fine old gallop, he could do with cooling down before you water him."

The lad watched him stride off, admiration plain on his face, before the horse nudged him for the apple core he knew was hidden somewhere on the boy.

"Yes, all right, you great beast. Here you go... I could do without the slobber, you know! Come on, let's go for a nice walk, then I'll rub you down. No, I don't have another one, piggy! We are lucky to have a master like Henri, aren't we, Nero. Not many young lords know the names of every one of the stable-boys; and he never mistreats his horses. Let's go and find some hay, then I'll draw you some water..."

Henri bounded up the stairs two at a time, still full of energy after his jaunt with Nero. This had the effect of bringing him into hearing range of the nearest conversation sooner than the participants had expected.

"... if he wasn't still just a boy!"

"Talking about me again, Your Grace?" Henri enquired lightly. Theobald, Archbishop of Canterbury, had the grace to blush.

"Am I right in assuming that you do not have concerns about my education, or my physical and intellectual abilities, and that you agree that I have a claim to the English crown through no less than seven of her previous kings?"

"No, my Lord, all - "

"Then you will not be alone in that assessment, I think. If I were not 14, but, say, 18 – would you hesitate to urge my cause?"

"Indeed not - "

"Your Grace, one day I expect men to follow me because I lead Anjou, or even Normandy or England. But at this moment, all I can offer them is a cause – a just cause! That duty to right a wrong, to put my Mother's heir on the throne of England, to fulfil the oaths the Barons swore to my Grandfather, King Henry - that does not change whether I am 14 or 40! We have a golden opportunity today, before the usurper Stephen can rebuild after my Mother the Empress' last campaign, and when he does not expect another assault until the spring. You know as well as I that the nobles are at the end of their patience with Stephen, and his mismanagement of the Church and exchequer. With you, and most of the rest of the clergy, unable to run the affairs of the Church without interference, England grows spiritually poorer every day. Let us at one stroke restore the Church and the Throne to their rightful incumbents. A relatively small, swift force, attacking Winchester and overcoming Stephen, could right all our current wrongs. If you were to put aside your visit to Rome and return with us to England, you could perform my coronation. What think you?"

"Indeed, my Lord, your argument is very cogent. I find myself becoming more inclined to it."

Henri bowed his head in thanks and farewell, and moved off into the throng to make similar pleas elsewhere. Behind him, the Archbishop turned to his companion. Henri strained his ears to make out the verdict:

"It is a good argument. Its flaw is that it relies on his ability to read a situation correctly, and change a plan in the face of enemy action – and that's still untested. Although he is competent in the hunt..."

"A man – or a boy – either has that ability, or has not, your Grace. You can train and prepare a man for it, but until his first battle, you cannot know in which camp he falls. Henri's years are against him; but he's right about a narrow window of opportunity. I say, back him; I will put 100 marks into the pot. If he succeeds, we all win; if he fails, he has two brothers in the same bloodline."

Henri bared his teeth in a smile totally devoid of humour. It was a prize worth the gamble. And he COULD do it!

He stood in the prow of the ship, relishing the wind in

his face, and the illusion of solitude. Behind him in his flagship, and the flanking ship, were his invasion force; a handful of knights, with their horses and squires, and all the mercenaries his credit could stretch to – a single company.

He was beginning to appreciate this quiet time before the storm. His growing experience with battles in France had taught him the value in using the time to envision his plan of action. Not that he had much of one, this time – again, he wished for more men; but the lack could not be helped. They would disembark at Wareham, and do some recruiting in the castles and manors in an arc to the north east, the ones where he'd had so much success as a boy. Then the strategy fizzled out; he intended to move in force and at speed to London or Winchester, or wherever the King was, once he knew the extent of his forces. *Fluid,* he thought firmly; *fluid, not vague. And if I say it often enough, I might even believe it...*

The wind shifted direction slightly, and a few drops of rain hit his face. He turned, and went to chat with his mercenaries. Paid swords or not, the better they knew him, and he them, the better they would function as a unit.

Henri lay on his stomach at the edge of the wood, watching the comings and goings of the castle at Purton. *How I would love to be in reach of one of those fires! It must be the forge to the left, and the kitchen to the right. I could really do with a big, hot bowl of porridge right now...* It didn't help that the bush he had chosen to wriggle under for concealment had developed a persistent drip down the back of his neck, which had become heftier and colder as the drizzle had changed to sleet.

He looked again at the approaches. The South and West were blocked by the moated ditch; possibly the castle's water supply, although the whole area was so low-lying that they could easily have a well inside too. *Must have the men pee in it anyway, just in case.* The keep defended the North side, with ample range for crossbows. Really, the only feasible attack was from the East, across the irritatingly large open space between the timber palisades of the bailey and the wood he was currently in.

Given the weather, there was no point in trying to fire the palisades; his best bet was to wait until dawn, hope for a repeat of this morning's mist, and try and time the raid so that the defenders' eyes were dazzled by the rising sun burning the mist off.

Another blob of freezing sludge plopped onto his neck. He suppressed the urge to scream his frustration, and crawled backwards, adding another layer of mud to his clothing.

"Gather round, men! We attack at dawn; let me talk you through the plan."

The thirty or so men were huddled under cloaks, and any scrap of natural shelter the wood provided. They did not look enthusiastic about moving. *Hell! What do I do if they just keep lying there? I need to get them moving somehow. Who looks least rooted?* Henri made eye contact with one leader after another, radiating expectation. *Thank God – here comes Owain – I shall never be rude about Welshmen again. Now, who's next? Come on, me hearties, come to Henri…* Slowly the group coalesced around him. It really was a pitiful little army, almost the same size as the one he had landed at Wareham.

It had been the same story at Corfe, then Salisbury, Devizes, and Marlborough; in each keep, the men had listened, but few had joined. One old boy had caught his arm in the bailey at Devizes, said that he had joined the call when Henri was a boy. He'd spent the last three long years fighting, and was sick and tired of it. Maybe he'd follow again when Henri had enough of a following to sweep all before him; but until then, count him out. The men around had nodded, and gone back to their quarters. It was all Henri had been able to do to keep from saying "but it's not fair!" The vision of the 9 year old he had been, who would have stamped his foot and said exactly that in a fit of temper, was all that stopped him.

The only ray of light was the letter from Ranulf of Chester that had reached him at Marlborough, offering to meet him with his knights at the Priory in Swindon on 12th night.

Finally, all the men were near enough to hear his voice, and he gathered himself to put some energy into his description of the plan of attack.

"So, we need to keep as low as possible and between the gatehouse and the sun. Owain, you and your bowmen are to hold your fire until you get a shot at both guards. Gary, your team is point; run through Owain's line on my signal and keep below his bow-shot. Knife the guards if they're still standing when you get there. The rest of the men will charge as soon as the guards are down, or if the cry goes up. You knights are to attack as opportunity presents. The end goal, of course, is the keep; but if that's not achievable, we'll set up a siege. Any questions?"

"What are we eating tonight?"

Henri's heart sank. To add weight to the question, his own stomach growled.

"Cold camp tonight, I'm afraid – all the more reason to capture the kitchen and their pottage tomorrow!" he pronounced cheerily.

Henri stood in the middle of the area where his vicious little Welsh knife-wielders had camped. They had left not a single item behind as they had melted away in the night; unlike the archers, who had politely arranged a few blankets to look like sleeping men. *By God I'd like to chase after those ignorant bastards and kick their balls through their teeth!* He shut his eyes for a breath and consciously unclenched his fists. *No time – I can chase the misbegotten cowards later. Right now, I need to decide what to do now. Retreat? Or press the attack with the remaining men?* He spat on a blanket. *Fluid, hah!* No choice, really; if he didn't try to get some momentum going, he would be one man fighting alone very soon. He went back to the main group, rapidly amending his plan.

The Eastern horizon was already aglow by the time they were in position. The weather too was mocking them, dawning clear and bright. A gate guard, coming out to relieve himself, saw them and raised the alarm before they were half-way across the distance; the gate had been slammed in their faces, and they found themselves beautifully backlit for the castle archers by the rising sun.

He'd lost another five men before they made it back into the shelter of the woods. Retreating and going back to recruiting was the only option, unpalatable though it was.

It was almost dark by the time they arrived at Swindon Priory, having made a detour to sweep through a village for some food. He rode through the gate at the head of his ragged little army, and dismounted in the courtyard in front of the Great Church. Ranulf was walking towards him out of the church, and he stripped off his gauntlet to clasp his arm in friendship. The gates started to swing closed behind his group – and there was a cry!

"It's a trap! They're armed!"

Sure enough, Henri saw one of the 'monks' closing the gate pull off his habit in one movement, draw his sword, and slash it across the neck of the boy who had cried warning. *NO! That's Jacques!* Ranulf had leaped to close the gap between them, and as Henri turned to confront him, he found his arm twisted up behind his back and a dagger at his throat.

"Yield, or your golden boy loses his life right now."

The group started to look around, gauging the opposition. Henri saw monk after monk transformed into armoured soldiers.

"Yield, my men! We are betrayed and overcome!" he roared, the dagger piercing the skin of his throat a little as he drew breath. *Come on, yield – there is no point in dying here. No sense in MORE people dying – poor little Jacques!* One by one, the knights saw sense and knelt, drawing their swords and placing them in front of them. The defrocked monks moved swiftly among them, confiscating the swords, and herding the squires and mercenaries into a corner. Henri felt his own sword belt being loosened and removed, and only then did the dagger withdraw and the pain in his shoulder lessen.

"So sorry, dear boy." Ranulf whispered in his ear. "I'm afraid your spy system is lacking; I swore fealty to Stephen a sennight ago. Foiling your little treason plot was part of the price." *You bastard turncoat! I will remember this.*

"Take the boy to the Priory cells." he ordered a passing soldier. "When we ride to the King tomorrow, he is to be in chains."

Stephen leant forward, propped one elbow on a knee, and rested his chin on his palm. The object of his close attention was kneeling, bound, in front of him – managing to look perfectly at ease, as upright as he could manage, with clear blue-grey eyes looking calmly back from a face haloed by red curls. Without breaking contact with that gaze, Stephen asked:

"My lord of Chester, what do you suggest I do with your captive?"

"He is a boy, Sire. Give him a good whipping, then ship him back to his father with a recommendation to repeat the chastisement."

The grey gaze did not falter.

"Robert de Ferrers?"

"Kill him, Sire. He has not yet attained his majority or his knighthood, so cannot swear any binding oath; and he is guilty of inciting treason against you. If you let him go, he will try again; and keeping him imprisoned would be a waste of money. Kill him, and be done."

"So, cousin. Which option do you council me to take?" The bound youth smiled.

"I prefer the first to the second, Your Majesty. There is a third route you may wish to consider, however; adopting me. Killing me would serve no practical purpose. I have, as you know, two younger brothers with an equal claim to your throne. However, making me your heir would neutralise the Angevin threat to you at one stroke."

The King snorted surprised laughter, breaking eye contact with Henri and looking round to share his mirth with his courtiers. To his astonishment, not all of them were laughing. Several – especially the older ones – were looking pensive; and only broke into dutiful smiles as they became aware of his gaze. Stephen's smile turned into a thoughtful frown.

"Clear the hall! - and loose his bonds."

"Father! You cannot be seriously considering this preposterous idea!" from Eustace. Stephen looked from one boy to another as the hall emptied. Henri's first act, on regaining the use of his feet, was to stand and make a formal bow to Stephen, then to rub life back into his wrists. Eustace was a couple of years older, but his chubbier features and lack of grace made that age advantage difficult to see. He was also going an unappealing blotchy pink, and looked as though he was just about to throw a tantrum. Henri was ignoring him, concentrating on Stephen.

"I am your son! And your heir! This is nothing but an idiot, a failed pretender who has no claim on you at all! If I were king, I'd have him whipped then cut his head off!"

"Actually, Eustace, I have not yet designated an heir. You would do well to remember that; and I do not recall inviting you to stay."

Eustace reacted as though he had been slapped, glared daggers at Henri, and half-ran to exit the hall just as the doors were closing. Stephen sighed.

"Oh, dear, Henri – I fear Eustace doesn't like you. However, a surprising number of my nobles did. Would you be kind enough to tell me who, apart from that wind-vane Ranulf of Chester, you approached?"

"I'm afraid, Your Majesty, that I cannot. I am, I remind you, a mere boy, and all the arrangements were made by my elders." Henri clasped his hands in front of him and looked at the floor, the picture of demureness. Stephen roared with laughter.

"Ah, boy, what an actor you are! Look into my eyes. Derby? Sussex? Leicester? No, I cannot tell, your face doesn't change at all. Perhaps I should give you to Derby and get him to torture the list out of you, before beheading you? No, I jest, I will not have you killed. Or whipped. I may live to regret the decision, but I think I will simply pay your bills and send you home.

Now, come and sit with me, tell me how your mother my cousin fares; we may have our current differences, but I was always fond of her."

HENRI, AGE 17

CARLISLE - 6-7TH JUNE 1150

Henri allowed himself a few more seconds luxuriating in the warm water, then heaved himself out of the bath. *Peh – I have not missed the climate here at all – I'm sure it was raining when I left England as a boy, and it's still just as cold and damp...* He waved away the servant trying to dry him off, and took the linen himself. Catching sight of his companion's expression as he climbed into the bath in his turn, he buried his grin in the towel and rubbed vigorously. *This Robert of Hereford clearly doesn't believe that bathing is good for you – or perhaps I left the water dirtier than I thought? Got to be some privileges of rank...*

Henry Murdac, the Archbishop, continued the lecture:

"- and so you cleanse your person, as later you will cleanse your spirit. You must be spotless, to show your purity, within and without. As a knight, you will serve God by protecting the bodies of those weaker than yourself, and to guard the corpus of the church -"

Henri had a sudden thought.

"Beg pardon, your Grace; you emphasise the body over the spirit. Why is that?"

"A perceptive question, young man. The holy

ceremony of knighthood is to prepare you to serve God through the concerns of the body. It is the exact equivalent of the ordination of a priest, whose duty is to the care of souls." *Ah. Interesting. I hadn't made that connection before.*

Robert heaved himself out of the bath, flicked a rose petal off his shoulder with great disdain, and allowed the maid to dry him and comb his hair. Henri tugged a comb through his own tight curls. *How does he manage to keep his prick still, when a pretty young thing like that is towelling him down?*

"Ah, you are both ready. Now to your clothing; in white, to show that your body is clean and your heart is pure." the Archbishop made the sign of the cross over the garments, and the two young men pulled on the outfits.

"A scarlet cloak; for nobility, and to remind you not to fear to spill your blood in Christ's service, for if you fall fighting His battle, you avoid purgatory."

Henri swirled the fine wool cloak around his shoulders, and fastened it with a gold pin.

"Black boots, to remind you of death, and that all men are mortal; do not commit the sin of pride, for death comes to all.

Now, confession; I will hear the Earl of Hereford first."

Robert and Murdac withdrew to the window enclosure out of earshot, Robert kneeling in front of the Archbishop. Henri amused himself by admiring the maids clearing away the bath. *Oh hell! I'm probably going to have to confess to the sin of desiring fornication whilst in a purified state.* He sighed, and waited for his turn with the Archbishop.

"Kneel, my son." Robert was on his own on the other side of the room, rosary in hand, working through his penance. Henri bowed to the inevitable and knelt.

"Forgive me, Father, for I have sinned..."

Some time later, the Archbishop continued the ceremony:

"I gird you with this belt to remind you that you are clean in body and free of sin. A true knight should always aspire to this state. A knight that dies in this state goes straight to Paradise; please take your ease on this bed, which is a pitiful shadow of Paradise, but the closest foretaste we can provide on Earth. I will return shortly." Murdac left the room.

Robert and Henri lay stiffly side by side on the plumped-up feather mattress, which was covered by fine white linen and more rose petals.

"What are we supposed to be doing here?" Robert whispered.

"Relaxing, and contemplating Paradise!" Henri said, in a normal voice. "It's the nearest we get to sleep until tomorrow night. And by then, we'll be knights... I think my uncle the King has arranged a tournament for the day after tomorrow. I'm really looking forward to trying the paces of that charger he presented me with earlier. He was indeed a royal gift!" Henri bounced, then remembered what he was supposed to be doing, and settled down again.

Robert sighed. "I do not approve of tournaments. I can't refuse without offending the King, though. I expect you go to them all the time, in France?"

"No, not really. Recently there has been no time for tournaments, my father has been keeping me busy with real battles. I do enjoy the chance to impress the ladies, though..."

"Hah! With those red curls, and those big grey eyes? You just need to raise your eyebrow and smile, and the women line up to swoon - what it is to be 17! I would prefer to spend the time with my lady wife, whom I have already won... Listen, do I hear the good Archbishop returning?"

"Now, my sons, it is time for your vigil; please follow me."

Henri's knees hurt. He shifted his weight slightly, and glanced over at Robert; he was completely still, with his eyes shut. *Is it possible to sleep, kneeling?* If it were, Henri hadn't got the knack of it.

He let his eyes wander again. Where the walls and ceiling of the castle chapel showed, the normally pink stone looked like clotted blood. He moved his weight on to his other knee, and looked for something more cheerful. His magnificent sword on the altar, lit by the sole candle, caught his eye. The light was glinting off the faceted ruby at the top of the pommel in a very pretty way. He settled his weight evenly, centered his spine, and allowed himself to imagine how he would use that sword.

He'd have to take that ruby off, of course, and get the pommel refashioned into something that could be used to strike a blow if necessary; but still, he could see how to wield it in God's service. His imagination shifted him outside into the golden sunlight, the warm colours of the countryside counterpointing the figure of a mounted knight in white armour. The figure seemed to be haloed with the light, and he could faintly hear some slow, sweet music. He flew towards the knight, and saw he was himself. He wanted to stay here forever.

The light turned back into the candle on the altar as the procession, led by the Archbishop, entered the chapel. *No! I want to go back – please let me stay!* Throughout mass, Henri tried to hold on to the image, but it slowly faded. Being allowed to sit to listen to the sermon – once the pain in his knees subsided – helped. He'd listened to this lecture, or variations on it, many times when squires were knighted in his father's court. He let his mind drift back to the light, only returning as Murdac was winding up in preparation for the oath. He knelt again in front of his uncle, David, King of Scotland, to take it. He felt buoyant, somehow, truly purified, and made the oath in sweet solemnity.

"I, Henri FitzEmpress, do solemnly swear on my immortal soul, that I will never traffic with traitors; that I will never give evil counsel to a lady; and that I will observe fasts and abstinences, every day hear Mass, and make an offering in Church. So help me, God."

David's dubbing sent him sprawling to the floor, shattering his newfound peace. *What the? – ah! My father does this. It's so the knight remembers all that he's learned during the ceremony. He needn't thump so hard though... Please God, I will always hold on to the memory of the light and the music; I don't care if the rest fades.*

BRIAN FITZCOUNT

WALLINGFORD - WINTER 1152

"Ad Henri, Dux Normaniae et Aquitaniae et Comes Andigaviae...

To Henri, Duke of Normandy and Aquitaine, Count of Anjou; from your loyal vassal, Brian FitzCount, Constable of Wallingford castle; greetings.

My lord, it is with shame and sorrow that I must beg your leave to surrender the castle of Wallingford to King Stephen. Our position is now hopeless; with the loss of the last bridge across the Thames to the enemy forces, we have lost all possibility of re-provisioning.

The fighting this year has been fiercer than any we have ever known. The King has built two castles right up against Wallingford itself, and from these, a host of mercenaries are conducting a now unbreakable siege against us.

The town, too, is suffering for its loyalty to you, and is

also surrounded. All entry and exit is prevented. I am much afraid that they are in a worse state than we are. We had a brief respite a few weeks ago when Roger of Hereford managed to get a single pack train through the King's lines. With the town's many more mouths to feed, and the early onset of winter, their plight is dire indeed. My estimate is that, on quarter rations, the castle can hold out until the end of January. The town may fall well before that, and without shame.

My liege lord, I beg you to either come to our aid, or allow us to surrender. We will hold out against the King whilst our bodies retain their strength, indeed, unto death if you so command; but failing an instruction to the contrary from you, I will surrender to Stephen when our ability to resist has gone.

Dated this third day of December, 1152."

The clerk finished reading, and waited for the Constable's comment.

"Bring wax so I can affix my seal. I will not fold it, King Stephen must read the letter or he will not allow it to go to Duke Henri. You must call truce to the bridge guards and demand access to the King; pray him to allow you to take the letter to Henri personally. If he refuses, as I think he will, beg him in any case to send on the letter with his best speed. This is a sad day, my friends..."

WIMER, AGE 18; HENRI AGE 19

FRAMLINGHAM & CAEN - DECEMBER 1152

The boy stood in the doorway of the little chapel, hopping from one foot to another and making urgent faces, as Wimer turned to bless the congregation at the end of Mass. *Good grief – is that another letter from the Duke? I wish Hugh wouldn't send for me in the middle of service! Although to be fair, I'm a bit out of the way down here. It may have taken young Fulk some time to find me. I'd better go and read it to him before he explodes.*

When was the last letter – yesterday? Things must be starting to hot up. Wimer skipped most of what he was planning to say as a closing homily, and finished in record time.

"Hello, Fulk! Another letter from the Duke of Normandy?"

"Yes – please hurry, Father – m'Lord is desperate to know what it says, and I took ages to find you."

The chapel was on the far side of the castle from the motte entrance, tucked under the wall, serving mostly the soldiers. The bailey was bustling with people coming and going. Hugh was calling up more and more of his knights' dues, and there was scarcely room to move without bumping into someone. There was a whole row of new kitchen lean-tos to their left, the earthy scent of pottage making Wimer's mouth water. A little way along, the farrier – who had attended the service – began hammering again, and the noise drove them away into the throng. They dodged a wagon loaded with beans of some kind heading for the kitchens, and climbed the motte steps.

The hall was heaving with people too. It was full at all hours, with nobles coming to confer with Hugh, or of knights pledging their service, or sending their clerks with gold and silver – and occasionally horse shoes - towards the campaign instead. Father John was sat by the door with a ledger, trying to capture all the contributions.

"Wimer! At last! He's been pacing round like a bear in a cage – for heaven's sake, get up there!"

Wimer was sweating by the time he had sprinted up the stair to Hugh's private chambers.

"Ah, there you are, boy – SO happy you could find the time to attend me, where the blazes do you get to when I need you! - read me this." and Hugh thrust a roll of parchment into his hand. The seal – Henri's smaller personal one, not the great seal of the Duchy of Normandy – had already been sliced in two.

"From Henri, Duke of Normandy, etc etc, to Hugh Bigod, Earl of Norfolk and faithful friend, greetings. -

He says about how he's managed to restore control over the last of his French lands, do you want the details?" - an impatient wave from Hugh.

"My lady wife and I intend to hold Christmas court at

our castle in Caen -"

"His lady wife!" Hugh snorted. "Louis' reject, more like! Still, she has brought him Aquitaine, and she is fertile..."

"- whilst I gather the last of my force and ships together. I intend to depart as close to Twelfth Night as may be, and expect to call upon you and your men to support me directly. I pray you, send by return a list of the forces at your disposal, so that I may better plan my options.

Your brother in Christ,

Henri FitzEmpress."

"Well, at last! A date. And close too, there's a multiplicity of details to complete, we'll be hard-pressed to call everyone in... I will not send a letter with the names of my men, it would be a noose around their necks if it fell into the wrong hands. You'll have to go, boy, memorise the ledger and recite it to Henri alone."

Me?! To Normandy! He wanted to run around and scream with excitement. He almost missed the rest of what Hugh was saying.

"Are you listening, boy? Add in the details we got last week from Roger of Hereford; and Father John will help me make a best guess as to Ranulf of Chester's numbers in the North. And you might as well stay with him, make yourself useful, until it's clear how his attempt at the throne is working out, then you can bring me news directly. Go! Go, and start learning the names. You can have three days to get it all in your head, then you'd better be off."

As soon as he was out of the solar, he leant against the wall and allowed himself an amazed puff of laughter. *I'm going to France! What an adventure!*

He stood looking at the little ship in disbelief. Even in the harbour, the swell was tossing it up and around in a very disconcerting fashion. A line of deck hands had made a chain and were passing bundles along. Wimer watched, fascinated, as the man standing on the edge of the ship effortlessly adjusted the height of his catch with each wave. *That man is a magician – how does he DO that?*

He heard a rider come up beside him and hail the ship. Half his attention on the display below, Wimer saw the man dismount, remove a saddle-bag, and hand the reins to one of the seamen.

"God give you a good day, my son; are you making the crossing too?" the stranger asked.

Wimer turned and looked at him, and noticed the tonsure.

"Good day yourself, Brother! I am Wimer, the Earl of Norfolk's chaplain. I must make the crossing, on my lord's business; but it is my first ever sea voyage, and I would wish for better weather! I've been stuck here for the best part of a week now, I was glad to be summoned this morning, but to be honest, I see no difference in today's weather, it's still foul..."

"The wind has shifted a point or two, that will have made the master's mind up. It will be a lively crossing, though! Ah, there goes my horse." and the two men watched as the blinkered palfrey was trotted smartly over the planks and into the shallow hold of the ship. The men ran one of the planks into the ship, and waved the clerics over the other one. To his surprise, Wimer made it across without falling in.

He staggered across the width of the ship following the monk, who plonked down against the far side. Almost immediately, the second plank was pulled in, the ropes cast loose, and the rowers began their task. The ship turned into the wind, and Wimer felt saliva pool in his mouth as she began to lift up and then slap down onto each wave. He swallowed, and swallowed again.

"Brother, as you love God, distract me! Tell me something of your life?"

"I go to find the Archbishop of Canterbury, bearing letters. You know he is in exile?"

"Yes, I heard that the King was insisting that his son Eustace was crowned, and the Archbishop refused to lead the ceremony? I never got the full story."

"Well, you know that only the Archbishop of Canterbury can crown a king. Stephen gathered all the bishops in London, just before Easter this year, and demanded that Eustace be crowned his successor. The synod refused; and Stephen imprisoned them all!" The monk made a dramatic pause, for Wimer to show shock. They had, however, just rounded the harbour wall, and met the gale. Wimer just managed to get to his feet and lean over the rail before he lost his breakfast. The monk made a rapid excuse to go and see to his horse. Wimer spent the whole, endless voyage throwing up, his stomach trying to turn itself inside out with every lift of a wave.

He almost cried in relief as the planks came out again

alongside the quay in Barfleur, and some blessed stability returned. He staggered across them, and leant against the quay wall, relishing the rain on his face. Dear Lord, thank you for safe deliverance. And, I suppose, for the realisation that I'm not a sailor! Please can it be calmer when I go home!

"An interesting trip!" grinned the monk, waiting for his horse. He passed Wimer a wine sack. He took a long swig, and started to feel a bit more human.

"I need food, and a horse, in that order. Could you recommend an inn and an ostler, Brother?"

The walk up to the inn was fascinating. By the time he got there, his neck was starting to ache, from turning so much at so many angles. Everything was so new! And there were so many people! Poole had been interesting, but he'd never felt right in the crush of things like he did here; maybe it was that the wide-open water at Poole gave you more of a feeling of space? Or maybe because it was the furthest he'd ever travelled in his life, and it felt so different... Whatever the reason, he felt completely alive – as well as hungry. He sidestepped a washer-woman with a big basket, danced an accidental step or two with the boy whose path that put him in, and went in to the inn with some relief. He'd only been sat at a trestle for a minute or two when the wench appeared.

"Stew, if you please, and a mug of ale; as soon as you can, I can feel my backbone trying to greet you!"

She snorted. "Oh, I thought you were just happy to see me... that'll be a farthing; if you want a room, talk to the bar man."

Wimer looked at her puzzledly for a moment – then blushed to the roots of his hair as he realised what he – and she – had just said. He reached for his purse to cover his embarrassment, and frowned. He stood up, and felt all round his belt. Nothing! My money's gone! The wench was watching him with a knowing grin.

"No money, darling? Hop it – we don't do charity here!" Before Wimer knew what was happening, she had expertly manoeuvred him back out into the street.

"Shame – such a pretty boy, too..." she murmured in his ear as she patted him on the bum, then sauntered back into the bar.

Wimer leapt away from the inn as though he had been burnt, almost under a cart. Suddenly the street felt like a much less friendly place. *What a fool I've been! I suppose anyone could have lifted my purse, whilst I was looking around like a new-born calf. And as for that wench! She's probably old enough to be my mother... what did she think I said?!* He could feel a blush growing again, and shook his head at his own stupidity. *Well, I'd better get back to the port and ask the way to Caen. At this rate I'm going to be walking all the way, unless there's a friendly carter. On an empty stomach too!*

Wimer leant against a wall in the great hall, arms crossed, watching the tom-foolery going on around the "court" of the Lord of Misrule, and trying to ignore the burn in his feet. Every so often he glanced across at the stair to the private chambers, willing one of the Duke's men to appear and summon him; but despite the intensity of his gaze, he was failing to conjure anyone up. It had been the best part of two hours since a page had taken news of his arrival up to the solar, with no response, and Wimer was beginning to wonder if the boy had actually delivered the message, or had been diverted by the mummery in the hall.

The volume of noise swelled, and Wimer became aware that the court's focus of attention was on him. A posse of young boys was heading in his direction, and the Lord of Misrule himself was standing on a trestle, pointing his sceptre of office at him. *Oh no! I don't need this. WHERE is the Duke?* Wimer straightened himself up and bowed, not wanting to get dragged into anything until he had seen Henri, but the Lord of Misrule had clearly decided that he was the next victim. The Boy Lord pranced up to him, and shook a bladder in his face.

"You, Sir, have a face like a boar! Only a bore would fail to join in the fun... Or perhaps you're a boor, not recognising my rule? Is that it? Bring up a board, men, and let this bored boor be borne away... Ah! Wait! Who's this on the stairs? It is the least of my servants, Henri! Here, Henri. Bear this boor to the boars; haul him from the hall. Um... Oh, enough wordplay. Both may expiate your sins by cleaning out the pigsty. Does my eye see your Aye?"

To Wimer's complete astonishment, the man ran down the stairs, shouted "Aye aye!", swept Wimer into a carry, upside down over his shoulder, and jogged out of the hall with him, to the sound of clapping and jeering from the mob.

He was set down in the fore-hall, at the top of the keep stairs. Wimer had had a chance to notice the quality of the cloth his nose was banging against, and when the man spoke in a hoarse, gravelly voice, he realised who his captor must be.

"My apologies, sir – that looked like it was getting out of hand a little. Do I guess aright, that I have liberated Wimer, Hugh of Norfolk's Chaplain?"

"Yes, Lord Duke. I have never been so swept away on meeting anyone before!" Wimer and Henri snorted laughter and clasped forearms. Wimer felt his earlier bad mood swept away with the pure silliness of it all, along with a strong wave of liking for the Duke.

"Well, I hate to say it, but we had better be getting on with our task dutifully; I'm afraid that young Andri is a thorough Fool, and may think to send someone to check the sties." Henri flung his arm around Wimer, wheeled him round, and swept him off down the keep stairs at a jog.

"Um... do you know how to do this?" Henri asked, as they stood leaning on the sty wall, looking at the enormous sow reclining along the whole of one side.

"Yes, Lord, I was a farm boy. The principle's the same as cleaning your hall; you get the inhabitants out, shovel out the smelly stuff, spread clean straw, and let the inhabitants back in. Moving her is going to be a problem, though."

"Oh no it isn't; we were tasked with cleaning her home, not babysitting her. Hang on..." Henri sprinted away.

Wimer grinned after him. *Is life always this exciting around Duc Henri? I could get to like it! Shame I have to return to the Earl soon.*

"Take her away, and don't bring her back until my companion and I leave." Henri ordered the two servants who trailed him. The servants' faces went carefully blank, but they obediently got boards and chivvied the sow away.

So Wimer briefed Henri about the likely placement, numbers and types of his troops in England whilst shovelling shit out of a pigsty, Henri matching him spadeful for spadeful, asking insightful questions about this or that magnate's intentions all the while. They were still discussing who might fulfil their obligations and who might not, when the sty had a thick floor of sweet-smelling hay, and the winter dusk was gathering. Henri took them back to the keep via the private stairs, avoiding the Fool, to continue the conversation in peace.

WIMER AGE 18, HENRI AGE 19

MALMESBURY - JANUARY 1153

They had an excellent view of Malmesbury Castle. *Perhaps too excellent?* Wimer had a sudden image of an archer appreciating the targets outlined so clearly against the skyline, and his palfrey took a step forward in response to his tension. He lost track of what Henri was saying for a moment, as he turned the horse and came up beside the Duke again, getting a good view of the siege castle behind them at Cams Hill in the process. He forced himself to relax, and listen to Henri. *My life might depend on the information he's giving me...*

"...the people will be in dire straits. Robert of Gloucester cut off their last supply route some time ago; I suspect the Abbot has been keeping them going out of his own supplies. You see how the wall follows that steep cliff on the west? It continues round the Abbey grounds to the North. There is a double gate at the north-west corner that serves as both town gate, and an entrance to the Abbey, can you see it? That's where you'll need to go in." *That looks a long climb, under the view of the defenders every step of the way. If it were any other man than Henri asking...*

"The wall on this side of the Abbey forms part of the bailey defences for the castle. There is a stream that flows under it, they share the same water supply, and that's one of the levers to move the Abbot; the castle has caused problems there, I'm told.

I want you to take the message we discussed to the Abbot as soon as may be, and see if you can persuade him to open the town gates to me. It will be a hard task, he's Stephen's brother Henry's appointee, and my sources say he's loyal to the King." *But a man who has compassion. He cannot approve of the King's actions.*

"I will have men waiting ready at the siege line there for your sign. If he can be persuaded, we will avoid much bloodshed – and time wasted. I will attack the town an hour after dawn on the day after tomorrow, so you do not have much margin. Are you still willing to take the task? I feel guilty about asking you to do so - you are Hugh's man, not mine - I should probably send you speeding home to him..."

Wimer shook his head, and smiled.

"Lord, when you have won the throne and my lord the Earl has done homage to you, I will be your man as well as his; you are merely anticipating my duty. I will go and see if I can persuade the Abbot to your cause, and will pray for your success when I am in the Abbey church. I think it best to approach on foot; has Earl Robert left me a bridge across the Avon?"

"Aye, the King's men hold the bridge down there, right by the scarp. I am indebted to you, my friend, whatever the outcome."

Wimer climbed the steps up from the river, sweat from the exertion warring with a very itchy feeling between his shoulder blades. He was in easy bow shot, from both the guards at the river, and the defenders on the town walls above. He sent up a short prayer of relief when he reached the Abbey's postern gate, and banged hard on it. The Brother Gatekeeper didn't tarry, opening it for him straight away, and slamming the gate closed tight behind him.

He had arrived just in time for Terce, so the monk showed him the way to the church. "Here we are, Father – in you go, and I'll tell the Abbot you're here."

He knelt, and prayed; *Lord, please help me to quickly persuade the Abbot of the righteousness of Henri's request. And thank you for this short respite, this chance to calm my nerves for the job ahead.*

With the opening words of the service he knew his sense of urgency was justified. He said the response with all his heart.

"*Dómine, ad adiuvándum me festína.* O Lord, make haste to help us."

After the service, Brother Gatekeeper came bustling back.

"The Abbot says that he will see you as soon as may be, and in the meantime, I am to keep you entertained. What would you like to do, Father? How about a tour of the public buildings?"

Wimer smiled politely and submitted to the tour.

Actually, he found it quite interesting – the Abbey was in the middle of a building phase, replacing earlier wooden buildings, and they stopped for a while to watch the stonemasons at work. They were checking the curves in a spiralling pillar with a template, and they were happy to chat for a bit.

The bell rang for Sext, and they went back to the church at the heart of the Abbey for the midday prayer. He could discern no particular message in the service or the psalms, but earned himself a glare from a neighbour in the church for laughing in the middle– he'd been trying not to think "Come on, Lord, hurry the Abbot up!", feeling it impolite to jog God's elbow, so to speak - and had snorted in amusement at the futility of hiding such thoughts from an omniscient being. He opened his mouth to explain, and shut it again, bowing in apology instead.

After the service, Wimer was introduced to Brother Cellarer and shown the lay buttery. As a guest of the Abbey, he was welcome to help himself to a meal there at any time. Brother Cellarer excused himself for a moment. *Not too much food here. And that acolyte is having difficulty putting that bread on the shelf and leaving it there...* Wimer poured himself a mug of small beer. On impulse, he broke a chunk of bread in half, and passed it to the acolyte, who looked as though he could hardly believe his luck. He took a big bite, and squirrelled the rest away under his robes.

"That's more food than I've seen for days, thank you!" he whispered, then hurried out with his prize as Brother Gatekeeper came back.

"The Abbot's still busy, I'm afraid. Would you like to see the herb garden?"

The plants were not particularly interesting in the middle of a chilly, damp winter's day, but Brother Gatekeeper kept them there until the mid-afternoon service. Wimer began to feel as though he would explode – as much from the need to make polite conversation about herbs, as the delay in seeing the Abbot.

"Brother, I beg you – speak to the Abbot again", Wimer asked as his babysitter appeared at the end of the next service. "The message I bear is time-limited, and must be delivered soon to be of any value."

"I will try, Father; please take your ease here in the Church, I'll be back shortly."

Wimer spent the hours between Nones and Vespers simmering gently, pacing up and down the nave and around the aisles, and distractedly admiring the wall paintings in passing. After Vespers, Brother Cellarer scooped him up again, and led him back to the buttery.

"Now, now, young man – don't fret; the Abbot will see you in his own good time. Brother Gatekeeper has passed on your messages, and as soon as the Abbot is free, he'll send for you. Now, tell me what's happening in the wide world outside our doors..." so Wimer found himself trapped into mindless chatter until Compline, after which he was firmly shown his blanket roll, with the promise that the Abbot would see him in the morning.

He tossed and turned until Brother Gatekeeper came to take him to the Night Service, and expected to do the same afterwards; but the monk had to shake him awake for Lauds.

As ever, the service calmed him; the Abbey had some particularly beautiful voices, and Wimer stayed for a little while after the service, giving thanks for the experience. As he rose, he became aware of a tall, slim, crisply-robed monk standing behind him, waiting patiently for him to finish. He took a guess, and went down on one knee.

"Father Abbot?"

"Yes, my son. My apologies for keeping you waiting for so long, but I was entertaining some visitors from the castle, and thought it best to keep you separated. They are breaking their fast, and will leave immediately afterwards. Please follow me."

They walked from the church into a part of the Abbey Wimer had been steered around yesterday, and soon were in the Abbot's private study. The Abbot waved Wimer to a chair, and stood looking out of the window. Wimer waited for the Abbot to speak, suddenly apprehensive; what could he say to this man to win him to Henri's side?

"Do you wish breakfast, my son? I can have some brought here. We monks are eating one meal a day at the moment, but I do not impose our routine on visitors."

"Thank you, Father Abbot, but no; I am aware of how difficult the current situation must be for you. Indeed, the message I bear from the Duke of Normandy is one of admiration for your steadfastness and support for the people; and he offers a potential solution for your consideration."

The Abbot turned, and started to pace, hands folded inside his sleeves.

"My people – the townsfolk, I mean – have suffered

much. This current siege has lasted on and off for, I believe, 9 years; but this last year, with the completion of the Earl of Gloucester's surrounding castles, has been particularly harsh. I bear no love for the Earl, who waited until the harvest was under way, then sent his mercenaries to wrest it from the villagers. Very little of God's bounty made its way to the town granaries this year. I had a small store put away, but with so many mouths to feed, that is trickling away fast. The Abbey itself is suffering, not so much from lack of food, but from lack of water; the castle garrison draws so much from the stream that little makes it to our side of the wall." He stopped, and faced Wimer. "If the Duke will allow some supplies through the siege line, it would be a Christian act."

"He proposes a more permanent solution, Father, with your help; to take the town, and to isolate the castle, forcing it to surrender."

"Hah! All that would do would be to put his mercenary wolves amongst my townspeople sheep; they would be worse off!" The Abbot started to pace again.

"Not so; he has very few mercenaries. The bulk of his army is liege clients fulfilling their service vows. Their aim is to complete this campaign and get back to their own lands by spring, rather than to loot. Henri will not allow ill-discipline!"

"And what is the aim of this campaign? Henri of Normandy may not have pledged allegiance to King Stephen, but I have! I will not break a vow."

The Abbot's hands were visible, clenched. *His vow matters to him. How does he feel about the King's behaviour?*

"What is your position with respect to the Archbishop

95

of Canterbury, Father Abbot? I ask simply because I do not know the answer, but I do know that he is currently in exile for refusing to crown Prince Eustace as heir. I heard that King Stephen arrested all the bishops in the land earlier this year, for suggesting that the King was an oath-breaker and that Eustace should not succeed him – have you heard the same?"

The Abbot tucked his hands away, and settled himself behind his desk. "Yes, it's true. A mistake on the King's part, I believe. Your point about Archbishop Theobald is well made; but I do not believe that England is best served by removing an heir. Normally the process goes the other way..."

"Agreed; but the person whom Stephen swore to put on the throne when King Henry died is the Duke of Normandy's mother. His refusal to observe that oath is surely part of the reason for the country's current woes. A neat solution would be to make Henri, Stephen's heir; to heal that wound, and the relationship between King and Church, at one stroke. Is that a cause you could support? All the Duke asks you to do is to open the double gate to his knights; to offer them entrance to your jurisdiction as Abbot, not to assist in the siege of the castle which the King's men presently hold."

"I will think on it, my son, and pray for guidance." He stood. "Now please return to the guest house."

Come ON... what else can I say to persuade you! Maybe nothing. I think I'll just retreat and let God and his conscience work. "Thank you for listening to me, Father Abbot. Please bear in mind that Henri will attack the town at dawn tomorrow, unless you have decided to grant him entry. There is not much time for thought..."

Wimer was expecting another full day of frustration, and was surprised when he was summoned back to the Abbot's study straight after Prime. The Abbot was standing waiting for him, looking very grave.

"My son, I have spent the time since our last talk in contemplation and prayer. It has become clear to me that King Stephen's reign has been blighted by his oath-breaking at the start of it, and unless that oath is redeemed through your Henri, relations with the Church will continue to deteriorate. The end-point might soon be that the whole land is put under anathema, and I cannot refuse any act in my power, and in my conscience, that will prevent that. Go to him now; I will open the town gates at his command at a time of his choosing. My monk-priests will then offer what comfort we can to the inevitable victims of the fighting."

As Wimer bowed and left, the Abbot turned back to his prie-dieu.

I shall pray too, Father Abbot... and perhaps I can be of use as a priest? I'd like to be there when Henri wins!

The dying man clutched at his arm, a pool of blood from his half-severed leg glinting darkly around him. Wimer put his thumb over the mouth of the tiny vial of holy oil, and turned his wrist in a practised flick. He smeared his thumb on the man's forehead. It was dry. *I'm out of oil! Will the words without the oil work?* He gabbled the rite anyway, in a single breath;

"Through this holy unction may the Lord pardon thee whatever sins or faults you have committed." *Please God, take this soul even if the rite is incomplete!*

He had lost count of how many such acts he had performed in the course of the night. He had followed a little way behind the invasion party, intending to offer his services to the Abbot; but almost the first act of violence he had witnessed was Brother Gatekeeper hit in the throat by a random arrow as he was administering the rite to one of the fallen gate guards. Somehow he had kept the vial of holy oil upright as he fell. Wimer had run to him, scooped it up, and said the rite in its emergency form for the first time in his life for the Brother, stumbling in his haste. The monk had locked eyes with him whilst he spoke, and only when the dying man's eyes had finally closed did Wimer remember to anoint his forehead. He hoped it still counted. He was not clear at all on what was essential, and what was not, for the Last Rite. Still, Brother Gatekeeper was probably recently shriven, so even with Wimer's bungling, should be due only a short term in Purgatory. *I just hope the soldiers have been able to take the same precaution.*

He looked around again. He was at the base of the Castle wall, underneath a tower. There were archers on top, using the burning buildings behind him to highlight their targets. The fighting was actually calming down a little now, though, as the heavy sleet began to douse the fire and the invaders' enthusiasm. As he realised that he could see by the early dawn rather than fire-glow, someone in authority yelled "Fall back!".

Wimer felt the hand of the man whose soul he had just

saved slip away, and got to his feet without looking down. In the Abbey the monks left inside would soon be singing Lauds. He felt the urgent need to hear it again, and pray his soul clean.

The siege had settled to a dull routine. In the few days since that first attack, the King's men in the castle had stayed where they were. Henri's men had cleared away the first row or two of houses, to get a bow's shot away from the castle defences, then spent the days dicing or whoring. The displaced townspeople were sheltering in one of the Abbey churches, and the peace of the place was in tatters.

Wimer had moved back to the wooden castle at Cams Hill, where there were fewer people. He was getting restless, feeling like he'd done his part, and should now be reporting back; but the weather was discouraging him from taking his horse and riding east to rejoin Hugh. The wind was roaring down from the North, full of wet sleet, the force of the wind preventing a full frost, so the land was sodden and dangerously cold. The River Avon running below Malmesbury was still within its ice-rimmed banks, but there was a thick curl of black flood water on the plain below Cams Hill.

One afternoon, Wimer came outside the keep for a breath of air and found both the guard and Henri watching something below. Henri caught sight of him, and waved him over.

"Wimer! Come and tell me who our visitors are, would you?" He moved away from the arrow slot in the palisade, to make room. On the far bank of the river, Wimer could see a line of mounted knights, and behind them, straggling in, groups of foot-soldiers. He strained to make out the devices on the knights' shields and pennants in the fading light.

"I see the white hand of Robert of Leicester... and there's de Ferrers... good heavens above, there is the gold centaur on a red ground! The King has come!"

Henri did a little gleeful spin, and thumped a fist into his palm. "Hah! I thought so! Got him! He must have pulled men from the siege of Wallingford, as I hoped; so Brian FitzCount has some respite. Now I need to set that in stone. Come, let's get the council together and start planning the battle order. We need to be ready for the morning! And if I am successful tomorrow, will you ride home as fast as may be, my friend, and ask Hugh to intensify his attack on the King's holdings across East Anglia? I shall want Stephen very busy all of a sudden." Wimer beamed at him in sudden excitement, Henri's expression matching his own.

Henri was holding on to the rags of his patience with grim determination. He had assumed that everyone was as eager as he was to win a decisive battle – but it became clear that many of the English lords were not at all enthusiastic about the thought of yet another encounter in the civil war.

The council had also been interrupted on five separate occasions during the course of the evening by clerks sent by knights in Stephen's army, with messages on a theme of "We're only here because the King has summoned us, but we don't want to fight you, and if it comes to a battle, we won't fight very hard." The messages were not helping his cause.

William de Mohun expressed the mood:

"By God's teeth, my Lord – you know there's none keener than I am to put you on the throne, and get the King's thugs out of my castle at Dunster; but fighting an anointed king is a sin. Besides, if we have any more of these" - pointing to the growing clutch of clerics awaiting Henri's pleasure out of earshot at the far side of the hall - "we will have more troops in Stephen's camp than he does; we only need to sit and wait."

His patience snapped.

"By God's bollocks, de Mohun – and the rest of you - the only reason those lily-livered turncoats in Stephen's army are sending messages of support is because they think we can beat them tomorrow! Stephen won the throne through perjury, and is the King who imprisoned an entire synod of Bishops! The chaos of his reign has been a mirror of his legitimacy; do not talk to me about opposing him being a sin, it is rather a duty! Now hear me. You are either with me on the field tomorrow, or against me, because I will not sit and wait for this opportunity, I will TAKE it!" - smashing his fist onto the table for emphasis, glaring round at them all. "Who rides with me?"

The Earl of Gloucester was the first to slam his fist down, with a not overly enthusiastic "Aye." One by one, reluctantly, all the knights followed suit.

"Now, perhaps we can get on with planning how we stand against Stephen on the morrow?"

Before daybreak, Henri's mercenaries were lined up three rows deep along the bank of the river, guarding the only bridge across the flood and extending some distance to either side. Wimer sat on his horse behind the mercenary ranks – he had been drafted as a messenger – and watched Stephen's camp stir.

Henri's knights, and Henri himself, were up on the slight rise to the left, on Stephen's side of the river but about a quarter-mile distant from his camp, blocking the longer route to the castle. They sat silently on their horses in the grey drizzle, pennants damply slicked to their lance shafts. The rows of motionless lances might have looked like a wood to the casual glance; it took Stephen's guards some time in the growing light to become aware of the threat, and sound the alarm. Wimer was close enough to hear the cries, carried intermittently on the biting wind.

Henri had wanted to sweep down on the King's camp with the dawn, but had been persuaded of the psychological advantages of waiting. Stephen's men were taking their time about reacting to the threat. Only the Earl of Leicester's men were fully formed up, under his distinctive banner. A page was holding an impatient charger by a mounting block, its saddle empty. A man in full armour burst out of the tent at the centre of the camp, and strode through the chaos to the charger. An older man in a bright blue robe, and a younger in mail, came out of the tent and watched him. Without looking back, the Earl mounted his war horse and led his force out of the camp at a canter.

Wimer watched, puzzled. Surely he wasn't going to

attack Henri's massed strength with just his own knights? It became clearer as he halted his men a bow-shot from the line, and went on alone. *Good Lord! Is he changing his alliance? That would be a great blow to the King!*

Robert, Earl of Leicester, one of the richest and most powerful men in England, displayed his choice of liege lord by dismounting and kneeling in front of Henri. Wimer looked across at the King's camp. The men outside the tent still watched the scene on the hill, their posture rigid. Henri had also dismounted, and was speaking to the Earl. He rose, and they embraced; Robert waved his men into formation on Henri's flank. In the camp, several richly-dressed men half-ran towards the figure in blue.

WIMER, EAST ANGLIA - 1153/54

Hugh Bigod was hanging on to every word of Wimer's tale, the platter of roast meat and bread going cold between them. Wimer eyed it sadly, took a quick gulp of ale, and continued.

"- there was no fighting at all; so few of Stephen's men were prepared to wage battle after the Earl of Leicester came over to Henri's side that he was forced to ask for a truce. Mind you, that suited many of Henri's men also. The terms of the truce are punitive; Stephen must tear down the defences of the castle at Malmesbury immediately, and has agreed to withdraw his siege forces from Henri's castle at Wallingford for six months. Of course, the Earl of Leicester's defection gives the Duke the control he needs in the Midlands, and puts the Earl's castles in his hands -"

"So has Leicester done homage to Henri?"

"Yes! In the Abbot's hall, after the truce terms were agreed, in front of everyone; and afterwards Henri raised him with the kiss of peace. Stephen's face was a picture – and his son Eustace stormed out of the hall."

"Mmmm, he's a problem, that one. He has a stubborn

streak, and a vicious temper – but he is actually a good field commander; he's had practice in Normandy and France, and men who have served with him rate him highly. We need to find some way of neutralising him. He's a year or two older than Henri, and would bitterly oppose any elevation of Henri. How did the younger son, William, behave?"

"A moderate, wanting a quiet life, I think. He accepted a place just below the High Table, and seemed to pay little attention to what was going on."

"That may have been a front, we'll have to wait and see. Wallingford relieved, for six months, eh? Brian FitzCount won't recognise the view from his walls without a siege army encamped. And Henri redeems his liege oath, that was a stroke of luck."

"No, my Lord, I don't believe it was luck. He had planned his attack on Malmesbury to force Stephen to withdraw from Wallingford. I confirmed for him that the King's banner was with the force; he was relieved and happy when Stephen appeared on schedule."

"Huh! Perhaps a stroke of genius then – we shall see; he now has the opportunity to build up his support in the Midlands. It may be that the next major battle will be at Wallingford in the summer." Hugh stood, and strode to the window. "So, Henri wants us to keep the King busy in the meantime, does he? Well, I've long felt that Ipswich Castle should be mine; it would allow me to protect my dock in the town nicely. Call in my Marshals, would you, boy?"

His tummy rumbled as he bowed. *Via the kitchen...*

Wimer stared blankly at the piles of tally sticks, the slates with scribbled notes, and the ledger scroll spilling over the side of the trestle table, and ground the heels of his hands into his eyes. It helped the burning a little bit; and eased the pressure along his cheekbones and behind his forehead. He sniffed hard, took a gulp from the flagon of small beer beside him, and started again.

Despite a head stuffed with wool, he had to sort out a plan for which of Hugh's men in the field needed what supplies over the next couple of weeks, or a lot of people would be seriously annoyed with him. He needed to make sure the blacksmith had enough time to make the lance heads, shield bands, arrows, or whatever was needed, and that there were carters ready to move it all around the countryside.

The job was complicated by the different kinds of troops. The foreign mercenaries had all their own equipment, of course, but needed renewables like arrow heads and spear shafts, depending on where they were deployed. Usually they were expected to sort their own food out, but where they were engaged in a long siege (and so had used up everything that could be got from the countryside around), or were in an area where Hugh didn't want the local lord upset, they also needed regular supplies of food – dried beans and peas to make pottage, mostly. At the other end of the scale were Hugh's household knights, who needed just about everything provided for them – and were quite likely to send a squire galloping home to demand a new tabard, a set of greaves, and a new cook pot, NOW.

Then there were the men who really gave Wimer a headache, the knights and their foot soldiers who were fulfilling their vows of military duty. It was Wimer's job to keep track of who had provided what kind of support for how many days, and to try and balance everything out so that all the farmers had a chance to get their fields ploughed and their crops sown. Most knights owed Hugh 40 days' service a year, and as it was now nearly Easter with no sign of peace, they needed to be called up sparingly. Wimer was quite sure that each of them were cutting notches in tally sticks of their own, and would pounce on any mistake. And then, when they had answered the call, the quality of the equipment they showed up with was completely arbitrary.

Wimer had had a bright idea on that one, though, and had recruited old Waleran – a sergeant who had fought under Hugh for old King Henry until a fall from a horse had shattered his leg and ended his fighting days. Waleran would look over each little troupe as it came in, make caustic remarks about their state of readiness, and send a page off to tell Wimer what they'd need from the household stores before they could be sent out to the field. The Earl was being generous with funds, thank Heavens.

It was one of these country troupes that was making Wimer's headache worse now. William of Peasenhall and his son were decently equipped enough – and met two of the four knight's fees they owed – but Waleran had disbelievingly reported that not one of the foot soldiers they had brought with them had any weapon other than their eating knives. The page had done an impression of Waleran that had made Wimer grin even through his cold -

"You're planning on cutting them into little bite-size pieces and eating them all up, are you? Your Mummies would be so proud!"

- but that left him with a problem. Tom the blacksmith had already complained about being overworked this week. Giving this lot swords sounded pretty pointless anyway, they'd be more danger to each other than the King's men. Maybe he should just issue them spades and have them spend a couple of weeks mending roads, now that would be actually useful. But he had the Acle contingent going home on Tuesday... Wimer groaned, wiped his nose on his sleeve, and glared at the scroll again.

"Ah, hang it all, why not..." and he made a notation beside the Peasenhall name.

The Earl and his men were on the way to Norwich, so Hugh could consult with the Bishop. Wimer was trotting along at the back of the group, enjoying the early spring sunshine, and savouring the sensation of breathing through his nose again. Up ahead, the vanguard had put up some crows; he idly watched them as he drew closer. One bold bird circled back to land again. They were feeding on something in a ditch. All of a sudden the smell hit him – *Dear Lord! That's not a deer, but the body of a man – no, several men!*

His voice went up into an embarrassing squeak.

"Hi! Come back and see this!"

One of the knights turned his horse and ambled back. "What's the problem, Father?"

Wimer held his nose, dismounted, and waved at the

bodies in the ditch. He could see at least five or six men, half-submerged in the water.

"Them! We must help them..."

"Too late for that, Father – they've been there a while, I noticed them when I was out this way a couple of days ago. Not sure whose side they were on, anyway."

Wimer spotted something lying in the grass, and picked it up.

"They were on our side! They were from Peasenhall – I sent them out road-mending only a week ago. Look – here's one of their spades."

"Well, there's nothing you or I can do for them right now. Come on, you can send people to bury them when we get to Dennington. Being alone out here isn't a good idea, the people who attacked these fellows might not be too far away."

Wimer reluctantly allowed himself to be persuaded back into the saddle. As he rode on, his mood grew blacker. *I sent those men to their Maker. I must take some responsibility for their deaths. Should I have given them a guard? What kind of scum cuts down men armed only with spades?*

He was jerked forward, as his horse put its nose down and grabbed for a bite of grass.

"Oh no you don't! Come on!" He hauled on the reins. They'd fallen well behind the main party. Suddenly the woods seemed nearer, and full of menace. He leant forward and kicked hard, and for a wonder the nag immediately went into a canter. *The quicker this vile war is over, the better, so law and order can return and it's safe to travel the highways! Those poor men. God rest their souls.*

The parish priest at Dennington got short shrift when

109

he tried to duck the job of retrieving and burying the men. Wimer stayed mounted, glaring down at the man until he ran out of bluster.

"Have you finished? Then I order you, in the name of the Earl of Norfolk and Suffolk, to send out a work party to retrieve the bodies and bury them in the graveyard here immediately. You will also send word to their families in Peasenhall, before this day is out."

He waited for the man's bow, then kicked his horse into a canter again to catch up with the Earl.

"Forgive me, Father, for I have sinned..."

The trembling rawness in his chest - that had been with him ever since he'd realised that he had sent the men out to die in a ditch - was making it difficult to get the words out. *I failed them. And myself. And the trust that was placed in me, to be a priest. I'm not worthy of that trust. I shouldn't be a priest.* He shook his head a little, to gain a little peace. *Well, I must simply tell the Bishop the whole sorry tale, then it'll be over. I can do whatever penance he grants me, then become a monk, and spend the rest of my life praying for their souls.* He licked his lips, and started again.

There was a long silence when he'd finished. Wimer concentrated on a single, rather battered, stalk of lavender poking out from under his left knee, and waited for the axe to fall.

"My son, I don't mean to trivialise your concerns, but I see no sin here? It sounds as though you were simply carrying out your duties?"

Wimer risked a glance up. William's brow was smooth.

I haven't explained it properly, he doesn't understand. He tried again.

"Father, they came expecting to fight. If I had issued them swords and put them in a battle line, they would have gone to a priest and cleansed their souls the night before. I sent them out to mend roads. Why would they bother to go to confession? I gave them nothing to defend themselves but spades, and they were cruelly cut down. They may have died unshriven – and it's my fault."

"Did you not say that you had instructed the Dennington priest to give them a Christian burial?" William asked, sharply.

"Yes? What of it, Father?"

"Are you sure they did not go to confession between leaving you and meeting their end?"

"I suppose they might have visited one of the village chapels..."

William became very stern.

"I think we had best hope so, as you had them buried in holy ground. I charge you to find out the state of their souls, before you confess to me again." He reached for a goblet to his side.

Wimer frowned up at the Bishop, confused. *What's he saying, that the state of my soul depends on that of those men's at the time of their death? Why? He understands that they were dead when I found them, doesn't he? Nothing I could do, except to give them a Christian burial, surely?* Then it struck him. *Ah! He must mean that they should not have been buried in hallowed ground if they weren't shriven!* He blinked, and briefly remembered an image of a crow pecking at the flesh from a shattered cheek. *Their bodies had suffered enough! I could not withhold their chance of resurrection too. Besides, they weren't suicides, or apostates; they were simple men, and they died doing what I sent them to do.*

William turned back to him, and smiled. "Now, my son - what else is on your mind?"

Wimer bent his head again to cover his disgust. *I have to get out of here! - I need to think what to do.*

He swallowed, to try and ease the dryness in his throat, then reeled off a short list of trivial sins, to get out of William's presence as soon as possible. Luckily, William didn't press for any details.

Dutifully, he professed contrition, accepted William's penance, and kissed his ring in parting.

The cathedral was bustling, so he walked the short distance to St Ethelbert's church, and found a quiet corner to kneel.

"Father, have mercy on my soul…" the prayer faltered.

He had no intention, ever, of risking finding out for sure that the men were unshriven. He had an image in his mind's eye of a grieving mother paying a pilgrimage to her son's grave, and finding that the body had been dug up and reburied outside the consecrated ground. It would rend her heart all over again, a greater loss of the soul on top of the death of the body, and no amount of prayers would be able to save the beloved soul from an eternity of torture.

He tried again. "Lord, forgive this miserable sinner!"

He thought back to the Bishop's instruction, trying to remember his exact words. *I'm probably due an extra spell in Purgatory for not knowing the state of their souls before ordering them buried – but I can avoid disobedience to my spiritual superior simply by never confessing to him again.* He felt a little better. *I'll ask Father John to hear me, that would work. I shall have to remember to confess again the sins William's just absolved me of, as well as the sin of lying about having contrition - because I most certainly am not contrite! May God have mercy on my soul.*

He started to stand, and froze as another realisation hit him. *Sweet Jesu! Until I can bring myself to confess to William again, I can't make him understand that I shouldn't be a priest!* He sunk back onto his heels, and rubbed his face with his hands. *I can't escape…*

He lifted his face to the chapel wall above him, a riot of colour. He became aware that the painting was one of Christ in Majesty, accompanied by saints and prophets, with little scrolls with their names above their heads. He was kneeling under Jeremiah. As he stared, it seemed to him that the saint smiled at him. *Oh my - Jeremiah - the man who said he was too young for the responsibility the Lord gave him! Well. I couldn't have a clearer sign than that!* He bowed his head again in thanks. *Thy will.*

He stood up, and took in a deep breath. *Then flawed as I am, I shall endeavour to do the job which Thou have entrusted to me.*

He crossed himself, genuflected, and marched off to find the Earl. He wanted to get home to Framlingham, to confess again as soon as may be…

When they passed through Dennington a few days later, Hugh's company were waylaid by the priest. To Hugh's surprise, the man ignored him and bowed to Wimer.

"My Lord, would you like to see how we have fulfilled your charge?"

With an apologetic look at Hugh, Wimer dismounted

and followed the priest to the churchyard. Hugh saw him bow his head to pray next to a row of fresh graves. The priest hovered to one side, fiddling with his rosary, and jiggling from one foot to the other. Hugh watched, irritation at the delay nicely balanced by bemusement. Finally, Wimer nodded to the man, and said something inaudible. The man's relief was clearly visible.

When Wimer returned to the company, the Earl raised a quizzical eyebrow at him:

"Been cracking the whip, have you, Boy? What was all that about?"

Wimer smiled, shook his head, and allowed his horse to move towards the back of the ride. Hugh looked thoughtfully after him. Was his baby chaplain developing the ability to command? He was certainly a useful addition to the household clerical staff. If he was becoming capable of more, perhaps it was time to expand his duties.

Wimer looked up from his ledger at the commotion. Two guards wrestled a skinny youth into the hall and shoved him to his knees at Hugh's feet. He tried to stand again. One cuffed him, hard, on the head, and he subsided, tugging his clothing straight.

The fat merchant puffing along behind started to talk as soon as he was near.

"My Lord, I demand..." the Earl flung up one hand, eyes fixed on the boy, and stopped him dead.

"Ah, young Piers." Hugh looked at the guards. "Stealing again?"

They nodded.

"I think I told you what would happen the next time,

didn't I, lad?" he asked, so gently that Wimer could hardly hear him.

The boy lifted his head and met Hugh's eyes. He'd been crying.

"My Lord, I beg you... my mother is deathly ill, and I cannot leave her for long enough to work. I did find some, as a stable-boy, but when Mother got so sick, I had to take care of her instead." He wiped snot onto the sleeve of his tunic, and managed a watery smile. "I was only stealing a few eggs to get some goodness inside her – and he looks like he could afford it."

Hugh sighed. "Ah, lad..." and turned to the merchant, who was almost dancing in indignation.

"You've heard the boy's tale, and his plight. Do you still wish to press charges?"

"Yes, of course, my Lord. The thieving little..." Once again, the Earl silenced him with a gesture.

"Take him and put him in the stocks. Fifty lashes at the close of the market." Hugh looked across to see that Wimer had caught the sentence. He nodded.

The guards tried to make the boy stand up, but at the Earl's words, he had collapsed inwards, crying again. He was half-carried, half-dragged off.

Wimer looked around the hall. There were still a few people waiting to see the Earl, although the day was getting late. Hugh was talking to his Seneschal, then stood and beckoned Wimer to follow him. Wimer could hear the seneschal closing the court as they climbed the stairs. *That's very early! Hugh looks tired, though. Who's the boy, I wonder? They clearly know each other.*

Hugh walked over to the solar window, and looked

out.

"A bad business with the boy. His father was one of my carters, the family used to live here in the bailey. The father was killed in an accident, crushed under a wagon-load of stones; young Piers was there and saw it all. He went a bit wild after that. He was caught trying to cut a purse a few months ago. He swore that it was the first time he'd done anything of the sort, so I just lectured him - "more in sorrow than in anger", you know the kind of thing." He shook his head, and walked over to his desk. "But he's out of chances now. I want you to see that it's done properly. Take this purse, and arrange for the herb woman to look after him, and his mother, afterwards. I wish he'd come to me, instead of being found a common thief."

Wimer bowed, and went back downstairs. *Too proud to ask for help, I suppose. He's lucky Hugh's fond of him, he could've lost a hand...*

In the market place, some of the traders were already packing up, and there was a crowd starting to gather in front of the raised platform where the stocks and the whipping-post were.

Wimer walked over to Piers. The young man – Wimer could see now that they were close to each other in age – was sat with his ankles trapped in the stocks, rubbing his hands over his arms, and weeping softly.

He looked up as Wimer came near. "Oh, Father, will I die? What will happen to my mother? I am so frightened!"

Wimer patted his shoulder, rather awkwardly.

"The Earl has given me some money for a healer, for both you and your mother." He scratched his head. *What kind of small talk can you make, to a man just about to be flogged?* "Um, I'm afraid you must be made an example of. Would you like to pray?"

The boy sniffed and nodded.

"Dear Lord in heaven, take pity on this your servant, Piers…"

Should I offer the last rites? Hugh expects him to survive, or he wouldn't have given me money for a healer, but he looks awfully skinny - what will fifty lashes do to him? Before he could make his mind up, a pair of castle guards came over.

"Come on, you!" they manhandled Piers over to the post and tied his wrists to the hoop at the top. One of the guards yanked Piers' head up by his hair, showing his face to the crowd, and shouted so his voice could be heard all over the market place.

"This wretched thief is to receive fifty lashes, by order of the Earl of Norfolk. Bear witness to the Earl's Justice!"

Some of the crowd cheered, and some booed the victim. The guard cracked his finger joints, and flexed his biceps, milking the cheers. Finally he uncoiled the whip hooked on his belt, and moved round to behind the post. Piers tried to follow him with his eyes, and flinched as the whip cracked in the dust, as the guard got the range. The next strike met flesh, and the boy screamed. Again. Again. The guard had found a rhythm, strokes coming at measured intervals, each one drawing a cry.

Wimer counted under his breath, eyes closed – then opened them again, remembering his promise to the Earl to bear witness. Piers' tunic was rags fringing the bloody mess of his back. Another stroke, and his knees gave way, forcing the guard to change his angle. At the count of twenty five the guards changed over. The boy made it to thirty-three before losing consciousness. The strokes continued to the full count, regardless.

When it was over, Wimer walked over to the post, and spoke to one of the guards.

"Help me to get him home, please. And then I need you to get the herb woman for him – on the Earl's orders."

The guard sawed through the rope at Piers' wrists, dropping him in the dust. Wimer started to try and work the rope over his hands, but the guard stuck his head in the loop of Piers' arms, gripped his wrists, and stood up with a grunt.

"Naw, leave him be, look – he's easy to carry like this. You go ahead and clear a path for us."

Between them, they got the boy to a lean-to hut on the edge of the village. Wimer ducked his head under the lintel, and tried to cough and hold his breath at the same time as the smell hit him. As his eyes got used to the dim light, he realised it came from the bed of straw in the corner, and the woman lying there in a fresh pool of bloody vomit. *She's very far gone – I don't think she stirred at all when I came in... The boy must not be allowed to see this!*

Backing out again, he told the guard to prop Piers against the hut wall, and to run for the healer. He himself put a fold of his gown over his nose, and went back into the hut to give the last rites to the woman. She was dead before he had finished.

Outside, Piers had fallen on his side; he was moaning

softly, still mostly unconscious. Wimer turned to find the herb woman, arms crossed, glaring at him.

"So, Father – our glorious Earl chooses to strip the flesh from the boy's back, and he wants me to tend to him so he won't have his death on his conscience. Is that about the size of it?"

Wimer lifted his chin and glared at her. "The boy has brought his misfortune on himself. This is the second time he has been caught stealing; he is lucky not to have been branded, or worse. Do you refuse the Earl's request? He sends money for your time."

The woman spat to one side, but hunkered down next to the boy.

"He's shivering with shock. We need to get him inside, and under a cloak. Is this his hut?"

"Yes, but I have just eased the passage of a soul in there – presumably his mother, he said she was ill. The air is foul, we must take him somewhere else."

"Bring him, then, he can have a corner of my hut for a while."

Wimer leant forward in his seat on the bench, listening to Sir Brian, one of the household knights, describing what had happened at Wallingford just a few days previously. The Earl had heard the news privately, from a messenger, earlier in the day. He had emerged from his solar only once since, to deliver the official version to the assembled castle folk in one barked sentence:

"A truce has been declared, making the Duke of Normandy the King's heir. Dismissed!" Wimer's first thought had been for the Abbot of Malmesbury. *Praise the Lord, the plan worked! I hope the Abbot feels vindicated... but why is Hugh so upset?*

The Earl had withdrawn to his solar, refused all visitors, and had all his meals sent up. The whole castle had been buzzing with rumour and gossip ever since, which Wimer had tried not to listen to. Brian was being much more forthcoming than the Earl, thank heavens, and had actually been there!

"So the two armies sat looking at each other across the bridge, for five days. The King had many more men, but our position was better – the Duke had taken the siege castle before we got there, and we helped build a rampart all the way round it; Stephen would have found it costly indeed to take that bridge, but it proved unnecessary. None of the nobles – except perhaps Henri! - wanted to fight."

Hah! I bet he did!

"Whilst we were baking in our armour, they were thrashing out the treaty terms in a tent. Basically, Henri replaces Prince Eustace as the King's heir. The younger son, Prince William, has already done homage to him. That's why the Earl is in such a vile mood – William keeps all the land that Stephen has granted him – and WILLIAM is named the Earl of Norfolk!"

Ah. Reason enough. No wonder he's furious!

"Our own Earl remains an Earl, by Henri's insistence, and keeps his own lands – but is an Earl without a name, can you imagine such a thing!"

A blessing on Henri for being true – and fast-thinking! At least Hugh keeps his lands. No wonder he's been in such a foul mood, though. He must feel that as a blow to his honour, as well as his purse.

"He's not quite as put out as Eustace, who stormed out of the hall. HE won't respect the truce, you can be sure, and he's a good commander. I remember when we faced him in Eu -"

Wimer attention turned to more pressing matters as Brian started to reminisce about his battles in France. *Would it be safe to start sending some troops home, or should I keep the numbers up for a little longer?* It sounded as though either of the King's sons might be headed in their direction. They might need a bit of muscle. He'd have to wheedle his way in and talk to the Earl. The world hadn't stopped, and Hugh's responsibilities hadn't gone away.

Goda sat slowly stirring some chopped beeswax into a pot of hot marigold ointment, observing the person for whom it was intended. Piers' scars were looking good, but the new skin got dry very easily. She suspected that he enjoyed the feel of the warm ointment, and the touch of her hands as she rubbed it in, although he would look away whenever she tried to make eye contact. He was turned on his side away from her now, as usual, staring at the hut wall aimlessly.

The frown line between Goda's eyes deepened. At least he was going outside to relieve himself now; but she was still having to put a spoon in his hand and tell him to eat. Time to do something about his mind, now his body had healed.

The beeswax was all melted in. She tested the

temperature with the crook of her little finger, and took the pot over to her patient. This time, her massage did not stop at his waist, but languorously drifted lower and lower, until she was cupping and lifting his buttocks with each stroke, then exploring further afield. Eventually, he responded, as she'd known he would.

Wimer paused in the act of knocking, puzzled by an unusual noise. He peeked round the door instead, then turned away hastily, face burning. With his back pressed against the hut wall, he tried to regain his composure. *Piers is recovering well, then...* He became shamefully aware of his own growing erection. *Huh, I thought I'd got over that.* He tried shutting his eyes and breathing slowly and deeply. The memory of Goda's amber-coloured hair waterfalling over her arched back distracted him. *Oh, for heaven's sake!* He pushed off from the wall and started walking hard, not caring where he was going, surreptitiously adjusting his gown every few steps. *Another sin for my confession list. So much for consecrating my thoughts to God.* He snorted laughter, spooking a foraging dog. *Not to God but Goda...* He stopped, appalled. *Dear Lord, what manner of priest am I, to think such thoughts!*

He thumped his groin, gasped at the pain, and stumbled off. *I must pray...*

WIMER AND HENRI - WINTER 1154/55

Wimer was grating a nut gall into a mortar and pestle, and concentrating on getting the results as fine as possible. It wasn't until the knife slipped and gouged a line of blood across his thumb that Wimer muttered darkly and raised his head – then leapt to his feet. Hugh stood, arms crossed, glaring at his household Chancellor and waiting for him to acknowledge his presence.

"I beg your pardon, my Lord – did you want me?"

Hugh looked him up and down.

"You look a mess. Your gown is threadbare; you've grown about a hands-breadth since it fitted you; you're covered in something vile – what are you doing, anyway?"

"Uh... making ink, my Lord."

"Good grief, man – get yourself a servant to do that. And get at least two decently smart black gowns made, not in homespun, please. I want you looking like a credit to this House, not like some Saxon peasant, when we attend the coronation next month." *Uh – I am a Saxon peasant? But clearly, no longer one in his mind! I'm flattered. I think...*

Hugh continued. "I intend to have the title of Norfolk restored to me, whether Stephen's brat wills it or no; and I have a job in mind for you. I need you to be dressed to inspire confidence." *Oh? What job? What's worth spending the money on black-dyed cloth? It costs a fortune!*

"Hmmm, get your hair cut as well, and new boots and shirts. Braies. I bet your braies are disgusting too. Just throw away your entire stock of clothing and get something decent. You're going to need a groom and a manservant, you're going to be out on the road a lot; take young Piers and your pick of the grooms – and DON'T suck your thumb, boy, for heaven's sake try to look like someone who can be trusted with the affairs of one of the richest counties in England!"

Wimer jerked his wounded thumb out of his mouth and surreptitiously wiped it on his gown, adding a smear of blood to the general grime. He belatedly bowed to the Earl's back; he was already striding off, shaking his head. Wimer could feel a broad grin growing across his face. *I'm going to Henri's coronation!*

There was an itch just under his right shoulder blade. As the Archbishop turned them to the North side of the Cathedral, Henri quickly shrugged his shoulder back and forward in a vain attempt to scratch it whilst the movement disguised the action, then composed himself again. His eyes were hot and dry too. *I bet I'm coming down with a cold – that damn ride through London bareheaded in the rain yesterday...* He sniffed surreptitiously as they turned for the last time. He was left alone facing the altar as Theobald escorted Eleanor back to her throne. He could see her in his mind's eye; her proud head already crowned with a simple ring of gold, her glorious red curls tumbling to her shoulders over the jewel and pearl encrusted collar of her silken robes. *I shall enjoy robing her in just that hair later. Perhaps a pearl in her navel... Hmm better keep my mind on the business at hand. Not every day one becomes a King...*

Two servitors came to remove his surcoat, blessedly relieving the itch; a third placed a stool in front of him. He knelt, and held his arms out to the side, wrists up. The servitor unlaced his linen shirt at neck and wrists, baring skin. The Archbishop processed round to face him, with priests holding the holy oil and the anointing spoon.

It was the oil – the Chrism, the same oil through which Bishops received their own mandate from God – that caught his attention. The light from the altar candles glinted a halo from the golden flask, as the priest with great ceremony poured a trickle into the anointing spoon. He could hear soft, sweet music in the background, swelling gently as the oil was placed on each wrist, then on his chest and shoulders; by the time his head was anointed, and the linen cap put in place, the choir in his head was singing "Gloria! Gloria!" at full volume.

He was barely aware of being led back to the marble throne beside his Queen, receiving his own crown, and taking the Archbishop's homage and oath of fealty.

It wasn't until it was the turn of Hugh Bigod of Norfolk to take the oath that he fully came back to himself – the old man had grunted in pain as he knelt. Henri had instinctively reached out to help, and as a result his hand had gone between Hugh's palms, rather than capturing his vassal's hands between his own. Hugh's eyes had crinkled with mirth, then he had straightened his face, moved to the correct positioning, and made his oath.

"I promise on my faith that I will in the future be

faithful to Henri my king, never cause him harm, and will observe my homage to him, completely, against all persons, in good faith and without deceit."

Eleanor commented acidly – just before the Earl moved out of earshot -

"Well, I wonder how long that will hold." Hugh's back stiffened, but he showed no other sign of hearing her as he made his way down the aisle past the long file of lesser lords. Not for the first time, Henri wished that his Queen placed a little less value on her wit. It was true that Hugh's power base was too large, and he had a reputation for switching sides with the wind. It was for that very reason he needed treating gently, at least until Henri was able to consolidate his own hold in East Anglia. A rebellion now might lose him everything.

"My Lady, I beg you – silence would further our cause better." He got a glare that declared later retribution, but to his relief, she remained decorous whilst the rest of the nobles swore homage.

Finally, the line came to an end, and Henri rose to make his own oath.

"- I do solemnly swear to protect the Church; to do justice to all my subjects, of whatever degree; and to suppress laws and customs that are evil. I further swear to protect the rights of the Crown, and to restore its honours and privileges to their state in the time of my grandfather King Henry. And finally – as I am now deeply honoured and proud to be *Rex Angliae*, King of England, and of the English – I too will take the English form, and be known as Henry, your King!" As he lifted his arms in the air, the cheers began, and swelled until the whole of the Cathedral rang with them.

The only sound in the great hall of Northampton Castle – turned into the King's court room whilst he was visiting - was a single set of footsteps falling impatiently on the flagstones. Henry had been pacing up and down since the bell for the midday prayer, after which Hugo FitzJohn, moneyer, had been scheduled to appear to answer a charge of underweight coinage. The tension in the room had been building steadily. Wimer stood stiffly at attention behind Hugh's chair, concentrating on being invisible, eyes fixed on the bead of sweat growing at the old man's hairline. Still Henry paced.

"Sire?" A cleric had entered the room. Henry whirled round.

"What?" he snapped.

"A messenger from FitzJohn has come, your Majesty. Will you see him?"

Henry nodded once, and stood waiting, smashing one fist into his palm, repeatedly. The young man whom the cleric ushered in took one look and fell to both knees.

"Mercy, Sire! M-my father craves your mercy! He lies ill in bed, and begs your indulgence!"

Henry walked right up to the kneeling figure. "Your name?"

"F-Felix, Sire..."

Henry's voice started softly... "I hate dishonest moneyers. Do you know what my Grandfather did with them, F-Felix? No?"... his voice started to rise in pitch and volume... "First, he cut off their right hands. Then he castrated them" - full scream now - "so that their line was ENDED! How DARE your father defy me?" and on the word 'dare', he backhanded the young man, and sent him sprawling. He lay there, snivelling.

Wimer looked from the unlucky wretch on the floor, to the King of all England. From deep inside him, his sense of fairness was rising. It was probably not a good idea, but he had to say something. *The father is the proper focus for the King's wrath, not the son...*

"Sire? I don't know if you know of it, but there is a fixed definition in Saxon law for when someone is too ill to attend court?"

Henry frowned, located the calm speaker, and waved him to continue – the glower still on his face.

"When the officers of the court arrive, the person must be in bed... under the covers... naked, or with only their braies on. It might be interesting to see how this man's father is dressed right now?"

The frown changed, one eyebrow lifting in quizzical amusement.

"You, and you – take F-Felix back home; do not let him cry warning, and approach the house quickly and secretly. I want the moneyer dressed exactly as he is, hands outside the covers, the covers tied down so he cannot wriggle, and the entire bed brought here immediately."

Henry stepped to the pissoir as the guards left, giving Hugh the chance to turn around and hiss:

"Are you out of your mind? What risk are you taking?"

Wimer smiled blandly, and went back to his parade rest as Henry resumed his pacing.

A short while later there was a commotion as the

guards returned, wrestling the bed and its occupant into the room. As they propped the bed upright, a purse fell from under the mattress. Henry swooped, hefted it, and chucked it on the nearest table, then turned to his victim. The unfortunate man's hands were tied to the bedposts, ropes holding the covers on at the level of his neck and waist. He was visibly shaking, face ashen. Henry danced right up to him, with a feral grin on his face. The man's ragged breathing stopped at the metallic sound of Henry's dagger being drawn inches from his groin; he strained to look down.

"Ah, yes; you know all about my Grandfather's treatment of corrupt moneyers, don't you." The man looked across at the King with a comically sad expression, speechless. Henry sliced upwards – and the rope across his neck was severed. The blanket fell to his waist. He was wearing a linen undershirt. Henry's eyes met Wimer's.

"I dislike liars almost as much as I dislike cheats. Are you wearing hose, Moneyer?" The dagger ripped downwards, taking the last rope. The first thing Wimer saw was that the man's legs were bare – but then Henry made a strangled noise, and stepped aside, letting all see that FitzJohn's hips were girdled by a thick blue ribbon, topped with a bow around his member.

Henry turned to the guards. "Was he in bed with a lady, perchance?" The grinning guards nodded.

"Wimer, my friend; what says the law now?"

Wimer's eyes went wide as he reached for words, but all that came was a bellow of laughter to match Henry's.

129

When he had recovered his composure, Henry retook his seat at the centre of the top table, taking the purse with him. He spilled the contents out and whistled soundlessly; a pile of gold coins - bezants - gleamed under his hand.

"Hugh FitzJohn. I acknowledge that you are sick, and I accept your fine of a purse of gold for failure to attend court. I will refer your case to the Exchequer to deal with at their earliest convenience. Be aware that failure to attend on their summons will accrue the death penalty. Do you understand?"

The unfortunate man swallowed and nodded. "Yes, Sire."

"Guards, release him and walk him, and his bed, home. Do not allow him to adjust his apparel until he enters his own door."

Wimer bit his lip, imagining the man's procession past his friends and neighbours. What an example of the dangers of defying the court! FitzJohn clearly got the point too; it was his face he was hiding with his hands as he left.

Whilst the bed was being wrestled out of the door, Henry beckoned the court clerk over and whispered something. He went back to the pile of scrolls on his desk and extracted one, which he handed to Henry. When decorum was restored, the King read it out:

"I, Henry, by the grace of God King of England etc., to all good men of his whole land, clerics and laymen; and to the future; greeting. Know that we have given, granted and confirmed by this our present charter to our most beloved Hugh Bigod and the heirs of his body the whole and entire earldom of Norfolk, along with all the lands, rights, services, fiefs and demesnes as pertained to that honour in the time of my mother the Empress Matilda, excluding only that land held by William of Blois. In testimony of which matter we have ordered our seal to be appended to our present charter."

At his name Hugh had stiffened, and as Henry continued, had fallen to his knees.

"Does that please you, my Earl of Norfolk?"

"Oh, yes, indeed, Your Majesty..." breathed Hugh. "I thank you with all my heart..."

"Good, that's that then." Henry said, briskly, putting the scroll back on the table and motioning for witnesses to come up and sign it. Seeing Hugh struggle to get back to his feet; "Wimer, help him back to his chair. Hugh, the job of Sheriff for Norfolk and Suffolk is attached for at least a year; am I correct in assuming that Wimer here will have a part in that?"

"Indeed, Sire. He will have my full authority in all monetary matters."

Wimer turned to look at him in slack-jawed amazement, then back to the King as he spoke;

"Here, then, Wimer - " and tossed him the purse of gold " – take this and find the Exchequer; lodge it as a fine into the King's purse from this court. You might as well start them off thinking kindly of you; it won't last!"

Henry was smiling benevolently as he bowed unsteadily and left.

...his full authority! For all Norfolk and Suffolk - dear Lord in heaven help me!

WIMER, BURY ST EDMUNDS TO FRAMLINGHAM, APRIL 1157

De Abbatis Hugonis, ad Henricus Rex…
From Hugh, Abbot, of the Abbey of Bury St Edmunds, to
Henry, King of the English, Duke of Normandy, Count of
Anjou, etc, etc…

Sire,

My apologies for troubling you; but I feel that I must
complain to you about the behaviour of two of your
vassals, to wit, Hugh, Earl of Norfolk, and William, Earl of
Warenne.

The rivalry between these two noble gentlemen has
once again, with the onset of spring weather, meant that it
is simply not safe to travel the countryside; armed gangs of
knights, of one faction or the other, ride out from their
lord's castles to terrorise travellers, demanding that they
declare themselves for one Earl or the other. Woe betide
any who guess wrongly the affiliation of their
interrogators!

I have in the Abbey infirmary one such unfortunate,
one of my own knights, who was travelling to the Abbey
for the Easter celebrations, and to pay his quarter-rent. He
was set upon by one of these gangs, and clearly displeased

them, as they left him by the wayside stripped to his skin and badly beaten. If it were not for the actions of his servant, who managed to borrow an ox and get him to the Abbey, the man would surely have died.

Sire, as the liege Lord of these rampaging Earls – I beg you, cause them to cease this rivalry, or at the least, remove from them the safe havens their men employ, from which to ride out and harass passers-by! It is a blot on your reputation that these two men have, between them, caused such grief and disruption in East Anglia.

The cost to the Abbey's revenues when men cannot travel to pay their dues is considerable; the same affliction must affect all those with wide-flung estates, including, I am sure, your own. Am I the only complainant? Surely not!

I shall pray that you are moved by this letter, and by the suffering of your subjects, to act against the Earls in haste, to lance this boil marring the peace of your realm. If you do not act, swiftly and with resolution, I fear a return to the anarchy that marked the reign of your predecessor.

I beg your pardon for speaking my mind so plainly; but the situation simply cannot be borne!

I remain your servant in all temporal matters,

Hugo, by the grace of God, Abbot of Bury St Edmunds.

Signed with the Great Seal of the Abbey, and the personal seal of the Abbot.

Hugh's every breath was hissed through clenched teeth. The old man was beetroot-coloured, with a vein throbbing prominently at his temple. *Is the stiff-necked old fool going to die of apoplexy in the street?* Hugh had his horse, and himself, under taut control as they rode through Bury. His people were still trailing out of the Abbey in a line behind him, taken by surprise at the speed of their departure from the Great Council, where the King was sitting in full majesty. Hugh had left the instant after he had knelt in submission to Henry, with scant reverence, and without leave to depart. Wimer had thought for a moment that Henry was going to call him back, and make him suffer some further humiliation; but he had relented and let the old man go without comment, flicking a finger to give Wimer permission to go after him.

As soon as they had cleared the East Gate, Hugh spurred his destrier into a gallop. *God help anyone on the road ahead of him.* Wimer, on a poorer horse, gave up the chase, and turned and waited for the first of the Earl's household to reach him – *ah, excellent, Piers, he can be trusted to organise things.*

"You heard what happened? - good. I think we ride for Framlingham. The Earl will push hard; no point in making the household suffer. Gather them all up, will you, and follow on in less haste. You might as well follow us along the Palgrave road, and settle people amongst our manors there; I will send word as soon as possible. I shall race after the Earl. Send a handful of men as an escort after us, and come yourself when everyone is settled. Good man!" and he spurred his palfrey into a ground-eating canter.

It took the best part of an hour and a half to catch up with the Earl, and when he did, Hugh's mood was not noticeably improved. At least he had slowed to a walk, and Wimer swung into place beside him silently. Hugh seemed to be glad of an audience, because it didn't take him long to start talking.

"I shall never forgive that jumped-up little upstart. Framlingham and Walton are mine! How dare he!" His voice had raised almost to a shout, then dropped again.

"de Warenne and Essex stripped of their castles, too, at least. I wonder if either of them would care for a bit of excitement in their lives? Henry will be busy with the Welsh very soon, far too busy to do anything about a little local rebellion."

Wimer, aware of the guards who could not be far behind, protested:

"My Lord! I pray you, do not talk of treason on the King's highway. At least the King, though harsh, was even-handed. And you do have the option to buy the castles back."

"For a ludicrous sum! I would beggar myself raising it. Which I suppose is exactly what Henry wants. No, I shall get back home to Framlingham, ensconce myself there, and see whether Owain ap Gwyneth is man enough to deal with our upstart Duke. I may well send him some encouragement."

"Please, my Lord!"

"Pah! Don't be a milksop, boy!" and the Earl kicked his horse to a canter. Wimer shook his head. *What will happen if the Earl rebels? I hope it's just his indignation talking. I'm not at all sure what my duty would be.* The word triggered a memory of shovelling pigshit, matching load for load with Henry. Wimer grinned, then shook his head again, and kicked his horse. *Let's hope it doesn't come to a choice...*

They arrived at Framlingham village in the very last of the daylight, having stopped only for a brief bite to eat and a change of horses at one of Hugh's lesser manors. The village was eerily quiet; there was no-one on the street at all, and the houses had their shutters closed. Hugh slowed to a walk, then pulled up in the middle of the market square.

"Halloo the village! Who will come and tell your Earl why we are boarded against a siege? Are we at war? Do we have the plague?"

For a while, the silence held; Hugh sat firm, sure that there were eyes on him, and with patience, one of his people would break. The wait was becoming long, though... There! Alward, his castle steward.

"Alward! What is going on?"

The man was more nervous than Hugh had ever seen him. It took a couple of tries for him to speak.

"My Lord – the castle is taken! A company of the King's men came two days ago, with a charter signed by the King, and the castle is in their hands now. No-one dared to resist, against a direct order from the King. I am sorry, Lord!"

Hugh sat on his horse without moving, anger and humiliation burning inside him. He was too late; Henry had outflanked him.

A gust of wind startled his horse into taking a sideways step, and brought him back to the realities of the present. Without access to his power base, he would need to make other arrangements – and build again. It would take time; but he could be a patient man, if required. They did say that revenge was best cold. He turned to Wimer, waiting quietly behind.

"Boy, I'm off to Manor Farm for the night. I fear we'll become a band of gypsies – I want you to go to the castle and remove my personal effects and the accounts, if Henry's captain will allow it. Meet me in the morning."

He turned his horse, and set off back down the street. At least in the dark, he could let the pain show on his face.

WIMER, EAST ANGLIA -
WINTER/SPRING 1165

Hugh absent-mindedly reached for his mug of mulled ale, and knocked it over – bandaged hands clumsy in their clover and bayleaf poultice. He swore quietly. He'd been in a foul mood pretty well all winter. The wet and cold was worsening his aches and pains, and moving to a new manor every few days wasn't helping either. *Has to be done, though, or I'll eat their pantries bare, I must still have a hundred or so followers, even with most of my people scattered. Damn Henry! I want my castles back!*

Every time he thought about the loss of his chambers in Framlingham, bright with his favourite tapestries and a roaring fire, he felt worse. All his delicately-worded approaches to people who might be expected to have a grudge against Henry had been for naught; the man was simply getting stronger and stronger, only his sons daring to oppose him. *When the whelps come into some power of their own, then perhaps I should re-examine that option; but for now, I am out of gaming pieces.*

He became aware that the ale had soaked through his gown onto his leg, and was chilling fast. *Enough.* He had had his fill of discomfort... He tried to click his fingers, and swore again.

"Woman!" he roared for the herbalist. "Come and take these damnable bandages off me!"

He waved a fist at a waiting page. "You! Go and find Wimer the Chaplain, and ask him to attend me, with his ledgers."

Goda was just leaving the chamber as Wimer came up, and they did an awkward little shuffle before getting out of each other's way.

"Ah, there you are, man! Stop by-our-Lady dancing and get in here!" Hugh bellowed at the sound of his step. "What took you so long? I need a thousand marks of silver, immediately; how long will it take you to get it together for me?"

Hugh snorted with sour amusement at the look on Wimer's face.

"A thousand marks! My Lord – I'm not sure you have anywhere near that in coin. It might take several months to raise it."

"Months will not do. I WILL NOT traipse around the countryside any more, going from draughty hall to wretched manor, all of them set up for some other man's convenience. By God's wounds, I want my castle at Framlingham back, NOW. I have decided to accept Henry's fine, dismaying amount though he demands, even if it beggar me. So, Chancellor; earn your keep, get me the money. How much can we raise immediately? Let's see the scrolls..."

Some time later, Wimer's estimate was proven. He could barely lay his hands on half the required sum. Hugh pushed back deeper into his chair, and rubbed the back of his neck. *God's blood, does any part of me not hurt? Old. Old and tired... but not past it, God damn it, not yet!* He slapped both hands down on the lion heads on the chair arms.

"Well, my boy, there's the Christmas rents to come in, and the Christmas court. The miscreants will be surprised how expensive their mistakes are this time round. I want you to write to anyone who owes me money, and call it in. Any other ideas?"

"It may well be worth suggesting to the King that we pay in instalments, my Lord? – his purse must be near empty after his latest campaign in Toulouse."

"Good idea. Do it. I want to be back in Framlingham before midsummer's day... I fear that another winter of this may kill me."

"Wimerus Capellanus, ad Prior et Canonici de Pentney...
Wimer the Chaplain, to the Prior and Canons of Pentney Priory, greetings.

Brethren, my Lord the Earl of Norfolk instructs me to repeat to you his earlier statement, that your founding charters were invalid, specifically with respect to your claim to the manor of Pentney; the reason being that his vassal Robert De Vaux did not, on any occasion, confirm the gift with the Earl his overlord. The Earl refuses therefore to acknowledge the gift, and demands the return of his lands, or your homage for them.

The manor carries a customary service of four knight's fees. On the assumption that you would not wish to provide this directly, he will accept a scutage payment in lieu, of 20 marks annually, payable in equal instalments at the major feasts. As an act of charity, he will not insist on back payment.

The first instalment of 5 marks will be due at Easter. If you refuse the offer to become a vassal of my Lord, he would expect you to vacate the land in question by Easter Sunday.

Dated this 2nd day of January, in the 11th year of our glorious King Henry."

"Wimerus Capellanus, ad Guillaume de Braham...
From Wimer the Chaplain, to Guillaume of Braham, greetings.

My Lord the Earl of Norfolk notes that you were fined 10 shillings at his Michaelmas court last, for marrying a daughter without your Lord's permission. This fine is unpaid, and is due immediately. Failure to pay in full by the Easter court will result in the Earl's extreme displeasure, and a doubling of the fine owed.

Dated this 2nd day of January, in the 11th year of our glorious King Henry."

Wimer inspected the quill. *It might take another sharpening...* The feather shaft split under the knife. He stood up and stretched, shaking the cramp out of his hand.

The manor folk were bustling around setting up the trestles for the evening meal, and the hall was beginning to fill up. *The light's starting to go - I'll do one more letter, then go back to the job tomorrow. Then I get a day off! Thank heavens for a travel day, this list of Hugh's debtors is never-ending* ... He rolled his shoulders, bones clicking in his back, then returned to the stool and reached for a new feather.

"Wimerus Capellanus, ad Hugonis de Almartune...
From Wimer the Chaplain, to Hugo of Attlebridge, greetings.

My Lord the Earl of Norfolk notes that your scutage fee of 5 shillings was unpaid at his Michaelmas court. The amount is due immediately. Failure to pay in full by the Easter court will result in the Earl's extreme displeasure, and a doubling of the fine owed.

Dated this 4th day of January, in the 11th year of our glorious King Henry."

It was the plight of the little people that was bothering Wimer the most. So far, in this session of the Bungay court, Hugh had reduced two widows accused of brewing sour ale to tears (three pence fine each), had extracted a shilling from a yeoman farmer who had married a daughter without Hugh's consent, and had just imposed a fine of a half-groat on an old man who had let his pig into the woodland to fatten a week before the agreed date.

Wimer carefully kept his face bland and noted the fine in the court roll. *This is getting ridiculous… Hugh's demanding coin for the most minor transgression! It's not the way to run things at all.*

Wimer supposed the old boy was lucky to keep the pig – but he was very, very tired of this endless round of tiny fines. It would take forever to raise the huge sums of money Hugh needed this way; all he was doing was making life miserable for his peasants. The Earl seemed to be enjoying the process, though. He had a whole schedule of county court appearances mapped out. Wimer was keeping a running tally for him; by Michaelmas, he thought they'd probably have around 650 pounds of silver. *Certainly a significant amount of money - perhaps enough to persuade the King to release the castles. Then maybe life can get back to normal again, for everyone!*

The monk cleared his throat, then began reading.

"*Ad Sanctissimo Patri Alexandro, de filiis tuis obediens…*

To our most Holy Father, Pope Alexander, from your obedient children, Gregory the Prior and the Canons of Pentney Priory, greetings. Dated this 7th day of February, in the year of our Lord 1165.

Holy Father, we are writing to you to beseech your aid. We believe that the Priory has had land stolen from it, by the rapacious and greedy Earl of Norfolk, Hugh Bigod – and so the thief has diminished the work of God that we are able to carry out. We have tried and failed to get restitution ourselves, and so are asking you, our last hope, to intercede on our behalf. I enclose the last letter we have had from the Earl, making ridiculous demands.

Our founder, Robert De Vaux, endowed us generously. We have charters attesting his gift, showing the manor of Pentney, with all its appurtenances, and with the mill of Bridgemill; with two salt pans, at..."

The Prior held his hand up, and the monk fell silent. For a moment, the only sound in the chapter house was the cawing of a crow far above; then the room erupted into cheers. The Prior waited until the noise had died down.

"I take it you approve, brothers! I will send a courier with the letter tomorrow, then. The dice are cast. "

WIMER AND HENRI WOODSTOCK
SEPTEMBER 1165

"Come on, race you back!" yelled Henry to the group of courtiers, setting his spurs to his horse.

Wimer's borrowed grey responded immediately, and he let it have its head, elated by its speed and power and the beauty of the autumn day. For a while he and the King were neck and neck, then the breeding of the Royal stables won through, and Henry pulled ahead by a nose, clattering into the courtyard of the Woodstock hunting lodge first.

As Wimer tossed the reins to Piers and dismounted, Richer de l'Aigle commented acidly, "That was foolhardy."

"What d'you mean?"

"Competing against the King is never wise. He should never be beaten." Wimer bowed, as much to keep the expression on his face hidden, and moved away – almost bumping into Henry, who flung his arm around Wimer's shoulders and walked with him in lock step into the hall.

"Don't pay any attention to old sourpuss Richer; he's cross because he wants his estates in Pevensey returned to him, and I haven't decided what it will cost him, yet... what do you suggest?"

"Whatever you decide, Sire, offer to halve it if he can

beat you at a challenge – and double it if he loses?" Wimer suggested mischievously.

Henry grinned, and turned them both to meet the man who was waiting for him at the entrance.

"Oger! How fares my favourite Sheriff-cum-Steward? You know Wimer the Chaplain, don't you?"

The fat man bowed low.

He isn't well, this Oger. His complexion's too ruddy – and he's sweating, even though the day is not over-warm. Wimer listened with polite interest to the conversation.

"I am glad to be in your presence again, Lord King; although I would wish I were serving you nearer home. I have just come back from a visit to the ends of the earth, a one-horse village called Holkham on the far Norfolk coast, and I thought I would never get back to civilisation." He mopped his forehead on the sleeve of his gown, not entirely for dramatic effect.

Henry laughed. "My poor servant! Was this on my business?"

"Yes, Lord King; I was seeing how the de Tosny heirs are doing. I had expected to find them at Flamstead, but found only the mother – the three children have gone to ground in their most rural manor."

"Three children? I thought there were only the two de Tosny boys?"

"Raoul had the two boys, yes, Lord King; Roger is the elder and the Baron. However, their aunt, Raoul's sister, is of an age with them; she and Roger must both be around twelve. You have her wardship. She is not quite budding, still a little early to make a match for her. Ida, her name is."

"When you think she's old enough, Oger, have her

brought to court, and we'll sort out a bridegroom for her. Well, enough of this; I-da better be off to see my own rosebud. See you at the evening meal." And Henry and his bad pun disappeared in the direction of the tower.

Oger turned to him, frowning.

"You're Bigod's man, aren't you?" Wimer nodded. "What did he mean, his rosebud? I thought the Queen was in France?"

"Rosamund de Clifford. The King breathes, eats and drinks her – he built the new tower over there for her; and he's with her every second he can spare. She's a pretty enough thing, I suppose; but then, I am professionally undisposed to appreciate the female form. It was a pleasure to meet you, Sir; God give you a good day." he sketched a bow, and went off to feed the grey an apple.

At table that evening Oger waved the wine server away, and claimed his own duty as Steward, pouring for the King. Henry had a brief word with him, speaking quietly;

"What do you make of young Wimer?"

"He seems sound enough. The Earl's accounts have become markedly more believable since he took over as his Chancellor; and he has a pleasant manner. Why do you ask?"

"Hugh is suing to pay a fine for the return of his castles at Walton and Framlingham, and to be allowed to build at Bungay. I set the amount at a figure I thought he'd baulk at, but apparently he's raised most of it. He's stronger than I thought. I'm minded to take his money and build a new castle at Orford, to keep him in check. I think Wimer may be of more use to me supervising its construction, than helping Hugh to raise money – but that would make him a junior to you; how would you feel about that?"

"Have a keen, bright youngster to do the running around for me? I would thank you from the bottom of my heart, Lord King. I have not spoken much of it, but I fear my health is declining rapidly. It would suit me well to manage affairs from Norwich castle, and let younger men do the travelling."

"I'll speak to him, then."

Wimer was almost ready to thump Piers, who was standing behind him guarding the money, an impressive pile of brass-bound boxes on a sack-barrow. Every other breath, it felt like, he rocked back and forward on his heels, and a floorboard creaked under him; Wimer was beginning to clench his teeth, waiting for it, each time. It was mid-morning by the time the clerk called them in, and Wimer was ready to scream.

Calm. I must be calm. Hugh's risking a lot on this throw of the dice.

He went to one knee before the King, sitting in state in a throne raised on a dais for this session of the Michelmas court. Henry narrowed his eyes at the chests, and waved a hand at him to speak.

"Your noble Majesty, my Lord, the Earl of Norfolk, Hugh Bigod, instructs me to appear before you to plead his most earnest prayer, that you return his castles at Walton and Framlingham. My Lord Earl is becoming elderly, and suffers badly from the ague; he wishes nothing more than to enjoy once more the warmth of the fire in his own chambers, and to lie in the same bed for more than a handful of nights. He particularly craves that you grant this boon before the onset of this coming winter, to save his old bones from more hard usage in cold weather."

Wimer bowed again, and waited, head bent, for Henry's response.

His voice, when it came, was cold.

"As I recall, there was a small matter of a fine, of a thousand marks? To remind him that his feud with William de Warenne must not interfere with the smooth running of the county. Has he learnt his lesson there?"

"Yes, great King. There are minor skirmishes, to be sure; but the Earls have been at peace for many years. Since, in fact, you imposed the fine!"

Henry snorted. "Good! Gave them something else to think about... and has your master spent his energy on raising the fine money instead, then?"

"Sire, my Lord Earl has liquidated all his ready assets, and called in every loan and fine due to him, over these last several years. He has raised six hundred and sixty-six marks of the sum, and begs time to gather the rest. He feels sure that, were he allowed to reside at his caput in Framlingham, he would be able to spend more of his energies in the task. Besides, he would be saved from paying the travel costs of his household."

Henry leapt off the throne and started pacing.

"He wants me to ignore a third of his punishment! The man has spirit... oh, no, I forget; your picture of an old and broken invalid was very touching, if wholly at odds with my recollection of your master!"

149

Henry paused, crossed his arms, and grinned evilly. He held the pose for long moments.

Come on, spit it out – I'm sure you've already decided on what you're going to do!

At last Henry spoke;

"I am reminded of some counsel you gave me a day or two ago. I might accept late payment of the balance, or even halve the amount owing, if you can best me in a trial. How say you?"

Wimer flushed, and wished the floor would swallow him. *The old fox! Serves me right, he's put me in exactly the same trap I set for de Aigle – How do I get out of this one?!*

"Sire, I am not authorised to gamble with the Earl's money. Um... If the stake were personal to me, I might be able to wager?"

Henry frowned down at him.

"I am, quite frankly, amazed that Hugh has raised the sum he has, in the time it took him. I think that your talents are largely responsible, and it would suit me well to remove you from that situation. How about this; you and I will arm-wrestle. If I win, you will leave the Earl's service and enter mine. In addition, I will accept Hugh's partial fine, and give him another three years to pay the balance. He should be able to manage that without starving his peasantry overmuch. How say you?"

Wimer blinked, becoming aware of a surge of elation at the thought of leaving Hugh's service – *Oh my. That sounds... fantastic! Am I really so uncomfortable as Hugh's Chaplain, that I would give it up without a backward look? Apparently yes, if it is Henry asking!* Without thinking, he blurted

"And if I win?"

Henry looked down at him in surprise.

"So, Chaplain – feeling cocky, are you? Very well. If you best me, I will serve you at supper, and sing for you too. And to add a bit more spice, if you lose, you shall sing for me!"

Wimer flinched. *Oh-oh. He would have to pick that. What chance have I against a man who does weapon practice daily? Ah well, if I lose, he suffers!*

"I accept, Lord King – but I do warn you, if you make me sing, you will wish you had lost the wager!"

With a broad grin, Henry leapt off the dais, and flung himself flat on the rushes. As Wimer turned to lie down facing him, he caught a glimpse of Piers' face, gape-jawed and bewildered at their antics, and his grin grew to match Henry's. They clasped hands and planted their elbows firmly.

"Come on then. Oger, you adjudicate; best of three. You ready, Wimer?"

Wimer nodded, and tensed his muscles. The King locked eyes, then calmly and slowly forced his hand backward. There was nothing Wimer could do about it; however he struggled, Henry's pressure was relentless, and his hand travelled in a smooth slow arc until it touched the floor.

"One to me. Again."

This time, Wimer started with his wrist tilted up a little, and found more leverage. He quickly pressed Henry's hand away from him, and managed a handspan of movement. He was rewarded with a slight frown, as Henry tried – and failed – to recover the advantage. With a last surge, he forced the King's arm into the rushes.

"Well done! One all. The decider."

Henry took no chances this time, Wimer having indeed surprised him, and slammed his hand backwards in a no-nonsense fashion.

"Ha! Got you! Your man can take Bigod's silver to the Treasury, and tell them the new terms for the fine."

They stood, and sorted their clothing out whilst Piers manhandled the sackbarrow out of the door. Henry picked one last piece of straw from his chest, and slapped Wimer on the shoulder.

"Kneel, and put your hands up." Wimer did as he was bid. Henry wrapped his hands with his own, warm and dry and comforting. "Do you pledge me all your loyalty, Wimer the Chaplain? Will you be my vassal, to serve me with all your heart and might until I, or my death, releases you?"

Wimer nodded, and swallowed. He had to try twice to get the words out. "I will, my liege."

"I in turn swear loyalty to you, and extend my protection to you, and I will provide for you until the end of your days, or mine. Amen."

Henry bent down, wrapped his arms around him, and bear-hugged him to his feet.

"Excellent! Well, off you go and practice your repertoire, my friend, I'll see you later!"

Wimer groaned, but bowed and left, walking on air. *I am the King's man! How marvellous! Deo gratia...*

It took several days of restless heel-kicking before

Wimer was summoned again to wait upon the King. Henry was pacing up and down the length of the chamber, scowling. Elderly Sir Bartholomew Glanville, Lord Bromholm, was leaning against the wall, clearly wishing for a chair. Robert, Baron de Valognes - and a third man whom Wimer didn't know - were watching the King, waiting for his reaction to something. The clothing of the men contrasted oddly; the lords were resplendent in brightly coloured long robes and surcoats, embroidered with jewels and pearls. As usual, Henry was in well-worn riding clothes, as was the other man.

"No! It won't do at all – ah! Wimer, there you are – you know Glanville and de Valognes, I assume?" Wimer rose from his bow and nodded to each. "And this is Alnoth, my master builder, my Ingenieur – not that anyone's being very ingenious at the moment! What do you say, eh?"

"Um, on what topic, Lord King?"

"On my new castle, of course! Oh, hang on, I haven't told you, have I – I'm thinking about a new castle at Orford. We're discussing what it might look like. Glanville thinks square; Alnoth thinks circular; boring, boring, boring! I want something new, a grand statement – what do you think?"

Wimer said the first thing that came to his mind.

"Why not combine them, then, Sire?"

"What do you mean?"

"Round and square. Um, build it in a circle but with defensive towers sticking out at the cardinal points."

Alnoth came forward.

"Like the Chrysotriklinos in Constantinople, then, Lord? Not very defensible, perhaps?"

Henry had stopped pacing. He thought aloud,

"Do I not recall that the throne room in Constantinople has echoes back to much earlier times? To the throne of Chosroes, emperor of Persia, and the Golden House of Nero? By God's teeth, Wimer, I think you have it! I like very much the notion of a building that draws its inspiration from the ancient Imperial powers, and not from Church architecture! Hmmm, to your point, Alnoth – I don't want a weak castle; the primary defence will be the curtain wall, but the castle must look magnificent. You two work out the details; let me know when you have a proposal. Good work." and the King favoured both Wimer and Alnoth with a pleased smile as he left the room.

Oh my! What have I just let myself in for?

Bartholomew sank on to the nearest stool with a sigh of relief.

"Much as I love my Lord King, I find being in his presence exhausting. So, Robert – did any of that mean anything to you?"

de Valognes moved to join him.

"Not a thing, my Lord." he said cheerfully. "However, it does look as though the King has chosen the right people. You and I have estates close enough to Orford so that a little light supervision will not be onerous; Alnoth is a master mason; and Wimer here will be our eyes and ears on the ground, as well as providing bright ideas in the nick of time."

What?! "My Lord, would you be kind enough to expand on that?"

"Ah, has our master kept you entirely in the dark? We –

Glanville, you, and I – are to be mutually responsible for the building of a castle at Orford, and for its completion to budget. Bartie and I cannot be present all the time, we have our estates to attend to, you know; you, as I understand it, are fresh from running the extensive affairs of the Earl of Norfolk, and are therefore superbly qualified to manage things on the ground. You are to up sticks and move to Orford; we will collectively answer to the Exchequer for the town as Sheriffs, under Oger the Steward's brief of Norfolk and Suffolk. Oh, and the Lord King has written to your Bishop requesting that you be created Rector of Orford. You've just become one of the busiest men in the kingdom!"

Rector! I will have my own parish! And what tremendous trust Henry places in me. Please God I am worthy of it – how thrilling!

Wimer took a swig of ale and poked glumly at the pile of bits of bread in front of him. Alnoth's expression matched his - they had been overcome by inspiration over dinner, and had destroyed both of their trenchers in the cause of illustrating it.

Alnoth plonked both elbows on the table, and rested his chin in his cupped hands. "It's no good – there's nothing here we can take to the King."

Wimer nodded. "Mmmm, you're right." In a sudden burst of energy, he swept the pile aside, leaving a light scattering of breadcrumbs.

"Let's start again. You like a circle, because of its defensive properties." - drawing one. "And the King likes the idea of a polygonal castle, because of its historical and mythical resonances. But we've tried just overlaying a square on top; it doesn't work." He used his knife to add four triangles onto the outside of the circle, as though they were the corners of a square, then used the blade to scatter the breadcrumbs again, without losing the circle.

"What if we made the square bigger in comparison to the circle?" Alnoth leaned over and drew bigger triangles. "No, that's pointless, you just lose the circle. How about smaller then?" and he drew shallower triangles. Hey, we could make it REALLY polygonal – how about this?" and added four more points, making a shape that was more point than circle.

"Well, I quite like that – it's elegant – but wouldn't it be awfully difficult to build?"

Alnoth sighed. "Yes; and expensive; and be completely useless defensively, the idea is not to give the enemy easy access to corners to chip away at. You couldn't build in arrow slots to defend the points, either, because the angles are too wide."

Wimer wiped the drawing clear, and put the circle back. They both sucked at their ale cups, thoughtfully. Wimer climbed over the bench, and started to pace up and down.

"Put the points in the middle? - no, forget that, it's a stupid idea. Tell me about these Persian kings' buildings, what do you know of them?"

"Well, the buildings are designed around number symbolism – so you might have three windows to symbolise the Trinity, for instance."

Wimer came to a stop as Alnoth finished talking.

"Oh! I think I have it!" he said slowly, and moved over to the table and the breadcrumbs, starting to wave his hands in the air as he went.

"Look! A circle; the Deity. THREE projections, not four; the Trinity. We can put them evenly spaced round the circumference, at 120 degrees – hey! Equilateral triangles! But who wants to live in a triangle, let's make the towers room-shaped..."

Robert de Valognes, who had wandered over to see what all the hand-waving was about, grimaced and backed away as Alnoth picked up the mathematical theme.

"Oh yes, I like that! And we could use equilateral triangles and their chords inside the circle, to divide it by 7 to give the width of the towers – the number of days of the week! We'll be able to have a domed ceiling at the top of the circle, between the towers, and give us the Dome of Heaven! And I'm sure it would work out really easy to measure if you picked the right radius... We could see if we could build in 13 of something, for Christ and his apostles, pillars maybe. I bet there's a LOT more we could do with this."

A couple of days later, the two men had worked out their designs on a wax table, where they could draw precise lines and circles. They were explaining it to the King, who was walking round and round the table, looking increasingly impressed.

Wimer was talking: "So you see, the public spaces will be in the circle; but each of the three towers will have a purpose. The main staircase goes up this one. This one will have most of the private chambers, and the main chimney flue runs up the outside, so they will be warm in winter.

The last has the kitchens, and the priest's quarters – near the chapel, which is above the entrance. There will be two main levels, and sub-levels in the towers. We will have a basement with a prison cell, so we meet your recent edict on prisons, and storage.

The base of the whole castle will be chamfered out, so it's difficult to undermine, and the entrance will be on the first floor, to make it easy to defend. There will be four more latrines than Norwich castle; I think it will be a very civilised place to live!"

Henry snorted at that. "How much would this richly symbolic fortified luxury extravagance with extra loos cost me, Alnoth?"

"Well, Lord King – it wouldn't be cheap – but the advantage of basing it on a circle radius of 49 feet, and then using root 2 and root 3 ratios, is that the proportions are pure; I can easily make templates for the master masons, and it won't need too much of my time. Wimer here completely understands the geometries, and can supervise on site.

I'm still working out final costs, but we've found a quarry just down the coast at Nacton for the bulk of the stone; getting it on to the site is always the biggest problem, so supply by ship saves money. We would use honey-coloured septaria blocks, with cream limestone facing; it will look magnificent...

However, you're not going to like the price; it's going to cost..." and Alnoth closed his eyes, so as not to see Henry's expression, and his voice got a little tense, this would be the most expensive castle in England "...around £660, as near as I can figure. That's for the keep alone, the curtain wall will cost more." When he peeked, he was amazed to see the King and Wimer grinning at each other like thieves.

"Go ahead, Alnoth; build me the most beautiful, spectacular castle in the land. I find that the cost is within my reach."

WIMER, ORFORD - SPRING 1166

It was so satisfying to see life and activity at last, everyone out enjoying the spring sunshine. From his perch on top of the huge heap of soil, surveying his little empire, he could see easily a dozen workmen's huts – almost as many houses as in the village proper. There was a constant to-and-fro of people in every direction, so different to how it had been all over the long, wet winter.

For months, it had felt like there was nothing much happening. *Although I've certainly spent plenty of Henry's money; I must write and warn him about that £200 bill for materials before it goes to the exchequer at Easter.* All of it had been preparation, though. It had been so wet that there really hadn't been too much that could be done. Two barge-loads of stone from Nacton had arrived, giving some unexpected unloading work to the village fishermen; and a couple of carpenters had busied themselves turning out wooden shovels by the shed-load, passing them over to a single blacksmith and his bored apprentices to fix an iron edge to each blade. Otherwise, there had been just the small gang of workmen wielding those shovels, preparing the ground where the castle would be, digging the mound of soil he was sitting on.

The sound had changed, too - instead of the

intermittent blacksmith's hammer, now there was a constant tap-tap-tap of mallet on stone, as the masons rough-cut large blocks of stone for the foundations.

There was no sign yet of trenches for these. Alnoth had said that he would start to lay the lines out for the diggers very soon, once the area was completely level. Wimer had found it very strange that they were levelling a plain where the motte and its castle would be; but Alnoth had explained patiently that they would build foundations and basement, then earth up the motte, and the rest of the castle would arise, as it should, from an imposing mound.

Good old Alnoth — he's so interested in the detail —wants to know every slight change of colour and texture in the soil. And he's happy to answer every stupid question I come up with! There he was now, walking up and down over the centre of the place where the motte and castle would grow, with a shabby-looking old man. What are they doing? Wimer stood up, dusted off his robe, and started down the heap to join them.

"There you go, Sir; just about here will do you." the old man dug his boot heel into the soil to make a mark, just as Wimer came up to them.

"God give you a good day, gentlemen. What are you doing? Is it something for the trenches?" Wimer asked.

"Finding the place where the castle well will be." Alnoth explained. Wimer must have looked as puzzled as he felt.

"Godric is dowsing for water. He's found it here; when we dig, we'll find water. He's very good."

"But how does he... Apologies, Godric, I should ask you the question; how do you know where the water is?"

"See these hazel twigs? I walk along holding them loosely in my hands. When they cross, that's where the water is. Easy, if you have the gift. Here, do you want a go?"

Wimer took the twigs gingerly.

"No, you're holding them too tight; just let them float in your hands. That's better. Now, walk around a bit... good. Just let your mind float..."

Wimer took a few more steps, and then felt the rods turn inward of their own accord. *How strange! I'm sure I didn't do anything.*

"Well, there you are, Master Alnoth; I reckon your friend has the talent too."

Wimer looked down. Right in front of his boots was the mark from Godric's heel.

The situation was just getting worse and worse as more and more people moved to Orford. There must have been thirty people rubbing elbows in the main chamber of Gedgrave Hall; all of them wanting some of his time, as Sheriff. *I am being nibbled alive, here – one petition at a time...I think I need to weed out some of the merely curious.* The argument going on in the small space in front of his table currently was between a baker and one of her customers.

"...and there was a pile of rat droppings in it! It were disgusting!"

"Oh, Lord, surely you don't believe him! If he found droppings in his bread, where are they? Why can't he produce them?"

"Because I spat them out onto the ground, you stupid

cow – what do you want me to do, ..."

Oh, for heaven's sake...

"ENOUGH!" Wimer roared. To his gratification, the entire room shut up and turned to look at him.

"As I understand it" - to the man - "Your case is that you had rat droppings in a loaf of bread you bought from this woman; but you cannot prove it. Is that so?"

"Yes, yer Honour, Sir – but..."

"Silence! And you, baker – can you find witnesses to vouch for the quality of your bread?"

The woman looked round the room. "Yes, Lord – there are some of my customers right here – him, and him... and her!"

Wimer stood up, and asked the crowd: "Has anyone here present ever bought poor quality bread from this woman?" He waited for a count of ten, but no-one put their hand up. He sat back down.

"Case dismissed. You – if indeed you had rat droppings in your bread, it sounds as though you were unlucky. To balance that luck, I won't charge you a fine for false accusation. Next?"

The woman curtsied and smiled: the man glowered, but wisely kept his mouth shut.

The next query was a question over where to site more workmen's huts, which was settled without too much difficulty. *Why has this case been waiting for a week for me to judge it? Surely the foreman could have sorted it out?*

Then there was the residue of a brawl – two workmen looking much the worse for wear, one with a black eye, the other with a bloodied nose. Wimer frowned.

"Why are you bringing this dispute to me, instead of to

your Master Builder? Do you actually want a Sheriff's judgement on this? Which of you wants to force the other to face a trial by ordeal over such a matter?"

The men shuffled embarrassedly. "Well, Lord, you were having a court, so we just thought..." the speaker trailed away under Wimer's glare.

"Yes, you didn't think, did you! Fools - wasting my time! I have better things to do than to wipe the noses of every pair of idiots who get in a fight!"

He sat quiet for a moment, irritation building up within him. *Hah! I have the solution! Let them pay for wasting my time. That should discourage them.* He stood, and rapped hard on the table, twice. Again, the noise level in the room fell.

"Now hear ye all. I will listen to local issues every Saturday morning here at Gedgrave Hall. It will be free for all to come; but I can spare only two hours, so perhaps only the first dozen cases will be heard. If you want a guarantee of a hearing, you had better get here early. Every third Saturday will be a Sheriff's Court, where I will only accept cases regarding the law. I will also hold additional local sessions on Tuesday and Thursday evenings; there will be a charge of ten shillings, refundable at my pleasure, to talk to me then. I will return the fine if I decide that you actually needed to speak to me. If it was a trivial matter, or if the case should have been heard by someone else, or if it could have waited until the Saturday session, I will keep the money." The room was completely silent.

"So, it not being a Saturday – do you two still want me to hear your case, and be the first to pay my fine?" The two bloodied workmen glanced at each other and faded back into the crowd.

"I thought not. Anyone else?" There was a general shuffling, but no-one stepped up to the table.

"Very well; this session is closed. Clear the room."

Only one person fought his way against the exodus to stand before Wimer; it was the carter's head man. He stood, twisting his cap in his hands.

"Lord. I need to speak to you about an urgent problem I need your help to solve, but I can't afford your fine."

"Don't worry, Aedgar – it's designed to deal with time-wasters, you get free access to me on work-related matters at any time. What's your problem?"

"Ah, thank you, Lord, that's a relief. It's the path between the quay and the castle – the stone carts have ripped it up so badly that it's becoming impassable, and of course it's only the start of the traffic we need to get up that rise. It's going to take time and labour to fix. We really need to dig out proper foundations, and build it up with rough stone then bedded cobbles, so it can take the weight of the carts. Some of the causeway over the marshes could do with reinforcement, too. Can I pull some of the workmen off the castle gangs?"

"No, I don't want to delay the castle itself at all, if I can help it." Wimer thought for a bit. "You don't need skilled people, do you? Just strong, willing workers?"

"Yes, Lord. Actually they don't need to be that strong. I'll happily take women and children when we start packing smaller stones into the rough ones, their hands are better suited to the job."

"Well, we have plenty of people coming into the village looking for work. Why don't you set up a hiring fair outside the bailey tomorrow morning, and see if you can get enough people that way? How many people will you need, and for how long, do you think?"

"I guess 20 or so for two or three weeks."

"What's the going rate?"

"A halfpenny a day for a man; a farthing for a woman or a child."

"Very well, then; I authorise you to spend 10 pence a day for 14 days." Wimer acknowledged Aedgar's thanks with a nod, and made a note on the long list of items he was charging to the King. "Oh, and Aedgar? Can you make the flat stretch of road a little before the bailey, double width? So you could have two carts passing. And I have been discussing sites for the church with various townspeople; I think the best site will be at the top of the causeway – so at least that will save you moving the stone along the top of the ridge!"

The hall on Saturday was crowded out. No-one at all had come to the Thursday session, and it looked as though the entire village had come today instead, to see what would happen. Piers and Wimer walked to the table in a little procession, Piers clearing the way; Wimer carrying a lit taper. When they got there, Wimer looked around, smiled, then ostentatiously lit the last two inches of a candle clock, and set its horn protector round it. He pinched out the taper and sat down.

"Who is first?"

The first few cases were straightforward. There was a cottage brewer accused of selling sour ale, whom Wimer fined two pennies as a second offence; a request for compensation from one of the fishermen, whose dog had been killed by a stone cart, which Wimer refused, deciding that the fisherman should take better care of his property; and a barge captain wanting payment for his latest load, the first delivery of limestone from Caen in Normandy, which Wimer paid with thanks.

As the captain made his way out of the hall, he was pushed aside by a group of liveried soldiers, who elbowed their way through to the front of the crowd. The old man who was just about to speak to Wimer glowered and stood back to let them in, before he was shoved aside too. Someone in the retinue farted, and Wimer could feel his temper rising.

One more piece of rudeness, and I'll do something about these arrogant fools.

There was a low grumble of disapproval, as the whole roomful of people waited for them to speak. The leader stood in front of the table and slowly peeled off his gloves, a sneer on his face. Wimer leaned back in his chair and concentrated on staying calm.

"My good man." the newcomer drawled. "I thought I would come and see what kind of operation you're running here. One of your workmen may be a villein of my master's; he wants him back. Line them up, if you please."

"My name is Wimer the Chaplain, Co-Sheriff of Orford. To whom am I speaking, and who is your master?"

"I am William, Master-at-arms for Guillaume of Felixstowe, Knight. The serf, man?"

"Master William; I believe that several people were ahead of you in the queue. If you'll take your place, I will assure you my full attention in due course. Perhaps I could ask my man to bring you some good Rheinish wine whilst you wait?"

The man pouted a little. "How provincial of you, to have a queue. Very well. Have him call me when you run out of peasants to deal with." William turned and flounced out of the hall, his men following him.

Wimer smiled widely, and invited the old man to take his turn, then the next case, then the next. All the while, the candle slowly burned. When it finally guttered out, Wimer finished the case he was dealing with, and then stood.

"Friends; that's all the free slots used up. Does anyone wish to pay my fee?" No-one came forward. "Piers, would you be kind enough to ask Master William to return?"

The man swaggered in.

"Master William. I hope the wait hasn't tried your patience too much. You are the next case, it seems. The fee is ten shillings for me to hear your case now."

The man's voice rose. Wimer noted that he was going an interesting colour, too.

"Ten shillings? Don't be ridiculous! That's preposterous! Who do you think you are?"

Wimer's smile went feral:

"I am the sitting Sheriff of Orford, Master William. Do you wish me to hear your case? You are welcome to take it to Westminster instead."

The man frowned, then flushed. One hand went to the sword hilt at his hip. Wimer held his breath. *Surely he wouldn't be so stupid… Perhaps I ought to have Piers start carrying the sheriff's ceremonial sword! Henry would skin him alive for such an insult to the Crown, but it would be a bit late for me!*

The man slammed his fist onto the table. "You haven't heard the last of this!" He almost ran out of the hall, his retinue hurrying to catch up.

Wimer breathed a sigh of relief. *Well, thank heavens for that. And with a bit of luck, that's the last we'll see of him - a runaway serf is not worth the expense of a trip to London.* He spent a few moments searching his memory for Guillaume of Felixstowe, then shrugged and called Piers over.

"Spread word around the master builders that they must be sure that they are not giving work to runaways. We got rid of this fool easily enough, but someone more persistent could give us a hard time. I do not want to spend days on end lining our entire workforce up for some petty lord to walk up and down checking for his villeins. Make everyone we're employing now – and all new people – swear an oath that they are free to leave their village. If they are serfs or villeins, send them back; we cannot afford to break the law on this."

Wimer failed to hop all the way over a puddle, and growled. A little ahead of him, one of the carters' mothers - *what's her name? Um, Wulfride?* - slipped and fell. He sped up as much as possible to help her up. *I suppose that I ought to be grateful that I can afford leather boots. I bet she can't, poor old girl.*

He got there just as she was going down for a second time, and grabbed her arm.

"Whoops! Hold steady, Goodwife! I've got you."

"Oh! Father Wimer! You are a Godsend - thank

you so much! It really is a trial having to come all this way to church, when the weather's being as wet as it has been - hasn't it been wet this year? We need a good, hard frost to sort this path out, don't you think? I…" The Goody didn't seem to want any response from him. Wimer stopped listening, and concentrated on steering them safely round the worst of the mud.

She's right, it's not fair to expect people to walk all the way to Sudbourne in this. I should have started building a church of our own a while ago, I've had the plans ready for months. But there are always so many other calls on my time… I wonder if I can use that as an excuse on Judgement Day. Well, you see, Lord God – I paid attention to my duties as a Sheriff and a builder of castles before my priestly ones… He winced. The Goody was looking up at him, waiting.

"I'm sorry?"

"I said, are you taking the service today? I do hope so. I'm sure Father Jehan is a very good man, but I don't understand a word he says, it's all so complicated! I like it much better when you give the sermon. Father Jehan does go on, you know - at least you're quick!" Her fist shot up to her mouth. "Oh! I didn't mean it like that, no offence, Father?"

He smiled down at her. "None taken, Goody!" She went back to complaining about the weather, and his thoughts wandered again.

He looked at the church on the horizon, and sighed. *I really do not want to sit through another of Jehan's sermons either…* Father Jehan was a little overawed at Wimer's presence in his church, and was compensating by preaching drearily long lessons full of half-understood theory mixed with some novel interpretations of scripture. His audience was split between those who were embarrassed for him, and those who had no idea what he was talking about, but had fasted for Mass and now wanted to break that fast as soon as decently possible.

He found a use for the predictably long sermon, and spent it fleshing out what needed to be done next to get his church built. Money was the biggest problem...

He waited more-or-less patiently until the dismissal, then quickly moved to the altar rail and called out to the congregation.

"Brothers and sisters..." he turned to Jehan and bowed, "With your permission, Father?" Jehan lifted an eyebrow, but waved assent. "Good people - I won't keep you long; but I need to talk to you about an urgent matter." He waited until most people had turned back to face him. Even more people than he had expected were crowded into the church; they could not go on like this much longer.

"My friends; we of Orford have presumed on the hospitality of the people of Sudbourne for far too long. We are just too many now to share a church; we need our own, as soon as can be." - There were a few growls of Aye! from the assembly – Wimer couldn't see if they were from his people, or from the Sudbourne crowd.

"As one of the Sheriffs of Orford, I can grant some Crown land to build a church on; the small meadow at the top of the causeway looks ideal. However, we need to pay for the cost of the church ourselves. I will contribute all the monies that I raise from people wanting to see me outside of the set court times, and any fines that are not owed to the King can go in to the pot. That will not be enough, however. I need your help to raise the money. My man Piers will stand by the door to take any donations you can give today, and you can make a donation at any court session. I will keep a tally, and let you know how we are doing every Sunday. Even if you can't afford money, you can still help by bringing in flints to build with - good big lumps, please, stacked in the corner nearest the causeway." People were turning and talking to each other, hands various distances apart. *Oh, rats - have I just made sure I'll get a mountain of flint, and no money at all to pay workmen?*

"Let us pray: Dear Lord in Heaven, please help us worship You better by building a beautiful church in Orford, large enough for all our congregation. We pray that we can raise the money quickly, and we will help you to help us by giving as generously as each of us feels able. Amen."

"Amen..." the crowd replied, and the church gradually emptied, past Piers and his outstretched hat. There were one or two clinks of coins, at least.

Wimer knelt in front of Father Jehan.

"Forgive me, Father, for I have sinned."

To my eternal shame, I'm getting rather good at finding ways around de Turbeville's injunction. This country priest can barely read the Bible; I can run rings round him.

Ever since the Bishop had effectively damned him over his refusal to investigate the state of grace of the men he had sent to die in a ditch, he had been very careful in his choice of confessor. Jehan met the main requirement;

someone who wouldn't ask too many questions about his life with Hugh.

What he was concentrating on now was a holding action, cleansing his soul of anything he could, whilst trying not to think of the purgatory in wait for him as a result of his decision not to obey William. It meant that he was as thorough as he could be when it came to confessing the minor sins he committed in the course of a day.

Normally, Jehan could hardly keep his eyes open to the end of the list, and gave perfunctory penance, delighted to see the back of this complicated priest who had been catapulted into his life. Today, however, he was listening hard, leaning forward slightly, on the edge of his seat. Wimer finished expressing contrition, and waited patiently for Jehan to speak.

"You forgot the most important thing!" he blurted, leaving Wimer completely puzzled.

"I'm sorry?"

"You were seen! You can't deny it!"

"Deny what, Jehan? What are you talking about?" Wimer, feeling attacked, got to his feet.

"Deuteronomy. Chapter 18. Verse 10. Divination is an abomination!" Jehan also was on his feet, spitting out the phrases. Wimer must have still looked completely mystified.

"You were seen with old Godric, holding his accursed divination rods! The Bible is clear, that is an abomination!"

All of a sudden, Wimer realised with a thud in the pit of his stomach what he was on about. A couple of other Bible references sprung to mind. Technically Jehan was correct – divination for the purposes of summoning demons was indeed an abomination – *but of course that wasn't what happened at all.*

"No, you don't understand – this was completely innocent, just a country skill. There was no invocation at all. Godric just held the rods, and handed them to me. I've no idea why they turned."

Jehan was not placated. "It's arcane! It's completely unnatural, knowing where to dig; there's no possible way of knowing that without asking for demonic help. You and your city-smart ways – I knew there was something unwholesome about you! Now we know! And I see no contrition at all – I will not shrive you. Get out of my church right now! Go!"

Wimer looked at the priest, shaking with his emotion and the righteousness of his position, and didn't even bother to try to change his mind. With a sardonic bow, he turned and started the walk back to Orford.

Oh, blow the man! I'm going to have to find somewhere else to hold services. Where's big enough? And what am I going to tell people? What a nuisance. Da – No! Don't swear! You have no confessor now!

He stopped suddenly. "Oh, dear Lord." *I have no confessor. I have - no - confessor. Every day I will build up sins that I cannot get absolution for.* He walked on. The wind was making his eyes water. *No prayers for the dead can ever wipe away the burden of sin I will accumulate. I will spend an eternity in purgatory.* He swiped angrily at his cheek.

"Lord, have mercy on me…"

Sleep was still as far away as when he had gone to bed,

hours ago. Wimer lay on his back, staring into the darkness: the tally of the day's sins, and his list of undone tasks, still churning in his brain. Every time he shut his eyes, images of devils with pitchforks appeared, and he could feel the fear churning in his stomach. *Good grief. Can't I come up with more intelligent tortures than that?* He rubbed his eyes, and turned over again. *Come on – think about the things you can do something about.*

Oger's summons from the Exchequer had come, and although it was of course expected, it meant that he had to set aside time to walk Oger through the castle accounts on top of everything else. *Yes. Think of the castle.*

He made a conscious effort to clear his mind, shut his eyes, and brought the castle into his thoughts. The lines of it were beginning to take shape nicely now.

He was following an empty wagon, which was going back to the riverbank for another load of stone. Its carter steered the team across the bridge over the ditch, round the outer defences, and out across the newly made road towards the causeway. Another wagon was coming up from the river, so the carter pulled over into the double-width piece of road Wimer had made expressly for the purpose. Wimer stepped off the road himself, to make way for the oncoming cart, and bumped into a woman carrying a wicker basket of moorhen eggs. He apologised and moved on.

He became aware that the wagons had disappeared, and in their place was a thriving little market; as well as the egg seller, there were boys selling the big pink-gilled marsh mushrooms Wimer had come to love, a couple of shepherds with spring lambs, a milk seller, and a cobbler. A few drops of heavy rain fell, and people moved under the eaves of the fine houses lining the market square. Wimer moved on to the side away from the castle, where the Ipswich road came in from the west and Quay Street turned down to the river, more well-built houses visible in both directions.

Across the cobbles was his new church, large and beautiful, sitting proudly in its spacious grounds. He walked up the path to the door, but his way was barred by one of the gargoyles, who stepped away from its gutter to block his progress.

"You can't come in, you're a sinner! And besides, you haven't paid for it yet!" the thing admonished him, poking him on the arm with a stony finger. "Go away until you've raised all the money!"

Wimer started to argue, but realised someone was calling him. *He turned around to find the source of the voice, but couldn't pin it down...*

"Father Wimer! My Lord! Please wake up! It's dawn... Father!" Piers was shaking his shoulder.

Wimer startled his servant by leaping up and rushing out of the door, "Thanks!" trailing after him. He wanted something he could shape with his hands – mud would do... where was a puddle when you needed one? He gave up, and veered towards the nearest carveable surface he could think of, the pile of blocks beside the castle. By the time Piers had caught up with him, he had scratched out the main elements of his dream, working as fast as he could to capture the essence of it before it faded.

"Ah, Piers – be a good fellow and get this block moved over to the manor, would you? Be careful of these scratchings! I don't want to forget any of it. The Lord has just given me the layout of the town to come." and he wandered off to break his fast and go back to his list of jobs, leaving Piers staring bemusedly at the stone.

The open-air service, with Wimer standing on the broad castle wall, was going smoothly. *I'm getting quite good at pretending to take the Eucharist...* He closed his eyes, and for a moment the dark welling of guilt from deep inside him threatened to overwhelm him. He forced it down, and calmed himself to pray. *O God of Mercy, I beg you, hear this sinner's prayer. Please God, let my blessing of your Body and Blood hold true, so that the people don't suffer for my fault.*

He turned back to the congregation, a goodly crowd. At least there was plenty of standing room, and the weather had been kind – something that could never be guaranteed, in April. Some people had gone over the fields to Sudbourne, but most of the workforce and the locals were here, staring up at him. There even seemed to be a couple of small groups of strangers here and there, probably people from one of the nearby villages, ridden in to see what Orford's mad Sheriff was up to now.

As he wound up, with the Dismissal and benediction, one of these groups made their way through the dispersing crowd towards him. The leader called up, with a smile in his voice.

"God's greetings, young Wimer, I see you're still coming up with new ideas!"

Wimer paused, robes half off his head, whilst he identified the voice – then whipped them off and turned round in the same motion.

"Lord Bromham! It's good to see you again! Let me come down..."

Wimer was fond of Bartholomew, who had visited several times over the last few months, and had been free with good advice. He sent a boy running to ask Goda to produce a meal, and escorted his fellow Sheriff home for some ale and a seat.

Once he'd brought him up to date on what had been happening with the castle – all good news, and all expenditure accounted for – he told Bartholomew about the drive to build the church. He was carefully vague about the problems he was having with the Sudbourne priest, and concentrated on the overcrowding, and the need for Orford to have a fine church of its own.

Bartholomew speared the last piece of meat from his trencher, chewed it thoughtfully, then washed it down with a swallow of ale.

"So tell me, how much have you raised through your subscription efforts?"

Wimer sighed. "About 37 shillings. Enough to dig out the foundation ditches. At this rate, we'll have enough to actually build a one-room hovel of a church in about ten years' time. I have plenty of flint, though…"

"I suppose you have the problem that you can't get rich people to help you to build a church, until you have a church (and the town that goes with it) to attract the rich… I tell you what, I've been feeling a bit guilty about leaving you with the full burden of everything here. If everything goes through all right at the Exchequer hearing at Easter, I'll chuck in a little something to the fund."

Wimer was preparing for the service – and being thankful that Saint Swithin had chosen to send fair weather – when a messenger arrived from Bartholomew. The squire handed over a heavy purse:

"My Lord sends a message, which he says you will understand: he says, *'Quietus Est'*".

Wimer thanked the man and sent him off to the kitchens for a drink, before opening the purse and spilling the contents onto the table. He stared in amazement at the pile of gold, the sight almost driving out the memory of the last time he had heard the phrase – in the Court of the Exchequer at Easter, when Oger's report of the King's farm of Norfolk and Suffolk (with Wimer's return for Orford nested within) had gone through without query. Oger had met his eyes and nodded grave thanks as the judge had announced

"*Quietus est*; the debt is discharged."

He stirred the coins with his finger, and then counted them up. Twice. It was an astoundingly generous gift. Bartholomew had sent around 100 marks; enough for a beautiful church.

WIMER, ORFORD - JANUARY 1168

"Wimerus Capellanus ad Henricus Rex...

Sire, I recently learnt with sorrow of the death of your illustrious mother. I have said Masses for her, and have added her to my daily prayers. Although I never met her, her deeds in a long and glorious life are worthy of study; and her spirit lives on, through you.

Indeed, the Lord gives, and takes away. I was overjoyed to hear of the birth of your son John at Christmastide, who I understand is a fine, strong youngster. I gave the castle workmen a holiday and some good porter to celebrate the arrival. We did not hear the news until the Thursday after Epiphany, so the workmen had been sober for a few days, to appreciate the gift a little more!

Work on the castle is of course slow now, with the frosts and winter weather, but Alnoth is content with the quality and speed of the build. Indeed, the shape and magnificence of it is becoming clear, even though only the basement and ground levels are complete. We are also within budget; although the costs for the Navy are beginning to mount up. I have a meeting planned with some of the local landowners in a few days, to discuss whether suitable wood can be provided locally, as we are currently shipping timber from much further north, at considerable expense. It may be that I will have to concede some minor rent rebates for a few years, but I will of course keep those to a minimum.

I'm sure that you will rejoice with me in the near completion of the village Church at Orford, funded by the generosity of Lord Bromham and by gifts from the local people. I hope shortly to be able to hold services there, relieving the villagers of the burden of a long, muddy walk across the fields to attend services. I am fairly confident I will be able to ask Bishop William to dedicate it this year – perhaps as soon as early summer.

The latest news from France implied that your difficulties with Archbishop Thomas have taken a more positive trend? - Although truth be told, the twists and turns of that situation are so confusing at this remove, that I simply hope for the best. I pray for both you and he, and for your reconciliation, daily.

There is no other business of note to inform you about. Crime in the county has fallen with the onset of snow; all I am dealing with is the odd drunken brawl. I am sure that will pick up with the turn of the year, but at the moment, I am enjoying the tranquillity!

Wishing peace and prosperity to you, and to your realm, I remain your faithful servant, Wimer."

He re-read the letter, then folded it in three, dripped wax, and used his new seal for the first time. He admired the design again; a cormorant, wings outspread to dry, in a small roundel. *The perfect image for my bustling little fishing port.* He wrote his name above it, to save the King a moment's puzzle over an unfamiliar seal, and consigned the letter to the messenger waiting to travel to France.

WIMER, ORFORD AND NORWICH
EARLY SPRING 1168

Wimer weighed down the corners of the parchment and carefully sprinkled sand on the wet ink. The letter could go to William de Turbeville with the next courier, he was expecting one within the next day or so. There was another to write to Lord Bromham. There really had been only one possible date to choose for the dedication of Orford's new church; 24th August, the Feast of Saint Bartholomew. There was still some minor pieces of work to be done – not least, the decoration of the walls – but Wimer's decision to build largely in Caen limestone (diverted from the castle) had sped up construction work considerably. The church would be ready for William, or his delegate, to consecrate. *Please God, let it be a delegate – if the Bishop comes himself, there will be that whole miserable business of the dead men to deal with. Although perhaps it would be best just to lance the boil – confess my knavery and sophistry all these years, and accept his punishment. Although what if he defrocks me? He must certainly take me away from here...* He shook his head. It was too painful to think about. *My beautiful church will outlast me, at least...*

The church had actually been in use for the whole of Lent. Wimer had blessed the building the day the masons had put scaffolding planks across the top of the walls in preparation for the next season's building work. They gave a bit of shelter from the rain, and the feel of a roof. The dedication date was a secret at the moment; Wimer hoped that he would be around Lord Bromham when he heard the news. He was sure the great man would be delighted – and he'd certainly earned the tribute. He made the sign of the cross over the letter, touched it for luck, then stretched and stood. A walk would be good, ease the kinks out of his bones. *I need to be out and about more, instead of spending my days crouched over a parchment roll!*

As ever, he walked to the castle first, duty taking precedence over pleasure – although it was beginning to be exciting, seeing the majesty of his and Alnoth's design beginning to take shape. They'd finished the ground floor just before the first of the winter frosts, and so now the weather was better, the workmen were laying out the chapel and the priest's rooms, along with the rest of the first floor.

Wimer briefly weighed dignity against the intense sense of freedom he got from the growing vista, hitched his robe up into his belt, and scrambled up the wooden scaffolding. He moved round the wall, close enough to grab the pole if he slipped, until he came to his own tower, with its endless, glorious view out over the marshes and the Ness. *I will wake up to this every morning, please God.* It was much easier to feel close to Him up here, where the petty issues of the day became very small in perspective.

A reddish-brown sail caught his eye, sailing round the point of the Ness into the calm, safe harbour behind. There was a growing flotilla there, as Orford Navy began to assemble. Wimer grinned at how grand that sounded. It only seemed like a blink of time ago when all you'd have seen from this height would have been mud and wetlands; now, the engineers were draining the marshes rapidly, and the outside of the Ness was bounded by a solid sea wall, protecting the meadows and arable fields they needed to feed their growing crowd of people.

Wimer turned, his gaze following another stone cart making its way up the causeway – now rising up above the land, as the marshes drained and shrank – towards the town. It could indeed properly be called a town, now. He could see smoke rising gently from perhaps twenty or so solid houses centered around the market place, including his own; more spilling down either side of the causeway.

Above them, his beautiful church stood, its fresh cream stone rising ethereal behind the wooden houses. He stood and gazed at it in pride for a few breaths, then bounced down the scaffolding again and strode towards it.

He almost had eyes only for his church – but scooped up young Jacky Williamson as he dashed out from between two houses, tossed him up into the air, then returned him to his frantic mother.

"He's becoming quite a handful, isn't he! No, Jacky, no more; you need to go back to your mother and practice being good!"

"Oh, thank you so much, my Lord! I swear, he went straight from crawling to running, and he's never still!" she turned away, burying her face in the boy's curls.

Wimer paused to watch them go. He had a particularly

soft spot for Jack, who was the first baby to be born in the workmen's camp, and so the first baby Wimer had christened as Rector. He was the best kind of sign of the town's success, with families happy to settle, and plenty of work for them. Wimer was himself employing Will the mason, Jack's father, on the church; the strong, simple zig-zag carvings, emphasising the perfect curve over the windows, were his.

As ever, he paused at the entrance to the churchyard to take in the whole picture. Unlike the castle, which mostly still showed the brown of the underlying mudstone, the church's cream-coloured limestone glowed in the sunshine. The builders were already hard at work, a chain of men tossing flints up to where the setter nestled them in the mortar. Another gang were working around the back of the church, putting the limestone facing up on last week's length of wall. The two teams were competing in strength and voice – Wimer blushed a little as the flint gang finished a verse with three fast pelvic thrusts and a huge cheer. No doubt about the topic then...

He ducked inside the church, and in his mind's eye, emptied it of scaffolding and piles of stone. What Bible stories should be painted where? Saint Bartholomew of course, holding his skin. Erasmus, for the sailors; perhaps Cuthbert or Edmund for the soldiers... his mental flood of colour was disturbed by one of the carvers.

"Excuse me, Father? Could I ask you to come and sit over here, in the sun?"

Wimer, a little bemused, allowed himself to be led to a perch on a pile of limestone. The carver adjusted his angle, turning his head slightly to the side, then bent over a plank with a piece of charcoal. Wimer stood it as long as he could, stealing sideways glances, but finally couldn't stand it any more.

"What ARE you doing?"

"Why, I'm drawing you, Lord. I think you're going on the chancel roof."

Wimer stared at him, none the wiser.

"Lord, could you..." and the carver gestured Wimer to resume his position. He did, although with a frown. Finally, he realised what the man was saying.

"You're drawing me for a gargoyle! Oh, my!"

"Yes, Lord. Oh! Hold that smile! That's a great expression..."

Wimer stayed where he was after the man had left, thanking him gravely for his time. His mind's eye went back to choosing colours and scenes for the walls of the church, now with the added image of a weathered stone gargoyle on the roof, mouth split wide in a grin that arched the rain far away from the walls. Once or twice, he shook his head in amazement at the thought of looking after his beloved church long after he was dead. *Who knows, maybe this tiny service may even count for something, in Purgatory?*

Piers found him there a little after noon, and reminded him that he'd wanted to ride over to Ikenhoe. The Abbot of St Botolph's was very fond of the pleasures of the table for a godly man, and was particularly partial to Goda's mushroom ketchup. The Abbot had been very sad to learn that he had finished the last of the year's store of the brown nectar when he had visited Wimer over the New

Year. Now the spring warmth had brought the mushrooms out in profusion, and Goda had packaged up several bottles for the good Abbot.

He walked his horse decorously over the tracks, mindful of the bottles nestled in their mossy basket, and arrived just in time to celebrate the mid-afternoon prayer with the monks. As ever, the beauty of plainsong filled his soul. There were only a handful of monks left to tend the little monastery that the saint founded, from which all of Christianity in East Anglia had spread; with the saint's relics dispersed to Ely and Bury St Edmunds, not to mention the bone in his own little altar, it was only the romance of the saint's history that still had the power to bring pilgrims. However, the voices of the few monks filled the church nicely, and the cries of the curlews on the river just behind were a perfect counterpoint. After the service, he asked a priest to hear his confession; and stayed to do the first part of his penance in that lovely spot. By the time he rose from his knees, he felt like a weight had been lifted from his shoulders.

On his way out, Wimer patted Botolph's great carved cross, covered with the dogs and wolves that were his emblems, for luck. Brother Cellarer caught him doing it, and smiled understanding.

"You know, I do the same, every day? I feel a strong connection with the saint when I touch his cross. Have you come to visit the Abbot? I'm afraid he's away on business. Is there anything I can help you with?"

"Ah, that's a shame, I've brought him some of the mushroom ketchup he loves – but I'm sure you can look after it for him, Brother! God give you a good day."

Wimer handed over the basket, gave the cross one last pat, and set off for home.

The breeze was picking up a bit, with the threat of a shower, so Wimer indulged his horse – and himself – with a good long canter on the way home, taking pleasure in the strength of the wind. He swung into the market area just ahead of a shower, and tossed the reins to a waiting lad. A sudden gust of wind slammed the door behind him, startling the young man who was waiting for him by the fire. *The Bishop's livery? What's this?*

The courier leaped round to face him, then went to one knee.

"My Lord Wimer, I am instructed by William de Turbeville, Bishop of Norwich, to put this into your hands alone." His voice was not quite steady as he held a rolled and sealed scroll in his cupped hands.

"Very formal, young Alan?" Wimer frowned. His joy in the day began to shred. *What is William up to?* He stripped off his riding gloves, and stepped forward to take the scroll. Alan, as soon as Wimer had it in his hand, stood, bowed, and almost ran from the hall. Wimer neatly cut the seal from the vellum, controlling his growing sense of unease. The light was poor, the sky outside an angry shade of bruise. He placed the scroll on the mantel, and lit a candle. In its light, he saw the scroll's single line:

"*Ego te iubeo statim ad ecclesiam Norwicum, et judicari.* - I order you to go immediately to the Cathedral at Norwich, to be judged. - *Willelmus, Episcopus.*"

Wimer leant against the mantel, and gazed into the fire. So, which of his spiritual crimes had William discovered? And what was he planning on doing?

"To be judged" - by whom? *And does that mean that the outcome is in doubt, or has he already decided what's going to happen?*

He stared into the flames. *Should I go? Or should I hide behind Henry's coat-tails?* He pounded a fist against the wood, gently. *Ah, I'm fooling myself, I have to answer a summons from my Bishop.* He pulled a chair close, and sat warming his hands. Perhaps it would be a relief to have it all out in the open, to accept whatever punishment William demanded, and then to be able to take a full, free part in the church again. *Even if it means giving up Orford?* Unable to bear the thought, he marched the length of the room and back. *Yes. Yes, I think so, even that.* He bent down and put another piece of wood on the fire. *It would be so good to stop being afraid for my soul.*

Wimer felt as though he was travelling in the eye of the storm – a quiet place, where people still smiled at him as he rode, and he was free to enjoy the spring breezes. Soon, though, William would judge him, and impose some sort of penance. It didn't really matter what it was, he'd accept it – but he hoped it wouldn't make things difficult for Piers and Goda, who were happily settled in to his little house in Orford. *I need to formally gift the house to them, especially now they've provided me with a god-daughter. I wish Piers hadn't insisted on escorting me! I'd feel happier if he were well out of this.*

His thoughts wandered again. *The worst punishment would be being sent on a crusade, away from everything I love* – no, thinking so was another sin, a crusader had their sins purged before they left. Dying on the journey would send him straight into a state of grace, he should wish for it, rather... it was all too confusing.

With a mental effort he turned his focus to what was going on around him. He held his horse in a trot, and as he relaxed, the animal stopped fighting the bit. Wimer reached forward and patted him on the neck, apologising silently. The little troupe moved on through the pale sunshine.

He stopped for a break at Framlingham around mid-day. The Earl wasn't there, to Wimer's secret relief – but his Steward was happy to give Wimer and his men a meal and fill him in on the local gossip. Wimer was only half listening, concentrating more on the fat capon he was making inroads on. Then the Steward grabbed all his attention with one passing remark about his daughter;

"Of course, it would be much better if Meghan could be wed, but with the Interdict, that's not possible. I pray Milord gets that sorted out in haste..."

Interdict? Wimer put a half-chewed leg down, and asked him for details. Apparently, the Archbishop of Canterbury had excommunicated Hugh, and put all his lands under an interdict, until a land dispute with a priory had been resolved. The priory had complained to the Pope, who had told the Archbishop to sort it out.

Wimer shivered. He supposed that Hugh wouldn't be too put out by the order – although even that brash old campaigner might be afraid of hell's fire - but for the thousands of people in his care, it was a harsh punishment indeed. There could be no sacraments except extreme unction, no marriages, and no baptisms. *How many innocent souls will be lost, as a result of Hugh's greediness for land?*

A messenger caught up with them just as they were preparing to leave Framlingham.

"Father? Lord Oger, the High Sheriff, sends word that he intends to pay a visit to you at Orford. He was planning to set sail from Ipswich this morning, so will be there imminently – I'm sorry to give you no time to prepare, but I wasted time riding to you at Orford."

"Ah, that's bad timing!" Wimer thought for a bit. "Piers, you must gallop back - I'll be fine alone. Tell Oger that I will hasten back as soon as I have obeyed William's summons. Show him around the castle, then settle him in front of the fire with the account scrolls, he'll be happy enough to wait for me there for a few days. I dare not delay William!"

Mulling over the implications of Hugh's indictment, Wimer rode on. The sky had clouded now, and the wind was getting up. He reached a farmstead just before the light died, and begged a bed in the empty hay barn in return for blessing the evening meal.

He filched an apple from the last of the winter store, and moved on again at first light. The weather had turned, with cold rain coming in gusts, and he and his horse made business-like progress, especially after they reached the Roman road. There were almost no other travellers, and he made good speed – Wimer had thought that he might need another night on the road, but he made it through the city gates just in time. He dismounted, and walked the horse through the well-remembered streets to a stable.

He cheerfully banged on the door of the Cathedral precinct. "Ho! Brother Gatekeeper! Here's a traveller looking forward to returning to his old home!" A hatch in the small side door opened abruptly, and a lantern had been shone rudely in his face.

A voice said "Wait here!" and the hatch slammed shut. Nothing happened for a very long time. Wimer was just wondering whether he should bang again, when the larger door was thrown open. Brother Gatekeeper – whom Wimer vaguely remembered as a novice – shone the lantern on him again, and then popped back inside. Two hulking lay brothers took his place, and without a word grabbed Wimer by the upper arms, and lifted him off his feet.

"Hi! What are you doing? Get off me, you great oafs! Don't you know who I am?"

"Oh we know who you are, all right. Shut yer mouth!" He kicked wildly, and connected with someone's shin. That proved to be a mistake, as one brother pinioned both arms, and the other sunk a fist into his gut. He hung quietly between them after that, concentrating on gulping breaths, thoughts whirring uselessly.

They took him, to his great surprise, into the Cathedral – and pushed him into the cell in the South arm of the cross. In Wimer's day, this was used as a penitential cell for a single monk, arranged so that they could see the altar and take part in services, but be segregated from both monks and laity. Now, the cell held two – no, three – other people, Wimer discovered, as they sorted themselves out, and he'd finished apologising for landing on a couple of them.

"Wimer? Is that you?" Wimer recognised the voice.

"Good heavens, Martin of Framlingham? What on earth is going on?"

"Well, we really don't know. We worked out that it has to be something to do with the Earl – and your arrival has put the seal on that – but what, exactly, is a mystery."

"But what have they said to you?"

"Nothing! Jean and I have been here for two whole days, Aefwyn for three, and the monks say nothing to us at all. They bring us water and one meal a day, and leave us completely alone. I hope that now you've come, whatever's going to happen will start – the waiting is driving me mad!"

Having run out of things to say, the four men claimed a corner each. The other men went to sleep. Wimer stayed awake, watching the candle light play on the painted walls beside the altar, as he had done so often as a boy. *What crimes have these young clerics committed?* William had clearly decided to purge sin from Hugh's household. For a minute, he had a brief flash of hope – *I work for the King now, William can't touch me!* - but it quickly faded. Whatever William had in mind, it was going to be settled in the next few days. No time for an appeal to Henry. After the trial, there would probably be no opportunity. Besides, the King could not intervene directly in a matter between a Bishop and a subordinate priest. He might complain to the Archbishop, but with relations between the Crown and

Canterbury as they were, he would get nowhere.

There was no doubt that William had decided they were guilty. Wimer knew he was, of course – he added up the years he had lived in direct disobedience to an order from his religious superior, and winced. William didn't even need the divining rod question, or the subsequent sins of holding mass without being shriven. He wondered again what young Martin had done. He was such a straight-laced boy...

The night was strangely peaceful. Wimer dozed, waking for each of the services, and watched them from outside the pool of light. After Prime, they were brought their meal; a bowl of porridge each, for which Wimer was very grateful. A short while later he began to notice that the lay side of the Cathedral was beginning to fill up. What was going on? Surely it was too early for Terce? *It must be the trial!* He sighed, and stood up.

"Brothers, I think that we are shortly to be on show. Best look our smartest..." and he took his own advice, trying to smooth his robe. Martin stood up too, and moved across to watch the growing crowd.

"What will he do to us, Wimer? I'm afraid..." Wimer put his hand on the other man's shoulder.

"So am I, Martin, so am I!" *Afraid, and strangely looking forward to it. I have almost forgotten what life is like, without this great burden of guilt and sin...*

Wimer caught sight of a group of hefty lay brothers heading towards them, the two who had manhandled him last night amongst them. He took a deep breath. It would all be over soon, one way or another...

"Well, lads, chins up, I think the show begins."

They were escorted out. Just before he was turned into the main body of the church, Wimer caught sight of the painting on the wall of Herbert de Losinga, the first Bishop of the Cathedral, facing his own trial, and felt a little better. Losinga had done very well afterwards, even though he had been found guilty.

That little glow of comfort evaporated as they turned the corner, and he saw the crowd. There were very many more people than he had expected, and as they saw him, the noise levels rose sharply. William had clearly been doing some pre-trial rabble-rousing. *Dear Lord! We are in the lions' den!* He could feel the noise in the pit of his stomach. He hoped he could keep his porridge down – his mouth went from dry to full of saliva in an instant, and he swallowed rapidly to stop being sick.

They reached the space that had been left clear in front of the high altar, and he was forced to his knees in front of it. Martin was pushed down beside him, eyes wide and terrified. Then the two boys went down, with a crack of knees on the tiles that made Wimer wince in sympathy. William, who had been standing with his back to the crowd facing the altar, dressed in purest white robe and surplice, turned round and raised his arms. The noise level dropped immediately. He held the pose for a few seconds, then lowered his arms and began to speak.

"Dearly beloved, we are gathered here today to witness the punishment of these four criminous clerics, whose sin has been so great that it has offended our dear Lord, Thomas, by God's Grace Archbishop of Canterbury and Primate of all England." He paused for more boos, whilst Wimer racked his brains to try and think what he might have done to upset Thomas a'Becket. He'd met the man once or twice, on the King's business, but had barely said more than "good day" to him.

"The leader of the vile affront against our beloved brothers of Pentney has already been excommunicated; now these men, too have been judged to have committed a mortal sin in the service of Hugh, Earl of Norfolk..." Boos drowned out William's next words.

Pentney? Why Pentney? What's going on? Wimer vaguely thought he could remember some dispute with the Priory *– wasn't it one of Hugh's vassals, giving away something he wasn't entitled to? –* but why was Becket involved?

Everything was moving too fast. When his head stopped spinning long enough to pay attention, William was reading from a scroll, presumably a letter from the Archbishop:

"- regard to our sacred duty and to the requirements of the law we have for just and manifest causes passed sentence of excommunication on you and cut you off from Christ's body which is the Church until you make condign satisfaction. We therefore command you by virtue of your obedience and in peril of your salvation your episcopal dignity and priestly orders to abstain as the forms of the Church prescribe from all communion with the faithful lest by coming in contact with you the Lord's flock be contaminated to their ruin."

Sweet Jesu! Excommunicated!

William snapped the scroll back into a roll and pointed it at the four kneeling men.

"You sinners; all four of you are barred from the community of the Church until such time as his Grace allows. May God have mercy on your souls. Go! Begone!"

No! This can't be right! I have to speak... "Wait!"

Wimer's cry was cut off as his minder monks lifted him to his feet and firmly moved him towards the main door. It wouldn't have mattered if he had managed to say something; the noise of the crowd had risen to a roar. People were spitting at him, and waving fists! Then they were at the entrance, and all four were shoved out of the door. It slammed closed behind them.

Wimer picked himself off the cobbles, and went over to Martin.

"What have we been excommunicated FOR? WHY?" Martin was curled into a ball, staring at nothing. He had to shake him and ask again before he replied.

"Pentney. What's this about Pentney! Come on, man, snap out of it!"

Martin's voice was strangely calm. "Didn't you hear? The Archbishop has decreed that anyone who helped the Earl to reclaim land from them is condemned. I wrote to the Prior and Canons of that stupid," he was getting louder and louder "third-rate, one-horse Priory, on Hugh's orders... now I may burn in hell for it!" His voice cracked, and he buried his face in his hands.

Wimer stared at him in disbelief. He vaguely remembered writing to the Priory a long time ago – he couldn't even remember the Earl's dispute with them.

"Me too..." he whispered.

Jean broke off sobbing long enough to say, "I carried a letter to them. I never even touched it; it was in my saddlebags. And now, if I die, I will burn in hell's fire. It's just not fair!" and he burst into tears again. The other boy, whose name Wimer had forgotten, was also crying. Wimer wanted to hit someone – preferably Thomas of Canterbury, *the small-minded, vindictive, little…*

A gust of wind chilled the spittle on his cheek. Wimer wiped it absent-mindedly, then remembered the hate in the woman's eyes. *We have to move…* "Lads – what will happen when the crowd comes out, and we're still here? I think we need to make ourselves scarce, and quickly. You clearly need to go to Hugh; he got you in to this mess, and he at least has the wherewithal to feed you until this has been sorted out. Who has money?"

Fear of the crowd was enough to stop the sniffles. All three lads shook their heads. "Why would we need money? We can stay at any religious house." said the unnamed lad.

Wimer shook his head. "Weren't you listening to William? The bit about abstaining from all contact with the godly? I'm afraid you're one of the peasants now, my lad; you have to pay your way." The boy looked as though he was going to burst into tears again; Martin got to his feet and pulled the other two up. Wimer undid his money-belt and poured out the contents into his hand. Not as much as he'd like; but then he'd only taken some money along on a whim. He quickly divided the pile into two heaps, put the smaller back in his belt, and climbed to his feet. He shoved the rest of the money at Martin.

"Here; you're in charge; get to Hugh as quickly as you can, and throw yourselves on his mercy. Try Framlingham or Bungay first; if he's not there his castellan will give you more money. Once he hears what has happened, he will write to the King and beg him to intercede with the Archbishop on your behalf." *Not that it would do any good.*

This is presumably all part of the Archbishop's dispute with Henry. We are just pawns that our beloved spiritual leader has crushed to dust and ashes as a by-blow...

"But, Wimer! Aren't you coming with us? What are you going to do?"

"Get away from this church! I advise you to do the same. Go with God's speed!" Wimer gave Martin and the lads a swift embrace, and walked briskly out the Bishop's gate. *If I walk far enough, fast enough, maybe I can make sense of all this...*

WIMER, ACLE - SPRING/SUMMER 1168

Piers looked down at the figure crouched vomiting in the gutter, wrinkled his nose, and moved up-wind. It took a little while for Wimer to notice him; but when he did, his reaction was fierce.

"Go 'way!" he slurred. "You mustn't talk to me. If you talk to me you'll catch it too. No. Mustn't talk." He tried to stand up, one finger pressed to his lips, but failed twice, and sat back giggling.

"Happy drunk, isn't he?" observed the tavern girl, leaning against the inn wall, waiting for a customer; not many around, at this time of the afternoon. "Generous with his favours, too." she smiled benevolently at Wimer.

Piers thought about that one, and decided he didn't want to know. "Young lady? Would you do me a big favour, and fetch me a bucket of water?" The girl stood upright, looking hopeful, but didn't move. Piers sighed, felt in his change pouch, and tossed her a quarter-penny. She smiled, and went into the tavern.

Wimer started singing. Piers was impressed; he remembered an evening when Wimer had sung for the King, and had been booed off half-way through the first verse. This was actually melodious. It was almost a shame to throw the water over him. This time, Wimer almost made it to his feet.

"Hey! Wodja do that for? Oh no, shhh! Mustn' talk!" and he settled back down, frowning, finger firmly in place.

Piers sighed, and turned to the girl. "Will you look after him for a bit? I'll be back with a friend as soon as I can." The girl looked sad. He muttered under his breath and handed her another quarter-penny. She blew him a kiss, and squatted next to Wimer. The prohibition on talking didn't seem to apply to her; when Piers glanced back before turning the corner, they were chatting away merrily.

Wimer looked up at the man walking towards him, and waved. "Hey! Bosh... boss! Come and have a seat, Shir Sheriff!" he patted the ground beside him. The girl stood, bobbed a curtsey, and disappeared.

Oger reached the same decision as Piers had, and moved up-wind before choosing a dry patch of dirt to sit on.

Wimer tried to smile and frown at the same time, finger to his mouth. Oger watched with interest.

"Can't talk! You mussnt talk to me or you'll get ex- ex-excombobulated!"

"Excommunicated? Don't be silly. With the Archbishop of Canterbury excommunicating anyone he can think of, if the rules were followed strictly the entire country would grind to a halt. Not that Thomas would be bothered – but the King would be annoyed. Do you want to annoy the King, Wimer?"

Wimer looked alarmed, and shook his head rapidly.

Oger wisely moved his feet, just before the movement made Wimer throw up again.

"How long have you been drunk, my friend?"

"Drunk? I'm not drunk! I had a little dink... drink hours and hours ago, none since, I'm thirsty now!" and Wimer looked at him owl-eyed and hopeful.

Oger thought rapidly. "Shall we go back and ask Goda for a drink then?"

Wimer beamed, and nodded enthusiastically – briefly!

"Come on, then, my friend." Oger stood, and extended both hands for Wimer to grasp. They linked arms; Oger counted, "One, two, three!" and pulled. Wimer came up like a rag doll, and ended up over Oger's shoulder. Piers, who had been watching from the corner as ordered, came up to help; and between them, they staggered Wimer back to Oger's rented house, and Goda.

She took one look at him, sniffed, and made for the kitchen. Two servants emerged shortly with a large wooden tub, and poured a bath. They helped Piers strip Wimer, and eased him into the steaming water. He was perfectly happy, singing away, still sounding half-decent! One of them produced a razor, and had a fairly successful go at shaving him, with not too many nicks. He was standing upright, swaying gently, and wrapped in a cloak when Goda returned with a horn beaker and handed it to him. He took a long swig – and would have spat it straight out into the bath, had he not caught sight of her face. With a huge swallow, he got it down, and looked piteously at her.

"What is IN that?" he shuddered.

"Drink it all up. It's chamomile tea to calm your

stomach, with a few drops of horseradish juice to help you purge the ale." She put her hands on her hips and glared at him until he gave in and drained the beaker. She took it from him and stomped out.

Wimer burped gently, and made a face. "That was Not Nice", he enunciated clearly. He looked around, vaguely waved at everyone, then wrapped the cloak tighter and lay down in a corner. He was snoring almost immediately.

He woke in the night with no idea where he was. The room was spinning round and round. He shut his eyes again. Now it felt as though his body was wheeling lengthwise as well as turning sideways. He couldn't help it; he was sick until he had emptied his stomach, then turned away and went back to sleep.

In the grey of early morning, the taste of his mouth disgusted him. He staggered to his feet, stepping in a pile of something cold and wet on the way – he stared at his foot, disoriented; then the smell of vomit hit him, and he threw up again. He wiped his mouth on the edge of his cloak, and noticed he was naked underneath. He quickly clutched the edges tighter, then almost dropped them in favour of his head; the movement woke a blacksmith's hammer inside. He must have made a sound, because one of the other sleeping bundles lying round the edges of the hall rolled over and sat up. Wimer licked his lips, and managed to croak a question the second time of trying.

"Friend, I need ale and to piss – can you point me at the right places?" He had a bad thought, and looked around him. Yes, his money belt was gone. Getting ale might be a problem...

The shadowy figure was back, with a beaker in his hands. "Here you go, my Lord; Goda said you were to have this, when you woke."

"Piers! Oh, watch the sick, sorry... Where are we?" He took a sip from the beaker, and made a face. It was the same potion as the night before, not improved by being cold. The events of the previous few days flooded back. "Oh! No, please, go away, you must not talk to me, on pain of excommunication yourself – you do know about that, don't you? Bishop William would not hesitate to punish you too!" and he made little abortive pushing motions, hampered by the need to keep his cloak closed, not spill the drink, and keep his head still.

"First things first, my Lord. Goda said you were to drink that down, before anything else."

Wimer looked at it dubiously, but obeyed. It didn't taste quite so bad if you gulped it, he discovered. Piers smiled encouragingly at him, and reached for something on the floor behind him. "Robe, then boots." Wimer struggled into the robe, took a boot, started to bend over, and changed his mind. Piers sighed, and steered him over to a bench. When he was dressed, Piers took him out to the latrine. Oger met them as they went back in to the house, took one look at his subordinate, and grinned evilly.

"How are you feeling today, my friend?"

Wimer winced at the volume, but tried to make his point again. "I've been better, Sir – but please, you must not talk to me; I don't remember too much about the terms of the excommunication, but the Bishop was quite clear about the duty not to drag any more souls down with me."

Oger shook his head. "It's not so bad as that. The court has done some extensive research on this, as you can imagine. Your servants, provided they were in your employ before the sentence, can talk to you on any matter, although you may not give them religious instruction. Any officer of your liege lord the King may talk to you about business; that's me, and of course the Exchequer. So can Adam of Weybridge Priory. I'm afraid you need to be careful with just about everyone else, at least until Thomas relents."

Wimer chewed this over, slowly. His brain didn't seem to be working too well – perhaps it was the pounding. He was very glad that he wasn't going to be completely isolated. *What was that about Weybridge Priory?*

He asked.

"That's where I'm sending you, my lad, up to St Benet's Abbey at Holme. You can't carry on as Rector of Orford, at least not on the spot." *Oh! Of course I've lost my people! And my beautiful church!* He could feel tears welling, and turned away. Oger busied himself with the lace at his sleeve cuff until he turned back.

"It's not so black, lad. Lord Bromham will install one of his clerics there temporarily, as a vicar, and he'll take over your castle-building responsibilities himself, until Becket sees sense." *And what if he never does? God bless Bartholomew, he'll look after my people… Good heavens! Does God hear me, whilst I'm excommunicate? Surely he must?*

Oger was continuing. "I have need for your skills in Holme. The Abbey is in the King's hands at the moment, until the election for the Abbot is completed satisfactorily.

You will have charge of its monetary affairs, and Adam, who is current Prior of Weybridge Priory in Acle and one of the Abbacy candidates, will have charge of religious matters. Solves two problems with one blow, I'm quite pleased with myself, he has nowhere near your fiscal and legal acumen. Now, how about some breakfast? I smelt bacon..." he lost his audience, as Wimer's face turned an interesting colour at the mention of food, and he ran out of the door again.

The journey to Holme was taking forever. Even though most of the party were on horseback, they rarely got above a gentle trot - and even then, the motion made Wimer clutch his head with one hand, and the saddle with the other. The horse, luckily, was perfectly happy to follow on in line, without any input from him. Whenever possible, he walked - it was so much gentler on his head; and besides, he could put the horse between him and anyone they met on the road. It was stupid, of course, but he felt sure that everyone could see his shame, like a brand across his forehead. *Maybe I ought to carry a leper's bell...*

The problem with walking was that it gave him plenty of time to think. He could recall no text that talked about God listening to the excommunicate, and plenty that discussed the eternal torments of Hell awaiting those who died in sin. *Am I really lost to God? Invisible to Him?* All his life, the certainty of being held in the hand of God - however stupid or sinning - had been a comfort. Now, there was nothing.

He was also exploring, as though it were a dark,

raw hole, the space that the loss of Orford had left in his heart. *They'll be talking about me, that's for sure!* He shook his head at the thought of the little knots of his former parishioners forming and reforming in the market square. He shook his head. *Nothing I can do about that, for the present, at least...* He remounted his horse and jogged a few steps, just so the pain could distract him.

He was feeling a little less delicate by the time they'd reached Acle, but no less wounded. He was trailing behind the main group, preferring his own company. Three of the village boys called out to him, some question about who they were and where they were going. He remembered just in time that he was forbidden to talk to them, and glowered instead. He must have tensed his legs – his horse broke into a trot, which he wasn't prepared for. There were a few head-jolting steps at sitting trot, with the boys jeering at him. He found himself wiping tears away as soon as he was safely past, first from the sudden increase in his headache, then at the thought that he might never be able to talk freely to anyone ever again.

He had more or less recovered his self-control by the time they had reached the Priory, but was still feeling very subdued. They stopped briefly to pick up Adam, then pushed on the three miles more to the Abbey of St Benet. He barely spoke to the welcoming party there, but made his excuses and escaped to the cottage he'd been allocated as soon as he could.

Adam was concerned on a number of levels. On a purely practical front, he was very aware of the need to deliver a full set of accounts to the Exchequer by the end of the month. He was also worried about the mental health of his accountant. Finance was not Adam's strong point – but so far, the top-of-the-range cleric who had been brought in to sort things out had spent his days in a wine cup. There was now only a week before Wimer would have to set out on his journey to Winchester, and so far as he knew, nothing was ready. He was going to have to practice another skill required of an Abbot, and have a stern chat with him.

No time like the present, he told himself bracingly, and set off to where Wimer would be – slumped in his usual corner of the refectory.

He stood and observed him for a moment. The man who had ridden through the Abbey gatehouse just a few weeks ago had been slim and lithe, and even though he had retired to his cottage almost immediately, Adam had got a sense of competence from him. Now he was puffy-faced, pale, and unshaven. Adam could not imagine how awful it was to be excommunicate, and to live with the mortal danger to his soul – but still!

"Adding to your sins will not make the burden lighter, you know."

Wimer looked up at him, through lids heavy from lack of sleep.

"What do you mean? I am avoiding everyone, as ordered."

"Yes, everyone – and every thing – including your duty to me, and to the King. How ready are you to present the accounts?"

Wimer shook his head, and raised the horn cup to his

mouth again. Adam backhanded it away, the cup clattering down the length of the table before crashing to the floor. Still with eyes locked with Wimer's, Adam called over his shoulder:

"Brother Cellarer! This man is to have nothing to drink but water, until I authorise it!" There was an acknowledgement from the kitchen.

Then to Wimer:

"You are in a sorry state. You are bounden in your duty to the King, but you have not lifted a finger to examine the accounts. You are letting your mind and your body rot in wine, and I have not seen you praying once. Well, I only have control over one of those things; if you want wine back, you will have to earn it."

Wimer looked at the blood-red trail across the table, and licked his lips. With careful gravitas, he stood, bowed, and left the room – with only a single stagger, swiftly recovered from.

He walked, blindly, out of the refectory, and simply carried on. It didn't matter where he went, but he had to get out, get away from there… one of the brothers tried to stop him, and he just brushed the man aside and kept walking, as fast as he could. His feet took him up the river bank. The tide was out, and the river bed was largely mud. A seagull cried, and for an instant he was back in Orford. The pain in his chest eased and he looked up in wonder - then the awful greyness of his life crashed down on him again. *It can only be a few hours' journey by boat, but it might as well be another man's dream...*

He carried on walking along the river bank for a while, lost in self-pity. The colour of the mud, and the leaden sky, matched his mood. *All I've worked for, all I loved, has been snatched away.* He had so wanted to present the town, whole and beautiful, with castle and church complete, to Henry; and to bask in his approval. Now Bartholomew would have that pleasure.

Was it really worth carrying on, and suffering insults like that ignorant priest had just inflicted on him? What was there to look forward to, except an endless stream of shame - or worse, pity? He looked at the mud with more purpose. There were stretches by Orford that looked firm, but would swallow a horse or a man whole. *That would, of course, be a mortal sin.* He snorted in sour amusement. *Well, yes - it would condemn me to eternal damnation. What's new?* It would be an awful way to die, though, the cold ooze pinioning your limbs, forcing its way up into your nose, that last desperate gasp of breath with your mouth open, lungs heaving with the heavy darkness. *It would be over then, though... Perhaps I deserve a bad death.* It would only be a foretaste of what awaited him in hell anyway...

As he stood silently examining the mud, looking for the tell-tale shimmer of water on unstable sand, a moorhen walked out from behind a clump of grass. It saw him, did a double-take, put its head down, and ran for safety. Wimer laughed out loud at its expression, and its blundering determination. *Oh Lord! I bet I looked like that earlier, running away from Adam!* A shaft of late afternoon sun turned the mud to gold, a group of water birds skittering across it. *How beautiful!* He stood still, remembering the scene in the refectory. *He had a point. I have been wallowing in self-pity.* He walked on until he found a dry-ish tree stump to sit on, and admire the view. *What an idiot I am. I have a lot of thinking to do.*

It was dark when he got back. He was hungry for the first time in a very long time, and went to beg some food from the Abbey kitchen door on his way past, to save putting Goda to trouble. He accepted the water that was handed to him alongside the pasty without comment, glad of the darkness that covered his blush.

In the morning, he cleared a corner of the kitchen table and started attacking the pile of tally sticks he'd been ignoring. Goda worked around him, hiding a contented smile. By the middle of the afternoon, he had developed a permanent frown. He stuck his head out of the door and sent a passing brother to fetch Adam. As soon as he came in the door – rather warily, given their last conversation – Wimer pounced. With no preliminaries, he barked:

"What is the value of the Exchequer summons?"

Adam blinked in surprise. "I'm not really sure? But it has to be answered on Monday next."

"Go and fetch it, please." Wimer dismissed.

When he returned with the scroll, Adam stood waiting for Wimer to read it, wondering why he felt so much like a schoolboy.

Finally Wimer burst out:

"This is impossible! You have less than a third of the required amount accounted for! I also have no record of who owes the King fines or debts." He shook his head. "I need to speak to anyone who buys goods or services for the Abbey; also to whatever sad excuse you have for a treasurer. We have no time to waste; please get them here immediately!"

"Um, I'm afraid I'm the sad excuse – at least, since Brother Denis died. He must have been sicker than we thought for some time before that, too, judging from his records. I'll go and get the others!"

Adam waved away Wimer's attempt at an apology, and left grinning. *At last, we have someone who understands the money side of things!*

Wimer looked round the roomful of monks with disbelief.

"Let me get this straight. None of you keep any particular records; you pay for what you buy by asking Brother Adam here for the money. If he gives it to you, it's considered authorised. You rely on your tenants to pay you the correct rent out of the goodness of their hearts, and on your servants to sell your goods at market for the best possible price and give you all the profit. Is that the sum of it?"

Adam flushed slightly. "It does sound a little... informal, doesn't it?"

Wimer looked gravely at him. "When you were running the place for yourselves, it probably worked well enough. However, now you are under the King's hand, I'm afraid it won't do at all. Do you remember some of the King's officials coming round, probably late last year, soon after the old Abbot died?"

There was some general muttering, along the lines of,

"Yes, I remember, nice chaps."

"They probably were very friendly fellows; their job was to assess the worth of everything you own, and to report back on that to the Exchequer. Brother Adam has seen the results of that assessment. The Exchequer expects you to return an accounting for the full amount, plus any debts that people in your jurisdiction owe the King, for court fines and the like. Actually, the Exchequer expects ME to make that return on your behalf, as I am the King's officer here, and if I cannot account for any sums, I will owe that amount personally." The brothers started to look worried. "The Exchequer is treating your estate like a miniature Sheriff's territory. Brother Adam, please could you read the summons you received from them?"

Adam cleared his throat, and began:

"Henry, King of the English, to Adam, Prior of Weybridge Priory, pro tem Abbot of St Benet's at Holme, greeting. See to it, as thou lovest thyself and all thy possessions, that thou or thine agent art at the Exchequer in the Palace of Westminster, on the day after St. Michael's day, and that thou hast there with thee whatever thou owest of the farm, of former years or of this year, and these debts mentioned here by name: and thou shalt have all these with thee in money, tallies and writs and quittances, or they shall be taken from thy farm, at the exchequer." He unscrolled a bit more. "It goes on;

Farm, 31 pounds and one penny; *in thesaurus* 24 pounds.

Fines for the marriage of daughters; 28 pounds 6 shillings and 8 pence; *in thesaurus* 20 pounds.

Osbert of Thurlton owes 40 marks; 10 pounds are *in thesaurus*.

Nicholas, cleric of the Bishop of Norwich, owes 10 marks; 5 marks are *in thesaurus*.

10 marks have been paid in full and are *in thesaurus* for the money owed by Placus.

For the relief of the son of Peter of Hocton, 5 marks are owed. 4 marks are *in thesaurus*."

He licked his lips, and looked around. "That's it. I'm afraid I don't understand it at all."

Wimer bounced to his feet and started to explain.

"It's quite simple. Those nice men who visited you last year estimated that your estate is worth £31. You paid £24 to the Exchequer at Easter; they wrote the amount in their account scroll – the Thesaurus – and gave you some tally sticks, which Brother Adam has kept, thank Heaven. The nice men clearly think you're dreadful at farming, because they said that you would make almost as much money from the fees for marrying a daughter as from farming; you owe 8 pounds, 6 shillings, and 8 pence more than you have already paid for that. The rest of the list isn't a huge problem, because that's personal debts; we're supposed to collect them on behalf of the King, but we can carry them over to next Easter. So in summary, you – or rather, I – need to find the best part of £16 in a week. Adam, how much have you got in your cash box?"

It took Adam two tries to squeak out, "I – I'm not sure. Maybe a couple of pounds."

"Oh, wonderful." Wimer waved his arms in disgust and ended up clutching his head. "Any hordes of fathers wanting to marry daughters in the next week?" The monks shook their heads. "So I am going to owe the King around a quarter of your annual income. They may just put me in jail and throw away the key!"

WIMER, THE EXCHEQUER, MICHELMAS 1168

The corridor was crowded with Sheriffs and their entourages. They had all been there for a while, and there was still no sign at all of the Exchequer clerks. Wimer leant against the wall next to the seat that Oger had managed to secure, darkly amusing himself by seeing who was refusing to meet his eye. Everyone was tense. They were gathered to personally present their summonses when called; then they would be called back over the next few days, in the same order, to defend their accounts. No-one was talking, really; except for a low, murmured conversation along the hall, just out of eavesdrop range.

Wimer caught himself biting the flesh on the side of his thumb, and went back to counting cracks on the walls instead. He started rehearsing his own presentation. *It can only be a damage-limitation exercise...* he found that his thumb was between his teeth again, when at last a clerk came out of the chamber. He clapped for attention, although everyone had noticed him almost immediately and stopped talking.

"London and Middlesex!"

The local team smiled and stood up. They were almost

always first. *Is that because they're the most complicated, so the Exchequer Barons get the worst out of the way first, or because they're the only people who are able to go home after their presentation, so the Barons are making sure they can travel in daylight?* Either way, who was going second was always much more interesting. Oger quite often managed it, by some trick Wimer had never spotted.

The London bunch left cheerfully. They knew that they would be recalled first thing tomorrow morning; no more uncertainty for them. The crowd waited impatiently. Finally the clerk appeared. Wimer held his breath:

"Buckinghamshire and Bedfordshire!"

Oger's magic hadn't worked this time. Richard son of Osbert winked at Wimer as he walked past. Wimer felt himself flushing – didn't Richard know about the excommunication? *Or maybe he doesn't care?* Wimer suddenly felt a lot happier. The glow lasted until the clerk came out again:

"Norfolk and Suffolk!"

Wimer pushed himself upright with his elbows, then courteously waited for Oger to move past. He clasped his hands together behind his back, to keep his traitor thumb away from his teeth. Andreas, who was doing Mildenhall straight after Wimer, grinned nervously at him, and let him go first.

Once in the chamber, they lined up in a row and formally bowed to the officers of the Court of the Exchequer. The clerk imperiously held out his hand for Oger's scroll, and read it out loud. Oger confirmed his name; then it was Wimer's turn. He offered his scroll. The clerk looked at it, then at him, and gestured for him to put it on the table. *He knows... he doesn't want to risk contact with an excommunicated man...* Wimer's stomach flipped. Out of the corner of his eye, he could see Oger looking at him worriedly, to see how he'd take the insult. *Well, he has no right to judge. His betters still have faith in me.* He fixed the clerk with a glare, and slapped it down. The clerk had the grace to flush – nearly as red as Wimer felt – and bent to pick it up. Wimer acknowledged his name, then stood stock still whilst Andreas answered his summons. When they were released, he took great pleasure in flicking the hem of his robe at the clerk's legs as he turned, and watching him flinch.

They entered the Great Hall, joking a little amongst themselves in relief that the first part of the twice-a-year ordeal was over. A man caught sight of Oger, and came across:

"My Lord, I have brought the de Tosny heiress, as you commanded."

Oger nodded thanks, and turned to his companions.

"Come and judge this girl's charms, my friends – help me choose a husband for her?"

Wimer laughed. "I don't think I'm qualified for that!" his mood went sombre again, as he remembered that he couldn't even perform the marriage ceremony for the girl and her intended. He slowed down a little, and let Oger and Andreas go ahead whilst he regained his composure.

He joined them just as the girl was rising from a curtsey. As she raised her head, their eyes met. His world narrowed to a pair of bright hazel eyes, and the perfect lashes that framed them. Oger said something Wimer didn't hear. It must have been an introduction, because the eyes closed demurely and dropped in another curtsey; then blessedly joined with his again. The cheeks below the eyes, and the tip of her nose, were freckled deliciously. He assumed her forehead was too, but on inspection – moving his gaze away from those eyes for just an instant – it was covered in a cream-coloured wimple. It became important to see the colour of her hair; there was a tiny strand, escaping by her right ear. It was a lovely warm brown. Wimer found himself smiling. Oger said something again, possibly to him, because his voice seemed louder. Wimer turned slightly towards him, without tearing his eyes away from that delicate little ear, and nodded. It seemed to be the right response, because the booming voice went away. Alas, the eyes were now modestly downcast. Following their direction, he became enraptured by the swell of her bosom, his member stirring in response.

No! This was wrong! He wrenched his gaze away from her, and the world clamoured around him again. Oger was speaking to his man, something about a horse. Andreas was clearly bored, looking around him – perhaps for the ale table. Wimer turned to the girl again.

"I'm sorry, I came too late to catch your name?"

The eyes looked up at him again. Wimer felt something melting and swirling in his chest.

"I'm Ida de Tosny, Father. It's kind of you to agree to show me around; I'm very grateful for a protector."

He winced. For the first time ever, he felt that his title was not apt, he wasn't feeling like anyone's protective father right now – then he remembered...

"Please don't call me Father. It's plain Wimer at the moment."

The eyes frowned a little in puzzlement, then her whole face broke into a smile.

"Oh, but my Lord, I don't find you plain at all!"

Wimer beamed back, inanely. Slowly his brain caught up with what she had said. *He'd agreed to show her around? Wonderful!* He cast around for something to amuse her with. Something that would let him get away from idiots like that clerk; there would be plenty more who felt the same way.

It was as though her thoughts were echoing his. She looked around the hall, frowning again.

"It's so stuffy in here! My Lord, would you think me forward if I proposed a walk outside?"

"My Lady, nothing could give me more pleasure."

He bowed formally and proffered her his arm. She made a deep curtsey, and rested her hand lightly on his forearm. Oger watched speculatively as they left the hall, then shook his head. Of course his friend would do nothing to sully the reputation of the King's ward.

They came out into the sunshine, and instinctively turned towards the great Abbey church. They were a little shy with each other, and were silent – until Ida noticed that their strides matched.

"Oh! I'm doing it again! Alda says that I walk like a man, and I must be more demure."

Wimer considered this. "Well, when the rhythms

match, it makes walking with someone very pleasant; it's conducive to both thought and conversation. Perhaps you could walk as the occasion demands; I do not need a demure companion." He smiled down at her, and then noticed that they were almost at the church.

"My Lady, did you wish to pray? I'm afraid I may not enter the church currently, but I should be happy to wait for you here."

She stopped and turned to face him, with that attractively puzzled frown. "I thought you were making a joke in the hall, telling me not to call you Father – but you weren't, were you!" Wimer shook his head. "What happened?"

He offered his arm again, and they walked on away from the church towards the causeway. It took him a little while to find the right words to start, but she was patient; and at last it all came tumbling out. They were walking fast and hard by the time he finished with the excommunication ceremony. Ida was silent for a moment afterwards. His heart was in his mouth waiting for her reaction. He didn't dare look at her. She swung round, and stamped her foot.

"How perfectly dreadful! What a horrid, mean, spiteful little man the Archbishop must be! I hate him!" Her voice had risen. Wimer glanced around, and was relieved to see that no-one was in earshot.

"Oh, my dear, you must not hate him; nor must I. He is our spiritual superior, and we owe him obedience."

She tossed her head. He noticed, abstractedly, that more of those pretty curls had escaped the wimple.

"Well, that's just wrong. He must know that you, and

those other young men, were just acting under the orders of your Lord; punishing you in such an awful way just shows that he shouldn't be anyone's superior. HE is the one who should suffer, not you!" The foot stamped again, for emphasis.

Wimer felt as though an enormous burden had been eased. He realised, with a shock of surprise, that Ida was the first person he had told the whole story to – and her reaction was like a soothing balm. It put her in danger, though. He put both hands on her shoulders, and looked her straight in the eye.

"Ida, listen to me, this is important. One of the strictures of excommunication is that I may not discuss matters of religion – including the shortcomings of the Archbishop of Canterbury-" he widened his eyes and smiled at her, and her frown lightened in response to the twinkle in his eye "-with anyone at all, or their soul will be in the same mortal peril as mine. I am more grateful than you can know for your support, but we must not discuss it again. And please, I beg of you – be more moderate and careful in your speech. The court is always full of envious ears, and if you had been overheard just now, it would go the worse for you. Promise me you'll be careful?" He held her gaze until she nodded, reluctantly, then took a half-step away and offered his arm again. He turned them round, and pointed them in the direction of the Palace. He cast around for a safer topic of conversation.

"I half recall Oger saying once that you had an unusual upbringing – would you tell me about it?"

He listened gravely whilst she described an unusual childhood indeed, allowed to run freely most of the time with her age-mate nephews, in their remote estate in Norfolk. Her whole face lit up when she described racing their horses on the beach, or flying their falcons on the marsh, under the limitless skies. *Limitless skies – just like my Orford...* He looked across at her in delight, and was in danger of being enraptured by her beauty again. He asked a question to bring his mind back to her words:

"Who is Alda, who disapproves of your walk?"

"Hah! She disapproves of a lot more than that! She's my nephew the Baron, Roger's, wife. She's three years older than we are, and very, very bossy. She thinks that I am not ladylike at all, and is always criticising me. She's very jealous indeed that I am a ward of the King, and so will marry well, when she has to stay in sleepy old Holkham. It's just as well I am, though, because she got my marragiatum – there's a piece of land in Suffolk that should have gone to me, but because my brother Raoul married before I was born, it went to his wife, and then to Roger, so Alda has it now." A frown crossed her face again. "Will the King think I am suitable to be a wife for one of his noblemen, do you think?"

Wimer looked her up and down, and could think of nothing more delightful than to be married to this young blossoming beauty.

"I am sure that the King will be enchanted with you. But it may be a while before he has a chance to meet you, he is very busy in France at the moment – interceding with the Archbishop and the Pope on my behalf, amongst other things, I hope."

"Oh, I hope so too! But I have been rude, and talked too much – please tell me about your childhood?"

So Wimer told her about Hervey, and growing up in Norwich, and how difficult it had been working for Hugh. He was just starting to tell her all about his beloved Orford when they entered the Palace grounds again, and they were surrounded by people. It was beginning to get dark, and Wimer realised guiltily that he had been alone with Ida for far too long, for the sake of her reputation. They both fell silent, until Wimer had a bright idea.

"My Lady, I have monopolised too much of your time today, I fear – but would you like to go riding tomorrow? I am sure I have no duties, whilst the Exchequer deals with the returns before ours in the queue."

Ida clapped her hands and bounced, most fetchingly.

"Oh! I should like that very much indeed!"

The next morning, Wimer was in the Great Hall almost at daybreak, in the smartest-looking riding clothes he could borrow at short notice, and with his hair still damp from the dunking he had given it in a wash bowl. *Will she come?* It could not have been more than a few minutes before Ida appeared. She didn't immediately spot him, and he had time to admire her vitality and trim figure. Then their eyes met, and even at that distance, he could see her happy grin. She half-ran across the hall, then slowed to a demure walk that even Alda must have approved of. As she reached him, she sank into a curtsey.

"Good morning, my Lord!"

He returned the greeting, and escorted her to the stables, where Piers was waiting with the horses. His time spent begging favours from Richard of Buckinghamshire paid dividends, as she ran forward and began to make friends with the rather fine animals he'd borrowed.

"I thought that Fleur could be yours for the day?" he asked, as she blew in the nostrils of a pretty bay mare.

"Oh, yes, please!" she beamed, and was up on a mounting block and in the saddle in no time. Wimer followed suit with the chestnut gelding, and they rode out towards the causeway side by side. Piers and her maidservant followed with the remaining horses and a picnic basket.

For a while, they rode through the bustling city, but soon came to more open countryside. He noted with approval that she sat well in the saddle, and was controlling her horse more with subtle shifts of weight, than through the light rein she was maintaining.

Ida had been drinking in the sights, sounds, and smells around them, happy to ride in companionable silence; but as they came around a copse and the view widened to show a gently-climbing grassed hill with a lone tree on top, she twisted round to face him, and impishly asked:

"How good a rider are you, my Lord? Do you think you can beat me to that tree?"

She needed no more reply than his answering grin, and kicked her heels and was off. Wimer thought that he had the better horse, but was making no headway on her at all, until she slowed to a trot, then a walk, short of the tree. He slowed too, and looked enquiringly at her.

"Oh, Wimer, she's gone lame! She was stretching out for me beautifully, then I felt her stride tighten." Her face was full of misery.

"That's bad luck! I tell you what, this is a pretty enough

spot, why don't we stop here for a bit, let her rest up, and see how she is later on?"

The smile came back, gratefully. "That's very kind, thank you." she had kicked her feet free of the stirrups and vaulted out of the saddle before Wimer could dismount to help. She slowly walked the horse up the rest of the rise, and tethered her within reach of some good grass.

The others trotted up, and they all helped to lay out a blanket in the dappled shade, and spread it invitingly with their picnic. The servants retreated discreetly to the other side of the tree trunk.

After they had eaten, they lay back and watched the sunlight play in the tree branches.

"You started to tell me about Orford, yesterday?" she prompted.

Wimer needed no excuse, and described church, and village, and sand spit so intimately that he found himself half-listening for seagulls. He wound up a little sadly, with plans for the future that could not now be realised, and they both fell silent. Ida sat up, and gazed out over the view.

"I'm sorry, I have spoilt the mood." he apologised, still prone.

"No; the fault is the Archbishop, and his... OH! Oh! Get it away from me!"

Wimer leapt to his feet and rushed to see what the problem was. She was flapping ineffectually at something on the blanket – a spider, he saw. Her face was white and strained.

"I have it!" he said, firmly, and bent down and scooped it into his hands. He trotted down slope a little, then opened his hands wide and threw the poor thing as far away as possible, very ostentatiously. Swallowing his smile, he went back to Ida.

"Thank you so much! I hate them – the boys were always teasing me with them at home!" She still looked pale – then brightened a little with a thought. "You see, you are my rescuer, as well as my protector! I have had so much fun today, it's delightful to find such a friend at court."

He bowed low. "My lady, I shall always be delighted to rescue you." they smiled at each other. Wimer let the moment stretch, then purposefully broke it, before he said or did something stupid.

"Shall we see how Fleur's leg is now?"

They decided that the mare was fine, but that they should walk back slowly so as not to risk her. They filled the trip with inconsequential chatter, mostly about horses they had known, Wimer listening more than speaking. They reached the Palace grounds in the last of the golden sunlight.

Oger swooped on Wimer as soon as they entered the hall.

"I'm sorry, my dear, but I have need of your protector now. Wimer, we are in court tomorrow first thing; come and rehearse..."

Wimer could do no more than wave, as Oger linked arms with him and towed him off.

"*Et Quietus Est.*" Oger bowed to the court, as they declared his account for the King's 'farm' of Norfolk and

Suffolk settled. Wimer's mouth felt dry as dust as he stood up.

"Who is doing the return for the Abbey of Hulmo? Oh, yes, Wimer the Chaplain. Up you come, then, and place your tallies."

The Justiciar's voice was in the same even keel as when he had dealt with Oger, and Wimer relaxed a notch.

"Thank you, Your Honour."

The Calculator was already consulting the Chancellor's Roll, and laying out the amount that the assessors had specified on his side of the chequered table. He was careful to keep like amounts in between the lines – so pounds, shillings and pence all had their own columns. Wimer watched him carefully, and then consulted his summons to see that the correct amount had been set. Only then did he lay out the tally-sticks that he'd brought from the Abbey in the matching columns on his side of the table, again careful to keep within the lines. When he had finished, and double-checked it, he nodded to the Chancellor's clerk, who read out the amount already paid in to the Treasury.

"In thesauro, for the 'farm', twenty-four pounds; do you agree?"

Wimer acknowledged that the amount was correct, and the calculator clerks began removing the amount specified by Wimer's tally sticks, the amount for one stick at a time, waiting for Wimer's inspection and nod before moving on to the next. When they had finished, there was a scarily large amount still to be matched on the Chancellor's side of the table. Wimer cleared his throat, and addressed the court.

"Your Honour, Barons, Officers of the court; I beg

indulgence for one mark of silver, for the construction of a mill in the Abbey demesne holdings."

The Justiciar raised an eyebrow at the Chancellor and the Bishop of Westminster, who both nodded. The Justiciar nodded at the calculators, who removed 13 shillings and 4 pence from the total, the going exchange rate.

Wimer closed his eyes. The moment that had been giving him sleepless nights had come. He opened them, sighed, and placed all the money left over in the Abbey coffers, after they had paid his expenses for the trip, on the board. A little ripple of laughter went round the clerks. The Justiciar looked down his nose at Wimer.

"Is that really all you can do?"

"Yes, Your Honour."

The Justiciar shook his head unbelievingly, but waved at the calculators to remove the paltry two shillings from both sides of the table.

The Chancellor stood up, and pronounced:

"Debet: Six pounds, eight shillings, nine pence."

Wimer felt sick, even though he had reached the same figure. He bowed acknowledgement.

The Chancellor sat down, and read the next amount out.

"For marriage fines; 28 pounds 6 shillings and 8 pence; in thesaurus 20 pounds. Place your tally sticks."

Again, the calculators laid the amount out on their side of the table, then removed the amount already accounted for.

The Justiciar gestured for Wimer to put down the rest of his fine money.

"Your Honour, I have no further monies at all." Out of the corner of his eye, he could see the Marshall's clerk – the nasty little toad who had snubbed him yesterday – sit up straight and grin. He would be the person who would take Wimer into custody, if the court decided to sentence him. Wimer stiffened his own back, and continued to look steadily at the Justiciar. He simply raised his eyebrows, and gestured to the Chancellor to continue.

"Debet: eight pounds, six shillings, eight pence."

Again, Wimer bowed. The Chancellor paused whilst he and his clerks all did the same sum, and compared the results. One of the clerks passed the Justiciar the total.

"Wimerus Capellanus, you are in debt to the Crown to the sum of 14 pounds, 13 shillings, and 5 pence. Do you acknowledge the debt?"

"Yes, Your Honour." Again, the Justiciar shook his head.

"Have you collected any of the debts owed to the Crown by individuals in your estate?"

"I'm afraid not, your Honour."

The Justiciar's frown was beginning to look fixed. He nodded to the Chancellor, who read the outstanding debts from the Roll. When he'd finished, the Justiciar called him, and the Bishop, over. The discussion was quite long. Wimer stood stoically, hands clasped behind his back, waiting for their decision. He could feel the clerk on his right metaphorically licking his lips. He used up a bit of waiting time thinking about what he would like to have happen to the clerk. He had just decided on suppurating boils up his nose, when the three Barons returned to their seats. The Justiciar spent an agonising minute just looking at Wimer. Finally, he spoke;

"If we had not had previous experience of your competence, when you did the return for Orford, you would have been dismissed and jailed without question. As it was, the vote was two to one." He let the tension build. The clerk leant forward in his chair. Wimer added everlasting toothache to his wish list for him.

"However, we have decided to give you a chance to redeem yourself. We will reassess your position when you present the accounts for the Abbey at Easter. We expect you to make considerable inroads into this debt, and not accrue any more. Is that clear?"

Wimer felt himself go cold, then hot, then cold again. He had not been at all sure that he would be allowed to walk away from the court.

"Is that clear?" the Justiciar snapped.

"Yes, indeed, Your Honour! Entirely clear! Thank you!" he hastily replied, then bowed low.

"Dismissed!" As he turned to go, he gave the clerk such a malevolent glare that the man flinched back, squeaking his chair a little on the tiles. Wimer bared his teeth in a snarl of satisfaction.

Wimer stood, fiddling with his saddlebags. The rest of the party were mounted, and beginning to look a bit impatient. He looked around one last time, and sighed. She wasn't going to come; he'd been stupid to hope for it. *Perhaps I made a fool of myself last night - I spent far too much time watching her at the evening meal. If someone noticed me moon-gazing, she may have been teased, and never want to see me again. Or, of course, I'm simply not important to her. Just one of Oger's men, and excommunicate, at that.* He turned back to his horse, and put one foot in the stirrup. Just as he did, her voice rang out.

"My lord Oger! Were you going to leave without saying goodbye? I have brought a favour for you to wear."

"That's very kind of you, my dear - but much as I love you, I have no intention of giving up my hard-won perch on this nag, my knee would never forgive me for the insult. Give it to Wimer to hold for me, would you? - as he's still on his feet."

Ida bobbed a quick curtsy, and walked round to Wimer, giving his horse's nose a rub in passing. *I wish that were me, under her touch*

They looked at each other a little shyly. *Her eyes are so beautiful...* Ida broke the silence.

"Thank you for a lovely walk the other day, my friend."

"It was my complete pleasure." *I must be beaming like an idiot - what can I say to her?*

They fell silent again. Oger grumbled,

"For heaven's sake, child – give him the ribbon, and let's go!"

Ida flushed, and thrust the favour at him. "Bear it for my honour..." she whispered.

He raised it to his lips and kissed it, shielded by the horse's bulk from the rest, then mounted. From his saddle, he leant down, and spoke for her ears only:

"My Lady – should you ever need rescuing, call on me; and I will come."

They looked at each other solemnly for a moment, and then she nodded, and stepped aside. The party moved out. Wimer looked back as they left the castle grounds. She was still standing there, her head held high, her dress the same warm yellow as the ribbon clenched in his fist. Wimer raised it to his nostrils again, inhaling the light, sweet scent of her, and then folded it carefully into his pouch. *Goodbye, lovely Lady - I pray we meet again soon.*

HENRI, BRITTANY - JANUARY 1169

"Henricus Rex ad Wimerus Capellanus:

My friend, just a quick note to let you know that I am still pursuing your cause with the Archbishop. I hope my patronage will do you more well than ill; you may be better advised to ride the Earl of Norwich's coat-tails, as the other clerks who were excommunicated with you are doing. Still, neither Hugh nor I are making any progress with the Archbishop, who remains obdurate.

I did have, for a few moments only, hope of reconciliation with him just this past month at Montmirail – I don't know if the tale has reached you yet? King Louis was brokering a peace, stabilising the gains I have made through might of arms over these past several months. Once we had dealt with my tenants, Louis listened again to the points in the argument with the Archbishop, and remonstrated with him. Thomas actually prostrated himself in front of me, and placed himself at my pleasure; then to everyone's astonishment, the man repeated that infuriating statement about 'saving his order'. I swear, if he had been standing, I would have hit him. At least Louis saw at first hand how obstinate he can be; but I'm afraid your cause was not advanced. Still, we shall continue to urge it, with both Becket and the Pope.

In the meantime, I hear that you are being suitably challenged by St Benet's! The Chancellor wrote to me saying that he had had the casting vote at the last Exchequer, and was still undecided as to whether or not he had made the right decision to continue your employment as Sheriff. I wrote back to reassure him; I expect that little corner of Norfolk has never been so well run as it is now.

Try to stay out of the Tower, my friend. I have need of you yet! And rest assured, I will do everything in my power to persuade my errant Archbishop to reinstate you in the Church.

Henry."

WIMER, THE EXCHEQUER - EASTER 1169

Wimer paced up and down the length of Adam's office – three strides, then a turn. *This isn't getting us anywhere: we've been at it for hours, and we're still no nearer working out how to clear the debt – or at least, raise enough money to keep me out of jail at the Easter treasury*! He marched up and down again, Adam watching him wide-eyed. *Gah! He looks just like an owl.* He briefly entertained himself by trying to work out how to make Adam turn his head upside down, then got back to the matter in hand.

"Look, let's try something new," he said, swinging back into his chair. "When you had money paid in last year, what amounts were a pleasant surprise?"

"Well, Sir Ricard's four daughters getting married at the same time was astonishing – although he looked rather more shocked than pleased!"

"Hmmm, leave marriage fees out of it – Sir Ricard's four daughters have given us a problem, the assessors have set that target too high, I'm sure. What else?"

"The Widow Edith gave us quite a lot of money for perpetual masses to be said for her husband's soul. I didn't think she was that well off."

"Bequests! Good idea. We will have to think how to get more of them over the winter. Can we sell burial space, too? Don't look so shocked, we have to make up that £14 deficit somehow! Anything else?"

"Well, the wool merchant was pleased with the quality of the wool, and said that he'd up his rate a little bit for us if the quality was as good again."

"That's interesting – why was the quality up this year? How many sheep do you have, anyway?"

"I think it must be because Brother Stephen joined us last year. He used to be a shepherd, over Norwich way, but when his wife died, he says he went a little mad, and lived rough for a while. He became a lay brother somewhere around Candlemas, I think. He spent a lot of time in the lambing sheds – I remember the old Abbot complaining about it, he missed several services – but he does seem to know exactly what he's doing. You'd have to ask him about sheep numbers, I'm afraid. I have no idea."

Wimer rubbed his nose. This was all very frustrating, with nothing he could really get a handle on.

"Let's try another tack. Who owes you money?"

Adam went to the sideboard, poured two ales, and handed one to Wimer without thinking. Wimer stared at it, nearly missing Adam's next comment, and then put it down untasted on the table.

"Almost everyone who rents lands away from the marshes, and doesn't have a pond. It's been so dry that the crops have been pitifully bad. I remitted a lot of payments..."

Wimer clutched at his hair, then relaxed his hand by force of will. No wonder he was in so much trouble.

"What grows on the higher land, then?"

"Sheep, mostly..."

The sheep were standing in a semi-circle, watching the shed beside the gate. Occasionally, one of the bolder sheep was taking a step or two forward. None of them were grazing. *Aha! Food on the way? I wonder?* Wimer walked round the shed, and peered in the open door. A man in a brown novice's tunic was high on the mound of hay, sending pitchfork-fulls of it downwards.

"Brother Stephen? Can I give you a hand?" he called up.

The man stopped, and leant on his fork. "Well... it's dusty work up here. Can you use a pitchfork? Then I'll go down and give some to the sheep."

In answer, Wimer girded his own gown, and scrambled up the pile. They worked in silence for a while, Wimer tossing hay down, and Stephen mounding it against the fence, where the sheep could take mouthfuls without trampling it. When they were done, they leaned companionably on the fence, and listened to the sheep munching.

"They look in good shape. I see you've got the rams in?"

"Yep. Just put them in today. Get some nice early lambs. Good price for 'em, at market."

Wimer leaned over, and scratched the back of a ewe, who moved closer without losing her place by the hay.

"The Priory has some money problems, just now.

In fact, we need to get hold of a lot of money next year, to pay taxes and fines to the Treasury - do you have any ideas?

Stephen kicked some hay back into the sheep's reach. "You need more ewes." he stated confidently. "We have three good rams. Keep them with the ewes, tup by November, lambs in March, job done."

Wimer shook his head. "I'm sorry, how does that help?"

"We shear before lambing. Wool money before Easter. Then we fatten the lambs over the summer, shear them and sell them before Michelmas, pay the bills again. Just get me more ewes, I'll solve your problems."

Stephen moved along the hay, kicking it firm against the fence, then tipped an imaginary hat to him and walked off. Wimer gazed after him, feeling hopeful for the first time in days. *Although where I'll find money for ewes, I don't know...*

Somehow, the need to pay off his debt, and the thought of Ida, became inextricably linked in his mind. He wanted her to be proud of him – and to be free to walk and ride with her again when the Exchequer met at Easter, without the threat of jail. She was often in his mind - that was both a joy, and a misery. He had long, internal conversations with her, telling her about his problems, or imagining her delight at a rising lark's song, or at the glimpse of a hunting owl at dusk. He would lie awake at night, sometimes unable to sleep for the sheer pleasure of knowing she existed, sometimes torturing himself thinking how few the hours they'd spent together, and how little he must mean to her. He filled these black nights with the memory of every word she'd ever spoken to him, hugging them to himself.

He felt as though the work of raising money for the Abbey was dedicated to her, which made it a pleasant job, to be done with vigour. He cheerfully threw himself into it. He was often away for days at a stretch, getting to know the people and the land. He was spending most time now, whilst the weather was good, riding out to the richer farmers bordering the marsh. Many of them owed the Abbey money, and he was happy to accept the promise of ewes instead, where pennies were in short supply. He was always careful not to break the terms of his excommunication, but simply asked how their year had been, and about the health of their families.

He was also doing a little gentle touting for the work the monks could do for the souls of the departed – no pressure, no scaremongering; just a light reminder that prayer could speed the passage of a soul through Purgatory, and masses could be bought for a small fee. Unbeknownst to him, he was doing an excellent sales job. Talking about Purgatory would of course bring his own eventual date with hell fire to mind, and however light he tried to keep the conversation, the look in his eyes was sometimes enough to send a shiver down the spine of the sensitive.

Both Adam and Stephen were waiting for him when he got back from one of these expeditions, sitting side by side enjoying the last of the pale winter sunshine on the bench that Piers had put outside the house. Wimer took care of Stephen first, telling him which farmers had promised what livestock whilst the list was fresh in his mind. In a day or two, Stephen would go and collect the new additions to his flock; he was looking more and more cheerful after every trip. Adam waited until he'd left, whistling, before speaking.

"You're certainly making him a happy man. We seem to have whole hillsides of sheep! The coffers are getting heavier, too, some people are actually paying their debts, and there's a steady trickle of people asking about masses for the departed. I wouldn't be surprised if you've magicked up a few spare marriageable daughters, too; you've been amazingly busy. Do you think we'll be able to raise the money?"

Wimer joined him on the bench, and eased his boots off. "Well, it's close, still. We need to keep the penny-pinching going; and I would be happier if there were a lot more marriageable young women out there. I think we can only count on two fines before Easter - although who knows, maybe one or two more will pop up. But the big money is all in Stephen's hands. I've done pretty well all I can, now, the rest is up to him."

"So are you planning on spending a bit more time at home, now?"

Wimer nodded. "I've been really lucky with the weather. I need to go and talk to your tenants in the West, too; maybe they've been blessed with more daughters! Soon the roads will be too muddy for travel, though."

Adam swivelled round to face him. "When you are

here, I'd like to see you spend some time in church."

Wimer stared at him, and then reached for his boots again. The blood-red velvet tide of despair, that had so nearly overwhelmed him at the time of his excommunication, was rising again. He pulled the boots on, slowly, before replying. He kept his head down.

"You know I can't do that."

Adam leaped up, and started waving his arms. "Actually, you can! I've been researching it. You can't take Communion, of course, and I can't hear your confession; but you can listen to the services. If you just stood at the back, it would almost be as though nothing had happened."

Wimer was still for a heartbeat or two, absorbing the blow, then heaved himself to his feet.

"Well, it has happened. And I can't forget it." Adam's smile was draining away. "I live with the threat of damnation every day; would you put water just out of reach of a man dying of thirst?" He shook his head, and turned away. "Good night, Father; I'll be off on the road again tomorrow."

He walked into the cottage and firmly shut the door behind him. Inside, he leaned on it, head back against the solidity of the wood. His hard-won peace, the safe place inside his head, was crumbling into the dark velvet pit. *So much for a day or two of rest. If he's going to try and force me into church, I have to get away. Now.* He sniffed, and swiped at his nose. *To have everyone pitying me, trying to be subtle about craning their necks to gawp at me... No.*

Adam had spent many hours on his knees, praying for guidance on how to help Wimer, and had worked out a plan of action. He had instructed his monks to keep an eye out for Wimer's next return. He wasn't particularly surprised when it was Brother Stephen who had spotted him. The shepherd had reported that Wimer had arrived at dusk, but had dismounted, gone into a small wood, and vanished, until the prayer bell could be heard across the causeway. Then he'd waited until all the small, distant figures had made their way inside the Abbey, and had crossed the causeway briskly. Adam briefly thought about asking Stephen why he had not been in church himself; but decided to fight one battle at a time. He dismissed his shepherd, and went in search of his accountant.

He did a bit of skulking himself, waiting until Piers left the cottage; a quick chat around the corner with him confirmed that Wimer was inside. He slipped in through the open door, and watched his victim for a while. He was slumped on a bench, half-lying against the wall; still in his muddy riding hose and tunic, eyes closed. Goda looked up from her sewing, and frowned; Adam raised a finger to his lips to quiet her. Wimer was oblivious. He looked exhausted. It was clear he'd lost weight, and in repose, his face was unbearably sad. He looked much older than a man in his mid-30s.

Adam abandoned his original plan, which was to give Wimer a lecture on what he risked to lose by not attending church, and the redemptive possibilities of excommunication. Assuming it was revoked at some point, please Lord… Looking at that face, Adam didn't have the heart to add to his burden; this man was clearly no stranger

to suffering. He should just go, and leave him in peace...
What was in the pouch, which Wimer was clutching so
protectively to his side? Just then, Wimer jolted a little,
settling in to sleep, and the pouch slipped a bit. The
movement jerked him awake, and Adam knew that he had
been seen. He watched, with some shame, as Wimer's
expression changed as he moved away from rest. He was
obviously dredging up reserves of cheerfulness. He sat
upright, placing the pouch carefully beside him on the
bench, and patted the wood next to him in invitation.
Adam came and sat down.

"Hello, Father! I didn't think anyone had seen me
arrive – come for a report, have you?"

Adam felt a little hot in the cheeks. Having abandoned
his prepared speech, he couldn't think of anything to say –
so leapt at Wimer's suggestion.

"Yes! It's been a while since you told me how we're
doing. How ARE we doing? Will we have enough sheep?
Have you found us any more rich widows, wanting us to
pray for their dead husbands? Any more brides?" He shut
up abruptly, aware that he was gabbling. Wimer gave him a
bit of a strange look, but patiently started to tell him about
their financial position again. Adam, who was really much
more interested in the state of Wimer's soul, let it wash
over him, waiting for a good place to make his excuses and
escape, and let Wimer get the rest he so obviously needed.
The speech finally wound up;

"So, you see, we will still be short of the marriage fees;
but most of the King's debtors have paid their fines. It all
depends on the wool money, now; and we won't know
how much we have until just before I leave."

Adam waved his hand. "Yes, well, thank you; I have complete faith in you." He stood up, and very seriously met Wimer's eyes; he was sure his cheeks were bright red, but he said it anyway.

"My son; I'd just like you to know that I pray for you every day."

Wimer closed his eyes, and Adam felt a wave of pity for him. He could stand it no more, and abruptly turned to go. From behind him, he thought he heard a whispered "Thank you".

He strode off into the night, grimly angry with a system that punished a good man so harshly. Well, if all he could do to help was pray, that he would do.

The sheriffs were gathered again, the corridor filled with a sea of fine, dark wool and furs. Wimer was on his feet, pacing up and down within the narrow confines of the space staked out by the Norfolk and Suffolk contingent. He was getting nearer and nearer to thumping the irritating little clerk, who was smirking at him every time he appeared to call in another shire. He was getting plenty of opportunity, as Oger's magic touch was failing badly – a good half-a-dozen groups had been called already.

Mind you, Oger was not looking at his best at all. He seemed gaunt, somehow, and his skin was almost grey. His eyes were shut; he was only opening them each time the clerk appeared. Wimer looked down at him again and frowned. He wished he could help... it was a welcome distraction from his own problems.

He hadn't seen Ida at all, even though he had been at Westminster almost three days, having galloped down from Norfolk. His mood had gradually changed, from being full of anticipation, to a black, sick nervousness. *Have I offended her in any way? Or has she simply decided that a defrocked Saxon priest is a liability, to be cast aside before he gets in the way of her court career? Maybe I've been deluding myself all along that she liked me?*

He swung round on his heel again, luckily for the clerk, who popped out just as he walked away. "Buckinghamshire..." Wimer clenched his jaw, and carried on pacing. At least the corridor was getting less crowded; almost half the shires had checked in and gone.

"Norfolk and Suffolk!" *Finally!* Wimer strode over to help Oger to his feet. The head Sheriff accepted the hand-up, but then shook off Wimer's proffered arm, and proudly walked in to the court at the head of his delegation. Each of them handed in his summons without incident. Oger led them out again, and round the corner from the holding corridor; then slumped. They started to gather round him, but again he pulled himself together.

"No, please don't trouble yourself, gentlemen; I'm fine; just a little tired. I shall go and rest, and if I don't see you before, I look forward to presenting the accounts with you in a week or two." His man had come up, and Oger allowed himself to be helped away.

What he'd said took a little time to sink in; but then Wimer realised he was right. It might be as long as a fortnight before they would be called back in to court. Just a few days ago, he would have been filled with joy at the prospect of spending the time with Ida; now he was terrified, not knowing how he would fill the empty days without her.

He wandered over to the ale table and took a mug, and people-watched whilst he sipped. At least this time no-one was obviously spurning him – but no-one was in a hurry to come and talk to him, either. It was astonishing how the Court had simply worked around the strict rules about excommunication, with the Archbishop producing new victims on a regular basis.

He finished the ale and decided to get some fresh air. He mooched out with no fixed destination in mind, and ended up perched on the causeway wall, watching the traffic and the wading birds on the mud. A serving-girl came up to him:

"Excuse me, my Lord – are you Wimer the Chaplain?"

"I am indeed?"

"Forgive the intrusion, my Lord; but she whose token you bear, begs a word, if you would be so kind."

Wimer leapt to his feet. "Yes! By all means! Take me to her!"

The girl curtseyed, and led off. She took him around the back of the castle, to an area he hadn't visited before, and then silently pointed to a bench half-hidden behind a clipped yew, before leaving him alone. He sat for a short while, then his nervous energy forced him to his feet, and for the second time that day, he paced for what seemed like an age. Finally, he turned round for another length and saw her watching him at the entrance to the garden. She looked pale and frail, and his heart dropped. *She's ill! Oh, I've been such a selfish fool, I never thought she might be ill! She looks so wan....* He stood still, hardly breathing, then knew that he must learn the worst. He half-ran to her, and went to one knee in the damp grass.

"My lady! Are you ill?"

Still she did not smile, nor speak, for a little. When she did talk, he had to strain to hear her words.

"Once you told me not to call you 'Father', because you had lost the right to the title. Now I can no longer bear 'Lady'."

He stood. "Mistress? Ida? I do not understand. What has happened?"

Again she stood silent, then shivered a little.

"Oh, this won't do!" he exclaimed. "Come on; let's get you inside."

He put his arm around her for warmth. She seemed to melt and turn in his arms, her shoulders shaking with sobs. *Oh, my very dear… how sweet your hair smells! And how I have dreamed of holding you!* He held her close, and then started to worry about someone seeing them like this. *Her reputation...* Patting her back seemed to help, and after a little while, the tears subsided. He gently disengaged, took off his surcoat and wrapped her in it, and led her over to the bench.

"Now, tell me what has happened."

She lowered her head and pulled the coat tighter, and for a second he thought she was going to cry again; then she lifted her chin and blurted out,

"I am with child."

Now her eyes were dry, and she waited for his reaction with her head held high.

This is not going to go down well with Henry. He put his hand over hers.

"My dear! Who is the father?"

She gulped back more tears.

"That, my friend, is the main problem. I do not know. I was raped."

Wimer stared at her in shock, then gritted his teeth instead of doing what he wanted to do, which was to leap up and hit something.

"Who? When?"

She lowered her head again, fighting more tears.

"Thank you for believing me. It was over Christmas; I left the hall to pee, after dark, and someone must have followed me outside. He held me against the wall with his hand over my mouth; forced me; and then threw me in the mud and left me. I never saw his face." She covered her own face with her hands, and took a deep breath. "I hoped that nothing would come of it, and that the loss of my virginity would be the only problem I would have to face; but I have missed my monthly courses twice now."

She put her hands in her lap, like an obedient child, and looked up at him.

"Oh, Wimer – what am I going to do?"

At this, he did stand up, and started to pace again. At a thought, he stopped and faced her.

"I don't know how to say this delicately – but my man Piers' wife is skilled with herbs. It would be a sin; but if you desired it, she might be able to rid you of the baby."

Ida's face tightened in shock, and her hands went protectively to her belly.

"No; I see that is not what you want. To tell you the truth, I'm glad; but I thought you should have the option. The sin of contemplating it is all on my shoulders. Very well; so, we need to work out what to do with a baby. I think that getting you out of court would be a good thing, too. You do not need the gossip as you swell. At some point, you're going to have to deal with the King when he returns and finds out that someone has deflowered his ward. If you are not the talk of the court, he may find it easier to, um, overlook some indiscretions."

Ida looked up at him and frowned in puzzlement.

"My dear, we still need the King's favour, to make you a good match; baby or not. In fact, more so, with a babe; it's just a trickier proposition."

Wimer went back to pacing, and they were both quiet for a while. Ida broke the silence, thoughtfully:

"My nephew's wife – Alda, I have spoken of her to you – is childless, after several years of marriage."

"Sometimes we just do not understand God's plan in these things."

"No – I mean, she is desperate for children. Of course, my nephew would like a son; but Alda yearns for a baby to hold in her arms. What if there were no baby when the King comes? What if it were Alda's?"

She stood up, pressed her fingertips together on her lips, and waited for Wimer's response. He took another turn to think about it.

"How would your nephew react? You can't exactly buy a baby with the same ease as a lap-dog. His neighbours would gossip. And we still have not solved the problem of your growing belly. We need to hide you away somewhere safe, as well as find a home for the baby."

"Home! Oh, Wimer, could I go home to Holkham? That would be wonderful... no-one cares whether I am here or not; perhaps I could catch a dreadful disease,

which might take several months of sea air to cure!
Perhaps Alda could catch it, too, and emerge with a baby.
Oh, Wimer, my friend - I think that could work!"

Wimer looked at her, feeling a heady mix of excitement
and apprehension. *It might just be made to work!* He had one
more go at picking holes in the plan.

"You realise, don't you, that you are talking about
passing off a bastard as the Baron's heir. And of course the
whole pack of lies depends on Alda's wholehearted
cooperation. It's very risky..."

Ida now was standing tall and confident. She ticked his
points off on her fingers;

"The baby would share his blood – if it's a boy, it
would actually be in the succession in its own right,
through me, should anything happen to my other nephew
– who is unmarried. Leave Alda to me; I shall write to her,
and put the idea of a holiday by the sea in her head. Then
when we are in Norfolk, I can speak to her in private, at
the right time. THAT is the terrifying part. I could do with
a friend by my side? And yes, of course it is risky; but if it
works, it's a marvellous solution! Do say that you'll come
and give me some moral support?"

Wimer looked into her eyes, and was lost. He would do
anything to earn the trust he saw there.

After Ida's little surprise, the long-prepared-for
Exchequer court was an anticlimax. They'd spent the
intervening week gently, talking over the possible scenarios
Ida might face, or simply enjoying each other's company.

When the summons came, Wimer was feeling calm,

and prepared. The only problem came during Oger's presentation; mid-way through, he leant against the table, his face ashen. He looked as though he was going to fall, and Wimer leapt up to help. The Justiciar ordered Oger to sit down, and Wimer acted as runner for him, placing his tallies and money as required. By the end of his account, Oger had more colour, and stood and bowed thanks to the court, and to Wimer, at the *"Quietus Est"*.

Wimer simply carried on in the same vein, answering count after count for the Abbey. The only moment he savoured was when his personal debt from the Easter court was called; and he placed a very satisfactory pile of silver on the chequerboard, clearing almost half. He could have cleared more, but he had held some back to give some to Ida, just to be sure she had a little cushion. He took his own *"Quietus est"*, and sent a mental message of thanks to Brother Stephen, who had made the bulk of it possible. Not only that, but his groundwork would guarantee a profit year on year; Wimer would be debt-free by Easter, or next September at the latest.

Finally, it was done, and they were free to leave. The next day, as agreed, Ida travelled with the party back towards Norwich, then split off with an escort of Oger's men to travel to Holkham. Wimer travelled with them, acting on Oger's behalf to see his charge safely home. They had simply told him that she had been invited up there for a holiday. Oger had accepted the statement without question, and was grateful to Wimer for his offer of an escort.

Alda arrived only a couple of days after they did, and immediately made her position as head of the household clear. The entire staff were lined up on one side of the drive to greet her, and Ida and Wimer took up position on the other. It was drizzling, a fine mist that was soaking everyone. Wimer was alternating between worrying about Ida catching a chill, and admiring the way the water droplets were silvering her hair. Alda made a royal procession past the staff, accepting their curtsies or bows, and saying a few words to the senior people. Eventually she reached Ida, who received a perfunctory hug. Wimer bowed, as Ida introduced him.

"A Saxon name? How quaint. I am hungry; I shall see both of you in the hall in a quarter-hour. I have instructed Cook to send up some pottage." *Quaint? I wonder if that translates to something like, oh look how clever, the dog can walk on its hind legs.*

The three of them sat in state at a table on the dais clothed in bleached linen. Below them, in the body of the hall, everyone was carrying on as normal - no-one else had been invited to eat early. *At least if everyone were sitting down, we'd be less of a spectacle...* He forced his attention back to his hostess, who was detailing, apparently yard by yard, the vicissitudes of her journey. He shaped his mouth into a smile *with luck, looking less glazed than Ida's* and resigned himself to listening, for her sake. At last, the servants brought bowls and an ornate tureen, and whisked off its lid. The earthy smell of the pottage made Wimer's mouth water; he realised that he was hungry too. Alda rapped on the table, making several people stop what they were doing and look round.

"My Lord Wimer; perhaps as our respected Sheriff's representative, and a welcome visitor in your own right, you would be kind enough to say Grace?"

Wimer looked at her, aghast, and then hurriedly explained the situation. Alda's expression, as he went on, became more and more pinched. She waited until he had stammered to a halt, and then pronounced in a voice that carried to the end of the hall:

"I do not extend hospitality to the godless. Be kind enough to leave my house forthwith."

Wimer sat stunned for a moment, feeling a flush burning its way past his cheeks to his hairline. *My God! She can't... Yes, she can. In fact, she should...* William's words at his excommunication struck him again. *"By coming in contact with you the Lord's flock be contaminated..." She's right, I have been putting Ida's soul in danger.* Wordlessly, he rose and bowed; first to Alda, then to Ida. He paused a moment at the top of the dais step, to compose himself, then walked steadily through the hall. People backed out of his path as though he were a leper.

He turned at the entrance to the hall, to fill his eyes one last time with Ida's beauty. She was looking directly at him, hands clasped to her mouth, looking as though she was just about to cry. *No, my Lady, you're better off without me - even though I've failed you.* He bowed again, then accepted the inevitable, and set off on the long road back towards the Abbey. *She will have to face that gorgon on her own. Damn Thomas a'Becket to the nether regions of hell!*

The summer dragged on, and on. He spent it out on the road again, spending a lot of time with farmers to the far North of the Abbey's estates. It was as near to her as he possibly could be, taking comfort from knowing that the same moon was shining on both of them. *What is her life like, so near and so unreachable? Has she managed to persuade Alda to look after the babe, or is that dreadful woman making life hell for my sweet Ida?*

The months were a slow torment of not knowing. Eventually, however, it was during one of his rare stops at the Abbey that a messenger brought him the news he had been waiting for, just before he was due to leave for Westminster again for the Michelmas court. The man found him leaning on a paddock fence with Brother Stephen, and handed over a sealed piece of parchment.

"*Ad Wimerus Capelanus, de Ida de Tosny*; He read the greeting, and folded the parchment away in his pouch, as nonchalantly as he could manage.

Stephen had been explaining an idea he'd had, to try and get a ram from a breed the wool dealer had been telling him about. Wimer tried to look like he was still listening.

"And this ram he can get us, a Clun Forest I think he said, should push up the quality of the wool - the wool's better for spinning than what we take off our old Norfolks. But he wants a whole silver mark for it! What do you think? Father Adam said I should ask you?"

Thank heavens he's finished - that must be the longest speech he's ever made... is something wrong? Why has she felt the need to write to me? "Do whatever you think is best, my friend. Excuse me, I need to go now." *Can I just nip behind a tree to read it? -*

no, he'd just keep talking to me about this ram - I need to get back to the house!

He walked back as quickly as he could, aware all the time of the letter just inches from his hip. Finally, he reached the house, and the sanctuary of his bench, and opened the letter again.

"*Ad Wimerus Capelanus, de Ida de Tosny*;

My friend, rejoice with me! My niece Alda is pleased to announce the arrival of a baby boy, who has been named Baldwin after his maternal Grandfather. Mother and babe are doing well. I shall stay here for a short while; then I will return to Westminster. Unfortunately, my nephew the Baron is in attendance on our lord the King in France at the moment, so you hear of his good fortune before he does. Alda begs your indulgence, and asks that you, in your capacity as Sheriff, send word to him with your official mail, so that he may most swiftly hear of his new heir.

I send this to you in good health and in good spirits,

Your friend,

Ida."

She was well; safely delivered; and the babe had been accepted as Alda's. Wimer, for the first time since the excommunication, fell to his knees. *Dear Lord in heaven, thank you for this great mercy!*

After the first flush of relief was over, he stood and read the parchment again. He admired the way in which she had never lied – she'd left that sin to him, as he passed on the news to the Baron. *Never mind, it's a burden I am happy to bear, for her sake.*

He touched the parchment to his lips, savouring the

thought of her hand touching it so few days ago, then forced himself to go looking for Adam to spread the news. The sooner as many people as possible heard that the Baron had a new heir, the better; let the truth about his parentage slide out of mind.

WIMER AND HENRI, THE EXCHEQUER EASTER 1170

Wimer was heartily sick of the sight of Westminster Palace. He had arrived a few days early, in the hope of spending some quiet time with Ida, only to find that the King had swooped in just a few days previously and the Palace was crawling with officials and hangers-on. There was no sign of her at all. He assumed she was, very sensibly, staying out of view, afraid of a repeat of her rape the previous Christmas. He thought it was desperately unfair of Henry – why had he chosen now to come back to England? He'd been away for four years, surely a few more days would have made no difference, so that Wimer could get the time with Ida he'd been craving.

Amidst all the noise and bustle, he felt very isolated. As ever, there were plenty of people who refused to talk to him at all, for the sake of their souls. When he got sick enough of that, and of the fruitless watching out for Ida or her maid, he went off on long rides, driving his horses hard and using their speed and power to relieve some of his frustration.

The sign-in of the Sheriffs had not gone to plan either. Wimer wasn't sure if he had been hoping to go first – to get the torment out of the way, so he could go back to the Abbey – or last, to extend his time hoping for a glimpse of Ida. As it happened, Oger's magic had completely failed him; of the 32 returns, they were 15th. Wimer resigned himself to about a week's worth of heel-kicking. He was heading for the stables again one morning when one of the chaplains assisting with the return of the Wiltshire sheriff hailed him in a corridor.

"Wimer the Chaplain, isn't it? I don't suppose you remember me, but my name is Brother Jerome; I remember your visit to Malmesbury with the King, when I was a young novice. This is my first trip to the Exchequer, I never thought it would be so momentous – what do you think of all the excitement?"

"Good heavens, that was a long time ago! What excitement? I'm afraid I've been a bit distracted... hang on, you're Wiltshire, aren't you? Didn't you present your accounts a few days ago? Why haven't you gone home?"

"Yes; haven't you heard? The King has decreed that no-one may leave the Palace until he releases us. He will hold a special Court after the whole Exchequer has finished. The rumour is that he will punish wrongdoers who have taken advantage of his long absence in France."

Just then the bell rang for Prime.

"Goodness, that time already – will you pray with me, brother?"

Wimer invented some excuse, and then bleakly watched Jerome bustle off down the corridor. So, his prison sentence at the Palace had just been doubled, if he had to wait until the last Return before finding out whatever Henry was up to. He was so tired of the whole business around the excommunication – he wasn't sure what was worse, being cut dead by the informed, or having to deal gently with the uninformed, like that boy Jerome. He set off for the stables again, desperate for some freedom of spirit, and wishing Ida was enjoying it with him; where WAS she?

The Great Hall had been cleared of all furniture and hangings other than the King's throne, which was the sole spot of colour against the dark stone. The Sheriffs and their retinues had been herded in by the Master at Arms' guards, and were being kept in a loose horseshoe shape in front of the throne, with a large open space immediately in front of it. The noise level had been rising. Wimer, catching conversations from either side of him, reached the conclusion that no-one else knew what was happening either.

He went back to fretting about where Ida was. He hadn't seen anything of her at all, through the entire Exchequer. Now he would be going back to the Abbey as soon as whatever Henry was up to had finished, and he was alternating between being really worried about her, and feeling sick and empty at the thought of going away without seeing her again.

One of the Marshall's men walked up to the throne, faced the sheriffs, and blew a blast on a hunting horn. The Marshall announced into the stunned silence that followed:

"Gentlemen! The King!"

All made obeisance. When Wimer raised his head again, Henry was sat fore-square in the throne, legs akimbo and arms crossed, looking quite magnificent. He was in a bright blue gown, embroidered in gold around the neck, and with an ermine-lined red surcoat. He was actually wearing his crown – the last time Wimer remembered seeing him in that was years ago, when Henry and Eleanor used to wear them at the formal feasts of the year. All that was well past, of course, with Eleanor in Poitou with young Richard.... whatever Henry's plan, he clearly meant to have the full force of the Crown behind it.

Looking more closely at his friend, Wimer noted that the once vibrant red hair had faded a little, and his face had new lines. His body looked thicker under the robe, too. Wimer sighed, and self-consciously ran his hand over his bald patch – he was most of the way towards never needing his tonsure shaved again himself. If he ever needed a tonsure again...

Henry waited until all the room had noted his formality, and then nodded to the Marshall. He banged his staff three times on the floor, and called:

"Dorset! Robert Pukerel, Archibald Pictus!"

Looking nervously at each other, the men moved into the open space in front of the King.

"Kneel!" the Marshall snapped; they fell to their knees together.

The King started speaking, very quietly. Wimer winced. This was not a good sign...

"I was dismayed to learn on my return from France, that certain of my Sheriffs, with whom I had entrusted the smooth running of the country in my absence, had abused that trust, and used my absence to grow rich at my expense, or that of my subjects. I am sure you are all aware that I have sent out a Commission of Enquiry throughout all the land, and their findings have been brought before me just in the last week." Henry held out a hand, and a cleric put a scroll into it. He leaned forward, unrolled it, and read:

"Robert Pukerel, Sheriff of Dorset; Item; that he did refuse the right of John of Wimborne the right to accuse his cousin Roel under the Assize of Mort d'Ancestor, said Roel paying Robert 5 marks to deny the case. Item, similarly that he did refuse the suit of Maud of Dorchester, instead asking 3 marks from her nephew William. Item... Item... Item..." Henry snapped the roll shut, and leapt to his feet.

"It goes on and on and on, Robert! Bribe after bribe, extortion after extortion! How could you do it? You have mired my name as well as your own. And where are these fines? I see none of them on your Exchequer returns. You have lined your own nest well, my fine friend! I cannot tolerate this!" Henry looked for a moment as though he was going to strike the kneeling man with the scroll, then tossed it to the Marshall, and turned away.

"Continue with Pictus."

As the Marshall read out the next unfortunate's audit return, Henry prowled round the little group. The crowd of waiting Sheriffs and retinues were absolutely still; the list of bribes dropped one by one into the silence. When he was done, Henry came to a stop facing the two men, his eyes fixed on Robert.

"Pictus; you are dismissed from office; I never wish to see your face again." The crowd waited to hear Robert's fate. Henry started pacing again, and then halted.

"I trusted you; I lifted you up into a high office; and THIS is how you repay me! You disgust me! Do you know how much you stole from me?" He bent over, and spat into the man's face. "DO YOU?" Robert silently shook his head, not daring to meet the King's eye.

"Over 15 marks! You will pay every penny of it back. You are dismissed from office; I take back the lands I granted you at Wareham into my own hand; and the Exchequer will have authority over your debt. Leave my presence, before I have a mind to brand you with a T, for thief!" Both men rose rapidly, bowed, and backed away. Henry turned to the crowd.

"Alured of Lincoln!" he called.

A young cleric whom Wimer didn't know edged his way to the front, and threw himself to his knees in front of the King, looking petrified.

"Alured; will you serve me as Sheriff of Dorset, acting as my eyes and ears in that county, maintaining my justice, and seeing that all things are done there according to my will?"

Wimer could see the man's tonsure turning red, as he flushed.

"To the best of my ability, Lord King!"

Henry smiled for the first time, and helped Alured to his feet. "So be it! Stand here on my right-hand side." Henry returned to the throne, and Alured moved to stand behind him, looking rather overwhelmed. Henry gestured for the Marshall to continue.

"Somerset, Wills de Capesuals; his servants Alan and Abel!"

de Capesuals was allowed to keep his job, but with a

hefty fine against his name in the Exchequer. The process went on. It was becoming clear that Henry was clearing the boards of anyone whom he considered had abused his position. Wimer began wondering what he would do if he was dismissed. *Would Hugh have me back?* Probably not, if doing so would incur the King's displeasure. The life of a landless excommunicate, with no sponsor, wouldn't last long. He would be reduced to stealing food, and the first person to catch him, could kill him. He became aware of a sharp pain, as he bit through to fresh flesh on the side of his thumb. Finally, they were called.

"For Norfolk and Suffolk; Oger Dapifer. Eye; Hodies of Eye. Abbey of St Benet's at Holme; Wimer Capellanus."

"Here we go, boys..." Oger muttered, as he led the way. They knelt, Oger grunting a little in pain. As the Marshall's recital went on, Wimer started to listen in horrified fascination. This was a side of Oger he'd never imagined. It sounded like half the county had a complaint! Finally, there was the damaging accusation that he'd tried to repay some of the money back after the King's officers showed up. Henry, back on his throne and listening to the list with his head lowered, lifted his gaze to Oger and shook his head. Wimer shivered, and hoped his friend would be spared the worst.

Hodies had only a handful of minor complaints, and then the Marshall closed his scroll and looked at the King. Henry frowned.

"What of Wimer the Chaplain?" The Marshall looked puzzled, unrolled his scroll, and shook his head. "No issues, Majesty, other than a single complaint of making a minor knight wait for justice. For several hours, his letter states." Henry's smile warmed Wimer through and through. *It was going to be all right.*

"Oger, you are dismissed as Sheriff. I should have you thrown in a dungeon; but in recognition of the many years you have served me, I shall merely demand repayment of the excesses listed here. Hodies..." Henry was interrupted as Oger fell forward. Wimer and Henry reached him together; Henry turned him over, and they exchanged relieved looks as his eyes fluttered open again. Henry stood, stern again, and gestured to the guards to help Oger out. Wimer went back to kneeling.

"Hodies of Eye; I thank you for your service in my name, and request that you continue to account for Eye. Will you do so?"

"Yes indeed, Lord King! Thank you!"

"Wimer the Chaplain; I need honest men like you. Will you bear the full burden of Sheriff of Norfolk and Suffolk? I will ask Bartholomew de Glanville and Willis Bardul to support you, but if you accept, yours will be the primary responsibility. Will you serve me?"

Wimer looked up at the King. "With all my heart." he promised. Henry smiled again, reached a hand to help him up, and then waved him to the group behind the throne.

Wimer paid very little attention to the rest of the proceedings, his head full of images of the land he now controlled. *Hah! I now have jurisdiction over the Bigod lands... I wonder if Hugh will be amused, or irritated.* Thoughts of Ida kept surfacing, and he kept squashing them, his head telling him that a Saxon boy like himself could not possibly aspire to her. Another voice suggested that the Sheriff of one of the richest counties in the land was not a mere country bumpkin. *Perhaps being excommunicate is the only real barrier. I could personally appeal to the Pope... Do I dare hope that she could be my wife? I know that priests who marry can't progress further in the church, but my career isn't exactly stellar anyway. Where IS she? I can't even judge whether or not to talk to her about it, if she's hiding somewhere!*

The inquest of the Sheriffs continued. Finally the King dealt with London and Middlesex; another complete change of officers. The guards cleared everyone but the chosen group behind the throne out of the hall. Henry made a short speech, again thanking them for their pledge of service to him, and telling them that they were the guests of honour at a banquet that evening. He left, and the group broke up. Wimer went to see how Oger was, then to borrow some finery.

He speared another juicy pigeon breast from the pie in front of him and bit in greedily. The unaccustomed aroma of the spices hit his nose again, and his mouth watered. His neighbour, young Alured, the new Sheriff of Dorset, also reached over, and picked out his own delicacy, a hand of pork. He bit off a chunk, made appreciative slurping noises, then used it as a drumstick to beat time to the music, as the mummers worked their way towards them again. Wimer raised his cup in salute to the lad who was playing the pan flute and dancing in front of them, and tapped his feet to the rhythm. It was his third or fourth cup of ale, Henry had toasted them at least twice already, and Wimer was feeling very mellow.

The hall looked magnificent, with the rich red and gold

banners of the King contrasting beautifully with the sombre stone. He wondered again at the cost of the lighting – every torch sconce was lit, boys were stationed around the hall with extra torches, and the top table had a thick candle for every pair of people. All the Sheriffs were there; he and Alured were sharing a trencher about midway down the right-hand side of the top table, with a good view of all the entertainment that was going on.

As well as the musicians, there were several dwarves, and a group of tumblers. The servants were still trying to bring in great platters of food, and the dwarves seemed to be trying to cause as much chaos as possible, without actually dumping food on the floor. Wimer watched a pair of them cavorting round a rather fine roast peacock, all its plumage back in place, carried by two nervous-looking servitors. One of its gorgeous, eyed tail feathers was already listing at an unusual angle; but they managed to skirt the dwarves, and placed the basket successfully in front of the King. One of the dwarves stuck his leg out and tripped one of the servitors on his way back out; Wimer snorted with laughter at the mix of relief and rage on the man's face.

His attention was drawn to the other side of the hall, where the tumblers were building a human pyramid, each choosing a more elaborate series of jumps, turns and flips to take their place in the structure. The last, a boy of about ten, executed a perfectly fluid set of backward flips, seemed to just touch the knee of one of the men at the bottom of the pyramid, and twisted up impossibly smoothly to stand proudly high at the apex, arms thrown wide. Wimer drained his cup, then banged it on the table, joining in with the applause. Just then, Alured nudged him;

"Oops, here we go, my friend – the King's new leman has arrived – best grab your supper before the King leaves; it won't be long now!" He gestured with a capon leg towards a woman moving up towards the top table on the other side of the room.

Wimer looked across idly. The woman looked of middle height; all he could see of her at first was the colour of her gown, a pleasing pale yellow. She passed under a sconce, and the gold net containing her warm brown hair briefly flared in the light. *Oh, dear God, no!* There were bands of iron around his chest. He waited grimly for her to pass the next torch, to be sure. As she did so, she looked across to the middle of the top table, and smiled at Henry. It was Ida.

The food he had eaten soured in his stomach. He swallowed hard to stop himself being sick. What had Alured said? That she was Henry's leman?!

"She is the King's ward, he would not take her to bed!" he snapped.

Alured looked up, a little puzzled at his vehemence.

"No, I assure you, friend, she is the King's new playmate. Her name is Ida de Tosny, a high Norman noblewoman. She might have been his ward, I'm not sure. Anyway, I'm told that bedding her was almost the first thing he did after he sent out the judges on the Sheriff's Inquest; they didn't surface for three whole days. Richard de Lucy was not amused, I think he wanted the King to spend just a little more time on affairs of state!" and he went back to his capon.

There was no coherent thought in Wimer's mind. A

black tide of pain was rising within him, turning his pleasure at his new office to ashes. Of course she would prefer the King. How could a Saxon peasant possibly compete? He sat very still, mastering tears, until a page leant over to refill his ale cup.

"Wine!" he grated, and the boy went off to fetch it. He downed the first cup before the boy had turned away, and held the cup out speechlessly for more. Half-way down the second cup, he noticed the taste and texture; it was like drinking sour river mud. He gagged slightly. Getting drunk on that was not an option. He had thought the tales of Henry's taste in wine were exaggerated! He reached for the nearest plate of food for something to take the taste away, and popped a morsel in his mouth without looking at it. He bit down hard on a pepper corn, which exploded heat into his mouth just as the Marshall cried for all to rise, as Henry prepared to leave. The King moved along the table towards them, Ida's hand firmly clasped in his, stopping for a word here and there. He jovially slapped the spluttering Wimer between his shoulder blades, and bent to whisper:

"I hope to have solved your little disagreement with the Archbishop of Canterbury very shortly."

Ida's perfume filled his senses. He was thankful that his coughing fit avoided the need for talk. He raised a hand in acknowledgement, head down, and Henry passed on, taking Ida with him. She trailed her hand across his shoulders, and briefly clasped his still raised hand; then was pulled out of reach. It felt like a farewell blessing. *Dear God, am I never to see her again? All my hopes...* He stayed stock still, tears welling up again, until the King had gone, and it was safe to leave. His shoulders burnt from her touch.

WIMER, NORFOLK - WINTER 1170

What is she doing, on this fine, chill day? He glanced at his shadow on the whitewashed wall, and worked out in which direction Westminster lay. He fancied he felt a line of connection between them. When he finally got to sleep at night, the line shone through his dreams, strong enough to be grasped. *Riding out with Henry, perhaps, in a gown of palest primrose?*

He stopped walking. *Ah! What an idiot I am! Henry could be anywhere – perhaps even back in France! Would he have taken her with him? If she were mine I would never leave her side...*

The man standing beside him coughed nervously, clearly wondering if the Sheriff had lost his mind.

"Lord Wimer? This way?"

Wimer mentally shook himself, and tried to prepare for what lay ahead. *Time to act the Sheriff... what a fine actor I am becoming...* Waiting for him in the hall would be the local great and good: at least one full knight, and twenty-four free men, prepared to recite the crimes of the neighbourhood. They deserved his full attention – even though the villages, and the petty crimes, were all beginning to blend together on this tour. Listening to people telling tales about their neighbours was not his favourite part of being a Sheriff. Still, it was undeniably efficient at turning up wrongdoing.

He dragged up enough politeness to go through the motions, shaking hands and smiling at each of the men, then as usual bowing his head and ignoring the priest's opening prayers. His mind drifted to his one perfect day with Ida, polished like a gemstone through frequent attention, whilst the priest took each man's oath in turn; then Wimer stood to make his usual speech, finishing:

"Please remember that you are an important part of the King's legal reforms, and that by fulfilling the terms of the Assize of Clarendon, you are doing your duty to King and Kingdom. You should not fear to report any crime, however small, however large, because by doing so, and helping to bring the criminal to justice, you are helping to rid society of transgressors. I thank you, both personally and on behalf of the King, for your service on the jury."

He noticed two of the men glancing scowls at one another, and raised an eyebrow – especially when the knight (he tried to remember his name, and failed) rose to his feet and glared the men into submission before starting to recite from a long list of petty evildoings. Wimer went back into his polite doze, only half listening to the names of people who had failed to pay one fine or another, or had ploughed too close to a headland, or some other trivial offence. None of these required the might of the Sheriff's resources; his clerk could note the names and dues and sort them out.

Wimer turned his thoughts inward. Sometimes, asleep or awake, he had a ringing in his ears, which waxed and waned without obvious cause. *Could it possibly be a result of her thinking of him? Do my thoughts likewise touch her? Her head must ring like a bell, if so...*

The knight finally wound to a halt and sat back down. Most of the jurors were relaxed, solemnly pleased with a job well done; but the two on the end were restless. They were a mismatched pair; one dark and slight, the other raw-boned, built along Viking lines. Wimer caught one man's gaze, then the other, and quietly said:

"Any crime, no matter how small – do any of you have anything to add?"

The hatchet-faced man at the end of the row pursed his lips and looked down, then stood with a show of reluctance. His larger companion tried to catch his sleeve and pull him back, but failed. He slumped back, arms crossed tightly in denial.

"My Lord, I have a crime to report." Even then, the man stopped, and licked his lips before continuing. "It concerns a ring that belongs to me, but was stolen."

Wimer's curiosity grew.

"Yes? Theft is a proper crime to bring to me; who is the thief?"

The man looked sideways down at his neighbour, and said softly.

"Gunnar, daughter of Ralph."

The seated man surged to his feet, crashing an elbow into the other man's stomach on the way up.

"You lying bastard! You promised you would not make an accusation you could not prove! What have you done to my Gunnar with your lie?"

Wimer's face grew impassive, as the issue between the two men started to become clear. He gestured to his sergeant-at-arms to separate them. He looked from one to the other. Ralph was struggling with the men who held him, and was visibly close to tears.

"You! What's your name? And tell me what happened."

The other man was still having problems breathing, but got out, jerkily: "G-Gavin, Lord... She found... the ring... on my headland. I took it from her... it was my right. Now it's gone... and my goodwife... saw her... running away from the hut... She must have taken it."

Wimer frowned. "Was the ring valuable?"

"It was silver, Lord... with a big red stone. Valuable enough... to be worth stealing."

Wimer turned to Ralph.

"Tell me about your daughter, and this ring?"

"She is just twelve, Lord! A good girl, and a Christian one! She would not steal. Gavin holds a grudge because I have refused him her hand. She is innocent in this!"

"Well, I think we will have to explore this further. Fetch me the goodwife and the girl."

The girl was tall and blonde, like her father; otherwise, unremarkable. She was dressed soberly, her hair in a wimple, and, except for one troubled glance around the court, kept her head down. The goodwife was all sharp eyes, drinking in every detail to relay to the village gossips. Wimer sat and watched the girl, whilst the priest lectured them both on the dangers to their immortal souls of telling anything other than the whole truth, and took their oaths. She clearly took it seriously – as well she might. *I wonder if she has ever seen one of the wretches missing a hand or a foot because of a conviction for theft; perhaps not, in this backwater.* The priest finished, and delivered them to the open space in front of Wimer.

"Gunnar, is it not?"

The girl glanced up at him, and nodded.

"You have been accused of stealing a ring from this man, Gavin. He describes a silver ring with a red stone. Does this mean anything to you?"

Again she nodded. Wimer noticed the goodwife peering curiously at him. *Ah, the gossip has reached here too... Don't worry, Goody, I only infect souls with my godlessness on alternate Sundays!*

He waited, but the girl stood silent. "Gunnar," he said gently, "I need to hear you speak. I want to hear your side of the story."

Her voice started as a whisper, then firmed.

"Yes, Lord. But I did not steal it from him! It was mine; I found it; rather he stole it from me!" she glared at Gavin, head up, completely sure of her case.

"Tell me where and how you found it, then."

"It was on the headland at the top of Gavin's strip. The plough had cut a little deeply into the headland. The turf gave way beneath my foot, and I fell. I saw a glint in the earth and plucked it out, and it was the ring. HE was coming up the other way, and ran to me. I thought he was going to help me to my feet; but no, he snatched the ring out of my hand, and ordered me home."

Wimer frowned. "Where exactly was the ring? In headland, or plough land?"

"He always cuts too far, Lord. He shrinks the headland year by year; this was a new cut into it."

"Very well; what happened next?"

"I tried to make him give me the ring back, but he spat at me not to be a fool, that the ring was his; and pushed me to the ground again. He knocked the breath out of me, and I started crying, so I ran home."

Wimer gestured for Gavin to be brought forward.

"How far away were you from the girl when she found the ring?"

The man frowned. "I was a little bit short of my strip. I was going to shout at the girl for stepping on my ploughed land, and then I saw her pick up the ring. No more than twenty or thirty paces away."

"Were there any other witnesses?"

"I don't think so, Lord; I don't recall any."

Wimer asked Gunnar the same question. She shook her head, then at his raised eyebrow:

"No, Lord. I didn't see anyone else."

"Gavin; what happened to the ring after Gunnar left?"

"I put it in my pouch."

"Did you show it to anyone?"

"Naw! Why get tongues wagging? I left it there until I got home that evening, then put it in my secret place."

"When did you notice it was missing?"

"The next day, when I got home. I wanted to see it, to hold it; and it was gone. I shouted to my wife to see if she had disturbed it, but she swore not; then she said that she had seen Gunnar running away."

Wimer turned to Gunnar. "Did you go to the house?"

She flushed, but answered steadily enough: "Yes, Lord. I wanted the ring back; it is mine, he took it from me. I was going to see if I could find it. But then she came back and shrieked at me before I even got to the house, so I ran away."

"Goodwife. When did you learn of the ring?"

"Why, just now, Sir! I mean, my Lord! I knew he'd been at the pot, but I didn't know what had gone in – or whether something had gone out; very private, is my Gavin, Lord."

"I remind you that you are on oath; did you look inside the pot when your husband was away?"

The woman twisted her hands together and looked sideways at Gavin, who was glowering at her.

"Oh, Lord – do I have to answer?"

Wimer crossed his arms and glared too. She looked from one to the other, then to the priest, and wrung her hands again.

"I did just have a peek – but I didn't see the ring; I heard him coming and put the pot back before he saw me. I'm not allowed to look in there, see. He'll beat me now..." and she flung her apron over her head and sobbed noisily.

Wimer shook his head in disgust, and motioned for her to be taken outside. When the room was quiet again, he stood up, and started pacing, thinking aloud.

"Gunnar admits to finding the ring, on land that may have been Gavin's, or may have been common ground, and thinks that it belongs to her. Gavin takes and hides the ring; Gunnar admits to searching for it. The ring is gone."

He walked further, thinking hard. When he was clear on what to do, he went back to his seat.

"The case rests on two facts; whether the ring was found on Gavin's land, and whether Gunnar took it from his house. If the land was Gavin's, the ring belongs to him as landowner, and Gunnar's attempt to recover it is thievery. If it was headland, the ring is Gunnar's, and Gavin is the thief for taking it from her. As there were no witnesses to the find spot, I can see no option but to put both to trial by ordeal."

The room was silent for a breath, and then Ralph tried to twist free of his guards and cried:

"Oh, no, Lord – I beg you! She is a child! If you must try by ordeal, let me suffer it for her! Please!"

Wimer motioned for him to be taken out.

Gavin was edging away from the disturbance, moving nearer the door. He turned and started to sprint, but bounced off the sergeant, who was coming to help regain control of Ralph; he grabbed Gavin by reflex. Gunnar sank to her knees, her face in her hands. Wimer stood.

"Waiting will serve no purpose. The trial will be by water, as soon as may be; Father, please prepare both candidates. Sir Knight, please instruct your household to bring cauldron, water, and linens."

He returned to his seat, and watched sombrely as the room filled with bustling servants. The priest had drawn Gunnar and Gavin into a corner, and they were both on their knees. He caught himself biting the corner of his thumb again, and moved over to the fire. He stopped the woman filling the cauldron when the water was at a scant wrist height. He moved restlessly around, fingering the linens and the stone set ready on the table, and out to stand looking out of the doorway. Ralph was still being held by a pair of guards. When he saw him, he tried again to burst free, and began to call out; Wimer hastily drew back into the darkness of the hall.

Eventually, all was ready. Wimer called a guard over, and told him to take a message to those waiting outside; that they could enter, on pain of absolute silence until the trial was over. Ralph almost ran in, his escort staying close. Wimer went to stand in front of his seat, and called the room to order.

"The purpose of trial by ordeal is not to punish, but to allow God to reveal the innocent. We cannot learn the truth of this case by questioning; so we refer it to God's grace and mercy. Each of you will be required to take the stone from the bottom of the cauldron. As this is the first accusation for each of you, the water is only wrist deep. The water is boiling. You should expect injury and pain; your hands will be bandaged, and will be examined in three days' time. If your wounds are healing cleanly, God has acted on your behalf, and you are innocent. If there is corruption, God has judged you guilty. The punishment the law demands for a guilty thief, who is proven so by ordeal, is to have a hand struck off. I ask you one more time; did you steal the ring? If you confess now, before the trial, I can impose a lesser punishment. Gunnar?"

Gunnar shook her head. She was pale, but spoke clearly: "No, Lord. I did not steal the ring."

"Very well. Gavin?"

"The ring is mine, Lord! I did not steal it."

"So be it. Father, will you bless the water?"

Gavin went first, driving his hand into the water and scooping the stone out with one movement. He stood with gritted teeth, breathing noisily, whilst one of the household women fumbled with the linens, dropping some on the floor, before managing to bind his hand. He stood cradling it, watching Gunnar hesitate.

She took so long plucking up her courage, that the priest spoke;

"Daughter, you must reach in and remove the stone. If you are innocent, God will protect you."

She drew in a ragged breath, and fumbled for the stone, her face tight with pain. Finally she pulled it out, and submitted to the bandaging. When it was done, she pulled her sleeve over the linens, and went to her father. He folded her in his arms protectively. Wimer sighed. *I hope she is a fast healer. I am less and less sure that these things are managed by the Hand of God. I suppose that's a sin too....*

He told the pair: "You are both charged to return here in three days, after Prime, when we will examine the wounds. If you do not return, you will be declared outlaw. Do not unbind the bandages in the meantime; your fate will be revealed to the full court." He bowed to the priest, and left.

As soon as he saw the girl, Wimer knew that his worry was founded. She was pale of face, bar two burning patches on her cheeks, and she came with her father; also clearly worried. Gavin, on the other hand, came alone, with confident bounding steps. Obeying some instinct that he couldn't articulate, Wimer delayed proceedings as long as possible, once more giving his speech about the meaning of the trial. Then he asked the priest to lead prayers.

When he could postpone no more, he called Gavin up and slit the knot closing the bandages. The man unwound the linens himself, and revealed clean, newly pink flesh. He held his hand up so all could see, and beamed proudly. Still Wimer wanted to prolong matters – was he missing something, that his subconscious was trying to tell him about? - so he thanked Gavin for his co-operation, and said that God had proven his innocence. Finally, he could delay no longer, and gestured Gunnar to come forward. Her bandages were discoloured, and smelt faintly of corruption. He knew it would not go well, but could think of no way out of cutting her knot. Her father tenderly unwound the bandages. As the damage became clear, Wimer hissed in sympathy; her whole hand was a discoloured, puffy blister, oozing pus at the edges. He stared at it for several seconds, trying to comprehend how God could wish her so ill, until Gavin crowded forward and shouted aloud in triumph.

"Look! Her wounds are unhealed, and foul! God has made clear the guilty party; Gunnar stole my ring!"

The room full of people murmured, many of them with sadness, and looked toward the Sheriff. Wimer knew himself caught, by the law, and by his own words.

"It is true; God's will is clear. The thief must lose her hand."

In truth, it might be a mercy. Perhaps better a clean amputation, than a lingering painful death from the corruption that would spread from the hand, left untreated. With a heavy heart, he ordered that the blacksmith's anvil be brought to the room, along with a brazier and irons to cauterise the wound. Through it all, Gunnar stood mute, lost in pain, sometimes swaying. Ralph was bearing the anticipation for her, making little hurt sounds and motions; but he was clearly overawed by the clarity of the judgement, and was being no trouble. Wimer made eye contact with the sergeant, and indicated that he should be guarded once the amputation was begun. He also called Piers over:

"Ride for Goda, as fast as may be. We will need her skills."

Finally, everything was ready; the smith, who would do the work, was sharpening a short-bladed but very solid dagger. Gunnar was led unprotesting to kneel beside the anvil, and the smith held her forearm firm on the flat top in one huge hand, readying the dagger with the other. In the hush, Wimer became aware of a noise outside, that had been gathering in strength for some little time, and held his hand up to stop proceedings. A strange silence fell, as all listened to the noise draw near. Soon it resolved into a woman's voice, jagged with effort, crying "Stop! Stop, I beg you!" All were still, waiting for the mystery to clear, except Gavin; he had clearly recognised the voice, and was becoming very tense. The sergeant noticed, and quietly moved to his side. At length, the voice resolved itself into the goodwife, bursting in to the room and searching faces for Wimer.

"Oh, please God I have come in time! I have run all the way – is the girl still whole?"

She stood clutching her chest, breathing in great draughts of air. She looked so dishevelled and upset that Wimer stood, and made her sit in his chair.

"Bring ale!" he commanded the room, and "Wait until you have collected yourself a little before you tell your news, Goodwife. There is no hurry; you have arrived in the nick of time."

"Thank the Lord... I was so afraid..."

The ale arrived, and he handed it to her with his own hand. When she had recovered a little he encouraged her to speak. She needed no urging...

"I found the ring!"

She displayed it in her open palm, standing up and turning so that everyone could see. It was indeed a thick, valuable-looking silver band, with a large red stone. She waited, smiling, until the murmur had died down. Wimer was silent, admiring her performance.

"I'm afraid it must have been me who knocked it out of the pot, when I peeked a few days ago. I am sorry to be the cause of such trouble!" she looked at Wimer, who waved her to continue.

"I only found it because He" - and she glared at Gavin - "beat me this morning. I knew I was in for a hiding as soon as he knew I'd looked inside his secret place; but it wasn't until today that his hand stopped hurting enough. Of course that meant that he was innocent, so he was in fine fettle; he even went to cut me a new switch, and laid it on well. He left me curled on the floor, weeping, to come up here and prove his innocence. I don't know how long it was before I stopped crying, and just lay there looking at nothing. Then I noticed that the nothing shone. When I reached out for it, it was the ring – and I knew I had to run like the wind, before Gunnar suffered for my mistake. It must have fallen on the floor and been kicked into that cranny; I've swept the floor every day since, and never even noticed it. I'm so glad I got here in time!"

There was silence following her speech, and then

people started crowding round her, congratulating her on her courage, and asking to see the ring. She was delighted with the attention, except when people slapped her on the back, and then apologised. In the background, Wimer noticed Ralph go and pick Gunnar up in her arms; she was cradling her wounded hand, clearly in pain, and not really present. Wimer hoped Goda was hurrying. Only one person was not happy at the news. Gavin's voice rose over the crowd:

"But God has shown her guilty!"

He was standing at the back of the crowd, pointing at Gunnar.

"Her wound has not healed, like mine has. What does it mean, if she is guilty, but the ring is found?"

He turned to look at Wimer, and the rest of the crowd followed. Wimer walked over to the anvil, slowly, frantically thinking. By the time he turned, he had an answer that he thought should satisfy them. He raised his arms, and firmly declared:

"Indeed, God is good! He has answered the first question I posed, not the second – do you all remember that I said the case turned on two points, of which the first was where it was taken from?"

His audience murmured, with the consensus being that, yes, they did remember that.

"If the ring was on Gavin's land, rather than headland, Gunnar took it unlawfully, because anything found on a freeman's land is his property. THAT, friends, is the answer that God has given us; that Gunnar was guilty of taking the ring in the first place! But Gavin took it from her straight away, so there is no further case to answer. We know now, thanks to Gavin's good wife, that she did not steal the ring, so Gunnar need not lose her hand. The case is closed! Praise be to God!"

The crowd happily chorused "Amen!" Only Gavin was still frowning, but stayed silent. Wimer felt a pang of pity for his wife, who would undoubtedly have another session with the switch as soon as Gavin got her home, and added:

"We should indeed be grateful to Gavin's wife, who has prevented a miscarriage of justice." and bowed to her. She blushed, and was again surrounded by well-wishers.

Wimer went over to Ralph, who was still cradling Gunnar.

"Get her home; my man has gone to fetch his wife, who is a skilled healer. She will do all that can be done to save her hand. I will also leave a gift with the priest to pray for her."

Ralph needed no more urging, and left immediately, carrying his precious burden. Wimer took one last glance around the room where he had so nearly presided over a horror committed in God's name, and went to saddle a horse. He needed some thinking time. *Was the explanation he'd come up with the right one, evidence of God's hand? Or was – heresy of heresies – God absent here, the outcome decided by blind luck? Or some other factor – perhaps the boldness of the accused in fishing for the stone?* Now he'd allowed the thought into his mind, there were a few cases down the years where the results were, at best, surprising. Had he maimed innocents, or even sent them to their deaths, because he had misunderstood God's role in the courtroom? Or trusted in Him too deeply? The more he thought about it, the more uncomfortable he felt. The ride did not improve his mood.

Wimer left his private chambers shaking his head in disbelief. Hugh Bigod was in amazing health for his age, and was as strong and forthright in his views as ever - it was good to see him in such fine fettle. But it really was more than a little stupid to pretend to Wimer that he couldn't afford to pay more than he was offering, to cover the monies owed to the Crown. *I could still probably work out to the nearest few marks what he's worth.* It was also foolhardy to lie to the Sheriff – but the Earl was stopping just short of outright confrontation. Wimer smiled wryly – the old fox would never change – then headed towards the nearest loo.

Coming out of the chapel was Martin, Hugh's clerk, who had also suffered excommunication at the orders of Thomas a'Becket.

"Martin! Well met, lad – how are things with you?"

"My Lord Sheriff! Well, thank you." he half-bowed, and made as if to walk away.

"Oh, no, you can't go yet – you haven't told me any of your news! And why so formal?"

Martin looked down, blushing. Wimer had to strain to hear him. "I have just been to confession."

Wimer looked at him, puzzled, for a few seconds – then the import of what he had said sank in.

"You – you have been accepted back into the church! When? - and who, and why!"

He could feel, welling up within him, a grey tide of hurt – and a small voice crying *It's not fair!* He stared at Martin, willing him to speak.

"A month since, my Lord Sheriff. The Earl sent me to France, to the Archbishop, carrying a letter begging clemency for all four of us. Thomas refuses a full restitution in the Church until he has spoken to each one of us, from his seat at Canterbury, nowhere else. That may be soon; his court was packing to go to Sens and wait for a favourable passage across the Channel. But as token of his regard for us, he has granted me, as the bearer of the Earl's pleas, a partial lifting of the sentence. I may not celebrate Mass; but I may make confession, and receive absolution. Oh, Wimer – I wish he had been generous enough to include you too!"

Wimer had gone cold.

"I had heard that he and the King had come to terms; but I do not believe that they will ever make peace enough for Becket to return unmolested to Canterbury. Each time they have come close, one or the other have proven themselves too proud to bend to the other's will. They will dance that dance until one or both of them is dead. I am glad, my friend, that some of the burden is lifted from you. For myself, I grow very tired of the waiting. My heart grows weary... I am not sure that, if Thomas a Becket restored me to the church this very day, I could find my faith again. It is sick and shrunken for lack of nourishment." He flicked his hand, to ward off the excess of sentiment. "Enough, I must be off. Pray for me, perhaps it will do some good." and he turned to go.

"My Lord?" Martin's soft voice halted him. "There's more; the Pope did as much for Jean, when he carried a similar plea from the King to our Holy Father."

The wail inside Wimer's head was threatening to burst

out. Without another word, he walked blindly off down the corridor. The unfairness of Thomas' action - saving a man just for carrying a letter, whilst leaving him damned - was almost as painful as the open wound left by the excommunication itself. And the Pope doing the same thing! This was God's shepherd, to whom he owed absolute obedience, and the Archbishop of all England, both behaving with no regard to his soul's mortal peril, and the weary months and years of living in fear and isolation. He angrily palmed his eyes, unaccountably full of stinging tears.

The hall was full of people, for the very last gasp of the Christmas celebrations. The priest had decided to hold the service of Epiphany from the balcony, so all could see. He had just called the crowd to order. Wimer had come to lean unobtrusively against the wall near his quarters, across the void of the hall from the Priest. He was waiting for the announcement of Easter's date, idly eavesdropping on the conversation between two lads in front of him -

"Did he just say Our Lord turned the River Nile into wine? Now THAT sounds like a good thing!"

"Urgh – don't talk about booze – I had way too much last night."

- when he saw the Sergeant come in to the main doorway downstairs, accompanied by a man in riding leathers. There was something odd about the man, and it took Wimer a few seconds of peering across the hall to realise what it was; his head was patchy, as though handfuls of hair had been pulled out. They edged their way round the hall and up the stairs, and waited at the top for the priest to close. When he had finished the blessing, they spoke just a few words to him. Wimer was near enough to clearly see the priest's face change colour, and see him stagger. He swiftly recovered, and went back to the balcony. The noise level had risen, and he couldn't get the attention he needed. The Sergeant used his parade ground bellow.

"News! There is dreadful news! Be silent and hear it!"

Wimer pushed himself off the wall and started to move down the side passage towards the priest, in case it was something that needed his authority, but the priest's first words froze him in place.

"My beloved children! Thomas our Archbishop has been foully murdered, at the King's hand! This man has come to tell us what happened!" and he moved aside for the messenger. Wimer stood horrified, his own words, not the messenger's, ringing in his ears - ... *dance until one of them is dead...* in a daze, he retreated back to his chamber door and closed it on the growing clamour outside.

Poor Henry! He could not, surely, have meant his one-time friend to have been murdered! Perhaps he had lost his temper, and some hot-head knight had taken too literally words spoken in the heat of the moment. *He must be devastated! And what now? What will the Pope do? There must surely be reprisals.* He snorted a bitter laugh. *Perhaps the whole country will be put under interdict. It would be nice to have some company...* He shook off the mood. He still had a duty to the King to fulfil. He opened the door, and sent the nearest person for the messenger. *I need the details. There's bound to be trouble...*

WIMER, EAST ANGLIA -
SUMMER/AUTUMN 1174

Wimer cursed under his breath, edging ever so gently further behind the thin screen of hazel leaves, moving as slowly as he dared to avoid drawing the eye. He noted abstractly that his urine stream was still flowing unabated, although fear had dried his mouth. By the time he had finished and adjusted his attire the dozen or so riders were perilously close, and he was sure of the identity of their leader; William of Framlingham – one of Hugh's men, through and through.

He stayed still as could be, trying to think tree-like thoughts, until the riders were past, then he started to make the return journey back to his men, moving as quickly as the need for silence allowed. His troops, and the horses, were tucked into a clearing further back in the wood, taking a rest break. If it came to a skirmish, he outnumbered William; but Wimer was very conscious of the chests of silver he had gathered. This war was being fought mostly by mercenaries, who were very loyal right up to the point where you were late paying them.

Wimer had been doing a tax-gathering sweep down the Suffolk coast, and was only a few miles from Cattawade, where he could ship the money to London and Henry. Losing the money now would put a big dent in the amount the royal purse could expect from Norfolk and Suffolk – at least, that part which was loyalist, given Bigod's defection to the rebels. It was the worst of bad luck to run into a party of Hugh's men here, on this minor path! They too must be making for the ford.

His luck worsened as one of his mares whinnied, scenting the passing horses. He was far enough into the wood by now to have lost the clear sight of them, but the enemy's reaction was swift, horses crashing through the undergrowth ahead of him. He gave up all attempt at silence, and ran the last few yards, throwing himself down behind a fallen tree at the edge of the clearing as it became obvious that his warning was too late. Only a couple of his men had managed to mount, and were fighting, outnumbered, at the far side of the clearing. The rest were ranged in a ragged circle, defending against William's charges afoot. Wimer was relieved to see that both his archers were at the centre, and using their brains; shooting at the enemy horses when they had a clear shot.

Just in front of him, a shaggy cob took an arrow in the chest, and reared up, screaming. It overbalanced, and the world slowed down whilst Wimer watched horse and rider growing hugely large over him. He scrambled backwards, as the rider kicked clear just in time, and smashed down across the tree trunk Wimer had been hiding behind. His sword spun out of his hand, landing just a little to Wimer's side. The man groaned, then shook his head and started to climb to his feet. He saw Wimer, and the sword, and lurched towards it. Wimer, still scrabbling backward, felt something smooth and hard under his hand, and desperately swung it at the man, one-handed. The branch connected with a robust crack on his forehead, and the man flopped face upward on the grass, eyes open, unblinking. Wimer came to his feet, and stared down in shock. He kicked the man. Nothing. *I've killed him!*

He looked around, dazed. In the clearing, two more horses were down, one of their riders engaged in a sword fight. As he watched, his man took advantage of a slip on the damp grass, and drove his sword into the other man's leg. William was crying the retreat, waving his men out of the clearing. In a few moments, the last of them were gone, the reverberations of their galloping hooves fading. Wimer dropped the branch, and stepped into the clearing. The whole encounter had taken no more than a few minutes.

"Are you all right, my Lord?" one of the men panted up to ask.

I killed him... Wimer looked at him, mazed, for an instant. *Well, what is one more mortal sin to my tally.* He rubbed his face, trying to force his brain to work.

"Yes, fine. Come on, let's move out, and get this money on a ship before anyone else tries to relieve us of it."

The beauty of the autumn leaves was beginning to look like a remnant, rather than gracing the trees by right. Wimer noticed it absent-mindedly, in passing, simply thankful that the roads were still reasonably mud-free. *The leaves on those beeches are almost the colour of her dress...*

His sergeant rode up alongside, and requested a rest stop for the foot soldiers. Wimer stayed a-horse, munching the last of the way food that the good Cistertian brothers at Sibton Abbey had provided, looking moodily along the road. *We can't be more than four miles out – but these are indisputably Hugh's lands, it would not be safe to ride on alone. Plenty of rebels still around who would love to take my head.*

When eventually they came in sight of the castle, it looked much the same from a distance. As they drew nearer, though, the familiar lines of the palisade was missing; and by the time they had ridden round to the south entrance the extent of the damage was clear. The King's carpenters had dismantled everything except the main keep, and an army of men were busy eating into the motte with iron-clad shovels.

He broke off his inspection, as the Sergeant bellowed "HOLD there!" at a couple of men half-sliding down the back of the motte, clearly intent on making a getaway.

"HOLD or I fire!" the Sergeant gestured the archers to string up. The two men looked over their shoulders at the group. One of them shrugged and sat down, hands on his head, to continue his slide to the bottom as a non-combatant. The other redoubled his efforts, lost his footing, and spun sideways down the steep slope. The Sergeant waved his men in to retrieve them, but the tumbling man scrabbled to his feet at the bottom and started to run again. The Sergeant's arm went up then down sharply; three arrows transfixed the man. His back arched, and then he fell, first to his knees then to his face, without making a sound. His companion gaped in horror, then stumbled to hand himself in to the approaching soldiers. The archers silently spread to cover the entire workforce, arrows nocked.

A figure in a workman's shabby cotte and hose came barrelling out of the keep. The men standing at the side of the slope made immediate way for him.

"WHAT is going on here?" he bellowed. *Alnoth! My old friend - What's he doing here? Of course, Henry must have asked him to supervise the destruction.* A tall, slender figure followed him out of the building, clearly an aristocrat from the look of his furred cape, but stayed silent. *Alnoth is not going to appreciate me shooting up his workforce...* Both men started down the motte steps. Wimer grimaced, but straightened himself in the saddle and rode forward to meet them. This was not the entrance he had been hoping for. They all arrived at the bottom of the steps together, and Alnoth and he spoke together as he swung down from his horse.

"Wimer? Good heavens, it is – WHAT..." "Alnoth, I'm most dreadfully sorry..."

Alnoth lifted his glower a little, and waved him to go on.

"Your man tried to make a run for it, even when he'd been told to halt. My Sergeant has standing orders to arrest anyone who may still be fighting the rebel cause, and to kill anyone who resists arrest. Despite the peace treaty, there are still many who would prefer to fight – or simply take advantage of a little chaos. You'd be surprised how many we come across. At one time, I would have thought nothing of riding over here with just a couple of men; now I need a small army."

Alnoth shook his head.

"Aye, lad. Or I should say, my Lord Sheriff. We've all

seen better times. Well, it sounds like the fool brought it on himself. Come up to the keep and wash the road dust down your throat, and tell me what you've been up to since I saw you last. You know Hugh Bigod's son Roger, don't you? GET back to work, you lot – the show's over!"

Wimer stood in his stirrups to call "Put up your bows, men! We are amongst friends here." Then dismounted, and held out his hand. "Sir Roger, it is good to see you again, painful though your father's disgrace must be…"

"-so entirely by accident, I killed a man. I'm lucky I found a branch, I could have gone for his sword instead – and been excommunicated for that! The closer I come to my own time of reckoning, the heavier my burden of sin grows. At times, I wonder that I can still move about under the weight of it. Certainly I grow desperately weary. Becket's death removed the last ray of hope." Wimer drew in a deep breath, and let it out in a rush. "Things were so much cleaner and clearer when we built Orford, weren't they, my friend?"

Roger was looking puzzled. "Excuse me – I don't mean to pry – but what has our newly-minted Saint Thomas' death got to do with you? Surely you weren't involved in his martyrdom?"

Wimer laughed, a hard, flat noise. "No. Much as I disliked our sainted Archbishop – and I have never known a man less saintly – I would not wish murder upon him. I am free of that sin, at least. No, his death set in stone my excommunication. His last letter to Bishop William confirmed it, just before his death; and Pope Alexander also ratified it, along with your father's sentence. I have actually therefore been excommunicated three times - so unless either Becket's successor, or the Pope, takes pity on me, I am destined for Hell, without hope of redemption. Neither of them appear to be in a hurry to redeem me. It is not a comfortable thought to live with."

The other two men were silent. Wimer began to feel the pressure of their pity, and suddenly wished to be elsewhere.

"Well, Goodnight, to you both."

He bowed and went off in search of an unoccupied bench to sleep on. As he left, he heard Alnoth say quietly to Roger:

"He has changed very much since I knew him in Orford. This business of the excommunication is desperately sad. I shall pray for him..."

Wimer had a sudden lump in his throat. It seemed that a simple act of friendship could still break through the grey film of despair that coated his days. He went to sleep with the memory of the gulls' harsh cries in the air around Orford Castle, and slept better than he had done in many months.

WIMER, NORWICH - AUGUST 1177

Wimer lay hidden behind his bed curtains, listening to the movements of the servants as they swept his fireplace and made his chambers ready for the day. He was often awake when they came, and would sometimes exchange a few pleasantries with them; but not today. He was sure his eyes were still red from weeping. He lay motionless, willing them to hurry up and go.

The girl clearing the grate found something, and hissed for the other servant to come over.

"Here! Elly! Come and look at this!"

"What?"

"A piece of parchment, with writing on, full of holes, and burnt – what do you think it is?"

"Dagger holes, those." said the other, judiciously. "Something's upset His Lordship – must've been bad, for him to take on so. But shh, nothing to do with us, and you don't want to wake him; best get back to work." and the brushing noises resumed.

Wimer lay rigid on his bed, aware that any movement would send a creak to the servants' ears. The day's mailbag had brought a letter that had turned his world upside-down. He didn't even need to shut his eyes to know what that particular parchment the girls had found had contained.

"Iohannes Episcopus, ad Wimerus Capellanus... John the Bishop to Wimer the Chaplain...

My son, when I was elected Bishop, I found amongst my predecessor's papers a letter from Thomas a'Becket instructing him to excommunicate you. Bishop William of course obeyed. There was a second letter from Becket, telling Bishop William that he intended to absolve all four of you clerics once he had spoken to you on his return to England; but of course his foul murder prevented that.

It was not until I by chance met young Roger Bigod just a few days ago, and he mentioned that you were still under interdict, that I realised that William had never removed your sentence.

I am deeply sorry that this unfortunate chain of events has kept you excommunicate for longer than necessary. I am happy to say to you with regards to the excommunication:

EGO TE ABSOLVO.

I urge you to go to confession immediately to obtain absolution for your sins. I am only sorry that I am required by the King to go immediately to France, so will not be able to hear your confession myself.

Yours in God,

John, Bishop of Norwich."

Wimer had read the letter a score of times, before to his horror bursting into tears. He had stabbed the parchment, over and over, before crumpling it and hurling it into the fire. He could feel the rage building up again. *All those years. All those years of fear, of shame, of suffering, bearing taunts and the scorn of little men. Were those three words supposed to wipe away the hurt? Dear sweet Christ, if that madman Becket had never cast that stain on me, I could have asked the King for Ida's hand the year we met.* It was a vision of unbearable sweetness and regret. He drew in a deeply shaky breath, and heard the maids scuttle out. For a while, he abandoned himself to self-pity.

When he could bear his misery no more, he swung out of bed in an attempt to fill his head with the concerns of the day. His foot kicked the mailbag, and he heard something else move inside. It was a letter, addressed to "Wimer the Chaplain", not to the High Sheriff. He slit the seal, and began to read.

"Ida de Tosny, ad Wimerus Capellanus…"

Jesu! It is from her! What can be wrong? Does she need me? He sank back on the bed to read.

"Greetings, my old friend. I hope this letter finds you well; I was shocked when I thought back on when we last met, and realised how long it has been! I recall very well your kindnesses to me, and am saddened that our paths have not crossed more frequently since. Of course, our Lord King has kept me with him in his lands in France these many years, with only the occasional trip back to England, and I am sure your duties as Sheriff keep you away from court in any case."

Come on – get to the point…

"I remember that the King was pleased to tell me of your elevation to Sheriff, and I was so proud of you! I envy you, living in Norfolk – give Holkham and the sea my love when you come near them next! I trust you are able to visit your lovely castle at Orford often, and hear the seagulls? You see, my friend, that even though we have not seen each other for some time, I remember our conversations together, and indeed the last letter I sent you, as though that were yesterday.

Oh, my love – I recall every word and gesture too...

The King promises me that I may accompany him on a visit to England, but there are so many other matters on his mind that it may not be soon. In closing, then, I write to you instead of perhaps having the pleasure of telling you my news face to face. It is my hope that you will rejoice with me in the birth of my son, William. The King has acknowledged him, so his future is assured. I so look forward to enjoying my baby as he grows, in honour.

Ah. A son – that she can keep; and that the King has acknowledged. Good. I am pleased for her.

I pray that we may be able to renew our friendship at some time in the future.

Yours,

Ida."

He stared at it for a long time, before kissing it awkwardly and placing it carefully in his locked chest, next to her other letter, and a faded yellow ribbon.

Two babes, two letters – I am so glad she can keep this one. She remembers me, and kindly! But she is so far away, and so unreachable.

He leapt up, and paced the length of the room and back. *What will happen to her when the King tires of her? Has some of her shine left her, for Henry, now she has had a babe? Dare I hope again, now the excommunication is lifted? She does write that she wants to renew our friendship!*

WIMER, BURY ST EDMUNDS - APRIL 1181

Wimer picked up his pace as he made his way towards Churchgate Street. It was getting late, and the clouds were threatening. He would prefer to be inside the Abbey before either the rain, or the night, fell. It was a courtesy visit to old Abbot Hugh, one he'd put off far too long – it was becoming clear that the old boy was losing his grip. He shrugged. *None of my business, at least whilst the Abbey meets its knight service obligations.*

A storekeeper wished him goodnight as he left the market square. It was his own fault he was late; he had remembered on the ride up from Westminster that Goda's birth day was imminent, and he might not be home in time to get her something from Norwich market. He'd sent his guard on to arrange lodgings at the Abbey, and walked into Bury. He'd been fascinated by a display of brooches that the stall holder swore were Roman, and had taken his time choosing one, shaped like a hare, or a racing hound, depending how you looked at it. Then of course he had allowed himself to be sweet-talked into getting a shawl to pin with it, by the woman in the next stall along. *Still, Goda will be delighted.* He was feeling pleased with himself, despite the lateness of the hour.

He had the streets to himself. The market was packing up rapidly, and everyone else was getting under cover. The magnificent Abbey gates at the bottom of the hill were just becoming visible, when he was almost tripped by a small yelping dog, careening out of a side street. He glanced down the street it had come from, and saw presumably its owner, a small girl, running towards him sobbing. He was just about to shout at her, for her uncontrolled dog, when his eye was caught by the scene behind her. Two men with quarterstaffs were beating a figure on the ground. One looked up the alley at him, roared something incoherent, and started towards him, waving the staff.

He rapidly weighed up his options. *Safety inside the Abbey gate; but it was a long sprint whilst carrying the girl, and what if Brother Gatekeeper was distracted?* Something nearer was required. He gave a great yell to alert the Abbey, and scooped the child up at the same time. *Choices.* Running down hill was easier, and nearer to safety, besides. He passed up the first dark entrance on his right, and then dived into the next. There was a shadowed space behind the great wooden pillar forming the opening to the courtyard beyond, and he ducked behind it.

Up the road, there was a cacophony of snarls, both dog and human. The terrier must have gone back to the fray. He glanced at the girl; she was listening intently, biting her knuckles. To distract her – that contest could only end one way, if the dog persisted – he whispered the first thing that came to mind;

"I am afraid too; if I die, I'll go straight to Hell."

He cursed silently, that could not be the best thing to

say to a young girl, unacquainted with the breed though he was – but it seemed to work; she turned to him, puzzled:

"I thought you Christians all went to Heaven?"

"Ah, that's only if you are clear of sin. I was excommunicated, you see."

She got to the heart of it immediately. "Was?"

He blushed, and hoped the gloom hid it. "Yes, well, the sentence was cleared some while ago, but I felt so angry at the man who imposed it – and at God, for letting him hurt me – that I haven't been to confession since."

Up the hill, there was a shout of triumph, and a yelp of pain, broken off at its height. The girl's face crumpled, and when she spoke again, it was clear that she was forcing her mind away from the scene up the hill.

"So it's your fault? I mean, your God could have let you die when you were in trouble, and you would have gone to Hell, but he didn't, and now you're punishing yourself?"

Wimer stared at her, dumbstruck. *Dear sweet Lord. Could it be so simple?*

He was saved from replying by a shout from the direction of the Abbey:

"Hoy! You! Hold where you are!" and the sound of many sandalled feet running up the hill. Wimer let them go past the hidey-hole, and then stood up. He offered the child his hand, and she took it gravely. He hesitated slightly at the entrance, then the memory of the deathly still victim lying in the side street made his mind up, and he steered them firmly down the hill to the Abbey gate.

The gatekeeper brother was hanging half out of the gate, straining to see what was happening. Bobbing over

his shoulder was another face, who as soon as he saw
Wimer, edged the gatekeeper out of the way and sprinted
across the width of Angel Hill to meet them.

"My Lord! Where on earth have you been! We've been
so worried about you!" then, noticing the girl, "And what
on earth is THAT!"

"That, Piers, is a young lady who has been
exceptionally brave through a very trying experience."

Wimer squeezed the girl's hand, and got a tremulous
smile in return.

"Please take a couple of the soldiers and see if you can
discover the fate of a small brown terrier, which held off
our attackers at a critical time."

He thought for a bit about how to send Piers to the
downed man, without alarming the girl.

"The main disturbance was on the second lane up on
your left. Oh, and look out for a large parcel, too – my gift
for your wife; almost as important as the dog."

Piers bowed and disappeared back through the gate, to
collect his escort.

"Are you someone important?" The voice was rather
small and hesitant.

"Right now, my dear, your safety and well-being is
rather more important than I am. Come on, let's get you
into the Abbey proper, and see if we can find you a
blanket and some food." He had a sudden thought.
"What's your name? I'm Wimer, from Orford. We missed
out on introductions!"

"I'm Rebecca, daughter of Elijah."

Wimer stopped, turned to face her, and swivelled his
hand around in hers to make a proper platform, then

kissed it.

"Pleased to meet you, Rebecca." Their hands clasped again, and they processed across the open square.

"Brother Gatekeeper, my companion and I are going to the Refectory. Please be kind enough to send my man in when he returns."

They were both devouring bowls of pease soup when they were interrupted by the arrival of a limping man, clothes and head bloody, who was quite successfully fighting off Piers' attempts to support him. Rebecca looked up, squealed, and surged towards him, sending bowl and soup flying.

"Papa! Papa!"

The man scooped her up and hugged her as though finding her made him whole. Wimer cleared his throat and looked away to give them privacy. *How I envy him! I wish I had someone who I could hug like that...*

Piers came up and gave him a swift brief:

"No sign of the hoodlums. This fellow has taken quite a beating, but should be all right. The dog is dead, I'm afraid; I think it gave a good account of itself, there's an abandoned stave beside it. I got your parcel."

Wimer nodded thanks, and then stood up as Elijah hobbled over, with Rebecca trying to support him.

"Sir! I'm very glad to see you in one piece; that outcome was definitely in doubt the last time I saw you."

"Lord, I cannot thank you enough for rescuing my daughter! She is my only child, and I could not live without her..." he stroked her hair for a moment, lost in his own thoughts.

"What did I witness? Was that a simple robbery?"

Elijah looked at him in surprise.

"Have you not heard about the martyr, Lord?" Wimer's face answered him. He sighed.

"Just a few days ago, on Easter Friday, a young Christian boy was found killed, with all the marks of Christ on him. The townspeople are convinced that it was a Jew who murdered him, and tensions have been high. I answered a knock on my gate without first calling for my manservant as backup, which was foolish. I nearly paid for my stupidity with my life. The dog tried to defend me, I remember that; then I took a blow to the head, and much of the rest is fuzzy, until I woke with your man bending over me. How did you come to be involved, my heart?"

"I heard Teasel barking, and followed her out onto the lane. There were two men hitting you with sticks, and Teasel was barking and barking at them. One of them hit her, and saw me and looked as though he would hit me too. Teasel yelped and went running off, so I ran after her; Lord Wimer was at the top of the lane, and hid us until the Abbey sent men. Teasel! Is she all right?"

Wimer knelt to her level. "I'm afraid not, Rebecca. She died attacking those men; she probably saved our lives, by keeping them busy until rescue came. I'm very sorry."

Tears were welling up in her eyes, but she sniffed once, and nodded.

Wimer stood, and turned his attention back to her father.

"I'm very glad that all except Teasel have survived this evening's work. I owe a great debt of gratitude to your daughter, who made plain to me the answer to a problem that has been gnawing at me for a long time. If you ever have need of anything I can provide, please let me know."

Elijah bowed. "Lord, you have already restored to me everything I love. I am eternally in your debt. My house is the sign of the apple tree in Hatter Street; please treat it as your own. Come, child – let us go home."

Wimer watched them leave, his hand still holding a memory of the warmth of Rebecca's hand in his. At the last she rewarded him with a wave and smile.

Goodbye, sweet maid – and thank you for your wisdom and insight.

He had almost tripped over the bitch, which had chosen to give birth in the corner of the castle stable. Forgetting the strap he was hunting for, he hunkered down and admired the puppies, and their mother. "What a clever girl you are! They look good and fat and healthy! And a good number too…" He continued to talk to her and stroke her, and she allowed him to check over the puppies. There were four altogether – no, five.

Wimer watched those puppies thoughtfully, over several days, happy that the negotiations were delaying his departure from Bury. At first, he wasn't sure what he was measuring them against; but it slowly dawned on him that he had, in his mind's eye, an image of some dark curls falling over a hugged pup. That made the decision easier; there was one particular brindled dog pup, with a cute patch over one eye, and an all-black bitch. *Not the brindled one, I think – too like the terrier.*

The bitch was the runt, and he was a little worried about her. So was the hounds master; Wimer came in one

Sunday morning after breakfast to find him examining the pups carefully. The little bitch was missing, and Wimer looked around frantically. There! A sack, in the corner, with something little in it – that was beginning to whimper.

"What are you going to do with the runt?"

"Drown it, m'Lord. No use to anyone, not worth it's feed."

"I'd save you the trouble? I know a home that would take it as a pet."

"Yes, take it and good riddance. It's old enough to leave its dam."

"Thank you!" and Wimer scooped it up straight away.

He had to do it himself; he owed her so much. Before he lost his nerve, he pulled his robe up a bit over his belt to make a pouch, popped the puppy in, and marched straight out of the Abbey's Norman gate and up the hill. There were still some signs of the recent troubles, with the odd broken shutter or smoke stains on some of the houses. The Abbot still had guards posted, to keep the peace; several burly lay-brothers, armed with solid-looking quarterstaves, were in sight.

He didn't slow until he was into Hatter Street. The brother on duty at the top of the street nodded to him, and let him past. He nearly missed Rebecca's house. The door to the yard had been hacked and burnt so badly that he walked past it twice, before realising that there was an apple tree under the charring. Then he realised that he had another problem he hadn't thought about at all. How was he going to give the pup to her? He couldn't just bang on the door, her father would never let him hand the pup over without a fuss. And he wanted to see her face when she saw the pup! He looked up and down the street. No-one was looking at him, so he went and leaned against the wall of the house, where he could peek in through one of the gaps in the door. There she was! She was hanging out clothes and singing.

"Rebecca!" he called, quietly. Again, louder. She stopped mid-note and looked around, but went back to her task. *Come on! How do I get her to hear me?*

Wimer suddenly felt a growing warmth on his stomach, as the puppy weed on him. "Eurgh!" he said, out loud – and then the door was yanked open. Rachel stood looking at him puzzledly.

"M'Lord Wimer! Have you a message for my father? What's happened to your robe?"

"Rebecca – have you finished hanging those clothes up yet?" came a woman's voice from inside the house, but coming nearer.

"Oh no! Here, take this!" said Wimer, thrusting the puppy into her arms and hastily backing away. He was rewarded with a look of sheer delight, and then the image he had been planning, as Rebecca bent over the pup. He retreated down the street grinning from ear to ear.

WIMER, ACLE PRIORY - SUMMER 1181

Wimer found Adam fishing, quite a way downriver from the Priory.

"This is a very peaceful occupation for the Prior! I had hoped to see you tallying your accounts!"

Adam had turned in annoyance to shush his visitor, but leaped to his feet to embrace him instead.

"Wimer! Um, my Lord Sheriff! How good to see you!" then more anxiously, "We're not in trouble with the accounts, are we? I'm afraid we've drifted towards informality again. Are you here on official business?"

"No, no, I'm teasing you. I'm here just for the pleasure of your company, now. Abbot Thomas seems to be keeping the Abbey's affairs up to date, I hardly worry about this little corner of Norfolk any more." Adam's face had darkened a little at the name. Wimer noticed.

"Don't you get on with Thomas? It's, what, ten years since he beat you in the Abbacy election, does that still rankle?"

Adam flushed. "A little, perhaps. But what really irritates me is that he interferes with every action I take. In truth, he runs the Priory in everything but name; there's very few decisions I am allowed to take without consulting with m'lord Abbot. I had charge of this place for years, before he was brought in; it vexes me. About the only use I am around here – apart from serving to the spiritual needs of my brothers – is putting fish on the table." He grinned wryly.

Wimer kicked his sandals off, sat down, and dangled his feet in the river. "Ahhhh that's good... Well, souls are what I came to talk to you about. Specifically, my soul. Could you bear to hear my confession?" Adam knelt beside him, frowning.

"My friend, are you in a position to ask that? Are you not still under interdict?"

"No. Bishop John wrote to me, absolving me from the excommunication sentence, some years ago." Wimer scowled, some of the resentment surfacing again. "He advised me to confess my sins at the time; however, I have had a crisis of the faith, and have never done so."

Adam took all this in, wide-eyed.

"Years ago! And to tell you by letter, not in person! Oh, Wimer, what a perfunctory end to such a bitter time, how galling! But you're ready to confess now? What's changed?"

Wimer lay back upon the grass, and put his hands under his head. After a second, Adam did the same, sensing that the telling of this tale would be easier if it were done to Heaven, rather than face to face. Wimer was silent for quite a while, but Adam made no move to hurry him.

"To get the easy matter out of the way, the Bishop had no choice but to write, rather than talk to me. The King has been sending him here, there, and everywhere on Court business. I believe he's acting as a travelling Judge right now. He did apologise in the letter." There was another long silence. "In truth, I hardly know where to begin with the deeper matter."

"Start with what prompted you to make the journey here, and work back?" Adam suggested.

"Ah, that was not so much a prompt, as a slap in the face, from a young Jewish lady I met in Bury this Eastertime. Never mind the details, but we were discussing God's love. She pointed out that I had survived the excommunication intact, and so God had intended it as a trial; and that my refusal to go to confession was a self-inflicted punishment, and a dangerous gamble, at that. Her argument is unassailable. But I am no longer sure that my belief has survived the trial. I have read and read, and thought until my head is nigh to bursting; and the more I think about it, the more sure I am that the girl was right. It no longer matters whether my belief is intact; I simply need to have faith in God's care, and do what is needful. I am ashamed of my sins... perhaps belief will follow. So, my friend, there's the short of it; will you still hear the confession of a perplexed sinner, and a non-believer?"

"When did you go to confession last?"

"Um... to a religious superior; shortly before the King's coronation. To a hedge-priest, whilst I was building Orford."

Adam sat up and stared at him, quickly doing some arithmetic.

"Are you telling me you have not been to confession with your Bishop for more than a quarter of a century? And William never forced the issue!"

Wimer flushed. "I was perhaps the least of his

concerns."

Adam shook his head in amazement. "Well, I think we'd better get started, then! But that was well before the Archbishop Thomas was even elevated, let alone estranged from the King and excommunicating everyone in sight – what stopped you going then?"

Wimer pulled his feet out of the river, stood, then formally went to both knees and bent his head over his clasped fists. Adam got to his feet.

"That must be part of my confession, I think." He made the sign of the cross. "Forgive me, Father, for I have sinned; it has been many years since my last confession. I can remember only one mortal sin..." and he told Adam all about the burial of the men he had sent out with shovels in the middle of a war, and William's instruction to find out if they had been shriven of their sins, before he next confessed to William.

"So in my pride, I decided that there was no purpose to be served by disinterring their bodies and reburying them outside of holy ground, if they had not been to confession; and I avoided the Bishop's intent by simply never going to him for confession ever again, choosing the nearest, not the greatest, priest instead. Now, of course, it's too late to either fulfil the task, or to confess to Bishop William. I deeply regret that sophistry."

Adam noted the careful use of words. "Any more?"

"There was an occasion during the Great Rebellion when I killed a man."

"Oh, my. Please continue."

"There was a skirmish, and I accidentally ended up hitting one of Hugh's knights with a tree branch, to stop him reaching his sword and attacking me. I just swung at him – and he was dead."

"Did you draw blood?" Wimer shook his head. "And were you in the battle?"

"No, Father; I was watching from the side – hiding behind a tree trunk, actually – and the knight was thrown from his horse almost on top of me."

"Thank heavens for that, I think we can ignore that one, as an unhappy accident. Do you wish to confess any venial sins, my son?"

Wimer nodded, looked him in the eye, and said: "Yes, Father; two. Firstly, I am beginning to doubt that God's hand is evident in trials by ordeal. I am increasingly uncomfortable about presiding over them, because I feel more and more that the outcome is simply a matter of luck." He stopped.

"And the second?"

Wimer bent his head over his hands again, lips to his knuckles. When he spoke, his voice was so quiet that Adam had to strain to make it out.

"I am in love with the King's mistress, the lady Ida, and have been since the first day I met her, several years ago. I have carnal thoughts about her often, and I am deeply envious of the King, who can enjoy her presence whenever he pleases."

Adam shook his head in wonder. "So, my son, to sum up; you disobeyed a direct order from your religious superior, for which you do not feel contrition. However, you are ashamed of deliberately avoiding the Bishop, so that you did not have to admit to disobeying his order. You are amongst a growing body of men who are becoming unsure about the divinity of trial by ordeal. And you are in love with a woman, although you are a priest under a vow of chastity. Does that cover it?"

Wimer looked up at him solemnly. "Yes, Father."

Adam had a sudden thought. "I assume you have not consummated this love?"

"Good heavens no, Father! I haven't even spoken of it with her!"

Adam took a pace or two past Wimer, and back.

"You haven't said anything at all of the sin which caused the Archbishop of Canterbury to excommunicate you?"

Wimer said steadily, "That is because I do not consider it to be a sin, Father. I wrote a simple letter, at the request of my employer; it was only later that the Earl's deeds were thrust into the political arena. The excommunication for the Earl, and three other clerics as well as myself, was the unforeseeable outcome. My actions were innocent."

"And yet it tortured you for, what, 15 years? God must truly love you, to test you so, my son." Adam ran his hand over his tonsure.

"Can we go back to the burial of those men? What did you understand William to mean?"

"That if they had not been to confession before meeting their deaths, that I should not have had them buried in the churchyard."

"But weren't they paying their Lord's knight service? Surely they would have attended a service and made confession before they set out. It was their Lord's duty to ensure that, not yours. It sounds to me like the Bishop was simply making sure that you were on top of things – but if they had only been in your care for a matter of days, it would be unreasonable to expect them to need shriving again so soon. I think you may have read too much into his demand."

Wimer shook his head in wonder.

"You may be right. Good grief, have I let a misinterpretation torture me all these years? William was just the sort of domineering superior who would give an instruction like that, with no explanation. Huh!" He sat back on his heels, literally taken aback by the force of the thought.

Adam, happy to have cleared up a minor puzzle, paced up and down again.

"I think that is the key, you know. Where you commit a sin, it is because you allow your intellect to undermine your faith. God has sent you a direct messenger in the form of that Jewish child; you must allow your faith to become childlike and simple again. The woman is another matter."

Adam thought for a moment, and then nodded.

"I will hear your Act of Contrition now, on those matters for which you truly feel regret."

Wimer knelt upright again, and stumbled through the prayer. What of the burials? Was that sin still with him, or was Adam's guess correct?

"*Ego te absolvo*. I would urge you to go to communion immediately. However, I require two penances from you. I recall you telling me once that Lauds was your favourite service."

Wimer nodded.

"Then I require you to attend it, whenever your duties

permit, for the course of an entire year; and to meditate on the simple faith of a child. I also instruct you to reorder your thoughts about the Lady Ida, and find some other way of regarding her, than as an object of lust. When you have achieved that, I want you to go and see her, to test it."

Wimer blushed furiously, but bowed his head in submission. Adam made the sign of the cross over him, and then reached down to help him to his feet. He glanced at Wimer's face, and gruffly suggested:

"Now, why don't you go away and have a think about all that, and leave me to my fishing!"

HENRY, WINCHESTER
FEAST OF THE EPIPHANY 1182;
WIMER, ORFORD

Henry drained his mead cup and leant back in his throne, belching gently. *Ah – good stuff!* He rubbed his full stomach. *How pleasant it is not to be at loggerheads with either my sons, or the Church. I must be slipping.* He looked round the crowded hall for those of his children present at this feast – a task made more difficult as many of the diners grew sated, and moved around to chat to old friends seated in different parts of the hall.

Easy to spot was his one legitimate son; John was still eating, hunched over his trencher, clad in a fine lambswool tunic. On closer inspection, there was a dark stain on his sleeve, which was shorter than it should be. Henry shook his head. The boy was going through a period of growth, making him even more morose than usual, and clumsy as a puppy. *Please God it be over soon.*

Also still seated, a few places further than John, was his acknowledged natural son, Geoffrey, whom Henry had recently elevated to Chancellor. He too had pushed back from the table, and, goblet in hand, was surveying the room. *Of all my children, he is the one who can be most trusted, and the only one who consistently uses his intellect to my advantage. What a shame he can't inherit! But he is a magnificent servant, and will continue to serve his brothers.* Henry smiled proudly, and looked again for the least of his sons.

It's a shame that none of the girls are here – it would have been good to have them, and their children, as playmates for young William. Henry spotted the boy in a corner, teasing a wolfhound with a bone. *He's taller than I remembered – he must be, what, five? Perhaps six? Definitely time to take him from his mother and get him some decent tutoring.* He was very like Ida in colouring. She was rarely far from him – *yes, there she is, leaning against the table, watching the boy. Looking a little careworn. This, too, is in my service – she has been at my side whenever I've beckoned for many years now. I should make some better provision for her...*

The thought of losing Ida brought his Rosamund to mind. He was going to make another gift to Godstow Nunnery when he distributed presents shortly. He urgently wanted to arrange the best possible provision for her, body and soul, and to minimise her time in Purgatory with prayers around the clock. There was the Abbess – hah! With young Roger Bigod sandwiched between her and the Abbot of Stratford Abbey, a Godly man indeed, but a crashing bore; and to be another recipient of Henry's generosity later.

Bigod looked as though he was bearing up well to the double onslaught of piety. No, be fair – he was making himself useful whilst waiting on Henry's pleasure for his inheritance, witnessing charter after charter. *In fact, he could witness the charters to the two religious houses. He is at least easier to spend time around than his father had been, and possibly more honourable too.* Not that he was going to get his Earldom back, nor indeed the bulk of his lands, until Henry was a lot surer of him. *Perhaps he was owed something on account, though...*

Henry slapped his slight but growing paunch, and leapt to his feet. He used the momentum to swing up onto the table and over to the other side. *Not bad for a man past the best flush of youth, my lad!* The noise level dropped gratifyingly fast, and soon even the servitors were still, having topped up everyone's drinks.

"My friends! We come to the end of another Christmas, and another year. And what a year it has been! We are at peace; reconciled with our Scottish and Welsh neighbours, and with Philip the new King of France. My son Henry the Young King is even now supporting Philip, and though we miss him greatly, his is an honourable task. My sons Richard and Geoffrey are firmly in control of their realms; my daughters all contributing towards the succession of their husbands.

I am blessed with three sons here with me tonight, and am surrounded by my friends. Tonight I would like to share some of these blessings, and distribute some gifts, as is my custom."

He beckoned over the servitor with his small chest, and put it on the table.

"I start with the Church, as is proper."

He took two charters from the chest, opened one, and laid the other on the table.

"Would the Abbess of Godstow please attend me?"

The elderly nun bumbled up, and curtsied twice in

front of the King. Henry bowed low, and handed her the charter with a smile.

"The lands as promised, good Abbess. "

"We will pray for her, Sire." she whispered.

Henry nodded formal acknowledgement, then returned to his task, a little subdued.

"The Abbot of Stratford!" The Abbot accepted his charter gratefully.

"And now, my beloved son John."

John stood, a trifle unsteadily. Henry realised that he'd taken a little too much wine, and moved down the table towards him, rather than embarrass the boy. He turned back to the room.

"I thought long and hard about a gift for John. I rejected clothes; because he's growing so fast that he'd need a new set next week."

There was a ripple of amusement, and John blushed.

"I'd give him money; but he'd only ask for more. I've raised sons his age before."

This time there was some outright laughter.

"Instead, I wanted to give him something to connect him to his heritage."

He stripped off a ring from the middle finger on his right hand, and held it up to the crowd. The large emerald caught the light nicely.

"This ring belonged to my father, and to his father before him. I think John has grown into it now."

He turned to his son, and slipped it on his finger.

"Wear it in good health!"

John bowed, looking a little underawed. Henry shook his head slightly, and went back to the chest.

"For my beloved Chancellor; a Book of Hours! Having just missed out on the Bishopric of Lincoln, he will need to sharpen his praying skills for his next attempt at the cloth..."

He lifted out a gorgeous book, wrapped in purple silk. Geoffrey took it reverently in both hands, and unwrapped it to reveal a gold and jewelled frontispiece.

"Sire! This is magnificent! My profound thanks!"

"And for my youngest son, William..."

William needed beckoning forward, this being the first time that Henry had singled him out in public. He watched with pride as the boy strode forward, carefully put out a foot, and bowed low.

"How old are you now, boy?"

"I am six, Sire."

"High time you had one of these, then."

Henry handed him a short dagger, snug in its own tooled leather sheath and belt. The boy crowed in delight, and strapped it on instantly. He looked round to show his mother. Henry followed his gaze, and bent to whisper to the boy,

"Go and fetch her."

He ran across, and pulled her over by her hand; she arrived in front of Henry laughing and protesting, then dropped a deep curtsey. He put a finger under her chin, and lifted her up.

"Not forgetting William's mother, the Lady Ida; a bolt of that very expensive silk she loves so much."

She blushed prettily, and curtsied again. Henry looked around for Roger.

"Stay here, my dear; Roger Bigod, step up, please."

He waited until Roger had bowed and taken a place beside Ida.

"I am not yet ready to pass judgement on your stepbrothers' claim to your father's lands and title; but in recognition of your services these last few years, I am returning to you the manors of Acle, Halvergate and South Walsham."

Roger bowed again, looking suitably grateful.

"And one other gift, greater than you know. The hand of the Lady Ida de Tosny, Royal ward, in marriage."

There. A neat discharge of my obligations.

It was more than strange to be riding into Orford, after all this time. Wimer reached the crossroads and halted, his guard pulling up behind him. *Left, to the church? Right, where I should be going, to the castle?* He shook his head, as a third alternative popped into his head. *Turn around, claim I'm ill, and not have to do this…*

He swivelled in the saddle, and beckoned Piers up.

"Take my horse, would you, and get the men settled? I'm going to pray, then walk over to the castle. You can take the rest of the day off, and give my love to your lady wife and beautiful babe. I shall be along to pay my respects in person as soon as I may." He dismounted, patted the grey's neck, and handed the reins over. The little troop clattered past him, and he took a deep breath then turned to face the church.

The sight hurt less than he thought it would. When he'd left, all those years ago, the place was still as much a building site as a church, with piles of rubble and mud everywhere, and the masons' marks sharp on every stone face. Now a neat gravel pathway ran between green banks, and the church had softened into the landscape. He walked down the pathway, then round to the back of the church. *Where is it...?* He moved into the churchyard a little, avoiding the flowers on a fresh grave, and looked up, and up... *There!* He grinned. *Hello, old friend - I'm glad you're still taking your gargoyle duties seriously!* He looked around, carefully; no-one was watching. He threw his head back and widened his grin to scary proportions, just as the mason had carved him, that summer's day when he was young. He laughed out loud at his foolishness, and carried on his inspection tour of the church.

Finally he reached the path again, and the door. He hesitated for a moment, but the onset of drizzle - and curiosity - got the better of him. *What saints have they chosen for the wall paintings? I do hope they've done justice to Bartholomew and his skin!* He dipped his fingers in the holy water stoup, made the sign of the cross, and went in. There was a woman kneeling at the left back of the church, so he moved as quietly as possible to the right, and admired the painting of Saint Nicholas supervising sailors along one wall. When he had finished, the woman had gone, so he walked across to inspect Saint Bartholomew. The artist had shown the saint with his skin folded over his arm, flowing onto the floor. *Ah, yes, good job with his insides! That's enough skin to cover a pair of oxen, though! I hope Lord Bromham was pleased when he saw it.*

The church was still empty, and so, feeling a little strange, Wimer made the sign of the cross again, and knelt in prayer. "Dear Lord in Heaven, have mercy on your servant Bartholomew, Lord Bromham, whose generosity made the building of this church possible." *And who was a thoroughly nice man, as well. I'm terribly rusty at this!* "Um, also, Lord, have mercy on the soul of Stephen of Glanville, whose untimely death has brought me here today." *Poor chap, could only have been in his 20s, and was doing all right as a sheriff.* There was a noise behind him, and Wimer leapt to his feet and looked round. It was the verger, lighting candles as the gloom grew. Wimer nodded to him, and left.

The rain had started in earnest, so he put his hood up, and half-ran down the street to the castle. No-one was about, and all he got was an impression of solidity from the houses lining both sides of the street. *Well. I'm glad I prayed for the old boy. I was very fond of him. And no better place than in his church; let's hope God was listening.* He hit a puddle and cursed; and was still shaking water from his cloak when he got to the castle entrance. Piers had had the foresight to send one of his men to wait for him, so he was escorted immediately to the keep. In the half-dark, all he got was an impression of towering power. *Have to wait for the morning to see how this has turned out!*

Glanville's chamberlain was more than delighted to see him, and insisted on handing over the accounts straight away. *At least the de Glanville boy finished collating them before falling off a hunter and breaking his fool neck.* Wimer bowed to the inevitable, and settled down to read through them before dinner, wax scratch-pad by his side. He was soon lost in the detail.

"How's it looking, Lord?" The chamberlain's question broke his concentration. He looked up, a little mazed. The servants were clearing the hall and putting the trestles out for supper.

"Yes, fine. I have one or two questions - for instance, why have the Bigod manors, um, let me see, Acle and two others, I'll find them in a minute - why have they been struck off the King's farm?"

"Acle, Halvergate and South Walsham, Lord, yes. The King gifted them back to Lord Roger on the occasion of his marriage, just this Christmas, that's why they've only just come off the register."

Wimer stood and stretched; he clearly wasn't going to have any more work time tonight. "Oh? Who's he married?"

"The King's mistress, Lord - Ida de Tosny, I think her name was."

There was a hissing in his ears, and his vision had narrowed to a pinprick. He could feel the room swaying, and sat back down hurriedly.

"Are you all right, Lord? Let me get you some ale!"

"No. No, I'm fine." He swallowed bile. "I must be more tired than I thought. I think I'll give food a miss, and go straight to my room."

"Yes, of course, Lord. I've put you in the priest's chamber on the first floor, is that all right? I thought you might want to be near to the chapel, being a priest yourself, although of course we could move you if..."

Wimer cut off the man's babble by climbing to his feet and aiming himself at the east stairs. Somehow he got up them, and into the hallway. *Chapel to the left; the priest's room to the right.* The memory of all those drafting sessions with Alnoth was still with him. He found his pallet, threw himself down on it, and gave himself up to the blackness welling inside him.

He must have slept, because a seagull woke him. It was a little before dawn, with only the faintest lightening of grey showing at the window slit. He got up, and went to lean against the cool stone, feeling the breeze on his cheek. One by one, deliberately, he ran through his precious store of memories of Ida - and said goodbye to each. He let a single tear trace its path down his cheek unchecked.

WIMER, MANOR HALL FARM, ACLE - APRIL 1182

He had spent the night at St Benet's, with Adam the Prior. Together they had rehearsed today's planned conversation until he knew exactly what he had to say. Adam had made him say it out loud often enough that neither his voice nor his words sounded strange in his ears any more. He'd left immediately after Lauds and headed for the Manor, recently returned to the Bigods.

He had arrived at the Manor just as the Lady Ida was preparing to ride out in the company of her maid. The terror that Wimer had suffered, every time he had thought of meeting her again in the last few months, had been swept away by the bonhomie generated by the stables. Very soon he and Ida were walking their horses out of earshot of Piers and the maid.

As always, it was easier talking a-horseback than face to face. There was always the opportunity to manufacture a need to check the horse from snatching a mouthful of grass, or from shying at a leaf... Wimer was talking full advantage of this shield, and was spilling his heart to Ida, whilst she observed him closely, listening sympathetically. He was just finishing telling her of the terms of his absolution:

"...and so that is what brought me to your door so early in the morning. I have attended Lauds almost every day since it was imposed on me as a penance, although truthfully it is more of a pleasure. I am beginning to regain some of the love of the monastic hours that I had as a child, and their gentle rhythms are restoring a measure of faith to me.

I have been thinking a lot lately about resigning my post, and taking a monk's vows. I have served Henry well for over twenty years, and I still love him; but his sons are another matter. I would not wish to work for any of them.

I yearn for the space to cleanse my soul through prayer, and prepare for God's summons. Henry and I both grow old – look, I already have a tonsure, God-given! He has achieved all he desired in life. I suspect that my worldly success is as naught, and that my life's great labour is still ahead of me." Wimer fell silent, and indulged in a little unnecessary stirrup resettling. Ida waited patiently, sensing more.

"There was one other condition of the absolution." He gathered his courage, and stared straight ahead. He could feel a flush building, and spoke before it crested his collar.

"I was to see you again, and test to see whether my feelings for you had moderated into something more appropriate, like... like..."

She took pity on him, and reached out to pat his forearm.

"I always knew that you carried feelings for me that I

was never able to reciprocate, old friend." she said, softly. "I hope our meeting is not too difficult for you? I would not wish to cause you any discomfort."

Wimer turned to her with a broad smile. "Oh, no, my Lady, not now – although confessing it to you is hard indeed. I shall always hold a place for you in my heart; but your marriage to Roger changed my thinking about you completely. Before, you see, you were always on the edge of being available, and always in peril. Now you are married to a good man, a powerful man, who will protect you far better than I ever could. And you are both young; there will be many children, and I pray, a growing love between you. No, all that feeling is behind me now, and it simply gives me pleasure to see you settled."

His smile turned warmer as he noticed her gesture – as he had spoken of children, her hand had lain lightly on her stomach for a moment. *The next Bigod heir is already started, it seems.*

"Well, I am glad to hear it – I think!" she said, with a light laugh. "It is always sad when a girl loses an admirer; but I could not bear to think of you suffering. I am indeed happy with Roger, and growing more so daily. The King made a wise choice, I am very thankful for it. The only sadness in my world is that my William has been taken from me; but that was inevitable as he grew older. I shall be allowed to see him on his birthday, and see how my baby has grown up!"

Now it was Ida's turn to be silent, and to pay more attention to her horse than to her companion. Soon, though, she picked up the conversation again, on a less painful topic:

"So tell me, my friend – how fares Wimer the High Sheriff in other matters? Are you still faithfully handling the King's business across your wide domain?"

He screwed up one side of his face, and half-shook his head. "In truth, all the joy has gone from it. I am afraid that the greater peril to my soul now comes from this duty to the King."

He looked across, and saw her frowning in puzzlement. He took a moment to gather his thoughts, the better to explain to her; then took the reins in one hand, and made a fist with the hand nearest her.

"I have several concerns." raising the first finger; "It is my duty to order, then supervise, trials by ordeal, whether that be by water, fire, or combat. You know that the Church teaches that the outcome of these is ordained by God."

She nodded, gravely.

"I no longer believe that to be the case. I have seen too many trials where the wrong person was unscathed, to believe that God has any hand in them. The outcome seems to be down to chance, or pure luck. So now I feel that I accrue sin whenever I hold a trial, and the law forces my hand often."

He checked her face; she was thoughtful, not dismayed, so he continued with his second item.

"There is also the question of how far I must go to satisfy the King's need for money. Again and again, I am asked to line the King's coffers by increasing the fines I impose; sometimes, that is simply not the just thing to do, but often I have no choice. It must be a sin when I fine a man so much for a trivial offence that he cannot feed his family, and so all of them become beggars. I have been known to pay part of a fine in such a case myself. It is no better if I am merely collecting the fines that the travelling judges set; then I am merely a party to arbitrary cruelty. Finally..."

He lifted a third finger, and glanced across in time to catch her smile, and then compose her features. He laughed.

"I'm sorry – you're right, I'm being pedantic. I'll be silent on the third count! The sin burden grows, and keeps growing, though; and I see no way out. Between my duty to the King, and the long years of excommunication, and then willfully refusing to confess even after being absolved of the sentence – I fear my soul is in danger of a sentence in Purgatory that makes me tremble."

His gaze rested on the horizon, deeply solemn. When he spoke again, it was to the far distances, not to her:

"When I was a youth – when Hugh Bigod offered me my first position, as his Chaplain – I came as close as you like to refusing him, and joining the novitiate instead. Perhaps I should have done... but I can't take the novice's oath yet."

"What is preventing you, my friend?"

"Pride!" He snorted. "Another sin... I feel strongly that the magnitude of my stain can only be cleansed by founding a small religious house, and ensuring daily prayers for my soul. That, I'm sure, is my great work. To do that, you need land. My brother left me a small parcel of land, at Dodnash, to my great surprise and pleasure; but it's only 70 acres or so, not enough to sustain a cell, let alone a Priory. I have saved some 400 marks over the years, which would buy me a little more, and pay for the building; but that is the extent of my wealth. If I am not privileged to be a monk in my old age, I shall need that little pot of money. So I dither; and daily the burden grows. I shall continue to wrestle with the problem." He shook his head, and brought his attention back to Ida.

"But my Lady, I have been remiss, and monopolised the conversation – what is your news?"

She was deep in thought.

"Well, apart from leaving the King to marry Roger – my major news is that my nephew the Baron has died."

He murmured sympathy. She continued to look thoughtful.

"Actually, that may play to your advantage. His death has had a strange effect on his widow, Alda – she seems to have found a freedom and relaxation of tension as a widow that she never had as a wife. Perhaps it is that her son Baldwin dotes on her, and has paid a fine so that she need never marry again, unless she chooses.

She has become quite mellow. Perhaps she has found a new depth to her religion herself. She wishes to pay debts she has accrued, including the one to you, relating to Baldwin. Just last week she wrote to offer me the return of my marriagiatum, which went to her instead of me – the land in East Bergholt, that I think must abut your land in Dodnash, it extends to the Great Way dividing the villages.

Her intention was to bolster the land grant that Henry has allowed Roger; but I have not spoken of her offer to him. He does well enough, and has hopes of persuading Henry to return all his father's lands before too long. How much land do you need? Would my thousand acres be sufficient?"

Wimer's horse jinked sideways, in response to his startled movement.

"My Lady! That would be a gift beyond price – I cannot..."

She held up a hand, imperiously.

"Wimer! Please do us the honour of allowing Alda – and I – to acknowledge the debt we owe you. What you did for us was a gift that can never be repaid; your act made possible the happy outcomes of both our lives. Baldwin, of course, has no idea what he owes you; but Alda can manage him. I shall write to her directly. I am delighted that we can do you this small service!"

It was her horse's turn to jink, as she forgot herself enough to do a happy bounce.

"And now that's settled; race you home!"

Wimer sat slack-jawed staring after her for a few heartbeats. *Dear Lord in heaven! What a gift! Am I dreaming?* He slapped his calf with his crop to check. His roar of delight spurred the horse faster than the crop would have done.

WIMER, DODNASH - SUMMER 1183

"*Sciant presentes et futuri*... Let it be known to those present and to the future..."

Wimer wrested the quick of his thumb out of his mouth and forced his hand behind his back. *Calm... I must look calm...* The land, and the beautiful little Priory he could build on it, meant so much to him. He took a deep breath to steady himself, and listened to the bored voice of the scribe start to read his charter.

"*Ad Wimerus Capelanus*... To Wimer the Chaplain... " would Ida's niece-in-law, Alda de Tosni, and her spoilt son Baldwin, do as his Lady had asked, and give the full measure? Wimer listened intently, and mentally ticked off the items.

"All our meadow from the gate of Adam de Bossuin; all the adjoining pasture down to the stream; and all our embanked fields to the alder grove at the side, all in pure and perpetual alms, free from all secular obligation..."

Yes, as promised, thank the Lord. Now, will the witnesses object? He had calculated finely the exact moment in the running order of the day's court listing to insert his charter, and had paid the clerk handsomely – seven silver pennies, a week's wage – for the slot he wanted; just after the midday break, when wits were dulled. He had so many enemies who might choose to damn his soul – obscurity was his best defence.

He bowed his head and prayed silently as the small crowd of witnesses milled round the scribe to get their names on the charter. No-one was questioning the terms, or the beneficiary; all looked to be local people doing their civic duty, simply hearing about the changes in local land ownership so they could testify to it later if needed.

"*Sciant presentes et futuri...*" The scribe started on the next charter. Wimer shut his eyes briefly in relief, then bowed to the Bench and left the court. *Henry next...*

"*Wimerus Capellanus ad Henricus Rex...*

Sire... I hardly know how to say this to you, so I beg your forbearance in advance. You would not believe the pile of scratched-out parchment I have accrued, trying to get the words right; so I shall simply be blunt.

I wish to resign my post as Sheriff and turn to the Church, as a monk if I am accepted. I can feel the end of my days in sight; and I urgently feel the need to come to terms with my long excommunication, and grow closer to God.

I would like to return to the village of my birth - a tiny little place in south Suffolk called Dodnash, which you will never have heard of - and found a Priory. I know just the man to be Prior, and I hope to live out my days in the service of God as a simple monk.

I beseech you, grant me release from your service!

Your humble servant,

338

Wimer."

"Henricus Rex, ad Wimerus Capellanus...

Ah, my friend, I envy you. What it must be like, to be able to just lay down your duties to man and be able to turn to God, I can only imagine.

Yes, go and found your Priory, with my blessing; you have served me long and well, and deserve my favour. For myself, I ask only that you pray for my soul occasionally; God knows, it needs the advocacy.

As does another poor soul, although that one may be beyond hope. The news of my son Henry's death may not have reached you, as it was only a few weeks ago. He died of a bloody flux, immediately after killing the inhabitants of an isolated Priory near Limoges and ransacking it.

I enclose a gift for you, my last if you insist on incarcerating yourself in a Priory! William Marshall brought the contents of the package to me, almost in tears, not knowing what to do with it. It was in Henry's possession, after that last fatal raid; but none of the brothers survive and he does not know who their mother house was. I want nothing to do with it, so I pass it to you. It would please me if I thought it was being used to sanctify your altar, but if you'd rather sell it, so be it.

Ora pro me – pray for me, and my poor, stupid Henry, God rest his soul.

Henry."

Wimer shut his eyes, feeling the pain behind his friend's

stark words. He remembered the two Henrys together, one sunny spring day at Clarendon. The boy was perhaps 8 or 9, revelling in the gift of a new pony; his father running alongside yelling approval, their matching flames of hair bobbing in unison for a few strides, until the boy kicked his heels and the pony leapt away.

He bowed his head and prayed, as asked, for both souls; the living and the dead.

Only when he was finished did he turn his attention to the parcel that had come with the letter; a lump about the size of his head, wrapped in leather, and lashed with thongs. *It doesn't look very prepossessing, for something that the Lord Marshall thought worth returning to the King from his son's death-bed?*

He picked up the pen-carving knife from his desk, and cut the knot holding the thongs together. A few tugs, and the leather fell open, giving a glimpse of the contents. He felt the air leaving his lungs, seeming to take all the moisture in his throat with it. He swallowed, and reached to flick the last fold of leather open.

This is exquisite… He reached out, and gently picked the reliquary up with both hands. The bright enamels, and the gilt metal, were pleasingly cool. He traced a finger, wonderingly, over the blue and yellow flowers bordering the pictures of Christ on the roof of the little church. *They are so smooth!* The flowers continued downward to the wall, spreading out at the bottom to form a carpet on which half-a-dozen saints walked.

He looked through the rock crystal set above the crucified Christ's head, and marvelled how anything could be so clear. There were holes left and right of the crystal with knife damage to the setting; someone had flicked out more crystals, or perhaps rubies or sapphires. He stroked a socket in apology for the insult it had received, and turned the reliquary round.

The roof was full of angels, the white enamels of their robes and trumpets dazzling against the blue enamel. The images on the wall were more martial, armed figures attacking someone. Wimer peered at it more closely, to work out which saint's story it was. A monk, kneeling... four knights, a head wound... *Becket!* All his pleasure drained away. He put the thing down on the table with a thump. *Henry could not have meant this insult? – no, of course not, he was grieving the loss of his son; he would barely have looked at it. The Marshall, too, would not have brought this to the King had he noticed the subject. He too would have been mourning his patron.*

He glared at it. The bright beauty now looked tawdry. A sudden thought made him flip the catches on the offending wall, and open the panel containing the relics. Two little packages were within; one labelled "A fingernail of Saint Thomas of Canterbury", and the other, "A piece of the habit of holy Thomas, Archbishop of Canterbury". He picked them out, and made to throw them on the fire. *No, I cannot. Whatever my opinion of the man, the Holy Father has ruled that he was martyred.*

He carefully replaced the scraps of cloth in their container within the reliquary, and turned it so the legend of Saint Thomas was to the wall.

It is beautiful. I wonder what it's worth? Henry is right. I must have some relics to sanctify my altar in the Priory. Perhaps I should go relic-seeking...

Around the edges of the square outside Norwich Cathedral, and lining the walls across the street, were stalls selling foods that the people who lived in the better quality houses around the close might need - milk and cheese, eggs, geese and chickens, baskets of peas and beans, fresh greens, the first of the season's apples. There was a little herd of piglets penned in one corner, bawling their hearts out, and adding to the odours.

The stalls right next to the Cathedral entrance were serving the needs of the devout visitors; candles for offerings, strings of rosary beads, and sacred images, jostled for space with stacks of tiny bottles of holy water and tiny relic packets. He glanced over at the relic stalls, and grinned, remembering the day when they had been perhaps 12 or 13, when he and Jean had seen the Pizzle of Saint Jerome on sale at two neighbouring stalls at the same time. *I need something a little more authentic today...*

All the stalls were doing good business on this pleasant summer's evening, and Wimer's escort had to clear a path more than once. Finally they reached the relative calm of the Cathedral precinct, and Wimer spotted young Brother Godric, the Sacristan, waiting for him by the great West Door. Before long they were tucked away in his office, small talk completed.

"So tell me, my Lord Sheriff – what is this mysterious package you wish to show me? I was most intrigued by your letter."

"Sheriff no longer, Brother – I wrote my resignation into the Court Roll myself, just a few weeks ago. I am plain Wimer the Chaplain now, and I hope very soon to take monastic vows myself. I will found a small priory very close to where I was born, and hope to live out my days there in prayer." He stopped to take a drink of ale.

"My thoughts have been full of the myriad of details required to bring such a project to completion. The King reminded me of a key detail recently, with a most generous gift – one which I fear is too sumptuous for the size of establishment I have in mind."

He nodded at his servant, who placed a table in front of him, and then the reliquary – covered by a square of cloth of gold. The sacristan leant forward. Wimer opened his hand.

"Please, my friend, remove the cover."

The heavy cloth slid smoothly over the shape within, then fell away. Godric sucked air between his teeth, then looked for permission to lift the little casket. He turned it one way then another, admiring the artistry. He was smiling like a shy boy when he finally looked at Wimer.

"This is indeed a sumptuous gift! Thank you for bringing it to show me. May I ask – does it hold a relic of the Sainted Archbishop, as it implies? I was so moved by his martyrdom, he has been an especial favourite of mine since his canonisation."

Ah, excellent. This is going better than I could have hoped. Wimer smiled back. "Open it, and see!"

Godric pulled out the relics, and went to his knees. "Oh! What a privilege you have granted me! To be so close to Saint Thomas – I – I am overwhelmed!"

"You see what I mean, that the gift is too large for a small Priory. Yet I must have a relic to sanctify the altar."

Godric was still kneeling, a relic in each hand, looking

from one to the other in wonder. *Come on, man, take the hint...* Wimer took another sip of ale. *Less subtlety, then...*

"Brother Godric, I wish I had another, more suitable, relic; then I could pass on this gift to a grander home. Would the Cathedral like it?"

The sacristan looked up at him, startled, then rapidly and reverently placed the relics back in their cavity. He touched the figure of Thomas once, then resumed his seat.

"The Cathedral would like it very much indeed." He felt on the floor beside him, still gazing at the reliquary, until his fingers found the cloth. He flicked it clean of dust, and carefully covered the casket. Only then did he look across at Wimer.

He stood up, and started to pace up and down. "You do realise, don't you, that these relics you are offering, as the holy remains of a martyr, are the most suitable possible relics for your altar? And then there is the beauty of the reliquary itself."

"Indeed, Brother. But I have in mind a small, humble priory, not a great Cathedral; I would be happy with something much more modest." *Besides, I have no intention of venerating the old goat.*

Wimer looked up to see Godric nod, once, decisively. He came back and sat on the edge of his seat. "There are currently 162 relics in my care. You will want a first-class relic for your altar, I suppose – bones, or hair; that brings it down to 30 or 40 objects. I am not prepared to release any of the major ones - not any of the pieces of the Cross, for instance, nor the limbs of any saint. But I have half-a-dozen lesser pieces that might suit. What exactly are you looking for, my friend? What kind of priory are you contemplating?"

It was Wimer's turn to stand up and move around, as though it would make the words come easier.

"It will be a small place, as I have said; very close to the place I was born, in the middle of the Suffolk countryside. It will follow the rule of St Austin, and will serve travellers and the local village people." He looked over at Godwin; he was listening carefully. Wimer could feel a blush grow, as he realised that he trusted Godwin. He blurted it all out, before he could change his mind.

"For the sake of my soul, I need a place within a firm discipline, with fasting and prayer the centre of my days, with fasting and hard work to purify my spirit. I would like the relics from a saint who can reflect that, one who the community can understand as well as venerate. A simple person, perhaps even a Saxon – although I realise I'm asking a lot."

Godwin also stood up. "I'll be right back, my friend – I think I may have something that will suit you very well."

Wimer sat down, and tossed the contents of his ale cup in one gesture. Was he being stupid? He was gifting the Cathedral something very valuable, in return for – what? He was pacing again by the time Godwin came back.

"Here it is – it's not much to look at, but I think you'll like it…"

He put a pressed-leather box into Wimer's hand. It comfortably covered his palm, but no more. The top had a picture of a man ploughing with a pair of oxen, the box's only decoration. The only sign that there was anything special about the box was the rays of gilding, set behind the man and oxen so that they looked like they were working at sunrise.

"Go on – open it!" Godwin urged.

Wimer carefully eased the lid open, and looked inside. The sides and base of the box were coated in white hair – presumably that of the original owner. It was beginning to feel all a bit cheap, compared to the Limoges enamelled casket he was giving up. There was a little packet of cloth inside, tied with a twist of straw. The attached label read, "Hair from Saint Walstan." He peeked inside – the hair was a curly brown, much like his own.

He looked up. "Who? – OH! I remember! He was the Saxon nobleman, who gave up his wealth to become a farm labourer, wasn't he! Isn't he from around here, too?"

Godric was smiling and nodding.

"I wanted a Saxon! And he blesses crops, and animals! Very useful for a country Priory. Hang on – wasn't his body pulled by white oxen, guided by angels? – is this reliquary MADE from one of them?"

Wimer could feel the hair rising on the back of his neck. *Oh my. I truly am in the presence of a saint. These relics have touched me in a way that Becket's bright casket could not – I would feel blessed indeed if I could venerate this saint every day, and call on his aid at time of need.*

He carefully refitted the lid, and kissed the box.

"Brother, you chose well. I am more than satisfied with the exchange!"

"Good! So be it. I shall pray daily for you and your Priory, with its new conduit to Heaven."

Ida's factor had met him at Cattawade with a map of

the estate. They spread the parchment on a sun-warmed rock at the port, and Wimer pored over it with the same feeling of awed amazement that had filled his soul since the land grant had succeeded. To his delight, he noted that his own bit of land did indeed abut it, on the Eastern edge.

Once he was sure that he had the boundaries straight in his head, he dismissed the factor and rode on alone. He climbed up from the river valley, the wind pushing him uphill, until he came to the old Saxon ditch and bank – the start of his new domain. *Now to find the perfect place for the Priory...*

He stayed on the Great Way for a while, following it over the sandy soil of the Heath. A little more of it was being farmed than he remembered from his boyhood, but still he caught sight of a hare sunning itself in a gorse thicket. He waved to a couple of distant figures working on their strips, and continued on.

After a mile or so, he followed a hunch, and took an old footpath down to the left. It wound through ancient woodlands, and then opened up to a wide valley. He dismounted and went on afoot. Sheep dotted the hillsides. *Brother Stephen would approve – this is rich land.* A rivulet cut through the valley bottom, the sound of it and the scent from an alder grove reached him on the breeze.

My boundary on this side is the stream between Dodnash and East Bergholt – is it this rivulet, or is the boundary further north? He climbed the hill. The line of trees in the far valley showed his border, hay meadows stretching steeply down to it.

He turned back to the broad valley, and lent against the trunk of a massive oak. He felt completely at peace – not sleepy, but invigorated by the view. A hunting sparrowhawk swung into place, almost level with him. It made eye contact with him, and cried once, insistently. "Here!"

He pushed himself upright. *Dear God, yes! Here! The church rising from the meadows, there by the alders. Dormitory and refectory next to it, forming part of the cloister square! Stables and fish ponds over there towards the birches, and houses for lay brothers and servants upstream!*

He ran down the slope, and paced out the buildings in his vision. *It can all be done, and more!* He fell to his knees in the middle of his church-to-be, and tried to find words for the emotions filling him. Instead of words, music came.

Praise the Lord! Rejoice! *O laudate dominum! Gaudete!*

AUTHOR'S NOTE

Somewhere around February 2011 I ran a metal detector over a mildly bumpy piece of meadow, and nearly deafened myself - there was a strong metal signal. Expecting it to be a lump of lead fairly close to the surface, I started digging; 18 inches later, I hit a shiny metal plate that extended well beyond the confines of my hole. Whatever it was, was clearly still in context, so I rang my contact in the local Archaeological Unit and asked them to come and do a mini dig. What they found was a large, and early, lead tile from a church roof. What on earth was it doing there?

With winter making a brief comeback, I retreated to my favourite wet-weather hangout, the Suffolk Record Office, and by chance came across a reference to my local Priory, and how Thomas Wolsey had closed it before the official Dissolution in order to pay for his school. There was a passing reference to the Dodnash Priory Cartulary. A bit of searching on the Internet led me to "Dodnash Priory Charters" edited by Christopher Harper-Bill, giving the history of the Priory, and handy English translations of the early Latin charters. As I read, I became more and more puzzled – the descriptions of the landscape around the Priory just didn't match the location of the ruins on the map. Then I found a throw-away comment about how the Priory had been moved, in its entirety, from its original site – and I started to get prickles up the back of my neck.

As soon as possible, I went back to the roof tile spot, and did some landscape archaeology. Looked at the right way, lumps and bumps resolved into three fishponds and the outline of cloisters and a dormitory building; more metal detecting, very carefully mapping the GPS co-ordinates of even the smallest finds, suggested stables, lay accommodation, and a series of outhouses. And reading the charters from this location, they made perfect sense.

So who was this Wimer guy who built it? And why did he pick one spot to found it on, and then move it? I had the date the Priory was founded, in 1188. An excellent source for the 12thC are the Pipe Rolls, which detail all the royal and court financial transactions of the period. And there was my man Wimer, the Sheriff of Norfolk and Suffolk! Following him back through the years, I could see the shape of his career. He was one of very few Sheriffs who survived Henry's clean-up of corrupt officers, and served in all the places I describe. Orford church lists him as its first Rector, to my huge delight.

He really did get excommunicated 3 times, as a result of the Earl of Norfolk, Hugh Bigod's attempt at a land grab from Pentney Priory. The Priory appealed to Thomas a'Becket, who responded with a hail of excommunication orders. a'Becket then refused to lift any of them – and reconfirmed all except for the messenger carrying his letter – using the victims as a lever in his dispute with Henry. Henry appealed to the Pope, who also confirmed the remaining excommunications, again excusing the letter bearer. So poor old Wimer was excommunicated 3 times; and there is no record of his reinstatement in the church. This must have been devastating in an era which believed in an immortal soul.

So I'm confident about his documented career as a Sheriff, and also that he was one of Hugh Bigod's chaplains, as that's documented in the correspondence with a'Becket. I don't know exactly when he entered Bigod's service, or how, but he must have had a church education in order to carry out his sheriff duties; and the simplest explanation is that he came to Bigod's notice via Norwich Cathedral, which had not one, but three excellent schools at the time.

The land grant is fascinating. I got thoroughly confused trying to trace Alda de Tosny's line back – the de Tosny or de Toesny or several other similar spellings did that infuriating thing of having the same name through several generations, and I gave up for a while.

Then I came back to it via a surprising route. I knew that the estate I was working on had been owned by an ancestress of mine, Edith Swanneck, at the time of the Norman invasion, and I was trying to follow her line forward in time. My lot are descended from her daughter who went to Russia; but to my great surprise, her other daughter's descendants get tied up in the de Tosny family tree – and it was clear that Ida de Tosny, Henry ll's ward and then mistress, was a direct descendant. And once I'd worked that out, it was very possible that Alda was a relation by marriage, to Ida's nephew. The possible birth dates (poorly documented as always for women) meant that they could have been contemporaries, fairly close in age.

Now, this is where it gets speculative – but what if Wimer's land was the marriagiatum gift, passed down from mother to daughter as land within the ownership of the female line? And if Alda had married the Baron de Tosny before Ida was of an age to inherit, perhaps she was in a position to influence its disposal.

(As an aside – if this supposition is accurate, I can trace the land ownership of this chunk of Suffolk countryside from 1056 to 1533, when Cardinal Wolsey comes along; and then there's a gap until the mid 19thC when it came into the current landowner's family. I plan more time in the record office Real Soon Now to close that gap!)

But coming back to Alda – why on earth would she give Wimer such a gift? It's a very generous one; the land owned 4 ½ knight's fees to the Bigod Earls, so would have been rich enough to amply provide for a small religious house.

There was a fairly large scandal when Henry took Ida as his mistress – it wasn't done, even in those days, to take advantage of your wards! Did Wimer and Ida meet at court? It's possible; Wimer is described in one document as one of Henry's "familiars", and although it's only a passing mention and he must have spent most of his time sheriffing – and Henry was on the continent for a great deal of time – I think that a possible friendship between them, and perhaps some favour that Wimer was able to do Ida, might have led to the land gift.

There is no evidence at all that Ida had a child earlier than William Longspee – but Baldwin seems to have been Alda's first child, rather late in life. So if I take two and two and make 47 out of it – I have the means and motivation for Alda to give Wimer the land he needs.

There is a thrilling entry in the Pipe Roll for 1188, in a different hand to the usual scribe. It might have been Wimer himself writing; it's a resignation letter, describing the money he's given in escrow to the King, to be used to pay off anyone who has a grievance against him whilst he was

Sheriff.

And one more miraculous survival through time. The Ipswich branch of the Suffolk Record Office have the original parchment charters, which you can handle and read freely. It took me some time to realise that they also have a box of seals which have fallen off the charters, or needed removal to prevent damage to them. One of these is Wimer's personal ring seal, a cormorant drying its wings – I've held it. It's amazing to come so close to him!

ABOUT THE AUTHOR

Nicky lives in the middle of rural Suffolk, UK, and is currently owned by a slinky black cat who's far too clever for her own good.

In her spare time, she's an amateur historian and archaeologist, and is often out on a field somewhere with a metal detector and/or a trowel. She's added quite a few things to the Heritage England Record and the Portable Antiquities Scheme; but what really fascinates her is the stories behind the artefacts.

Her first historical novel is about the story of a local boy made good - Wimer the Chaplain was born in Dodnash in Suffolk of a poor Saxon family, but made it to be a confidant of Henry ll, holding down the job of High Sheriff for all Norfolk and Suffolk. Then he gave it all up and came home to found a Priory... finding the original site of that Priory (not where it's shown on the map) is still one of her proudest discoveries.

The follow-on novel, in production, explores the mystery of why the Priory apparently moved itself lock, stock, and barrel from a perfectly good site close to every amenity, to the middle of a stream valley that floods every year without fail...

She also writes children's short stories about Henry Baker, a boy who finds a magic pencil on the way to school - and who has lots of adventures as the pencil makes anything he draws, become real! He generally draws things to get him out of the sort of trouble any 9 year old boy can find – but occasionally he draws some historical artefacts too :)

Find out more about Nicky and her writing at
http://nickymoxey.com

Made in the USA
Monee, IL
19 November 2020